Love Interrupted

Written by
Kimberly Ann Dockter

Cover concept by Sara Nichols

Cover designed by Georgia Dahler

Contact Information:
www.kimberlyanndockter.com
contact_me@kimberlyanndockter.com

ISBN# 978-0-615-38740-6

Printed in the USA by
Vision Van Gogh
11521 Eagle St. NW Suite 6
Minneapolis, MN 55448
www.visionvangogh.com
1-800-368-6701

This book is dedicated to those who have lost all hope. God has not forgotten you! Just remember what the apostle Paul said in Romans 12:12, "Be joyful in hope, patient in affliction and faithful in prayer."

Acknowledgements

Jesus Christ: The author, perfecter and finisher of my faith. Without You this book wouldn't have been possible. Thank You for the many gifts You've given me. I wasn't blessed with the ability to draw a stick figure, work a paint brush or sculpt a statue, but You've worked through my hands doing hair for the last seventeen years and have blessed me by bringing many incredible people across my path; and then You gave me the ideas for this story and the know how to translate it from my head onto paper. My goal is to honor You in all that I say and do. Thank You for Your unfailing love!

Justin: My husband and best friend. Thank you for your patience and support while I've spent countless hours on this book. I'm so grateful that God brought you into my life. It's been an incredible journey that I couldn't imagine doing with anyone else. I love you so much!

Mom and Dad: Thank you for making me go to church every Sunday as a kid. It took a while, but those seeds of faith took root. You are the best parents in the whole wide world and I don't tell you enough how much I love and appreciate you!

Sara: my cousin and visionary behind this cover. I gave you many off the wall ideas and you got it on the first try. I'm just sorry that I couldn't use what you originally designed, but I think what they came up with did your vision justice! Thank you for your many hours of dedication to this project and putting up with my crazy thoughts; there aren't enough words to describe how awesome you are!

Jan: my 'knit-picker'. I can't thank you enough for going over and through this and asking numerous questions, making me ponder things I might not have before. It helped make this book what it is today.

Jerilyn, Karen, Mom, and Marian: Thank you for taking the time to read this book and giving me your great insights and support! This is a fun but scary adventure and I needed every one of your encouraging words immensely. I appreciate you all so much!

Roxanne: my photographer extraordinaire. Thank you for sharing your gift and working your magic!

And last but not least I'd like to thank Guy and Georgia at Vision Van Gogh for helping me in areas which I was clueless and putting up with my impatience. God knew what He was doing when He led me to you!

But those who hope in
the Lord will renew their
strength. They will soar
on the wings like eagles;
they will run and not
grow weary; they will
walk and not be faint.

Isaiah 40:31

Chapter 1

Ten minutes to one. Only four hours and ten minutes left to go, Eva Wahler thought to herself. It had been a slower day at the salon. For the past hour she had been reading about the latest Hollywood crisis and she couldn't help but feel sorry for the people involved. See? Money sure didn't make one happy, she consoled herself. She'd take her mediocre paying job, handsome husband of ten years, and two Irish setters over the cameras, fame, money and highly exposed drama. Eva had her share of troubles, but none could compare to any one of their problems.

Tick...Tick...Tick....Time sure stood still when you fixated on the clock. Why couldn't Charlotte, Eva's one o'clock appointment and best friend of eight years, come in early for once? The standing joke between them was that Charlotte would be late for her own funeral. But with four children under the age of eight, Eva over-looked her tardiness. She always enjoyed the tales circling around Charlotte's family, usually leaving both of them in hysterics. Even though Eva was a fast efficient stylist, when it came to doing her friend's hair, she tended to go over with her time...mostly spent in conversation. Eva needed a pick-me-up after sitting for so long and just knew that her friend would wind her up and lift her spirits again.

Thirty seconds to the hour, the door of the salon flew open, and in came the tornado which was Charlotte. "Hey, Eva, sorry I'm late...." She plopped down into Eva's chair as if it had her name written on it.

"Hey, Char. You aren't late. In fact, if you need thirty seconds to catch your breath, take them. After all, you have them to spare, not to mention the fact that I have nothing the rest of the day," Eva added with a giggle.

Charlotte's shoulder length, thin, curly, mousy-brown hair

looked as if it had seen better days. Her appointments had been more sporadic than in the past due to her crazy schedule with the kids. "Oh my goodness, I didn't think I'd make it! I had to get Indy to a doctor's appointment this morning. So after I dropped him off at school, I brought the twins and baby Brake to my mom's house so I could run some errands for Charley. This is my last stop. I don't mean to hurry you, but I gotta get back and relieve my mom. The baby looked as if he was giving her a run for her money before I even left."

"How do you do it, Char?"

Smiling peacefully, she said, "Only by the grace of God!"

Eva snapped the cutting cape around Char's neck and felt through her hair. It was really dry and brittle. "Did you run out of your professional products again?"

Looking guilty, she said, "Yeah, that's what prompted this visit. Is it beyond repair?"

"No worries. I'll put on one of our Hair Masks for a few extra minutes and that should help. Why don't you come on back?" Once back at the shampoo bowl, Eva gave a quick shampoo and then massaged the deep conditioner into her hair. While Charlotte was reclined, Eva asked, "So what else is new in the world of Charlotte, Charley and the Factory?"

"Well, other than I'm pregnant?"

Eva stopped what she was doing and said, "What???" She had to have been joking, Eva thought. After all, Charlotte said she was done after the twins, and that was one baby ago.

Sighing, she said, "Yeah. I'm four months along apparently. It was quite a shock, since it was just last month that I missed my monthly. I swear, Charley just has to stand near me and I get pregnant."

Eva envied her more than anyone knew, but she gave Charlotte an encouraging smile. "Well, you sure have your work cut out for you! But, four months? How did you not know you were that far along?" They headed back to Eva's station and she started doing the usual cut, knowing that Charlotte had the same style since Eva met her eight years prior, and knew without asking that she wasn't interested in something new.

"Well, it was kind of weird. When I got my period a few months ago, my usual PMS symptoms never left. You know, the usual boob hurting and queasy stomach, so I just thought I was coming down with something." Eva gave her a skeptical look. "What?" Charlotte asked. "When I get sick, that sometimes happens, but I ruled out pregnancy because of the whole getting my period thing. Well anyhow, as soon as I missed last month I went to the doctor and told her what was happening. It was baffling really because I tried to remember when Charley and I had last, you know, and if I remembered correctly, we were playing it really safe. But nope, I'm not only pregnant, but four months along to boot. I was relieved that it wasn't something serious, but Charley didn't see it that way. He was just a wee bit upset, but the way I see it at this point, what is one more, right?"

Eva was always amazed at how her friend could find the silver lining, no matter the situation. "Well, congratulations. Maybe it will be the girl you always dreamed of."

"Ha! I don't think I'd know what to do with a little girl now! Frankly, I'd be afraid to bring a girl home, not knowing what the boys would do to her! After all, I had older brothers and I'd rather not put someone through that if at all necessary."

"Well, God knows what you need, and I know that either a boy or a girl, everything will work out just fine."

"Always does....Hey, before I forget, would you and Eric like to come over on Sunday afternoon for the races? Charley is having a few of his associates over with their families. Thought you two would like to join us."

"I'll have to ask him. He's been working a lot of overtime lately, and Sunday has been his catch-up-with-things-around-the-house day. But if anything, I may come over."

"That would be great." Eva was concentrating on the haircut, or so she wanted Charlotte to think since her mind ventured elsewhere. It was getting harder and harder to put on such a brave front every time someone told her that they were pregnant. After six years of knowing that she would probably never be able to conceive, and giving that burden over to God, she still got upset from time to time. Satan loved to rear his ugly head, knowing that having a baby meant so much to her and he made sure to discourage her every chance he could, by telling her that slim chance would never happen. Eva still clung to hope, where her husband, Eric, didn't. As far as he was concerned, fertility and adoption were out. And faith that God would provide their miracle was an all out joke to him. There was no talking to him about any of it. Eva would have gone through fertility, even though they only gave her a thirty percent chance of conceiving that way. To her, it was still a thirty percent chance. Eric wouldn't have that, not with the high risk of cancer involved. The fertility activated certain cells it needed to stimulate egg activity, and cancer cells that everyone had in their body sometimes were affected by the drug. He wouldn't take that chance. She was too important to him he said. And adoption was out because if their child wasn't of his blood line, he wanted no part of it. He loved kids, but he wanted 'his own' and 'not someone else's problem'. This killed Eva. Her one and only desire since the day they decided it was time to try for a baby was to be a mom, so she busied herself in everything she could think of until it happened and hoped that one day God would hear the cry of her heart. She really tried keeping positive about the whole subject to the outside world and when anyone ever asked her when they were going to have kids, which made her heart ache each time they inquired, she would just say, 'We don't know yet,' which was usually effective from any further inquiries. Besides Eric and the doctors, nobody knew her burden. Nobody knew the shame of not being able to do what women throughout the ages were able to do or the emptiness she felt inside every time she saw another woman with her child or the strain that it had on her marriage. Eva couldn't even count how many arguments she and Eric had over the subject the last few years, which had the same outcome every time. She walked away frustrated and hurt, and Eric was resentful that she kept bringing it up. They were at a standstill with little hope of either one giving up their stance.

Eva hated being reminded of her inadequacies, not that anybody knew how their words were affecting her. Luckily Charlotte jolted her out of her stinkin thinkin by asking, "What's wrong?"

"What? Oh, nothing. Just a little tired is all. It's been a slow day. Maybe when Barbie comes in at three she'll let me go early. I forgot to take something out for supper, so maybe I could go to the store and get home before Eric and throw something together. I've been really trying to do what we've been learning in our Bible study, but I find it challenging to do stuff for Eric lately, because he's always so short with me. I wonder when the appreciation will kick in. The lady who wrote this *How To Be The Wife of a Happy Husband* must either be married to an amazing man who is receptive to what she suggests or is working hard towards sainthood. Following this book is making *my* husband anything but happy lately. It's like the more I pray and am obedient not only to God but to Eric, the more he resents my presence. I don't even talk about Jesus around him anymore, and I've long since asked him to go to church with me because I know the answer will be no anyhow; and when I'm kneeling for my bedtime prayers he just rolls his eyes at me and says something derogatory like, well, when you and Jesus are done with your moment, could you shut off the light?"

Eva knew she said too much because Charlotte threw a sympathy glance her way, and she detested pity! She tried hard to avoid conversations and situations that would lead to her complaining, like this. But given their friendship and the lack of people in the salon at the time, her mouth was faster than her brain. Charlotte approached her carefully when she said, "This is just a suggestion, because I've been there before. Maybe refrain from kneeling when you pray to when you are alone; at least until Eric realizes the reason behind your actions. And he will one day," she added optimistically before going on. "Keep praying and believing. Faith is a powerful thing. Satan will use everything and everyone, even those closest to you, to crush that faith and your hope. Don't let him. You do what God asks of you, and it will never come back void. Remember, all things come together for good for those who love Him."

Somehow, Eva managed to cut, dry and style Charlotte's hair without even thinking about it. Just when she felt a moment of despair, God sent her encouraging words through her sister in Christ. God had a way of doing that which always restored her sense of hope; solidifying in her heart and mind how real He was. There was so much to remember about Christianity, which she had found and received almost eight years before. To her, it was a simple message, however very challenging to live it. But it sure kept her going in the midst of her trials.

"Thanks, Char. You are a blessing!" Eva said. Once her cape was off and Charlotte was standing, she gave her a sisterly hug.

"No, you are! Not only a blessing, but a miracle worker! See how fabulous you make me look? And here I thought only God could make a miracle out of a mess!"

"Oh please! You give me too much credit."

Once they got to the front desk, Charlotte set her purse down on the counter, rifled through it like a madwoman and patted her jeans as if they were on fire. "Oh crap!"

"What?"

"My cash card! Wheeler was playing in my purse earlier and I knew he would get into my wallet so I took it," she paused as if retracing her steps in her mind, and then snapped her fingers. "Oh! I know where it is. Oh my goodness, Eva! I'm a total mess. If my head weren't attached I think I'd lose it. I just don't have enough time in the day," she said looking at her watch. "Could I run by a check later? Oh!" she slapped her forehead in haste, "I need products desperately too!"

Calming Charlotte's fears, Eva said, "How about this, take the products and I'll collect your money when I see you on Friday."

"I won't be there. Charley and I have a dinner to go to with

14

his company."

"Well then, Sunday. It will be an excuse to get out of the house and come over."

"Really? Barbie wouldn't mind?"

"Not a problem. I'll cover it for you. After all, I know where you live," Eva added with a chuckle.

"Oh double crap!"

"What now?" Eva said, trying not to laugh too hard at her friend's behavior.

"I at least wanted to give you a tip! I don't even have two nickels to rub together."

"You know you don't have to tip me. Your advice is tip enough, believe me."

"No, it's not, but thank you for making me feel better." After gathering her products and getting a total for her bill, to pay later of course, they hugged again and in the embrace, Charlotte said, "I love you and I'll be praying for you and Eric."

"Thank you, I appreciate it. And again, congratulations on the baby."

"Lord have mercy!" she said jokingly, walking out the door.

Eva had been holding down the fort since nine in the morning, and ever since Char and her energy departed, she had done everything to make time fly. After cleaning the salon from top to bottom, she looked at the clock. Two thirty. *What?* She couldn't believe her eyes. It surely felt like hours had gone by. Nope, with a double take, her eyes hadn't failed her; it only took her fifty minutes to shape up the salon. She was half asleep reading *The Ladies Home Journal* (yes she was desperate) when the receptionist, Stephanie, walked in. She had a cute little figure that any girl would be envious over, beautiful big blue eyes surrounded by long black eyelashes, thick hair that was brown as milk chocolate with a few natural vanilla strands which highlighted her heart-shaped face, and a smile that could always light up a room. Not to mention an awesome personality that the clients just loved.

"This isn't a good sign," Stephanie joked.

"For me it isn't, but you girls should keep busy tonight.

How was school?" Eva asked with a little anticipation.

Stephanie's face lit up. "I have some exciting news!"

At this point, Stephanie set down her bag and took a seat next to Eva in the reception area since it was dead. They usually held their gab sessions in the back room where Barbie expected all non-work associated conversations to be held. Eva loved Stephanie, and vice versa. The two of them had so many great conversations and was one of the best perks of Eva's job there. Stephanie was the only person there who let her chew her ear off about her faith without discord. If she disagreed, she never let on. If she had questions, she asked, but other than that she just listened which Eva appreciated. Eva saw a lot of herself in Stephanie, and Eva was young enough to where she was still 'cool' in Stephanie's eyes.

Eva pleaded, "Oooooo, do tell!" Moments like these, she felt as if she were in high school again. Talking about the mundane things like the dances, the music classes, the boys, the hanging out with her girlfriends and talking about boys because actually dating them seemed so out of reach, and envisioning the future through rose colored glasses. There were so many possibilities and it never occurred to Eva that some of them wouldn't turn out the way she planned. But, unlike some of the adults in her own life, she encouraged Stephanie to follow her dreams and if she wanted something, to seize the day and fight for it.

"Remember when I told you about that Justin kid last year?"

"You mean the kid who intentionally ruined your new shoes in that mud puddle?" With an enthusiastic nod from the girl, Eva continued, "How could I forget that? It had you wondering about him for weeks afterwards. What about him?"

"He sort of asked me out," she said with an enthusiastic grin.

"What do you mean by sorta? He either did or didn't."

"Well, listen to this and you decide. Today Mr. Wilber had us pair up for the solo and ensemble contest coming up in December, and just as I was about to ask my friend Renae to be my partner, of all the people to come up to me and ask me to sing with him was Justin Twilliger!"

16

Eva had to laugh at Stephanie. "Why do you find that so unbelievable? You are a great singer, and from what I hear so is he." Not to mention it helped that Stephanie had every asset any boy her age would be drooling over. She was popular in her own right and had confidence in every way except with boys. If Eva had to guess, boys were too intimidated to ask her out and she was to shy to make a move so there she sat; a dateless senior. Little did they know her ache for a boyfriend was almost intense as Eva wanting a baby! Her young friend was always in Eva's prayers, that she would meet someone who was worth her wait. Patience was a virtue, she kept reminding Stephanie, and that sometimes God's plan and our plans were a little off. But Eva was so happy that the stars had finally come together for the bubbly teen. "Still, I wasn't expecting it! I almost died," Stephanie exclaimed, holding her petite fingers to her collarbone for effect and added, "I was so nervous."

"So I take it you said yes?"

"Without hesitation!" Stephanie giggled. "And get this, after I said 'sure' to his inquiry he wiped his brow and said 'Whew!'. Can you believe it? The hot football stud was relieved that I said yes! Well, naturally that rendered me speechless for a second, but I came back with an ever so brilliant, big old blush. He gets me so tongue tied! People were looking at us. I could feel their stares, and I felt like the biggest dork. But then, the next thing I knew it was our turn to go in to meet with Mr. Wilber. So after deciding on our piece and we were walking back to our seats, he asked me if we could get together after school sometime, 'you know, to practice'." Stephanie added hand quotations for the last part.

Laughing, Eva said, "He totally asked you out."

"Do you think?"

"Heck, yeah! I'm sure you will have time to practice at school. Why else would he ask to see you outside of school?"

"True," Stephanie agreed, and then said animatedly, "*Oh*, and oh! Before we left for lunch, he said that he was really sorry about ruining my shoes last spring. I told him it was really no big deal, not to mention it was so last year. He said he felt like a big time jerk, and after reassuring him that the slate was cleared, his smile literally jolted me. I know, it's probably nothing, but dang, a girl can dream, can't she?"

"You sure can, Steph. Don't underestimate yourself. You are a beautiful, sweet, talented girl."

"With no chest to speak of," she added with a giggle.

"Oh shut up!"

"I'm serious, Eva. I went into 'The Gap' the other day to look at bras, and the sales girl directed me to the training bra section," Stephanie joked.

Laughing to the point of her eyes watering, Eva said, "Oh come on! You aren't that small."

"Well, I certainly have a ways to go to catch up to you! And yeah, I know, you were small too in high school. But it still doesn't help me when all I need is band-aids to cover mine up!"

"Seriously, you have to stop! My bladder can't take this!"

Just when the fun was getting started, Barbie walked in. Fifteen years older than Eva, you would never know. Her short spiky red and black hair screamed fun, unlike Eva's boring, conservative natural light brown with highlights that hung past her shoulders in layers. Safe. Comfort zone. That's what it was. Not much changed there since beauty school twelve years prior. Like her friend Charlotte, she was okay with same old, same old.

Was it three already, Eva thought. Man, Stephanie needed to come in earlier next time! Time flew when she was around.

"What am I missing?" Barbie asked.

"Oh, nothing much," Eva and Stephanie said in unison, but then burst out laughing again.

"Yeah, sounds like it," Barbie said sarcastically. She made her way over to the books and sighed. "That fun, eh Eva?"

"Terrible, but at least I got some cleaning done. You're welcome by the way," she teased Stephanie. "Don't expect that all the time. You both just caught me on a good day."

"Well, you can go if you'd like. Or you could help Stephanie with inventory."

"And I'll take that as my cue to go!" Eva said quickly. "Think I'm going to make Eric his favorite manicotti."

"Wow, is it his birthday?" Barbie asked.

"Nope, it's just because I love him. He's been working so hard. Good food puts a smile on his face and lately I live for them."

"Ahhhhhhh, how romantic," Stephanie joked. "Just remember me if there are any leftovers."

"Ha! Very doubtful, but I sure will. See you guys tomorrow."

Chapter 2

Eric Wahler was spent and all he wanted to do was go home, fill his empty stomach, put his feet up and relax. The last three months of working sixty hours a week was catching up with him. But knowing that this was the only weekday night he had with Eva, he knew that relaxing wasn't going to be any part of his evening. He cringed thinking about what kind of mood she'd be in because lately it was hit or miss, and there always seemed to be something else added to his already long list of 'to do's around the house. Years ago he couldn't wait to come home (the one he had slaved to get before they were married) and into his wife's inviting arms. Of course they were only nineteen then and still wet behind the ears in puppy love. They both thought they knew what they wanted, and that ultimately was each other. Yes, they both had dreams of careers; hers in cosmetology and him of becoming a mechanic. But ultimately it was to be together. He asked her to marry him the night of their high school graduation, after dating for two years, six months and two days. To him, she was the best thing that had ever happened to him. He was just this gangly boy with no real sense of home; 'nothing special' he would say. In his early days of high school, people saw him as a rebel. Not that he was looking for trouble, but trouble always found him. Having no parents to keep him in line, he and his brother were on their own a lot. His uncle Ben, his mom's brother, took them in when he was ten and his brother was fourteen after his mom died of breast cancer. Their dad left the scene before Eric had a chance to know him. The only thing he knew of his father is what his brother, Barton, remembered of him and none of it was good. Memories of his parents rarely were talked about however, especially their mom because it was just too painful. Uncle Ben was there physically and financially, but emotionally he was unavailable. He was a Vietnam vet and he had a hard time dealing with people, let alone two snot nosed kids, and unfortunately up until Eric's brother went to college the only sense of parental guidance Eric knew was from him, which wasn't saying much since his brother was just a kid himself.

His brother butted heads with his uncle all the time and had left for college as soon as he could manage it. Eric always stood in the background trying to remain invisible until Bart brought him into the argument. As far as his uncle could see, they were cut from the same cloth and stuck together like thieves. But little did his uncle know he was more scared to cross Bart than he did his uncle. The worst his uncle would do to him was insult his gene pool, which they shared, so by the time he was a teenager it was a running joke between the two boys. Bart, on the other hand, would've beat him to a pulp if he'd side with his uncle. By the time Eric was a sophomore in high school, Bart had left for college along with the trouble and he and his uncle got into a comfortable routine and kept out of each other's hair.

But it was when he met Eva that his life changed forever. In his opinion, she was the prettiest girl that ever acknowledged him. He had never seen her before, but he noticed her right away. She was always smiling and had the prettiest blue eyes he'd ever seen. They sat next to each other in history the first semester of their sophomore year, and since they both were a little shy neither of them said a word to each other. He still remembered the day she first spoke to him. She sat in front of him and her long brown hair was having some static cling issues, to the point that every time she ran her fingers through her hair to calm it down, the louder the crackles from the electricity became. He tried holding back a chuckle, but obviously she must've heard him. When she turned, her face was bright red. "I have *no* idea what's going on with my hair!"

"I think you just need a negative charge to counteract it." With that, he touched her hair and after a quick shock between her head and his hand, every fly away hair settled down. "There."

"Thanks." Her smile jump started his heart, and a few days later he worked up enough nerve to ask her out. Even though she was an orchestra and choir girl, not the usual kind of girl he had dated, he liked her instantly. And she had talent, so much in fact that she could have gotten a musical scholarship to any college. But as much as she loved to play the violin, she didn't want to pursue it other than a hobby. Making people beautiful was her passion. In fact, she had been cutting his hair since they started going together that fall of their sophomore year. He loved her energy, her friendliness, and most of all the way she made him feel ten feet tall whenever she was around him. 'When had that changed?' Eric asked himself now. They had meshed so well together all those years ago. What had gone wrong? So what if they couldn't have kids. All he ever wanted was her; to belong to someone and somewhere, happy. That was more than his parents had by far. If kids resulted from their love, it would only be an added bonus to him; not a necessity. But not to Eva. Ever since the doctors told her that her chances of conceiving were slim to none, she was on a mission to prove them wrong. Her plight was a silent one to the world around her, but she was constantly doing research about her condition and praying to a God he doubt cared about their little problems. Eric knew how badly she wanted a baby; especially every time she got around kids. It always fueled her cause, and often times it got them into a heated dispute that drove a further wedge between the two of them. At first, he was sad too that it didn't come easily to them and may possibly never happen, but if he had to be honest about it he was more relieved; relieved that he didn't have to assume responsibility for another person, other than Eva and himself. Eva put on a good front for people, but he knew how much she blamed him for their predicament deep down. Unfortunately, not even that guilt trip would ever change his mind over their alternatives.

And then there was the issue of him not attending church every Sunday. So what if he didn't? He simply didn't believe in it. It wasn't as if he didn't believe in God. He just didn't need to talk about Jesus every five seconds or spend every free moment he had at church or doing church things. It had been a while since they had argued over that actually. Maybe his point was made that people didn't need it to believe. He worshiped in his own way. Her holier-than-thou attitude really wore on him. Yes, she stopped talking about Jesus this and Jesus that twenty four hours a day, but everything about her radiated an air of arrogance and she had this know-it-all attitude which drove him crazy. No matter what problem he had, she always had some great Godly wisdom to give him. His once comfortable home now made him feel not only uncomfortable, but unwelcome.

Ever since Eva started putting in more evenings a few years ago, Eric got accustomed to slipping on over to Jake's Tavern and Grill in Cannon Falls for a drink with his buddies after work. It was a block from Solid Steel, and since it wasn't in the same town as they lived he knew Eva wouldn't have a way of finding out. He knew how she felt about drinking, and especially about bars. It was something she had always stood by. He was never much of a bar goer when he turned of age, and he gave up the hard partying when he started going out with her, but over time he looked forward to the escape. It was a place where he could let loose and listen to people talk about things other than babies, 'to do' lists, and religion. Needless to say, due to her being home, he skipped Jake's on Monday nights.

As soon as he turned off his truck, he could hear the dogs go crazy inside. Their attached garage opened right into the pantry way where every day he got an onslaught of wet kisses. That was the only inviting thing about his house lately and it always put a smile on his face. No matter how mad they made him, just the look in their amber eyes and the circular motion of their tails erased any ugly memory of their previous behavior. Sure enough, as soon as he was in the door, barely getting off his work boots, Reddog took a flying leap at him.

"Hey, buddy! How you doin?" he asked, petting him roughly. Rounding the corner came Bruiser, Reddog's litter mate brother. "Hey pal..." They were both attention hogs and if not paid attention to properly and divided up evenly, a fight would soon start. It was never a pretty sight in the small mudroom.

Suddenly tomato, garlic, basil and oregano flirted with his nostrils. He loved that smell, and apparently his stomach caught up with his brain, letting out a loud growl.

"Hey honey! Great timing. Supper's almost done." Eva smiled at him in the entryway.

"Hey! Smells great. I gotta take a shower quick."

"All right," she said and sailed back into the kitchen with Bruiser at her heals. That dog loved her, where Reddog pledged allegiance mostly to Eric.

Years ago he would have skipped the shower and gone right in for a kiss but now he'd rather get the steel dust and grime off his body and forego the kiss.

The warmth of the shower felt so good on his aching body. He didn't know how long he was in the bathroom, but half way into the shower he remembered the delicious meal waiting for him, which made him hurry. Eva was an awesome cook, when she chose to do it. Lately it had been more frequently, he silently noted.

After slipping on a pair of running shorts and a clean tee shirt, he went into the kitchen where he found his wife standing at the stove reading. He went behind her and kissed her neck, which made her flinch and hold the book against her chest. Instead of trying again for a proper kiss, he went to the refrigerator and extracted a beer. "Sorry. Whatcha reading?"

Flipping over to the cover, she read, "PCOS: The Facts."

"Oh," he said without interest, grabbing a plate for himself. This was not a discussion he wanted to start tonight. So instead he walked up to the food, took a whiff and commented, "If this tastes as good as it smells, my stomach will be forever in your debt."

"I just have to get the garlic bread from the oven. It will be done in a minute. Go ahead and grab your manicotti. I'll bring the bread out to you." After dishing out a healthy portion, and grabbing his beer he made his way to the living room where they always dined and flipped on the TV. Reddog sat with his head resting on Eric's knee, drooling. "Sorry buddy, this is for me. I'd share with you, but you are on a diet." He laughed as Reddog's eyes turned sad. Man, that dog got to his heart every time, but not enough to cave in.

Just as the six o'clock news came on, Eva, trailed by Bruiser, came in with the bread. "Here ya go, hon. Need anything else?"

"Nope, I'm good, thanks."

A minute later she was next to him on the couch, watching the evening news in silence. During a commercial, she asked, "So how was your day?"

"Tiring. At least today wasn't as physically draining as most days, but learning this new machine is frying my brain. Cramming two weeks of training into two days is too much. The weekend guy really screwed the machine up, so they called the guy from Malmac to come and fix it. He has to come all the way over from Norway, so I decided to see if I could fix it to save him a trip overseas. Well, I got it up and running..."

"Wow hon, that's awesome!"

"Yeah, you would think my foreman would have thought so too, but he jumped my crap because if anything would have happened to the machine in the process of me 'fixing it myself' it would've cancelled the warranty. I just hate waiting around for someone to fix it. Every other day there is something going on with it. Then right before I left today, Lars finally came."

"Lars?"

"He's the guy from Malmac, Inc. He was impressed with my knowledge of this machine. After I punched out, he caught up with me and offered me a job."

"Really? Doing what?"

"Doing what he does. It would be a traveling job fixing machines like the one I work on, and the money is out of this world. But as soon as he offered me the job, he kinda discouraged me at the same time by saying that if I was in a relationship or had a family that I wouldn't want it. Apparently he is going through a divorce."

"Oh, that's not good. But I guess it's good to know that you have an option if you don't want to work at Solid Steel anymore," she added positively.

"Yeah. I'm glad *someone* recognizes what I have to offer. I work ten times as hard as the rest of those guys and know every machine in that place, but do they appreciate that? Heck no!"

"Oh, hon, I'm sure your bosses see that and so do your coworkers. They probably just don't want to show any favoritism," she said, trying to raise his spirits and then added, "I'm very proud of you. I wish I had half your work ethic and stamina!"

He smiled over to her. It had been a long time since he heard an actual compliment come from her lips that wasn't laced with an undertone of something she needed on top of it and was the first time in a long time that he had the stirring in his loins towards her. "Thanks. Speaking of work, how was your day?" he asked, suddenly not remembering the last time he actually asked and was surprised that he sincerely wanted to know.

"Long and boring. Charlotte was my only client."

"Oh boy! And what have the kids done now?" Eric jokingly asked, knowing how chaotic that household was.

"We really didn't talk much about them. But she did have some rather shocking news. Just take a guess at what it was."

"I don't know. She's pregnant again," he said off the top of his head.

"Yup," Eva said with a giggle. "Can you believe it? She's on her fifth child! She's already half crazy. But like she said, what's one more?"

Shaking his head, Eric said, "Five kids. They are nuts, but then again so are the vast majority who have more than two. But whatever. Thankfully that's them and not us." He said that before he thought about how it sounded. Looking over to Eva, she turned her head quickly, got up and headed to the kitchen with her half empty plate. Dang it, he scolded himself, not again! What was meant for a joke never came out as that around her. One of these days he would learn to think before speaking. He heard the clink and clank of dishes and knew she wasn't going to come back into the living room anytime soon. So after quickly finishing up his meal, he collected his thoughts and joined her in the kitchen.

"Babe, that came out wrong. You know what I meant, don't you?" He couldn't see her face, since she had it down and was concentrating on washing the dishes, but saw her nod reluctantly in response. "But you are upset with me," he concluded by her actions.

"No, I'm not," she whispered.

Hugging her from behind, he said, "You can't do this to yourself every time you hear of someone having a baby. You have to face the fact that we may never have children."

"I can't...I can't give up hope, Eric. Not yet..."

Seeing the tears streaking her face, he wiped them away with his finger. Placing his lips at her temple, he asked, "Why can't you just be happy with the two of us?"

"I am happy," she said, turning to face him. "I just want your child too. Is that too much to ask?" Stepping into his warm embrace, she placed her head on his shoulder. "I just hate feeling this selfish."

"You need to get past this, Eva. I have."

Eva took in a deep breath, pulled away and paused before saying, "Let's not go there tonight. I don't have enough energy."

"I agree," he said, relieved.

"I love you, Eric."

He heard the passion behind her words, but he could feel the weight of her sadness looming between them. Looking past her, he placed a kiss on the top of her head and sighed into her hair, saying, "I love you too...." He had to get this load off her mind, and the discomfort in his shorts notified him the direction he needed to take her. "Forget these dishes..."

"But Eric..." she said, turning away from him.

"No buts. I need you...." he started to say, claiming her lips. "Right. Now." As he pulled her towards the bedroom, he showered kisses on her as their clothes were shed along the way.

Chapter 3

Business at The Beauty Spot was unpredictable lately. Twenty years ago they were one out of five salons successfully inhabiting Red Wing, but now it seemed like every time they turned around another chain was showing up, stealing their business. Feast or famine was the name of the game. Famine was on Monday for Eva, but the rest of her week was a feast to beat all feasts! One of the newest chains was giving $7.99 haircuts which resulted in a business boom for the girls at The Beauty Spot; fixing the damage that is. After the fifth person who needed a repair left, Barbie had the best marketing scheme ever. Sure it was a bit cheap and unprofessional, but it sure rounded up business. She called her printing company to make up a huge sign that read, 'GET A BAD HAIRCUT? CALL US FOR A HALF OFF FIX IT NOW!' Eva didn't know where the girls over at their competitor learned how to do hair, but whoever gave them their licenses should be fired.

The first client for Eva on Wednesday was a man she guessed to be in his early forties. She had never seen him before, because with a face like that she knew she would've remembered. Very rarely did any man other than her husband make her turn her head, but this man was *handsome*. His blue eyes were in such contrast to his black hair, that they illuminated the smile that he gave. Eva was almost too transfixed to notice the chop job on his hair, that is until she took him back to her chair and was half way through asking, "So, just a trim today," and then she gasped when she saw the mess. "Oh my, did we get a little happy with the razor?" she asked jokingly.

He winced. "That bad, eh? I knew the front looked a little off. I hadn't even taken a look at the back."

"Well, let's just say it's a good thing. Let me guess, this is the product of Cheap Cuts?"

"You got it. Apparently I got swindled too huh?"

"I don't know about swindled, but you, along with a lot of

other people sure didn't have luck in getting the right stylist over there." She studied his hair closely, sucking in her lower lip subconsciously. "There is only one way to make this cut better, but I have to warn you that I'll be going really short."

"H-How short you talking?"

"Well, not military short, but enough to hide these nicks in the back of your head. And judging by the top of your hair, I'm going to have to take it down to about an inch and a half if you want everything to be symmetric."

For the first time since he walked in the door, he wasn't smiling, nor did he have a twinkle in his eye. "Do what you have to do. I'm in town on business, and I have a meeting in..." He looked at his Rolex watch. "Forty five minutes." Even with a terrible haircut this man exuded confidence.

"No problem. Let's get you shampooed."

"I should have known I was going to get what I paid for. That girl didn't even use a water bottle to mist down my hair. But when I'm in a hurry, I take what I can get."

"Well, when you are done here, I'll give you a receipt and when you have time you can bring it over to them. By law, they have to give back your money."

"Go through all that just to get back my eight bucks? Forget about it. I should have just waited and sprung for my usual twenty dollar haircut!"

Back at her chair, she started cutting and asking her usual bout of questions; What do you do for a living? Do you live close? Are you married? Do you have children? And hasn't the weather been wonderful? if all else failed. She guessed he was a professional, judging by his suit. When he mentioned he was an accountant, she was surprised by the fact that he had a fun personality unlike most of the bean counters she'd met over the years. Every girl in the salon was gawking at him, as if they had never seen a Greek god or anything. If it were a professional thing to do, she would yell at them all to mind their own business. More times than not though, depending on the person sitting in her chair, she found her client and herself engaging in conversation with the rest of the salon. But that

wasn't the case this time; at least, she should say, she and her
client weren't engaging in other people's conversations. The
rest of the salon, however, seemed to have gotten instantly
quiet and hung onto their every word. After finding out that he
wasn't a local, a few of the girls continued on with their own
conversation, losing interest. But when she asked him if he
were married, Eva noticed a few of the girls strain to hear his
answer out of the corner of her eye. Come to find out, he had
been happily married for eighteen years with two little girls.
Eva hoped that he didn't hear the groans of the girls as loudly
and obnoxiously as she did.

He was quick to fire back questions to her just as fast. Yes,
she'd lived in Red Wing all of her life. Yes, she was married,
although she didn't add happily because at the moment she
wasn't exactly. She and Eric had a shaky start to their week,
with her getting emotional over the baby thing again, but it
ended up all right. It had been weeks since they were intimate,
and him initiating it was a shock to say the least. After all,
lately, the more she went in for a touch, the quicker he pulled
away. She knew she was repulsive looking to him. Since she
got off the pill seven years prior to start a family she had
gained almost eighty pounds. They sure sneaked up on her
fast, and before she could do anything about it, it was already
way out of control. Now, just getting up in the morning took
more motivation than she had. One of these days, she was
going to get in shape again she kept telling herself.

And then it came to the dreaded kid question. She simply
smiled and said, "Nope not yet," and was grateful that he let it go.

It's amazing how much a person could talk about in a mere
fifteen minutes. His hair wasn't perfect, but it was a vast
improvement. Her handsome client smiled once again. "Do
you have a card?" he asked when they got to the front desk.

"Sure."

She handed him her card and he studied it. "Eva Wahler."
He then looked up to her, put the card in his wallet, handed her
thirty dollars and said, "Keep the change."

"But it's only a ten dollar fix."

He winked, and she was positive her cheeks reddened. "But it was worth thirty. You did a great job! I'll call the next time I'm in town. I'm excited to see what you can do on a fresh pallet."

"That sounds great, Mitch. Have a great day!" Eva had to get out of his presence soon. It had been years since anyone had flattered her like that; and never by someone so handsome.

Barbie stood behind her and whistled as he retreated out the door. "That man can have free haircuts for life if he comes back! I think he fired every one of these ladies' engines, and that's saying a lot since I think some of them haven't been behind the wheel in a veryyyyyyyy long time!"

Eva chuckled. "Well, all I know is, I'm going straight to Hades with the thoughts that are going through my head! I need water. Is it hot in here?" she asked on her way to the back room.

"Yes," all ten people who were there said in unison.

Eric warned Eva that he was working overtime all week again, including ten hours on Saturday. And no, as much as he'd love to watch the races at Charlotte's, he didn't think he'd be up to being around that many screaming kids. After telling him that she'd be going anyway, he just shrugged his shoulders indifferently, rolled over and went to sleep. This schedule of his was killing him, and them, Eva thought. Something had to change, because if she had to hear one more thing about that machine and how big a pain it was, she was going to throw him off a cliff, or jump off herself. She always listened, trying never to say anything but encouraging things. One of them had to keep their chin up, she thought.

Saturday rolled around, and Eva was looking forward to getting her grocery shopping done, cleaning a little and if there was time, a little reading which she had been neglecting for some time. Saturdays never failed to be busy at work, and this Saturday they were two girls short. Luckily, they had Stephanie. She worked like a little church mouse; things always got done, but no one ever saw her do it. It was hard to find a good receptionist and they would miss her when she went off to college.

Her last client of the day was a no show, and where the other girls would be bent out of shape about it, Eva was elated because she could finally sit down! Eva remembered the day when she could work twelve hour shifts, be on her feet all day and feel no pain, where girls who were ten years older than her worked six hour shifts and were complaining about all their aches and pains. At the time she scoffed at them; now she wanted to contact them and beg for forgiveness for being so insensitive!

Eva was working on her daily figures when Sheena the nail tech came up behind her and said, "Jonas is out of town tonight. Let's go out for a drink and appetizers at Liberty's."

"Oh, Sheena I'd love that, but I'm dead on my feet and I have a million and one things to do before Eric gets home!"

"Eric Schmeric! Let him fend for himself for once. What you need is a little time to yourself. Amber and Julie already said they were in. Come on!" Sheena urged, blinking back at Eva with her cat eyes and her you-know-you-want-to smile. The last thing Eva wanted to do was go out. If she had a choice, she'd go home right now and forego the grocery store even though they needed food badly at the house.

Just then, she heard her friend Julie gasp and say, "Eva, just say no."

Thinking that Julie was referring to going out with them, she uncomfortably chuckled and asked, "Why?"

Julie nodded towards the front door, where it faced Main Street. The buzzing of traffic muted out the clicks of peoples' heels on the sidewalk so when she turned to face it, she knew what Julie was warning her when she said, "Look."

Sheena clicked her tongue in a tisk fashion and said, "If you say no to us, you are definitely saying no to her!"

Sun glared in Eva's eyes from the silver dangly earrings of the incoming subject. In tow were her three kids, the two oldest were of course fighting ahead of the woman and the baby was slung on her hip like an unwelcome attachment. Eva, for some reason, got an instant headache. The door opened, and the clang from the bell hitting the door sounded like a gong. Seth and Noah, the two oldest, came screaming in excitedly, running towards Eva. "Auntie, Auntie! Mommy says we gonna stay with you!" said Noah, the blonde haired three year old.

"She did, did she?" Eva asked through clenched teeth, towards her sister-in-law Natasha. She remained smiling for the kid's benefits, but what she really wanted to do was choke her worthless sister-in-law. Natasha pawned her kids off so often it's a miracle that the kids knew she was 'mommy'.

Natasha held back her wild curly Julia Roberts mane from her perfect angular face with her sunglasses and said, "Something came up. You don't mind, do you?"

Eva looked over to the girls watching the scene, and with an eyeball nod, Sheena was basically saying, "Go ahead, tell her no."

"Well, actually, I have a lot on my plate tonight," Eva said fairly confidently.

Natasha snorted and flung back her head laughing, and said sarcastically, "Like what? Putting your feet up from working all day?" That coming from a stay at home mom (if you could call her that). Eva had to hold her bite back. Natasha's idea of a long day was trying to find someone to watch her very active kids while she lived out the life she would have had, had she not met Eric's brother, Barton six years prior. She was twenty; he was twenty eight, and after dating (but most people would consider it friends with benefits) for three months, she ended up pregnant which ended her modeling career prematurely. In Eva's opinion, neither of them were really ready to settle down to start a family, but there they were six years and three kids later. Somehow they made it work, but it baffled their family how.

Shaking off the urge to tell her sister-in-law to get a clue, she politely responded, "As a matter of fact, I'm going out with the girls after work."

Lydia, who was ten months old, was on the verge of having a melt down having to be in her mom's arms when her brothers had full range of the salon. So, doing the typical Natasha thing, she set her down where she could get into anything while she talked with Eva which made the baby happy instantly but made

Eva instantly on edge. Getting serious, Natasha said, "Barton has been delayed in San Francisco until Monday morning and I've had plans for months to go out tonight."

Eva never was bold around her sister-in-law, but having her army of friends behind her, she felt empowered at the moment to say with a shrug, "I guess you'll have to change them. See, that's what being a mother is all about. Self sacrifice. Your life is no longer your own."

Natasha looked like Eva had just punched her in the face. "Not in my household. I will *not* conform my life to my children's schedule. They will conform to mine!" Her confession made Eva speechless, which prompted Natasha to go on. "Come on, kids. Let's go visit your uncle Pete. Maybe *he* will want to spend some time with you." She spat that out just to get a jab in at Eva, knowing that would stir her.

And it worked. Alarm bells went off in Eva's head. Barton hated his brother-in-law Pete. If he found out that Natasha sent his kids there, World War Three would erupt! Maybe she should just let that happen. It was about time that he found out about Natasha's abandoning her kids almost every weekend while Barton was away for work. After all, having the kids over that much was starting to wear on Eric and Eva. But she also knew that if Eric ever found out that Eva knowingly let Natasha bring those kids to Pete's, World War Three would erupt at her house too. She was backed into a corner. The girls would never understand, but she had to spare those kids from Pete's influence. It was bad enough that they had to be around their own mother!

"Wait!" Eva said, "For how long?"

Smiling with satisfaction, she said, "Until tomorrow afternoon or so."

"I have commitments tomorrow. I have to play in church, as well as something in the afternoon..."

"The kids love your church, don't you, kids?" The kids stopped what they were getting into and nodded excitedly. "See? Boys, tell auntie how much you want to stay over at her and uncle Eric's tonight."

34

"Stop!" Eva said, holding her head. She just hated how she used her kids as pawns to get her own way. "Fine...fine! They can go to Charlotte's party with me. There should be other kids there for them to play with."

"Great!" She picked up Lydia, who just knocked over a whole row of shampoo and conditioner and handed her to Eva without even a hug goodbye. The baby melted right into Eva's arms and then planted a big raspberry kiss on her mouth. "I'll put the kids' overnight bags and car seats in your car."

"You are leaving them with me right now?"

"No better time than the present. Thanks!" Natasha said quickly, before bolting out the door without even hugging or kissing any of her kids goodbye. Little Noah stood by the door looking out, tears in his eyes and lower lip trembling. He didn't cry, but he sure looked like he was going to at any second. Those poor kids! There had been so many times Eva had wanted to call social services and report her, but it was those kids who would suffer.

Feeling a hand on her shoulder, Julie asked gently, "Why do you always let her win?"

"It's not about her winning. It's about the welfare of these kids! I'm sorry guys, there's just no way I could let her take them to be with their unc-...." Eva stopped short when she saw Seth and Noah's eyes on her. So with Lydia in her arms, she sat down on one of the chairs and both boys found their little nook on either side of Eva. She loved those kids so much. "Auntie has to get her stuff ready and we'll get some groceries so we have something for you to eat, how does that sound?"

"Can we make that special chocolate milk again, Auntie Eva?" asked five year old Seth with big blue eyes.

"I think we can arrange that."

"Auntie?" Noah, her three year old nephew with the most innocent face she had ever seen, asked.

"Yes, darlin?" Eva responded, brushing his blonde hair back with her fingers.

"I don't want hotdogs."

Eva chuckled. "Then we won't have hotdogs. We can

decide what we are having when we are at the store, okay?"
And in unison, they yelled, 'Yeah!' Even the baby piped in
with a clap, smile and a coo, which made the boys laugh.

Eva never had all three kids at once when doing her grocery
shopping. It wasn't an experience she cared to repeat. In fact,
she didn't get half the things on her list, because the boys were
fighting to the point that Eva had to threaten to take away toy
and chocolate milk privileges. It worked just long enough to
get the essential items she needed. She didn't blame them for
their behavior. Eva blamed it on their parents; or at least the
one they saw all the time. Punishment for them came in the
form of spanking whether they were naughty or not; they just
had to be in their mom's way for them to get swatted. Eva
believed in the whole 'spare the rod, spoil the child' bit, but
she felt Natasha took it too far but didn't say anything due to
keeping harmony in the family. As for herself, she never had
to do it yet with them. They listened to her and if they didn't,
things got taken away or they had to sit quietly, away from
each other for twenty minutes. That was effective. A part of
her thought the kids minded so well for the fact that they feared
never coming back to stay with them. Eva suspected that it
was just another way for Natasha to keep the kids in line;
warning them that they better be good otherwise there
wouldn't be any more stays at "Casa 'de Uncle and Auntie's".

By the time they reached her house, she was so tired that she
was afraid to sit, fearing she would fall asleep on impact. And
with the kids crazier than a wind up toy at Christmas, that
couldn't happen. Eric wasn't home yet, which meant she was
going to be the sole person to let the dogs out as well as
provide the dinner and entertainment for her overnight guests.

Plopping Lydia in the highchair Eva had found at a garage
sale for five dollars, she told the boys they could go play with
the dogs in the living room. But if she heard any
roughhousing, it was going to be time out for both of them.
The boys sauntered off quietly, giving Eva a moment of rest.
At the grocery store they decided that spaghetti and meatballs
would be all right, so Eva starting rolling the meatballs, and

frying them up while the water boiled for the noodles. Clomp, clomp, clomp came from Lydia, who banged her fists against the tray. Music! That's what Eva was forgetting! Turning on her radio in the kitchen, she started singing along. "My Jesus, my Savior. Lord there is none like You! All of my days, I want to praise the wonders of Your mighty love..." Eva was so immersed in singing that she didn't hear the front door open. It was when the boys screamed, "Uncle Eric!" and hearing him scooping both kids up that alerted her.

"Hey, buddies. What are you doing here?" he asked joyfully.

By this time, Eric had walked into the kitchen with both boys in his arms and both dogs at his heels. Seth pulled off Eric's work hat and put it on his own head, saying, "Mommy brought us to Auntie's hair cutting place."

Eric sent Eva an expression as to say, 'I really don't appreciate this'.

Noah giggled, taking Eric's hat off Seth and said, "This is Uncle Eric's hat."

"Well, put it back on my head then silly." Which Noah then did, but cockeyed so he looked like a rapper, making Eva chuckle. "You boys are getting so heavy! Why don't you take Red and Bruiser back in the living room while I talk with Auntie?"

After letting them down, they yelled happily, "Okay!"

Once they were out of sight, he glared at Eva. "What in the hell is going on here? I told you, Eva. No more. I love them kids, but they are not our responsibility!"

Meekly, Eva said, "I know, and I did say no. But then she threatened to take them to Pete..."

"Oh for Chrissakes, she is a real piece of work! Where is Bart?" he asked grudgingly, raking his dirty hand over his tired face.

"Delayed in San Francisco."

His eyebrows scrunched together in confusion. "I thought he was in Dallas."

"Nope, apparently he's in San Francisco."

Shaking his head as if his memory had lapsed, he asked, "And where is our worthless sister-in-law going tonight?"

"She didn't say. All she said is that she had this planned for months and she actually had the nerve to say that those kids need to fit *her* schedule, not the other way around. Those kids don't deserve that, Eric. And I wouldn't see them going with Pete; no way, no how!" Eva tried keeping their conversation just above a whisper, but she just about shouted that last part.

Lydia decided that she wasn't getting enough attention, and let them know by starting to whine. Eric must've blanked out that she was even there, because where there was a scowl on his face a second ago, was now a shiny happy face. "And who do we have here? Is this Lyddie Mynickie?" And with those few words, Lydia stopped crying and reached out for Eric, smacking her lips. This warmed Eva's heart to see. Those kids clung to Eric as if he were their saving grace and she knew if they were ever blessed with kids, he'd be such a great dad. Lydia was now in his arms, and she too grabbed for his hat. To make it easier on her, he placed it on her head, making her giggle. Smiling at Lydia, Eric addressed Eva, "I'm done playing her game. My brother is going to hear about this one."

Chapter 4

"Where the heck are you?" Eric blared into his portable phone as the call connected. He was stalking to the side of the house, phone in one ear and a lit cigarette in the other.

"On a business trip. What's it to ya, hot head?" his brother shot back smartly.

"It's to me because while you are off livin' it up in sunny San Francisco, I'm here with your kids. Again..."

"Where's 'Tasha?" Bart asked with obvious confusion.

"So I take it you didn't know of her big plans that she had for months and months and would never think of abandoning for the sake of her own kids?"

"Don't get testy, bro. I was just asking, and no I had no idea she had any plans for tonight. As far as I knew, she was patiently awaiting my arrival. She didn't even seem that upset when I told her I'd be delayed until Monday."

"I bet," he added sarcastically. "Well according to Eva, she was very eager to get rid of the kids. This is the fifth time in the last six weeks, Bart. I realize that your all-so-important job takes priority in your life, but don't you think at least one of you could make the effort to be with those kids?"

"Like you would know what it's like to have the job that I have, be married to the most high maintenance woman alive and have the three busiest kids given to man. Before judging, little brother, stand in my shoes for an hour and you'll know why I cherish these little escapes."

"They're certainly becoming more and more frequent lately. Where are you, really?" Eric asked skeptically.

"Er—San Francisco."

"Why did I think you were in Dallas?"

"Because that was last week. This week is San Francisco, and next week is Los Angeles."

"Jeez, Bart! Why don't you just move to the west coast?" Eric asked in haste, annoyed.

"Because our families are in Minnesota."

Eric chuckled sardonically, "More like, your permanent babysitters are here. All I'm saying is I'm getting tired of coming home after a long freakin' week and finding your kids standing in my doorway waiting for me to play with them. They aren't *my* responsibility, bro."

Bart sighed through his end of the phone, "No one said they were. I'll handle it when I get home. So I take it that you took the kids overnight?"

"Its 9:30 at night, bro, what do you think?"

Quietly, Bart said, "I'm sorry about this, man. Really, I'll take care of this when I get home. Maybe I can find an earlier flight..."

"Do what you have to do," Eric said, exasperated. "I just don't want to see those kids go through what we did. They deserve both parents in their lives. Don't be a deadbeat dad like ours was. I don't think I could ever forgive you for that."

"Jeezus, Eric. Excuse me for wanting to provide for my family. Don't make me feel guilty for doing what I have to do to make that happen! I'm not going anywhere! And the next time you *ever* compare me to that swine, make sure you say it to my face so I have the chance to kick your ass!"

Eric almost smiled. Good, he thought. At least he expressed some emotion. It's more than he could say for his brother's sorry-for-an-excuse-wife. "Sorry, man. Just get home. Your kids miss you." And the call was disconnected.

By the time he got inside, he was two cigarettes short and the tension in his gut was released; somewhat. Eva was pacing across the living room floor with an almost sleeping baby in her arms. She looked so beautiful, Eric thought. How natural she was with kids. Times like these pained him to know he would never see his off-spring in her arms, but the thought quickly vanished. Eva smiled, blinking her crystal blue eyes over to him and whispered, "Where did you go?"

"I needed a smoke," he admitted nonchalantly.

"And?" Her wide eyes prodded him.

He couldn't get away with anything, he sighed deeply, so he confessed, "I talked with Bart."

"You didn't!" When he nodded, she groaned, "You said you wouldn't do that tonight, Eric!"

"I had to, Eva. It was either confront him, or take it out on you. And I'm sick of taking it out on you."

Walking over to him, she turned so the baby faced him. "Is she out?"

Eric brushed his finger against Lydia's cheek lovingly, and said softly, "She's out like a light."

Eva gently put the baby down in the make shift crib that was propped up next to the couch, and after making sure she didn't stir, she met Eric in their bedroom. She closed the door behind her, watched as he stripped down to his boxers, and applied a silly smile to her face.

"Why are you looking at me like that?"

"You know, after all this time, you are still the most handsome man I've ever seen."

He appraised his body, trying to remember what he looked like at sixteen. There was a little more chest hair that camouflaged his matured chest muscles, and a few added scars from work and home accidents; other than that he still saw himself as a youthful looking kid. "Oh yeah?" he asked, enjoying the compliment.

Eva came a little closer and said with a twinkle in her eye, "Oh yeah." She then ruffled up his light brown hair that was flirting with his dark blue eyes, "But you need a haircut bad!"

"I'll have to schedule some time with you," he remarked dryly, turning off the closet light.

"Oh don't give me that, Eric. I'd cut it for you now, but I know you'll say-"

"I'm not in the mood," he finished for her. "Well, I'm not, Eva. It's been a long week and I'm exhausted!"

"I know," she said sincerely, and then started to disrobe all the while staring at him with hunger.

"What? Oh come on, babe. Not tonight."

She met him beside the bed and started to caress his chest. "You don't have to do a thing. Just let me love you," she said as she replaced her lips where her fingers just were.

"Eva, I don't think..."

She silenced him with a kiss to his lips, pushed him back onto the bed, and said, "Don't think."

Eric knew that moments like these were few and far between. It had been years since they had made love more than once in a week, and even longer since he welcomed her advances. There was a danger of doing it with the kids just feet away which turned him on, heightening the sensation and before long he was controlling the situation, loving every inch of her. She was very responsive, which only urged him to please her more. Just when they were going to make the most intimate of connections, one of the boys started to cry. "Oh, for the love of God!" Eric groaned.

Kissing him quickly, she pushed him off her, and she quickly threw on a robe. But not before whispering, "I'm sorry, hon. Be back as soon as I can!"

Eric ground his teeth to the point of his jaw hurting. His brother owed him *big time*! And so help him Natasha better stay far away from him because the verbal onslaught she had coming from him would blast her into next century! It was moments like these that he felt so lucky to have a wife like Eva who was loving, considerate and down-to-earth. Her patience calmed him down; usually. Twenty minutes had passed since Eva had left to see what the crying was about, and from what he could detect she at least got the situation calmed down. But he was getting impatient so he thought he'd see what the hold up was.

Eva had three year old Noah curled up in her lap, tears streaming his face. Eric took a close seat next to them and said, "What's wrong, 'lil man?"

"I want my----m-mmmmoomyyy!"

"Oh, buddy. You'll see her tomorrow, and if you fall asleep it will come a lot quicker!" Eric said smartly, hoping his suggestion worked. But one look at his nephew's eyes which were filling up once again, he tried another approach. "How about calling your daddy?" He asked, glancing at the clock. Twelve thirty-five. It would only be ten thirty-five in California. He went to the kitchen, grabbed the portable phone and dialed his brother's number. It went straight to his voice mail. That rat-bastard, Eric thought venomously. Well, I'll show him. "How about we leave your daddy a message, Noah?"

At the mention of that, Noah stopped crying for the first time and gave a half smile while nodding. Eric waited for the operator's instructions and then handed the phone to Noah. "Now wait until it beeps to start talking, okay?" At that, Noah nodded again.

"Hi, daddy. I want you to come home..." Eva kissed the side of Noah's head while Eric messed up his hair, making him smile. "Auntie Eva said that I am going to a party tomorrow so I can play with Wheeler and Chase. But please come home. I miss you," he said and then handed the phone back to Eric.

"Feel better, champ?" Eric asked while hanging up.

"Uh, huh."

"So do you think you are ready to try to go back to bed?"

"Uh, huh."

Eric picked Noah up from Eva's arms and settled him next to his brother who was dead asleep on the queen size bed in their extra bedroom. He wasn't out of the room before he heard the deep sounds of the three year olds slumber.

Eva was back in bed, sprawled out, when Eric came in. "Oh, are you still wanting to play?" he asked with a devilish grin.

She wiggled her eyebrows at him and crooked her finger, motioning him to join her. Following her nonverbal command, he was atop of her, assaulting her with his all powerful kisses. "Now, where were we?"

Kissing him in intervals, she said, "Right. About. Here." Then she reached with her feet and pulled his behind to meet her, making the connection they starved for.

Chapter 5

Even though she only had six hours of sleep, Eva felt alive and well. Lydia woke her up around six-thirty, and Seth and Noah weren't too far behind her. Eric was dead to the world, and she left him to sleep. It had not only been a long week for him, but a long night she remembered fondly with a flush to her cheeks. She couldn't remember the last time that they made love like that. When she woke with a smile, she knew it was good.

After fixing the kids breakfast, Seth helped Noah get dressed while she got Lydia ready for church. Eva was doing a mental checklist on her way out the door, reviewing all the tasks she had that morning. Slapping her head, she said, "My violin! Be right back, kiddos!"

Luckily, when she arrived at church, Gloria, one of her choir friends, saw that she needed an extra pair of hands and came to the rescue. Since the kids were shy, they hovered around Eva like static cling. So she excused herself to drop the kids off at Sunday school until they were acclimated. Even though technically Seth and Noah were two years apart in age, the teachers agreed that it would be okay if Seth stayed with his brother in the preschool room to adjust easier. And since the nursery didn't open up until the service, she had the choir director's teenage son watch Lydia while she practiced with the choir. Luckily Lydia was at an age that didn't take too much to adjust to people, which helped out Eva in situations like these. Lydia's low grade fever had dropped, due to the medicine she had given her for her teeth. Hopefully it wouldn't wear off until after church, Eva prayed.

*   *   *

Eva's mediocre-sized church seemed rather crowded. On an average Sunday they had about one hundred and fifty people attend, but today it seemed like the congregation had doubled in size. They had two Sunday morning services, and twice a month they had a Saturday night service. At the time she decided to shop for a church, she didn't know what she was looking for. She grew up in a big Lutheran church, but after confirmation she stopped attending because she didn't have a family who urged her to go, and it wasn't important enough to her to continue. As far as she and her parents were concerned, she fulfilled her spiritual duty. At the time, Eva didn't think it was fair that her parents pushed religion and church on her and her sisters, yet they themselves didn't darken the doorway except for Christmas, Easter, and an occasional wedding. However, after she was married a few years, something compelled her to find a church for her future family to be brought up in because it was the responsible thing to do. But what she found in her search was a small, non-denominational church that was just getting started. Pastor Rob, who was in his late twenties at the time, founded it. It was young, with very few elders. She liked how different it was to the stuffy church she attended when she was a kid. Everyone was super friendly and genuine; and as for the service there weren't any written prayers or Bible verses on the bulletin, recitations of creeds to be spoken in mass or even a title of the sermon the pastor would be speaking on. He preached right out of the Bible, and for the first time it started to make sense. And he not only encouraged bringing your own Bible to church, but to actually read it and meditate on it on your own. Sunday school wasn't just for the kids in this church. There were three classes for adults; one for beginners and two intermediate classes. That was two more than when Eva first started going there. At first she lived for Sunday school, but now since she had been part of the choir, singing mostly alto when she wasn't playing her violin, she hadn't been attending Sunday school like she would have liked. Those first few years she dove in, learning every thing she could about what it meant to be a disciple of Christ.

But it was a few months into attending faithfully that she felt like she was hit by a mack truck of Truth during one of Pastor Rob's sermons on the second coming of Jesus. "Would she be ready if Jesus came for her today?" was the question that piqued her interest. She'd always known that there would be The Great Judgment when she died, which would determine if she was good enough to make it to heaven. Eva always wavered when it came to her eternal destination, not quite knowing if her good was enough to outweigh the bad. But she finally understood when she heard that God had a certain standard; a Holy standard that no one could ever come close to full filling on their own. All she had to do was place her trust and life into God's hands and receive the simple plan of salvation through Jesus Christ's sacrifice. And needless to say she gave her heart right then and there that day, securing her a place in heaven. Her spiritual eyes were opened wide to the world around her from that point on, and it not only changed her life forever, but it helped her through some of the roughest times she had ever faced. Eric went to church on occasion, but he felt really uncomfortable at Crossroads Assembly. Eva was really discouraged at first that he didn't share the same excitement in her new faith, but with the help of some wise friends, they always gave her hope and reassurance that through her, Eric would get there eventually.

*   *   *

Eva had called Eric from the church to invite him to lunch, but after a few snide comments over the fact that *her* 'to do' list wouldn't get done on its own and the cost factor (you know, one more big mac, large french fries and a coke would push them over their budget, Eva thought sarcastically), she held her tongue. Yup, she thought, the afterglow of last night was definitely over. Times like these, when he got so defensive, she had a hard time not taking it personally even though she knew it was just exhaustion talking. Having the kids around sure made it easier not to overreact to his words. Before she hung up, she reminded him that she was heading over to Charlotte's and would drop the kids off at his brother's after the races. He said a hurried goodbye, which frustrated Eva even more.

What ever possessed her to take the kids to McDonald's on a Sunday afternoon, Eva had little idea; quick and easy, not to mention it was a good way to ensure good behavior, she finally reasoned as they entered the kid haven lobby. Lydia was borderline crabby and running a low grade temperature again, causing her not to eat and whine; unfortunately it was too soon to give her more medicine. Eva just prayed that she could keep the poor baby hydrated because she remembered Noah at this age and how sick he got from dehydration on top of teething; she didn't need a repeat of that! Luckily, Lydia was enthralled by watching the million and one kids running and screaming on the Play Land jungle gym. Seth and Noah knew they had to eat everything in their happy meal or else no play land. For little tykes, they sure packed away their food quickly for the sake of getting their fifteen minutes of fun. They started to grumble when Eva told them it was time to go, but cheered up instantly when she reminded them that they were going to see Charlotte and the boys.

How she was going to get through the next few hours without taking a mid-afternoon nap was beyond her. Bart's kids were busy, and knowing Charlotte's household Eva knew it wouldn't be a relaxing adult time.

On the way to Charlotte's, Lydia fell asleep and hearing the boys singing along to the radio didn't leave her much hope at them doing the same. One down, two to go. Fat chance at that, she sided. It was only a five minute ride, and once Seth and Noah saw Indy and the twins, it was going to be a free-for-all.

Charlotte's driveway was crowded with cars when Eva pulled up, causing her to park in the street. Meeting Charley's colleagues would be something new, and already was proving to be interesting. Without interrupting Lydia's slumber, she carried her as the boys followed up the winding cement driveway, passing by a couple BMW's, Lexus, Jaguar and an Audi. Eva appreciated nice things, but never craved them for herself. Charley was the sole provider for his family, working hard as a corporate lawyer for a few local chains. Charlotte had a degree in history, and was working at a library when she met Charley. He insisted that when they had children that she stay home, which she didn't object to. It worked for them.

Their house was equipped for not only a dozen kids, but also for a small party of adults. Charlotte must've been watching out for guests because as soon as Eva was on the steps, Charlotte opened the door.

"Hey, Eva. I didn't think you were going to make it!" She said, hugging Eva and the baby for dear life. "But I'm so glad you are here!" Letting go of them, Char smiled and remarked, "I didn't know you were going to bring guests! It's so good to see you! Come on in, boys!"

"Hi, Mrs. Featherstone!" the boys replied.

Once inside the spacious entry way, the boys kicked off their shoes, threw their jackets on the floor and chased after Charlotte's twin boys as they were being pursued by Indy, Char's oldest. Lydia didn't stir once in all that racket.

"Indy! You boys take your craziness into the playroom! No running outside those walls otherwise I'm taking away your Play Station for a week!" Charlotte said sternly. The boys came to a halt and made their way back to the playroom. Leverage was a great tool, Eva thought.

"No Eric, huh?"

"Nope. He had stuff to get done. Having the kids there would only delay him, so coming here worked out great!"

Charlotte admired the baby resting peacefully in Eva's arms. "It sure would be fun to have a little girl..." Shaking her head as if it were the craziest thing to say, she asked, "Do you want to put her down? I could put her in Brake's crib. He's taking a nap on our bed right now. One of the older girls has his baby monitor. I put her in charge in case he wakes up and I'm not around."

"No, that's okay. I rather not jinx waking her up. She seems pretty glued to me at the moment, and she needs a lot of rest."

"Oh! Before I forget..." Charlotte started, while walking over to the commode, opening one of its hidden drawers. "Here's for my hair and products. Thanks again for doing that for me. I'm such a scatter brain!"

Taking the check, Eva shoved it in her pocket, trying not to disturb the baby in her arms. Unfortunately it was too much of a stir, because Lydia's eyes went from slightly open to almost a shocking look, realizing that she wasn't in a familiar setting. She didn't cry, but she certainly was up now.

Charlotte and Eva went to see what the kids were up to, and what a zoo that was! The room was the size of Eva's entire first level of her house. Balls of every size were being flung around the room, a train track with a boy running one of the trains was in the corner, a glassed in cubicle area where the video game/movie watching area was nestled into the corner and there were five shelves full of toys for every age kid. Eva would've been surprised if she ever heard a child complain of boredom.

There were eight boys inhabiting the room ranging from age three to seven, so it was nice having all that space for them to run, and there were two teenage girls minding the fort. The older of the two teenagers was a cute, petite red head with the clearest blue eyes she had ever seen. The other girl had jet black hair with a darker complexion, but her eyes matched what Eva assumed to be her sister.

The redhead walked over to Eva and smiled at Lydia, who buried her head in Eva's neck. "What's her name?"

"Lydia. She's just waking up from her nap."

The teenager snuck behind Eva, playing, "Peek-a-boo!" and within minutes Lydia was giggling, deciding she liked that game. "May I hold her?" the teenager asked, holding out her hands. Before Eva could answer, Lydia was leaning towards her new friend.

"What's your name?" Eva asked.

"I'm Peyton. That's my sister, Shayla," she added, pointing to her sister who was on the ground playing trains with Noah. "You are so cute, Lydia. Do you mind if I take her over there to play?"

"Sure."

"And don't worry. I've been babysitting for over a year now. I know CPR and have taken all the classes for watching babies and toddlers," Peyton said so maturely, you would've thought she was on an interview.

Eva almost laughed at her matter-of-fact statement. "How old are you, Peyton?"

"Thirteen."

"Well, you seem really responsible. My name is Eva. If she becomes a bother, please bring her to me. She's been a little fussy because she's teething."

"Okay," Peyton said with a perky smile, and then walked away with Lydia towards the toys.

Charlotte had sneaked off in the midst of Eva and Peyton's conversation, settling a dispute between her twins. Once she made sure everything and every one was all right, she made her way back over to Eva. "Everything seems to be in order. Shall we go to the adult room now?"

"Lead the way!"

Turning towards Peyton and Shayla, Charlotte stated, "If any of those boys cause problems, come and get me."

"All right, Mrs. Featherstone!" they said in unison.

Charlotte was excited for female conversation. No other wife showed up, but the kids came in droves with their fathers. Luckily one of Charley's new associates brought his two teenage daughters, which helped her out a lot. And now with Eva there, she would have a good time.

"So where are Bart and Natasha?" Charlotte asked as they headed to the adult room.

"Sore subject right now, Char. Bart is in San Francisco, and I don't know where their mother is."

Shaking her head, Charlotte muttered, "I don't know how a mother could just up and leave those kids as much as she does. They are so precious."

"Yup, it's frustrating. But what can a person do? Yelling and confronting only works on people who actually care."

"That's very true. But bless your heart, Eva. You always come through in a crisis."

The sound of men's laughter and glasses clinking hung in the air as they approached Charley's Race Room. A wooden sign hung over the door indicating just that. Charlotte and Eva quietly entered the room, trying not to draw attention to themselves. NASCAR and NHRA banners hung on the walls, along with Ford emblems and shadow boxes of model cars of Charley's favorite drivers. Rusty Wallace had a whole wall to himself, along with Jimmy Johnson and Ricky Rudd. Eva had heard of these men, but wouldn't know their history like The Featherstones. Off to the right, an oak wood bar ran along the entire wall aligned with eight tall stools. A few men were sitting and sipping on their beers while a man with his back turned behind the bar was mixing a drink.

Charley, looking prim and proper even though he was in jeans and a NASCAR tee shirt, waltzed over to the ladies and swerved in for a kiss from his wife. "Glad you could make it, Eva. Eric didn't come?"

"Nope. He said to say hi, and that next time he'd be here."

"Well, that's too bad. But since you are here, I'd like for you to meet some people." Charley was always very friendly and out going which was why he made a great lawyer, Eva often thought. "Hey guys, I'd like for you to meet a friend of ours. This is Eva Wahler." Her cheeks were fire red as soon as eight sets of eyes were suddenly on her.

"Hi," she said with a smile, and hoped that she didn't have to catch all of their names! She wouldn't have remembered them anyhow. Luckily, they nodded a quick hello and had turned around, continuing to watch the race.

"Would you like a drink?" Charley inquired.

"A water would be great, thanks."

Taking his wife's hand, he escorted the women to the bar. "Hey Carter, would you go in the fridge and grab a water for me?"

"Sure."

By this time Eva wasn't paying attention to the bar, but

instead was studying all the memorabilia that hung on the walls. Out of the blue, the man behind the counter declared, "Hey, you found my life saver!"

Charlotte sounded confused. "What?"

Laughter filled the air, which made Eva turn her head toward the familiar voice. She was having a de-ja-vu moment. Then she saw those entrancing eyes...and that hair... "Wow!   Hi, Mitch, isn't it?" Eva asked, not quite believing her eyes.

"You two know each other?" Charley asked.

"Yup. She saved me the other day. By the way, I've never had so many compliments. I guess that little fiasco made for a great discovery." His smile made her heart pulsate, and it shouldn't, she scolded herself; she was a married woman for crying out loud! But the way he spiked the front of his new style sure made him look, well, younger and too dang sexy for his own good; far better than when he left the salon!

Trying to distract her thoughts, Eva said with a smile, "Well, I'm glad to be of service."

"Well, your great service may get you a lot more people coming your way. I should've gotten more of your cards to hand out. As it is, I've been just giving your name and number to anyone who compliments my fabulous haircut."

"Wow! That's really nice of you.   No better way of advertising than word of mouth," Eva replied, half shocked and half appreciative. "If you send as many people as you say, there just may be a free haircut in it for you," she added, settling herself on an empty barstool.

"All the more reason to continue spreading the word then, eh?" he said with a wink.

"Of course! Very rarely does anyone get anything free in this world without strings attached, outside of God's salvation that is," she added with a chuckle.

Resting his elbows on the bar, he leaned in and said respectfully, "I take it that you are a Christian."

"Was I that obvious?" Eva giggled.

"Well, regular people just don't blurt things out like references to God's salvation, and if they do they sure don't put it into the free category..."

She didn't know what compelled her to open her mouth, but the words just flew from her before she could stop. "I guess I see my business as a gift from God. The regular people of this world give us free hand outs, but it's usually for personal gain. I, for one, love to give back because I figure it's just a little of what God has first given to me."

Mitch smiled appreciatively. "You are a wise lady, Eva Wahler. I wish my wife shared your views, but I guess we all have our crosses to bear, don't we?"

Something in the way he commented alerted Eva to some thing amiss. Could he not be so 'happily married' as he made it sound the other day? It intrigued her to dig deeper, to find out where he was coming from not only a spiritual standpoint but as a person as well, yet she knew it was wrong. Talking about marital issues with the opposite sex who wasn't your spouse wasn't wise; especially when lustful thoughts were on the forefront of your mind. If she wanted to play with the devil she would've taken the bait, but it would only fuel the fire in her mind, not to mention her hormones. This was definitely not from God, and she needed to get far away from it. Knowing what she should do, she simply said, "Yes, we sure do."

Shaking his head in disbelief, he remarked, "What a small world. How do you know the Featherstones?"

"We met in church a few years back." Speaking of the Featherstones, Eva thought as she looked around, where did they go? In a matter of seconds, they were left alone at the bar. But she would not get sidetracked. "They are really great friends."

"I just met Charley this week. He mentioned this party he was throwing, and I thought it would be a great opportunity to get to know him and my other colleagues better." He glanced around, making sure no one could hear him and once he knew that the coast was clear, he leaned in and in a whisper, admitted, "Don't tell anyone, but I'm not a race fan." And then he did his signature wink, which made Eva's heart skip a beat.

"Your secret is safe with me. In fact, I'm not much of a fan either. I'm here for Char. She usually doesn't get to watch much of the race, so I like to come and relieve her from watching the kids."

"Well, that's real nice of you."

Flushed faced and messed up hair, Charlotte made her presence known again. "I'm baaaack," she declared, jokingly stretching her arms out as if she just orchestrated a grand entrance.

"And where did you go?" Eva asked sarcastically, as if she didn't have an idea seeing the state of her dress.

"I went to the kitchen and got the food if you must know," she said exasperatedly, while pushing her wild hair off her face.

"I could have helped you, Char, had you let me know you were going to do that!" Eva said with a quick half smile, notifying her friend that she didn't appreciate the disappearing act.

"Yeah, well, Charley wanted to help and you and Mitch seemed to be okay in conversation so, well, you know...."

Mitch chuckled while he busied himself behind the bar. When his back was turned, Char grabbed Eva's arm and mouthed, "Doesn't he look just like Alec Baldwin?"

Eva took a longer look at the man in question and smiled, whispering back, "Now that you mention it, he does."

"Shhhhhhh! He's coming back."

Eva turned towards him and said, "Well, Mitch, it was great talking with you again. And I'm glad that your haircut worked out. I'll leave you to your bartending abilities."

"Enjoy your water," he said again with another wink before she walked away.

There were two black leather couches encompassing the fifty two inch screen TV which looked inviting. Unfortunately, the only seats available were the leather recliners which were moved in as an afterthought from the living room. So, after grabbing some snacks, Eva and Char took a seat on them, chatting about how great the sermon was that morning when the redheaded girl who was minding the kids' room pushed through the door with a screaming Lydia in her arms.

"Eva, she won't stop crying. And she feels really hot."

Eva took the baby, holding her in her arms and pressed the back of her hand to Lydia's forehead. "She needs her medicine and it's in her bag in the entryway; will you get it for me please? It's purple with white kites on it."

While Peyton went to search for it, Charlotte said, "I think I have something for her to chew on. It works great for teething and I just hope it's still where I think it is. I'll be right back."

"Thanks, Char."

Eva went out into the hall because the men looked at the crying baby like a boil they'd love to pop. While she was waiting, Mitch came out, shutting the door quietly behind him. "Is everything okay out here?"

Lydia wasn't relenting in her wailing. "She's teething."

"Ohhhh..." And instead of leaving like any other man would, he stayed. "I don't miss those days," he remarked.

Eva smiled over to him, but he looked perplexed. "What?" she asked.

"I. Just. Never mind," he said, holding the back of his neck as if he were distressed about something.

"No, what is it?" Eva encouraged.

"I just thought I remember you saying you didn't have kids."

"Oh. I don't. This is my niece, Lydia."

"Oh, sorry about that. She looks a lot like you, so I just assumed she was yours."

Eva chuckled. "Yeah, the funny thing is, she's not even blood. She is my husband's brother's daughter." Before Mitch could comment, Peyton showed up with Lydia's things.

"Here you go, Eva," Peyton said, handing over the diaper bag. "Oh, hi daddy!"

Hugging her close, Mitch said, "Hi, princess."

Eva placed Lydia on the carpeted floor while she dug for her medicine, but when she heard Mitch's greeting to the teenager, she looked up and asked with interest, "This is your daughter?"

"One of them. If you have met her, I'm sure you have met Shayla as well."

"Wow, when you said you had little girls, I was imagining 'little' as in three and four."

"Nope, they are little as in pre-teen and teen and the reason for my prematuring grey hair!" he laughed, pointing out the few silver flecks on the side of his head.

Playfully hitting her dad's stomach, Peyton smiled and said, "Oh, daddy!"

Eva smiled at them, and realized quickly that she was getting distracted by the scene. She quickly gave Lydia a few drops of her medicine, positioned her back in her arms and then started to rock her. Mitch patted his daughter on her seat and said, "You better go and help your sister out."

"Okay. I hope Lydia will be all right."

"She will." Eva said with bright eyes. After the young red head retreated, Eva turned to him and said, "Thanks for your daughter's help."

"Don't mention it. It's nice to know something was ingrained after all we've taught them."

"So where is your wife?" she blurted out so quickly that she didn't have time to recover other than to add, "Sorry for being so blunt. I'm usually not that rude."

"No worries. She is out of town with her girlfriends. Once a month five of her girlfriends get together somewhere. And since I had nothing to do, I thought I'd bring the girls down here. It's getting harder and harder to find things to do with them now that they are getting older."

"I can imagine." Eva loved her dad, but he was never the type of dad to take her anywhere or do anything with. He was their provider, and that's it. She always wondered if he would've been different had they had a boy in the mix. Rarely did he have a comment over anything in his girls' lives. All he ever said was he wanted them to be happy. Stress wasn't in his vocabulary, and that said a lot since he was married to the most contentious woman alive. "I think it's great that you make the effort to spend time with them. They may not appreciate it now, but years down the road they will remember that more than anything."

Charlotte had Noah in tow on her way back from the entry way. "Sorry, Eva, couldn't find that teething ring, but look who I found!" When Noah saw Eva, he ran to her and his lip was quivering. "Auntie, Seth pushed me and said I couldn't play with Tate. But I wanna play with Tate."

Kneeling down to him, she hugged him. "Why don't you hang out with me for a while?"

His tearful eyes blinked, and he nodded sadly. They may not be her kids, but anyone could see that she loved them as if they were hers, which wasn't lost on the present company. "Hey, 'lil guy, why don't you come in and watch the cars go in a circle on the TV with us?" Mitch asked.

"Noah, this is Mr. Carter. His daughter is Shayla."

At the mention of her name, Noah's eyes lit up. "Really?"

"Yup."

Looking from his aunt to Mitch, Noah took his hand and Eva followed with a now content Lydia. Mitch sat in one of the recliners and signaled for Eva to take the other one. Noah climbed onto Mitch's lap and appeared content as can be with his pretzels and water.

"Noah, honey, why don't you come and sit with Lyddie and me? I'm sure Mr. Carter would like his lap back."

"Nonsense. I don't mind at all. It's been a long time since I've done this, and quite frankly, I kind of miss it."

Noah smiled up to him, then over to Eva. "Well, all right, as long as you don't mind. But the moment he starts getting too heavy, he can go back to the playroom, all right, Noah?"

"Okay, auntie."

There was nothing more handsome than a man holding a child. Eva tried everything to look away, but there was something so peaceful about that man. It's like he had no worries, and if he did, he had a great way of hiding them. "Thank you," she mouthed over to him when Noah's back was turned. Mitch just smiled and then returned his attention to the child in his lap.

Voices erupted right outside the room, causing Mitch and Eva to look. Charlotte and Charley were escorting in a few new people, which in Eva's mind was no cause for more gawking so she turned back around. Eva knew introductions were going to soon be made anyhow.

"Hey, Charley, just comin' for my kids."

"Hey Bart. Well, two of them are in here."

At the mention of her brother-in-law's name, she whirled around and stared not only at him, but Eric as well. Her husband didn't look happy either as he glanced her way.

Chapter 6

To say that Eric was irritated was a mild understatement. All he wanted to do was wake up to a peaceful house, which he had thanks to Eva, rest a little bit and get at least one thing off his long list of 'to do's. His rotten mood started after being interrupted the first time by Eva's mom. Almost every Sunday was the same routine; she would call, and he would remind her that Eva was at church and to call back in the afternoon. Then she would make some snide comment about him not being there with her, as if it was the most unforgivable sin in the world, when she, in fact, wasn't now nor had ever been an avid church goer. How Eva ever turned out all right after being raised by an overbearing mother as she, he'd never know. He just hoped that his wife would never take on her mother's personality, and the minute she did he would make a run for it.

Then two telemarketers called one right after the other, making him want to pull the phone from the wall. But then he wouldn't have gotten the last call (the straw that broke the camel's back) from Eva. He almost called her back after his rude behavior, but number one, he was still angry, which never proved to be an appropriate time to settle any matter between them; number two, she called from the church and had probably left already and number three, he would've had to take the time to repair the wires which were disarrayed when he finally *did* pull the cord from the wall, and he just didn't have time for that *plus* the first initial task at hand, which was the leak under the kitchen sink. Then to put the icing on the cake, the dogs were overly rambunctious, so he locked them in the living room while he tried tackling the leak. Hearing the drip, drip, drip night and day was almost annoying as finding another one of Eva's 'love notes' lying on the counter for him. They usually said something to the effect of, 'Eric, the washer isn't cycling out right or the furnace is making a funny noise' and it always ended with 'love, Eva'. Once upon a time she used to verbalize the request, but she must've gotten sick of seeing the look of disgust on his face every time she brought up an issue so slipping a note on the counter was a lot easier than dealing with his response. Her facial expressions told a thousand tales when things weren't getting done and the list just seemed to get longer and longer, and just seeing the disappointment in her eyes when she saw him resting when he knew she thought he should be busting his butt around the house not only hurt him, but made him angry. How much more did she expect from him? He was only one person after all.

He was bitter over the fact he did so much, while from his perspective, she wasn't pulling her weight around the house. Sure he knew she worked. But her thirty-five hours were nothing compared to his sixty. And more times than not, he was the one cleaning up the house when she had all the time in the world to do such a menial task. Doing things for other people ranked number one on her list of 'to do's', which prompted many arguments over the years. Taking the dogs for a walk had been his job for the last few years. He remembered the day when they would take them together. Back then, they didn't have the stresses or problems they did now. And back then, she couldn't wait to get home and spend the night with him, no matter what they might do.

Now it seemed like she had time for all her friends, but for him? One, maybe two days they spent together. And sex? Well, this week sure was a jackpot week, he thought sarcastically to himself. But that, he knew, was a fluke. For years her response to it felt as if he were forcing it on her. The enjoyment of the act wasn't there with her, and hadn't been for a long time.

Things started to change in her libido once she went back on the pill after the doctor said it was the only way her body would get back to normal. They were in a catch 22 situation. When she wasn't on the pill, she had no chance of getting pregnant due to the cysts on her ovaries. Being on the pill shed the cysts but put her in the same predicament of not being able to conceive. After that, sex had almost become non-existent, and temptations for him started to spring up everywhere. He met a lot of women at the bar, and had many chances to stray. And he almost did once, but in the end he loved Eva and could never do that to her.

He had been wrenching on a pipe, working out all his frustrations of life, when he heard the dogs signal an intruder bark. Eric was just about on his feet when his brother, dressed like he just got off the golf course, walked in.

"Jeezusss, Bart! You scared me half to death. What are you doing here?"

"Nice to see you too, little brother," he shot back derisively. "If you can recall, you are the one who insisted that I get back here as soon as possible. I'm here to retrieve my kids." And when Eric just stood there with an evil look on his face, his brother added, "Oh and by the way, thanks for putting my kid on the phone last night. You're a real douche bag."

"Maybe, but it worked. You are here now." Eric said with disinterest, opening up the refrigerator and extracting a beer, adding, "And they aren't here."

"I can see that. Where are they?" Bart asked with a scowl.

"With Eva. They are at the Featherstones."

Retrieving Eric's phone, Bart asked, "What is their number?"

"Why?"

Bart looked at his brother as if he were the dumbest man in the world. "Because I'm going to have Eva bring them here."

Slamming the beer down his throat in seconds, Eric crushed it between his big hands and said, "No, you're not. You are *not* going to inconvenience us any more than you already have. If you want those kids now, you are going to go pick them up yourself. Otherwise, you will either wait here for them or go home and wait. The choice is yours."

"I really don't have time for this," Bart said exasperatedly.

"Tough. Neither did I last night, or the last month of week-ends. If it weren't for those kids, I wouldn't have time for you," Eric said through clenched teeth and the fire in his eyes should have warned his brother to just leave.

"What is your problem? You told me to come back, and

here I am. What else do you want from me? Damn!"

"What I want is for you and your wife to grow up and take care of those kids. You hide behind your job. To me, that is no better than how our dad walked out on us. And your pathetic excuse for a wife..."

He didn't have time to get that last part out because Eric's face met up with Bart's huge fist. "You. Are. Dead." Eric fought back, bringing both two hundred pound men down on the floor. Eric had a few inches and twenty pounds on his brother, but Bart was a scrapper; nothing intimidated him. If you were a stranger looking on this scene, you would think they were two overly testosterone teenagers the way they were fighting, rolling around on the kitchen floor and calling each other every foul name in the book. The dogs must've sensed danger, because before they knew it they jumped over the gate and Reddog was nipping at Bart's feet.

"Get that mutt off me or I swear I'll kill it after I kill you!"

"Not if I kill you first!" Eric got on top of Bart and tried punching his brother's face again, but with every punch, Bart blocked. Red was getting in the way of the punches, so Eric yelled, "Red, back off!" and the dog obliged.

Both men were breathing heavily and after realizing what he was doing, or was about to do, Eric rolled off his brother and sat on the kitchen floor holding his knees, staring at the kitchen sink that was still in need of repair. Bart was on his feet again within seconds, and had jammed his balled up hands in his pockets. And in a quiet voice he said, "I love my kids. I will never abandon them like our lame ass father did. *Never* disrespect my wife again, or we *will* be through. That's not a warning, it's a promise."

Eric just sat there, but nodded his head in silence.

"I don't know what is going on with you, little brother, but I'm sure it's more than dealing with me and my kids. I need a cigarette. Do you have one?" Still seated, Eric pointed to the counter where his Marlboro's sat. Shaking his head at his brother's stubbornness, Bart asked, "Would you care to join me for one?"

After a few seconds of pondering, Eric got to his feet, reached for his jacket and his pack of cigarettes at the same time and walked out the kitchen door without looking at his brother. Bart followed silently.

Eric already had a few deep inhales of his cigarette before Bart was handed one. And the first time since rolling around on the ground, Eric said calmly, "This was part of the problem."

"*Huh?*" Bart asked, confused.

Holding out his cigarette, he said, "I was having a nic-fit right before you came. Our argument didn't help. Just fueled the fire, ya know? Sorry for what I said..."

A few seconds later, Bart said, "Yeah, I know what you mean. Sorry about punching you. It's been a stressful weekend. And don't worry, Natasha won't be bothering you for a long time with those kids."

"I'd rather watch them than seeing those kids in her brother's hands, Bart. We will always be there for them, but seriously man, this every weekend thing has got to stop."

"Oh, believe me, *my* kids will never be left alone with that meth head Pete. She knows that if I hear that it ever happens, I will quit my job and stay home with them. I've threatened that before and as far as I know she has never resorted to using him as a sitter. She likes living in style too much to risk me quitting my job to stay at home," he said, knowing his wife better than Eric thought he did.

"Well, that's a relief."

Snubbing out his cigarette, Bart asked, "Want to head over to the Featherstone's with me?"

"Naw, I have stuff to do."

"Whatever, man. Your wife is over there, having fun, while you slave away? When was the last time you had fun?"

"I have fun all the time." But Eric thought long and hard, and it saddened him to think he couldn't recall the last time he did; the after work bar escape hardly constituted fun. It was what it was; an escape.

"Bull, you are coming with me. Change your clothes and

let's get going."

"Naw, you go ahead."

Grabbing the almost full pack of cigarettes out of Eric's hands, his brother said, "You are going to come with me and your cigarettes. Now, let's get a move on! I want to see my kids!"

So, there they were, standing in the entryway with the always happy-go-lucky Charlotte and her excitement over their appearance. He was trying very hard playing the part of a cheerful person, when inside he was seething over the fact that Bart still had his cigarettes in his pocket and if it weren't for him and his kids, he would have been peacefully doing his own thing at his own quiet house.

"Eva's in Charley's Race Room. Follow me!" Charlotte said enthusiastically. "She'll be so shocked to see you!" she added towards Eric.

And that she was, Eric thought as he spied her out behind his brother's back. Sitting with her back to him, she seemed in deep conversation with some guy holding his nephew. That didn't bother him as much as her guilty face when she saw him.

"Daddy!" Little Noah screamed cheerfully when he heard his dad's voice. He wiggled out of the man's lap who was sitting next to Eva.

Bart scooped up the little version of himself and hugged him tight. "Hey, tiger! Miss me?"

"Yes! I missed you soooooooooooo much!"

By this time, Eva had made her way over to the little party and Lydia, recognizing her dad, squirmed in Eva's arms. "Hey, 'hon! Hey, Bart! You are home early!" Eva said with an open smile.

"I just couldn't stay away from these little monsters one day longer!" Bart said as he tickled his three year old. "Come here, baby girl." He then reached with his free arm for Lydia and the baby slid into his embrace and planted a wet kiss on his cheek.

"I didn't think you were coming, Eric," Charley interjected, but appearing genuinely happy that he did.

"Well, Bart wanted to come get his kids so I thought what the heck? Watching the races sounded a lot more entertaining than working on my leaky sink!" Eric said, lying through his teeth. Eva came to his side and slipped her arm around his narrow waist. "Well, the leaky sink will always be there. I'm glad you're here," she said, beaming.

He smiled briefly down in reaction to her sweet words and when he looked back up, the man who was sitting next to Eva when he came in was standing next to Charley. "Eric and Bart, this is the new accountant issued to us indefinitely."

The man introduced himself as Mitch Carter, shaking both Bart's and Eric's hands. Eric was put off by the fact that he looked his brother square in the eye, but when it came to him he glanced away, giving him the impression that something wasn't right.

"Well, as much as I'd love to stay, I have to get these rug rats home," Bart said.

"Of course. Let me go find Seth. Last time I saw him he was playing video games with Tate and Indy," Charlotte said, while motioning for Eva to join her.

Kissing Eric's cheek, Eva whispered, "Be right back."

As soon as she left the room, Eric felt uneasy. It wasn't as if he didn't know Charley, but being around a bunch of stuffy professionals always made him feel inadequate. You know, the people who actually got a degree, and we aren't talking just a two year education. These are the kind of degrees that give 'job security' a whole new meaning. Although he didn't have a degree, working with his hands made him happy, and knowing that he could provide for Eva and him made him proud. But standing amongst these so called scholars made him question his worth as a man. Standing back and listening to Bart make idle chit chat with this bean counter, and his host, who was known to be a powerful lawyer behind some very reputable businesses, made Eric wish he had something intelligent to interject. Where his brother was more the outgoing talker in a crowd, Eric enjoyed the shadows and his attempt at a conversation would be transparent so he wouldn't even bother the embarrassment of joining in. These men seemed nice enough, and maybe if they were on his turf they would get along great. But in this setting, at this time, even with the strength of Bart at his side, he just felt like a shell of a man. Every once in a while those old feelings of nothingness would pop up, crippling him.

"Would you like a drink, Eric?" Charley asked.

That sure came at the right time, Eric thought, but the need to escape was still on the forefront of his mind. "I'd love a beer, but I'll see my brother off first and then I'll be ready for it!"

Eric lifted Noah into his arms and Bart followed with Lydia in tow. Over his shoulder, Eric spoke just above a whisper, "I'll take my cigarettes *now*, man!"

Chapter 7

Eva rested the back of her head against the soft leather seat while Eric took the wheel of her vehicle. Although she didn't feel like she did much, she was exhausted. She kept replaying the way Seth reacted to her telling him that he had to go home in her head. Knowing it was a typical response for a kid his age, it shouldn't have bothered her. Especially when she knew how much he got into his video games. More times than not, tearing him away from it was near impossible without a tantrum. But there was a part of her that thought it had something to do with the anxiety of having to go back home, because after telling him that his dad was there which would excite almost any child who hadn't seen their parent in almost a week, Seth practically ignored her and dove more into his game without any backfire at all. But luckily for everyone involved, with gentle probing from Eva he politely set down his controller and took Eva's hand.

"But auntie, can't I stay with you and Eric tonight? I promise to be really good."

His face was priceless, but not enough to sway Eva. Crouching down so she was eye level with him, she hugged him in close and said with a loving smile, "You are welcome at our house anytime, Seth. But it's a school night and I know for a fact that your daddy missed you so much that he did everything he could to get back to you earlier than planned."

"He did?" he asked as if not truly believing her.

"Yes, darling, he did. And he's anxiously waiting to see your handsome little face. Let's not make him wait a moment longer, all right?" And that is all it took for him to let go of her hand and race into the foyer where Bart and Eric stood waiting for them. Bart just ruffled his hair and after saying a quick, 'Hey son!" and then turned his back on him to help Noah get ready and added impatiently, "Let's not take forever getting

our jackets and shoes on. Mom is waiting for us at the house."
The mention of 'mom' made Seth pause for a moment, but
when Eva gave him an encouraging nod, he hurried into his
gear and was soon ready to go. When Lydia saw Eva, she
started to whine and reach for her, so Eva said a quick
goodbye. It killed her every time she had to leave them.

Eva had resumed her conversation with Charlotte and Mitch,
sitting in the middle of them at the bar as she waited patiently
for Eric to return from saying his goodbyes. Eva really hated
talking bad behind anyone's backs, but when it came to her in-
laws she vented a lot, mostly to Charlotte and Stephanie whom
she trusted with the information. When Charlotte inquired
about what Bart's arrival was all about in front of Mitch, Eva
was hesitant to say anything, due to Eric hating airing dirty
laundry about his dysfunctional family. If he were to overhear
Eva mentioning anything about their business, there would be
hell to pay. Just when she was in the middle of saying that she
had no idea why Bart was there, Eric walked in and for the
second time that day she felt like a deer caught in headlights.
And she recognized that quick raised eyebrow that meant that
she was off the hook now, but she better believe she would be
asked about it later.

Over the years Eva had learned to become a good abstainer
of the truth, as unchristian as that was. Not that she made a
habit of lying, but some things were best left, well, unsaid.
Like for instance, there had been months she purposely 'forgot'
to take her pill so maybe an 'accident' would happen like some
of her friends and clients. Oh how she prayed that that
'tragedy' would occur. However, all it did was prolong her
monthly to the point of figuring that method just didn't seem
worth it.

And then there were those times when she just couldn't
stomach seeing how her mom treated Eric at family gatherings,
so she made excuses for Eric's absence every chance she
could. It was blatant how much her mom disapproved of him,
so when Eva made the suggestion all those years ago that he
just not go to one of their get-togethers to avoid the scorn, he

didn't even balk in disagreement and before long it became the norm that he not be there; well, outside of holidays, that is.

Eric had vocalized how he had noticed that it wasn't just himself who Eva's mom sought to ridicule; she had a way of belittling Eva as well. It hadn't always been like that between mother and daughter. They had a great relationship, that is, until Eva decided to make her own choices; mainly about her future and it happened to be around the time she started going out with Eric. Needless to say, it didn't settle well with Bonita 'Bunny' Johnston. Her mother was all about control, and the more independent Eva had become, the more they butted heads. All it did was push her more towards Eric, which infuriated her mother even more towards him. Eva could just shrug it off when her mom's words were aimed towards her, but knowing Eric's background with abandonment issues, she knew that any hope of a connection between the two would be totally cut off if he heard the things her mom said about him when he wasn't around; he was already offended by the things she said to his face. After fourteen years of being with Eric she had hoped that her mom would've accepted him as the man she devoted her love and life to, but all her mom saw was a man with no hope of a real future and the one who helped her daughter chase away her dreams of becoming an accomplished musician.

"So, who is that Mitch guy? You seemed to be having quite the conversation with him," Eric said, jostling her thoughts back to the present.

"He's the accountant working with Charley."

"Don't treat me like I'm stupid, Eva. Both times when I came into the room today, there he was, talking with *you*. Why is that?" he asked, with calm intensity.

"Not just me, Eric. Charlotte was there too," she brought to his attention, and then asked him flippantly, "Since when do you play the jealous card?"

Whipping out a cigarette and lighting it, he said, "Don't evade the question. I just want to know who this man thinks he is talking with *my wife*."

Eva's heart started racing, because Eric always trusted her.

69

She was prepared to explain what she and her friends were talking about when he came in, but wasn't expecting the Spanish inquisition about Mitch Carter. So as calmly as she could, she explained, "I met him earlier this week actually, but at the time I had no idea he was tied to Charley. He came in for one of our 'fix it' promotions, so when I saw him we were like old friends, and since he wasn't interested in the races he hung out with Charlotte and me."

"It wasn't just you and Charlotte. When I first came in, he had Noah in his lap and you guys looked like you were having an in-depth conversation. I also noticed the way he was looking at you."

"*Wow*, Eric. I think you are reading wayyyyy too much into this!"

"No, I'm telling you how I saw it, Eva. Who is this guy really? He sure as heck wasn't there for the races, but yet seeks out to talk with the only women in the crowd instead of his own colleagues? Either he's gay or he's got a thing for you!"

"Okay, I think you have gone overboard there, Eric," Eva began, holding back her temper, "Mitch is a happily married man I'll have you know. And our conversation that you are so concerned over? It was about kids' and God. I should probably be honored that you hold me up in such high esteem that I could turn the head of another man, but right now I'm hurt and utterly confused as to why you are acting like this."

Inhaling a huge puff of his cigarette, he took his time blowing it out. "I just didn't like how he was looking at you, and the fact that the guy couldn't look at me in the eyes told me he was guilty about something."

"Nothing was going on, Eric, for goodness sakes!" When he didn't say or look at her, she added desperately, "I swear!"

Finally, shaking his head, he said, "It wasn't right. It was a little too cozy a scene to drop in on, and I could've sworn that it looked like you were talking about me the second time."

"But I-"

"Whether I'm overreacting or not, I just want you to know that I didn't like it, not one bit. I don't care if he is a boring bean counter. I don't trust any guy who would cozy himself up to another man's wife!"

"It was all innocent, Eric. You don't even know him. He's not a bad guy. You really need to give people more of a chance before you start judging them." That was one thing Eva had a hard time understanding about her husband; Eric was always on the defensive with people. It took a while for him to warm up to anyone.

"I just call it like I see it!" he yelled, red in the face.

Uh oh, Eva thought, that was the wrong thing to say. "Look, I'm sorry. Let's just cool off before we say things that we will regret later and not talk until we get home. I'm getting a headache."

"Well, isn't that convenient," Eric muttered under his breath.

Instead of answering, she just closed her eyes. A few minutes later, they were home and as soon as she walked in the door the phone was ringing. But by the time she got past the dogs, it quit so she looked at the caller ID. It was her mom. Eva hadn't talked to her in a few weeks because of her busy schedule, and when they did it was usually over something dramatic, so she figured she better return her call before her mom exploded.

Her mom answered on the fourth ring.

"Hi!"

"Who's this?" her mom asked cordially.

"It's Eva, mom. What's up?" Eva looked over to Eric who was petting both dogs at once while giving her a questioning glance.

"Didn't that husband of yours tell you that I called this morning? He does have a bad track record with that you know."

Ignoring her last remark, she said, "I just got home. What's going on?"

"Your father and I will be in Minneapolis on Tuesday. We'll be staying with Andrea and David. We were thinking about getting everyone together Friday night. Heidi said she'd get there around six and I haven't heard from Joelle yet. But I don't figure she'll want to come this way for a long weekend, but anyhow, we hope you can make it."

"Well, I'm sure I'll be able to, but Eric has been working a lot of overtime lately-"

Her mom cut her off by quickly saying, "Oh, that's no problem. Tell him we understand. Let your sister know ASAP if you are coming."

"All right mom. Talk to you soon. Say hi to daddy for me."

After hanging up with her mom, Eric asked, "What was that all about?"

"They invited us to dinner on Friday. I guess they are coming up on Tuesday and staying with Andrea."

"Well, thank God for small miracles!" Eric joked, but then got really serious when he asked, "They aren't expecting me to be there, are they?"

"No, hon, that's why I said you would be working."

"Well good. I'll be just too exhausted."

"We all understand that. Until your overtime slows down, I won't expect too much out of you," Eva said sincerely.

"Why, thank you mother," Eric shot back sarcastically, which told Eva that she again had said the wrong thing. Knowing that responding back to his snide comment would be another error in judgment, she stifled it.

Eric plopped himself on the couch and said, "I'm going to take a nap. Wake me when supper is done, all right?"

"Sure," Eva said between her teeth. She looked at the clock. Twenty to five. Bruiser whined next to her and Reddog waited by the mud room door. Time to let them out. For the first time in years, her frustration gave her the energy to go for a walk. After putting the phone back in its charger and hooking their leashes to their collars, Eva led the dogs on a mile walk.

*   *   *

"Oh my god, Evalynn! Are you pregnant?" Bunny Johnston shrieked, gawking at her daughter as soon as she took off her jacket.

72

Blushing profusely, Eva retorted sarcastically, "No, mother I am not. I'm just fat, but thank you for pointing it out and making me feel oh so much better about myself."

Bunny's mouth gaped open as if she wanted to say something more, but couldn't. Her mother was speechless and Eva gave herself credit that it only took two seconds to do the task. She never knew what her mother would throw at her, and Eva always had to be on her toes. Loving her mom was the hardest job she had in life, and a lot of the time she just asked for God's love to shine through her because she had very little lately for her mother. Maybe being sarcastic wasn't the best way to deal with her, but it was the best defense mechanism for Eva.

"Eva? Is that you?" her sister Andrea asked as she came from the kitchen, wiping her hands on her apron. Her sister reminded Eva of a 50's icon TV mother with her perfect house, perfect husband, perfect kids, perfect job, perfect hair, perfect body(after having 2 kids) and just an all around perfect life... perfect, perfect, perfect. Andrea was six years older than she, and had always been the mothering type. Even though Eva joked about how 'perfect' her sister was, they had a great relationship and she really looked up to her (with an exception of a few annoying habits like being anally clean and having semi-control issues that she picked up from their mom).

"Hey," Eva said with a smile as she hugged her. As usual her sister was wearing a knee length modest dress with pearls and sensible matching dress shoes, Eva chuckled to herself. If she wore a beehive she would've fit right in to the set of *Leave It To Beaver*.

"No Eric, huh?" She looked disappointed. Andrea and her husband David got along the best with Eric and always treated him with respect.

"No, I thought mother told you."

"No, mother told you to call your sister to make final plans," Bunny hissed from behind her.

Momentarily forgetting, Eva said, "Yes, you are right. Sorry Andie. I hope you didn't plan extra for him."

Batting her hand in the air in front of Eva, she said, "Oh, it's nothing. Better to have extra than not enough. Come on in. We are just waiting on Heidi."

The grandfather clock dinged in their sitting room (you know, the room where no one walked, sat or breathed in even though it was fully furnished) and alerted them that it was six o'clock. Her black sheep of the family younger sister, Heidi, would soon be there. She was two years younger than Eva and had always been an element of her own. Art was Heidi's world. Didn't matter what it was, she dabbled in it. The last time anyone had heard or seen her was Memorial Day when the entire family got together to celebrate birthdays, and she was getting ready for a big show in Chicago to debut her body painting canvases. Heidi explained with enthusiasm that its where she lathered herself in different colors of paint (sometimes she used two or more extra people as well) and rolled around on a canvas, calling it art. Somehow, Heidi always got by. She lived in a studio apartment in South Minneapolis. Family was never her thing.

Eva and Heidi got along when they were younger but once Eva started high school, their relationship changed. Heidi slowly, but effectively, detached herself from not only Eva, but the rest of her family. They saw Heidi maybe twice a year, but she was the type to only speak when being asked a question. Heidi was the one sitting in the corner reading a novel or sketching in her notebook. Rarely did she have something to interject. Heidi was mellow and nothing ever bothered her. Eva presumed that it was because of all the pot she smoked. Where most kids in high school smoked it at parties to enhance their fun, her sister smoked it to 'heighten her creativity'. After being punished (not so severely in Eva's eyes) when her mom and dad found out she was smoking it in their house her freshman year of high school, her sister just became more of a recluse from the family. Heidi spent a lot of time at her friend Lola's house, who could have been her twin; they were both dope-smoking art recluses. Eva's dad, Richard, was oblivious to her sister's pot addiction and was proud of his 'artistic' daughter, and somehow Bunny just didn't notice her daughter's segregation from family until it was too late.

Richard Johnston got up from the bar stool he was sitting on in the kitchen when the group entered. At sixty-three, his short silver hair was a complete contrast to his smooth tanned skin. If it weren't for that hair, he could have passed for a man in his late thirties where as Bunny wore her beige blonde hair in a shoulder length bob, which Eva had been trying to get her out of for years. It was no secret that her mother colored her hair and would until the day she died. If she kept this look up, she'd always look like the professor of literature that she was (she had retired two years prior).

"Hi, daddy," Eva said as her father enveloped her with a hug.

"Hi, sugar plum. It's great to see you!" her dad said, and then added as he glanced around the room, "It's too bad Joelle couldn't make it to round out the bunch."

"Well, a week's notice isn't a long time to make arrangements, daddy."

"But she knew about this a month ago," her mother stated.

That irritated Eva. "Why did I just find out about it on Sunday?" Eva didn't know why she was even surprised that her family would keep her out of the loop, since it happened frequently, but it hurt nonetheless. Maybe if she had kids they would be more apt to involve her more, she thought bitterly.

"Well if you'd return my phone calls-"

Andrea, the peacemaker, interrupted before WW3 erupted, "Oh, you two stop! It doesn't matter! I'm just glad you could make it, Eva. I talked with Joey a week ago and she said she would've loved to be here but Gavin had a tournament in New York this weekend." Joelle was her youngest sister, and at one time the sister with whom she got along the best. But with their hectic lives and the separation in geography their kinship grew apart over time. Her little sister had been a tomboy and very much a jock all her life. Sports came naturally to her and she had a full ride to the University of Colorado for soccer, where she had met her now husband Gavin. They resided there with their little girl, Tyla. Her husband played soccer professionally, which cramped their free time because of them traveling the world. They did try to get to Minnesota at least once a year; this year she was planning to come for Christmas. When Joey was around for family events, things always seemed more balanced.

Andrea's kids were so disciplined that a person rarely knew they were in the room, so it took Eva a few seconds to notice that they were there. With their perfect postures, eight year old Ryan and six year old Alyssa sat silently, drawing pictures of some sort.

"Whatcha doin?" Eva asked, coming up from behind them.

Half turning to meet her eyes, they both smiled and Alyssa said, "We are working on our books."

"You are making a book?" Eva asked, impressed.

"Uh huh," Ryan said, getting back to his illustration. She noticed that on his, there were words above his picture.

"For school?"

"No. Mommy gave us the assignment. See what I have so far?" Ryan asked with his brown eyes shining, lifting three pieces of paper towards Eva.

"Wow, Ryan. It's about a boy with superpowers? Were you inspired by Harry Potter?"

"What does inspire mean?"

"Did you get that idea from reading Harry Potter?" Eva asked, making her question clearer.

"Nope. Mommy won't let us read that. I thought of it on my own. My boy gets his powers every time he does a good deed. But they don't work when he does something bad."

Eva kissed the side of his head and said, "That sounds like its going to be a great book! I want a copy of it when you are completely done with it, ok?"

Smiling from ear to ear, he said, "Ok!"

"Auntie Eva, my book is about a princess."

"Let me see," Eva said, appraising her niece's picture over her shoulder. "Wow, Lyssie, she's almost as pretty as you. What's your story about?"

"It's about a princess who gets to play with dolls all day and doesn't have to go to school!"

"That's stupid!" Ryan blurted out.

"Is not!"

"Is too!"

"Then your super hero story is stupid too!" Alyssa spat out, pouting.

"Hey you guys, stop. Both of your ideas sound great and I really look forward to getting a copy of both of them. Maybe they will be ready by Christmas. I'd sure love that as a gift!"

"Really?" they asked in unison.

"Yes, really." That seemed enough to pacify them to get back to their project.

Eva made her way over to the stove where her mother and sister made the final preparations for supper. Her mom was pulling the roast beef apart while her sister was mashing the potatoes. "Is there anything I can do to help?"

"You could take the corn out of the oven. It should be done."

"I sure hope that sister of yours hurries up; otherwise this food will get cold, "Bunny said with irritation.

"No worries, mother. We'll just eat without her. It's not as if she would care. After all, she'll only be eating salad, or have you forgotten that she's a vegan?" Andrea said.

"But still," her mom was about to continue when they heard the doorbell.

"David? Will you get that please? I'm a little busy in here!" Andrea asked her husband in desperation.

"Sure." Good ol' whipped David, Eva thought. What Andrea wanted, Andrea got when it came to getting what she desired from her husband. One thing she could say about Andrea though was that it didn't go unappreciated.

Once Eva put the food on the table, she wandered over to the commotion in the entryway. "Oh, my god!" she heard her mom shriek again.

"What?" Eva asked as she came upon the crowd, but she didn't need anyone to answer her question because it was quite obvious as to what her mom was having a conniption fit about.

At first Eva thought her mom's reaction was over Heidi's new waist length brown dread locks and her matching-haired

77

male companion. He wore what looked like women style jeans which were so tight that they looked painted on his scrawny legs with a Mexican knitted poncho topping the ensemble off, while Heidi was wearing a floor length tie-dyed dress covered by a multicolored handmade sweater. It wasn't until her sister turned that Eva saw what the rest did. Her sister was full blown pregnant!

Eva's head started to swim. No way was her pot smoking, artsy fartsy, I-could-give-a-crap younger sister going to have a baby. Why, God, why? Eva wanted to scream. Instead of reacting one way or another like everyone else, she announced that supper was ready and escaped the room.

As usual her family skipped grace, but Eva bowed her head and thanked God for the food, her family and all the blessings in her life. She also made a desperate plea to get through the night without having a breakdown. That could wait until she was out of their presence. Eva knew conversations were going on around her, but when she was with God, no one and nothing else existed.

"Earth to Eva," her mom joked.

Lifting her head up, she asked, "What?"

"I said that you'll be the next to have a baby around here!" She gushed with excitement.

Little did her mother know, that was the last thing Eva needed to hear at the moment. So instead of responding, in 'Eva fashion' she shifted the focus back to her younger sister. "So, when are you due?" she asked, trying to sound as sincere as possible.

Rubbing her stomach with her ringed fingers, she said proudly, "End of November."

Eva almost choked. "That's like five weeks away."

"Yup. And if I'm reading my charts right, little Moon will be born on November 14th." It bothered Eva that her sister was so much into astrology. Horoscopes and the stars was her guide instead of God's Word. Eva tried witnessing to Heidi when she first became a Christian, but it just wasn't Heidi's thing and she asked Eva respectfully not to come at her anymore about the subject. Eva respected her wishes, but never gave up praying for her.

"Moon? That's what you are naming your baby?" Bunny asked in disgust.

"Yes. It only seemed fitting since there was a full moon out when I found out I was pregnant and her due date is also scheduled on one."

"What is this, the seventies?" Andrea joked. "You do know that the hippy era is over, right, Heidi?"

"Joke all you want, but Moon is going to be his or her name."

"You don't even know the sex?" Andrea asked in astonishment. The control freak that she was had ultrasounds until she found out the sexes of both her babies. Eva was surprised that her kids didn't come out radioactive.

"No, I don't. And while we're at it, please don't plan one of those stupid showers for me, Andie."

"Well, you just ruined her day I hope you know," Eva joked. After all, her older sister lived for bridal and baby showers.

"Does Arthur agree with the name you picked out?" Bunny inquired, not giving up.

"Well, mom, I don't think it really makes a difference if he does or not. I'm the one having the baby here, not him."

"But certainly the father has a right-"

"Sure the father has a right. But Arthur isn't the baby's father," Heidi said nonchalantly as she continued eating her salad.

For the first time since dinner, her dad spoke up and asked, "Well then, who *is* for crying out loud? Certainly it wasn't another immaculate conception!"

"His name is Sebastian, and yes he knows about the baby but doesn't want anything to do with it. That's okay with me. I'm all right being a single mom," Heidi stated matter-of-factly.

"So, who are you then?" her dad asked her sister's companion, confused.

"I'm just a friend of hers," Arthur spoke up quickly, yet seemingly unaffected by the scene around him.

"We met in Chicago at the body paint expo back in June. His work was out of this world! And he liked my pieces, so we've kept in touch. He's living with me until he can find his own place and I just thought it would be nice to invite him to a home cooked dinner. Sorry if you got the wrong impression," she said unflappably.

By this point, Eva found it so funny that she didn't have time to be sad, praise the Lord! What a mess her little sister was in, and yet she hadn't a care in the world. Not that it was surprising coming from her floating-through-life sister, but a person would think at this stage in the game she would be getting a little reality check. It wasn't gas she was going to pass very soon after all; it was an actual human being.

After supper was done and plans were made for the holidays, Eva made a quick escape, but not before she was stopped by Heidi. Tears that threatened towards the end of the night from the events filled her eyes as she reached her car and were about to spill until she heard her sister's voice behind her.

"Eva! Wait up!"

When Eva glanced back, she almost felt sorry for her sister as she held her bulging stomach while she sped wobbled towards Eva's car. "What?"

"I need to ask a favor of you. I know it's totally unlike me and I'm out of my element here, but you are the only one I know and trust who won't give me a hard time about it..."

Heidi looked so unsure of herself, which she hadn't seen for a long time. So, to end the uneasiness between them, Eva asked, "Well? What is it?"

"I need a birthing partner. I have specific plans; no drugs of any kind, that sort of thing. I'm considering a water birth. Well anyhow, I just need a coach. And since Sebastian is way out of the picture and Arthur has no interest in being it, the only person I thought of was you."

"What about Andie? She'd be better than me. She's been through it twice after all."

"Are you kidding? *No way!* She'll order everyone around and I do not want to piss off the nurse or doctor who will deliver my baby! I don't need a control freak, I need someone who will be calm and collected like you!"

Eva should have been honored, but something inside her snapped. "Me? Why me? Sheesh Heidi! We haven't been close in years. You are my sister and I love you, but you are the most selfish person I know. I mean, who comes to a family gathering, after not speaking with any of us for months mind you, and show up pregnant of all things! I'm just a little frustrated with this family right now. Mom and her snide comments about my weight and my choice of husband...And you; when things happen to upset the scales for most people, they would freak out or have some reaction to it, yet you are so float-through-life with no care in the world about everything it makes other people worry for you. And to be quite honest, I don't know if I can handle your stresses too." Eva was breathing hard and clenching her fists as if she were ready to punch someone.

"Wow! Hey, listen, I don't react to things simply for this reason. Look at yourself! You are going to give yourself a heart attack. I'm not asking you to take on my life. Just be my birthing coach. But I see that it's too much to ask. I'll let you know when I have the kid. Take it easy, Evalynn. Sorry I asked anything," Heidi said, deflated. Eva hurt her sister, which she didn't think possible. For to hurt someone, someone would have actual feelings.

As Heidi turned away from her, Eva said calmly, "Heidi, I'm sorry. I'd...I'd love to be your coach..."

"You sure?" her sister asked, uncertain. "Because I'm really okay with doing this on my own."

"Again I'm so sorry, Heidi. You shouldn't have to do this on your own. I want to be there, really I do."

Smiling, which made Heidi glow, she said, "Thanks. I'll call you when I schedule the classes."

For the first time in years, Eva went over to her sister and gave her the biggest, longest hug. It startled both of them, but they kept hanging on as if they discovered they liked the feeling. The flutter against Eva's stomach made them separate. "Wow! It is pretty active I see!" Eva exclaimed, rubbing Heidi's stomach.

Catching Eva's hand in hers, Heidi led her fingers to where the movement was. "It's the most incredible experience, sis. To think that there is an actual human being in me. It's freaky, yet quite incredible. And to be honest with you, I did freak out when I found out. That's why I didn't say anything to anybody for a long time. Arthur figured it out a few months ago when one day my belly popped out. And before you ask, he's A-sexual." When Eva gave her a quizzical glance, she said, "He's not into men or women. He has no desire for a relationship of any sort, which works for me. I love him as a friend and our situation just... works," Heidi said, shrugging her shoulders.

Tears were about to spill and a pity party was about to begin so Eva said quickly, "That's great. Well, I hate to run, but I want to get home before Eric goes to bed. I don't get to see him much. Call me, ok?"

"Ok." After another quick embrace, Eva hopped in her vehicle and drove away fast, all the while sifting through the strange course of events of the night in her head.

Chapter 8

By the end of the November, Eric was beyond exhausted, stressed and disturbed. Life in the last four weeks had been nothing but a crazy turn of events. First of all, when Eva returned from her 'family gathering' he knew it was going to be a long night with one look at her red-rimmed, mascara-free eyes. Finding out that her care free sister was ready to pop with a child was unbelievable in itself, but hearing that his wife agreed to be her birthing coach was mind- boggling. After all, Eva and Heidi were the two sisters who rarely spoke, let alone had anything in common. But it was just like her to say yes without discussing it with him first, and she never understood why he got so upset over such things, which made him even more furious. In her eyes, she was doing something charitable and out of the kindness of her heart. He saw it as just another thing keeping her away as well as people taking advantage of her generosity. That was one of the first things he noticed about Eva all those years ago. She was such a giving person, and he loved that about her. He would have never guessed that he would come to resent it.

Then, after hearing the highlights of her evening (which he inwardly thanked the stars that he didn't have to suffer through), the dreaded 'I want a baby' subject came up again. He tried to think positively that it had been months since their last debacle, where they agreed to wait on a miracle. Although, in his mind, miracles were rarely dropped off at his door step so his words were void of truth. Hopes had been up since that day six years prior when finding out that her chances of getting pregnant were slim to none. And Eric wasn't stupid enough to believe that it would be the last time they would discuss it, especially after all her friends, not to mention family members, were showing up pregnant left and right. Her argument now was that she had been waiting on a miracle, but now God was telling her to be proactive about it and not just rest on her laurels. She cut Eric off as soon as he started objecting to fertility for the millionth time.

"According to the newest research, I shouldn't have to go on fertility. All I'll have to do is control my eating and exercise and once the weight starts falling off I can get off the pill and we can start trying again," she said optimistically.

How could he argue with her on that? Fertility was something he was opposed to with a passion. He'd lost one too many women in his life to cancer, and just the chance that it might increase Eva's chances of getting the terrible disease, there was no way he'd go for it. But dieting as the cure all? He didn't quite buy it.

"If you think it will be that easy then go for it." His words, not to mention his tone were a little pessimistic, but he knew his wife. She tried diet after diet, but she never stuck to it. And the most he'd ever seen her exercise was taking the dogs for an occasional walk. Yeah, he hadn't been the best encourager. Until lately he'd never thought of her as fat. Curvy, yes. Unhealthy, no. But now, he did notice she was getting a little more than curves around her middle. Not that he would ever say anything to her. He wasn't a complete idiot.

"But are you willing to help me? I need support and if we are going to make a baby together, I need you with me on this," she said desperately.

Even though he knew she had been crying her mood was anything but solemn now. In fact, it had been years since he'd seen any fire within her like what he was seeing now. However, he was reluctant. Maybe it was fear that their efforts would fail again. Maybe it was because he liked his life, being care-free and having his independence. After all this time it would be hard to adjust to a kid, he thought for the hundredth time. Sure they both had good careers to support a child right now, but how often would they get to see it? If one of them was to cut down on work, how would they be able to afford it then? Absent parenting resulted in major problems down the road. How could he relate all that to his over anxious wife without her getting her feathers ruffled? Reluctantly, he said,

"Of course you have my support. In anything you do. But about trying again, we can cross that bridge when we get there. Getting healthy is the important thing." There, that should do it, Eric prided himself with his noncommittal charm.

Eva rose from the chair she was perched on and started pacing. "I want a child, Eric," she stated with determination. "I'm sick of talking this to death. I need action. Miracles don't happen on their own, you know." She stopped and looked directly at him, crossing her arms. "We are a team, and if you aren't totally in this with me I don't know if I can do this. I need you!"

"Like I said, babe, you have my support. I want what you want. Get healthy. Get happy." Now he was standing in front of her with his hands on her shoulders, staring directly into her eyes. "I know you want a baby, and I wish I could grant it to you right this minute," he said, not quite meaning every word. "But like my uncle always said, it's more fun practicing for one."

Smiling at his flirtatious joke, she said, "You're a pig."

"Oink, oink," he said, wrinkling his nose.

"I'm serious, Eric. I'm sick of wasting time while everyone around me is getting pregnant. I want this more than anything."

Rolling his eyes, he gave her a light shake. "Eva, for gosh sakes, I know! The more you rehash it, the worse I feel for not being able to give it to you. Why can't you be happy for what we have and if a baby comes along, great! And if not, great! After all, you are the one always quoting 'everything happens for a reason'."

"Because everything *does* happen for a reason. But I'm just saying, why not help God along with that miracle and do what I can to make it happen?" she asked with a smile.

Pulling away from her because he was annoyed that she destroyed any chance of decent foreplay, he said, "Whatever, Eva. Do what you want. I'll support you. I gotta take the dogs for a walk.' And he started to walk away.

"Wait! I can go with you. It will be a great start to my workout plan!"

And that it was. For the first time in a long time, Eva took the dogs for a two mile walk before and then again after work. She picked at her food, which he chastised her over. He insisted that she needed to lose the weight in a healthy way or not at all. After the first week, she came running in the living room, squealing, "Eric! I lost six pounds!"

Of course, Eric had just gotten home from a long day at work and had his feet up, resting when she bolted in, jerking him out of a comatose state. "What?"

"I lost six pounds!"

"Great! Keep it up, hon," He said with as much enthusiasm as he would towards a turn your head and cough physical exam.

"I think I'm going to check and see how much a gym membership will cost. Maybe we'll get a family discount."

"Eva, when will I be able to fit time in for a workout? No, you go check it out but count me out." He thought that would lead to an argument, but she must've seen the exhaustion on his face because she didn't pursue it.

Rumors around his work were circulating, which was stressing him out. He didn't know if he should confide them in Eva or not because he didn't want to worry her if they were just rumors.

Even though he had twelve years seniority he was still on the chopping block if this outsourcing talk were true. He kicked himself over and over for not going back to school when Eva had completed her licensing, but he had been making more money working for that factory than he would've in any trade field he was interested in at the time. And he didn't mind his job. Most of the time he was his own boss, except for the times they had to call in Lars from Malmac Inc. to fix his machine. The last time he was there, Lars cornered him with conversation. Eric really liked Lars, even if he was Norsk. After all, Eric was almost all Swede so the competition between the better nationality was a standing joke.

"So, I'm hearing rumors about this place," Lars said out of the blue while they were out on a smoke break.

"Yeah, you aren't the only one."

"What are you going to do if this place folds?"

"Honestly? I have no idea. I'm trying hard not to think about it."

"I've been talking to my partner about you. He's really interested to talk with you."

"I don't know, man. It sounded like my cup of tea until you mentioned about how much strain it was on a relationship."

Lars exhaled a plume of smoke and said, "Forget I said anything. Brigit and I are working things out. I was very bitter at the time. But listen, we are a five year old company. It started with my best friend, his brother and myself. Now we have expanded to twenty employees and are looking for a few more quality people. Jessup, my friend, wants me to concentrate in Europe, which will let me be closer to my family. So I know he is looking for someone to take my job here in the states. Give him a call and feel him out. He's desperate for dependable help. The money is great and nothing has ever been boring about this job!"

Eric laughed. "Are you trying to sell me on your company?"

Winking, Lars said, "Is it working?" When Eric wasn't saying anything, Lars handed him a card and said, "Just give him a call. You never know, Swede, you might actually like what he has to offer."

And that he did. It was an attractive offer, not to mention that Jessup Totiono was a very upbeat and down-to-earth man. He liked how this CEO got right down to brass tacks by asking if Eric was interested at all in the job. After being honest about his reservations, Jessup put almost all his worries to rest, to the point where Eric was seriously debating over quitting his job regardless of outsourcing. The only drawback was he would have to be gone for three to four months for training....in Italy.

Eva was enthusiastic about it, but then again, these days she was excited for everything. It almost disturbed him how much she was becoming so absorbed in this new lifestyle that little else mattered, but to be that supportive husband she required he zipped his lip and let her do her thing. Within a week, she had joined the gym and was there every day, even hiring a personal trainer. Eric hadn't seen much results in the way her body looked, but he could tell that her attitude was different than any other time she had tried in the past. And he knew she would need that more than anything to keep this momentum going.

Eric had been so exhausted that going to the bar after work didn't hold its appeal anymore, so he would go home, let the dogs out and then zoned out on the couch until Eva got home from working or from the gym. Their conversations were held five minutes before bed and a few before he left for work in the morning. At first he was honored by the fact that she started waking up with him, making him breakfast before he left for work and then taking the dogs for their two mile walk after he left. But after a week or so, breakfast was forgotten and she was out the door with those dogs before he even got out of the shower. Bitterness worked its way into his heart and as much as he wanted to confront her on it, he couldn't. She was on a roll and he didn't want to get blamed for her falling off the wagon.

Even Monday nights were becoming a thing of the past. Even though he belly ached (to himself) over having to be home, instead of the bar with his work friends, he missed their time together. But again, he remained silent. The more absent she was, the more he thought about taking the job with Malmac, Inc. Eva obviously didn't need him, other than to repair what needed fixing around the house and now to be her weight loss cheerleader. Maybe it was the sign he was looking for. Maybe the time away would do them some good. Eva already told him to go for it if that's what he wanted to do. He knew the money would be great and the traveling would be different in an adventurous sort of way. And since they didn't have a family, he had no obligations; this would be a great time to try it. What did he have to lose?

Eric was in the position he loved best, between his two dogs with their heads resting on his lap while he was lounging on his couch, daydreaming over what could be when the phone rang. It woke him up instantly.

"Hello?"

"Hi, Eric. This is Lars."

"Hey Lars, what's up?"

"I hate to keep bothering you, but I want you to know that Jessup was really impressed with you. He wants you bad, Swede. He's in China for the next few weeks and is making me do his dirty work. He has interviewed over thirty people and you were the only one he talked about with the board of directors. What can we say or do to get you to take this plunge?"

Wow! Eric thought. If this wasn't the answer he was secretly hoping for! Clearing his throat, he said, "Every holiday off and five weeks of vacation a year and you got yourself a deal!"

Confusedly, Lars asked, "Didn't Jess go over the benefit package with you?"

"No, he didn't."

"Well let me then. After your training you will automatically receive six weeks of vacation and full medical. So I can call him and tell him that you are on board?" he asked, presumably.

After a few seconds of realizing what he was about to agree to, he said, "I'm on board. When shall I put in my notice at Solid?"

"New training starts on January second. That will give you a little over a month to make the arrangements. We will mail you your plane tickets. If you don't have a passport, I'd get one ASAP! It's been taking up to twelve weeks to get them due to the new border regulations. If you need to expedite it, do it. We will reimburse you for everything."

"No worries. I already have mine."

"Great! Call one of us if you have any questions or concerns. You will never regret this decision, kid. This is a ground floor opportunity."

"Yes, well, I hope my wife is excited as we are. I'll talk to you soon, Lars."

After he hung up he exhaled deeply. Oh man, what did he get himself into?

Chapter 9

"Just twenty more seconds!"

"I'm dying!" Eva screamed as her legs turned to rubber beneath her.

"Fifteen seconds! Stay in there! I know you can do it!" Bryce, her personal trainer relentlessly encouraged.

Sweat pouring from every pore of her body, lungs on fire, muscles aching but enough determination to get the job done, she completed her sprint on the treadmill and took it to a light walk, sucking in deep breaths of air. "Good job, Eva. We will walk it out for five minutes and do it over again," Bryce said casually.

With big eyes, she asked disbelieving, "What???"

Chuckling, he said, "Why do you look so surprised? You should know me by now. I'm going to take you past broke. It's what you signed up for."

Actually, what she signed up for was to lose weight, she grumbled to herself. In four weeks she had lost, yes, but not the numbers she was hoping for. Seventeen pounds was not substantial. The rate she was working, in her mind she should've lost at least half of her goal, which was a total of eighty pounds. But as her rock of a trainer told her, it's about taking it off slowly and smartly. It's a change of life, not just something you do for a quick fix. Well, in Eva's mind, this was definitely not a quick fix. It was more time-consuming and energy-sucking than she had imagined. At first it was more physically draining than mental, but now it was becoming the opposite. Everything revolved around her workouts and food intake. When she signed up for a personal trainer, she lucked out in getting the number one man for the job. He was a few years older than she, lived and breathed fitness and she knew he was hand delivered to her from God. Every now and again, she would argue with herself that he was sent from Satan to kill her, but she knew better. She didn't do well with constructive criticism and more often than not in the past, she would quit before she would do what was suggested. But there was something in the way Bryce communicated with her. He pushed her beyond her comfort zone in a way she felt empowered. Ninety percent of the time she wanted to give up, but he had a way about him that made her feel that she had wings. A lot of the times, it only took him staring intently on her, as if he were giving her some of his strength to move forward. She could only surmise that it was God working though him. It was a month into training with him where she hit a plateau with her weight, which discouraged her beyond measure. He took her aside, sat her down and asked what she was so upset about. After telling him her frustrations, he said, "You have to look on the bright side, Eva. You didn't gain. Sometimes it takes your body time to adjust to the changes you are making. How is your diet? Are you following the plan I gave you?"

"To the tee. I eat a big breakfast, and then do the small snacks throughout the day and then I have a good-sized supper. Well, when I have the time. Work has been crazy for the holidays so all I can do on my nights that I work is try to eat more protein and veggies. Other than that, I haven't even had a sip of pop or a bit of chocolate, which has always been my downfall, especially this time of year."

"Well, you just keep doing what you are doing, and in a few weeks if we don't see results we will just change your plan a bit. You work with me, do what I ask you to do, and I'll guarantee results." She knew he was also a believer, so what he said next made sense and was valued. "It's like becoming a Christian. You make that choice to follow Him, and step by step you learn how. It's not about being perfect, but perfecting what it is you're trying to accomplish. If something isn't working, change it. Don't put too much emphasis on losing the pounds. It's about getting healthy one step at a time. You have to remember that the slower the pounds come off, the longer they will stay off. Maintaining is a plus, losing is a bonus. Just remember that."

"I will. Thank you."

"You're welcome. Now, let's get back to work!" And as quick as they had a little moment, it was gone and it was back to business. That's what she liked about him the most.

Her goal was to lose thirty pounds by Christmas and she was almost there. The holiday season would be the great test, since normally her house would be full of cookies, bars and candy. This year it would be fruit, even though Bryce said it would be all right for her to splurge on something sugar free or a cookie or two. But she knew herself. It was all or nothing, so she stuck with fruit and veggies. So far, so good. It was a blessing in disguise that she was taking weekly trips up to the cities to be with Heidi for birthing classes, because not only was she getting to know her sister all over again, but she didn't have time to bake.

The night her sister went into labor, she and Eric were having a serious discussion about his current job and whether or not he would be taking this new job with a European company. She was in full support for whatever he wanted. It sounded like it was right up his alley, being the technical person that he was. And the extra money would be great; especially when they tried for a baby. When, not 'if' this time, when she got pregnant she could stay home with the baby or at least cut down to part time and be able to afford it with this new job. Of course, she wouldn't tell Eric that was where her thoughts went to because she knew he was sick of hearing about everything pertaining to kids. The only down side to this offer was that he had to go so far away for his training and for so long. But in her mind it could be perfect timing. By the time he'd get back, she would be at her destined weight, God willing, and they could start the baby process. God was sure working everything out, Eva thought enthusiastically.

Up until the moment Heidi called when she went into labor, her sister exuded nothing but serenity and a spooky calmness. Her roommate Arthur had the same relaxed aura as Eva got to know him a little better, which was probably why he and her sister got along so well. Eva bet that if she mentioned to them of doing a baby body art feature, using the newborn and the afterbirth as their 'paint' she would get some sort of excitement from them. But she didn't want to give them any more 'creative' ideas. Cringing at the sarcastic thought, she instead zipped her lip about Heidi's indifferent attitude. If she didn't know the sound of her sister's voice, she wouldn't have guessed the freaked out person on the other line was her. Heidi was in panic mode, which Eva was somewhat grateful for, yet alarmed about. Not only was it a few days before Thanksgiving, but Eva couldn't have been busier. She had only started training with Bryce a few weeks by this time and trying to fit in her workouts was a challenge with work as busy as it was. She could have worked twelve hours a day and it wouldn't have been enough to get all her clients in. Then there were the choir practices at church for the holiday season as well as her commitment to help organize a trip up to Minneapolis to volunteer at the Feed the Starving Children foundation between Christmas and New Years. So far they had thirty-two volunteers and they needed fifty by the first week in December, and she was the person in charge of finding those people. Then there was Eric, always holding on while she ran here, did that, volunteered here and organized that. She could feel the exhaustion, tension and frustration every time they were together. If there was something major going on in his life, she wouldn't have a clue. Good thing she had enough time to find out about this new job prospect, she thought. At least that was something. She missed him, and by the time Heidi's baby was born, she hoped her life would be calm so they could get together again.

After packing a few things, she kissed Eric, patted the dogs quickly on their heads and ran out the door. Eva hated city driving, especially at night because she wasn't familiar with the highways and streets. She pulled into the North Memorial Hospital parking lot an hour later and found her sister waiting in the entryway bench with her hand on her belly, sucking in air as if all those birthing classes never happened.

"Why haven't you been admitted?"

"They are full."

"What do you mean, they are full? They don't have a room anywhere? And why aren't you breathing like you were taught?"

"It hurts really bad, Eva! When the contractions hit, the last thing I'm thinking about is breathing! Arthur had to go to work, so I told him to go because I knew you would be here soon. But I wasn't counting on them being full. They called ahead to Abbott North-western and they have plenty of openings. So help me up and we can get going." Eva extended her arm and Heidi clasped onto it just as a contraction hit.

"How far apart are they?" she asked when she sister relaxed.

"About ten minutes."

"Let's get going!"

En route to the other hospital, Heidi asked, "Did you call mom and dad?"

"No, should I have?"

"*No*! I'll call them and the rest of the family when this is all over. In fact, I'd be just as happy if I waited until Christmas to let them know."

"Heidi! That's not nice. Even though we were all shocked to know you were having a baby, we are all excited for you. They love you, just as I do."

She sneered. "I see the way all of you look at me, Eva..." When Eva gave her an astonished look, she said again, "Yes, even you do Eva. Although you are the only one who makes attempts to understand me. Ever since we were kids, I felt different from all of you. The others find ways to make fun of the way I live my life, and I hear when they talk about me when they don't think I'm listening. It does hurt, you know, even though it doesn't seem like it bothers me. At least you are honest with me in what you think. And that's why you are the only person in our family whom I trust. You are flawed, just like me; unlike the rest of them..." Eva was taken back by that statement. She wondered what imperfections she was referring to.

"We are all flawed, Heidi," Eva said lightly.

"Yes, but they don't appreciate it like I do. To be flawed is what makes humanity beautiful. Mom and Dad and Andrea aren't human. Flaws represent failure to them. They are robots, living...." Another contraction hit, causing her to pause and take in a deep breath. "...living for what other people think of them. I refuse to live up to a certain image. And my baby won't ever feel unwelcome in my home like I did growing up. Whatever his or her dreams are, I will support them. I won't ever make them feel beneath me. They will know what love is." Tears were streaming down her face when Eva looked over to her.

Clasping her hand around her sister's, Eva said, "I have no doubt that you will be the best mom."

Smiling through her tears, Heidi whispered, "Thank you." Another contraction hit, this time making her sister double over. "Oh my god! This hurts so bad! Make it stop!"

While driving with her left hand, she rubbed Heidi's back with her right as well as she could under the circumstances. "I wish I could. We are almost there. Breathe in deep and one. Two. Three..." The breathing exercises helped a little, but Eva knew her contractions were getting closer and closer.

By the time they reached Abbot Northwestern, Heidi was complaining that she felt like she needed to push. The nurses put her in a wheel chair and Eva followed closely behind until they got to the birthing room. It looked like a mini hotel room, all except the hospital bed that the nurses were hoisting Heidi up onto.

"Hi, I'm Lucinda. I'll be your nurse. Think you will be able to change by yourself? Or would you like me to stay and help?"

"I'll be fine. My sister can help if I have trouble."

"All right. I'll be back shortly. Put this gown on, with the opening in the back. You may leave on your socks...." and the fifty some year old nurse looked down at her sister's open toed Birkenstocked foot. "Oh, I see that you aren't wearing any. Well, anyway, I'll be back soon!"

Once the door was shut, Eva asked, "Do you need help?"

"Please..." She unsnapped her overalls, which fell to the ground. All Eva did was be her sister's support by offering her shoulder and tried like mad not to look at her sister in an undressed state. It had been years since they had seen each other naked, and even though modesty flies out the window when the birthing process starts, it was still a private thing to Eva and she would rather not see her sister's naked body.

They had just put her gown on when she doubled over again. "I really, really have to push, Eva! Get someone quick!"

Once she had her sister on the bed, Eva ran to the door and saw their nurse a few feet away. "Please come quick! She feels like she has to push!"

Within seconds, there were two nurses and one doctor situating Heidi while Eva held her sister's hand. The doctor was a handsome man in his early forties, if Eva were to guess. His green eyes smiled back to both sisters. "Well, lets see how far along you are," he said calmly. After a brief checking, he said, "Whoa! Lucinda, we are ready to go!"

"Already?" Eva asked, shockingly.

"Looks like. I see the baby's head. Okay, Miss Johnston, start pushing."

As Eva encouraged, Heidi sucked in a deep breath and pushed with all her might. "Looks good. Let's do that again."

After another long push, Heidi really started to sweat. "Oh my god, this hurts!"

Eva had a hard time holding back something sarcastic like, 'What, did you think it wouldn't?', but decided it would probably be better to encourage her. And after three pushes, Heidi's little girl was laid on her stomach. At least that's what Eva thought she was under all that blood and white gunky afterbirth. But still, she was beautiful. So beautiful that it brought tears. "You did it, Heidi. She is perfect!" Eva said, kissing her sisters cheek.

Staring at her new creation, Heidi said, "She is, isn't she?" Just then, the change of cold atmosphere must've awakened the baby, and they got to hear that her lungs worked well.

Lucinda took her and explained, "We have to weigh her and clean her up. But congratulations, mom, you did a great job!"

The doctor came into view, and with a smile he said, "Well,

you have been by far the fastest delivery we've seen this year. Five minutes after admitted. You did great! If they were all as easy as you, I'd never tire of my job!"

"Thank you, doctor," Heidi said with reddened cheeks.

"It was my pleasure. Take care of that little girl now. I'll check on you two later," he left with a smile.

"Seven pounds, ten ounces and nineteen inches long," Nurse Lucinda announced, bringing the baby to Heidi. Once the nurse left and they were alone, just the three of them, they just stared at the baby as if they couldn't believe she was here.

"So, are you still going to name her Moon?"

Admiring her daughter, she said, "Moonae Tian Johnston. And yes, she will be Moon for short."

"Well, she's cute enough to pull that name off. Where'd you find those names?"

"Moonae came to me the other night when I was laying in bed, and then I wanted her to have a part of her dad somehow. And since Sebastian isn't female sounding at all, I thought Tian was cute and it went with Moon and Moonae. But now that I'm looking at her, she looks like a Moonae, so if she doesn't like my nickname for her, she can use it."

"Good thinking, sis. You did good. You did real good!"

"Will you call mom now?"

Taking in Heidi's peaceful state, she said, "Yeah. Sure."

For the first time since she got to the hospital, she felt envy fast approach. Oh, how badly she wished it were her baby she was announcing to her family.

Yup, and now you are going to be the black sheep of the family. Now that Heidi has something that your mom, Andrea and Joelle share, you will be the only one without. And what do you have, Eva? A falling apart marriage to a man your mom doesn't like, an over weight ugly body who can't produce children, and a wavering faith. Where is God now, Eva? He said all you had to do is ask and you shall receive...well? What has he delivered?

Stop it!' Eva scolded herself. 'I'm a child of God. He will deliver in His timing, not my own.'

'Give me peace, Lord', she prayed silently. 'Banish these thoughts that I know aren't from You. Help me be a good servant for you. Remind me of Your way and Your will. It's not about me. Thy will be done. Without you, I am but mere skin and bones without direction. With you, I am complete. In my weakness, You are strong. Let my sister see Your hand in all of this. Give me the right answers when she has questions. Love her as you love all Your children. May Moonae be the one to bring her to You. In Jesus name, amen.'

She needed some air, so she made her phone calls in the lobby while her sister got a little nap. Eric wasn't answering, so she left him a message. Her dad answered on the second ring, and after relaying the message, he said that they would call Heidi right away (since they were back in Florida). Both Andrea and her youngest sister, Joey, answered right away. Andrea came right over, since she only lived twenty minutes from the hospital. And Joey was again bummed out that she missed yet another birth in the family and wouldn't be able to meet Moon until Christmas. Poor Joey. She was the farthest removed from the family, distance wise. But they were all encouraged that it would only be a few weeks until they saw each other again.

It was going on one in the morning when she finally said her goodbyes and made sure Andrea was there for Heidi before she left. That day was the tip of the iceberg when it came to being busy. The next month would prove to be her hardest yet.

* * *

Christmas came upon Eva like a whirlwind. Just a few flurries, but no real snow which made it harder to fathom that it was even that time of year. Since Christmas landed on a Wednesday, she and Eric didn't have a lot of time off work so they decided to stick close to home and invite Eric's family over for Christmas Eve. Her family had decided to get together over the New Year so that was one less thing to make time for. They hadn't seen Bart, Natasha or the kids since Eric and Bart's blow up almost two months prior and Eva was looking so forward to seeing them; the kids, that is. They always made the holidays special. Eric's uncle was an undecided guest up until the night before due to recovering from the flu bug that he had around Thanksgiving, but thought he could venture out for a little bit.

Eva was busy preparing her homemade augratin potatoes when she heard the dogs bark at the front door. Bruiser's high pitched bark muted every other noise in the house. Seconds later, the sound of Noah's voice erupted in the kitchen. "Auntie Eva! Look what I made!"

Hanging from Noah's little three year old hand was a piece of blue yarn holding a yellow star made out of construction paper with dots of red glitter around the edges. Eva knelt down so she was eye to eye with her nephew. "Wow, buddy. Did you really make this?" she asked suspicious, but playfully.

With big eyes, he nodded while saying, "Yup! Seth teached me how." When Eva didn't make a move to touch his gift, he said, "It's fo you. It's fo your twee!"

"Why, thank you, sweetie! I love it!" She exclaimed, while hugging him close. "You should go show your uncle Eric and have him help you find a spot to put it on the tree. Somewhere where Red and Bruiser won't get a hold of it and eat it!"

"Ok!" he said before shooting out of the room like a cannon.

Luckily the potatoes were ready, so all she had to do was put that and the corn in the oven, then wait an hour. Eva was deep in thought, mentally going over a check list when a shrill voice behind her jarred her thoughts.

"Lydia! You get back here!"

Eva turned around just as her niece ran into her legs. Her precious little niece had her chubby little arms up, signaling to Eva that she wanted up, so Eva obeyed willingly.

"Well, look who started walking!" Eva said excitedly.

"We're trying to break her of that, you know," bellowed the rude voice of her sister-in-law.

Lydia petted Eva's freshly done hair, which kept her attention on her niece when she responded, "Break her of what?"

"Of her begging."

The briskness of her answer made Eva look at Natasha to see if she was serious. "She's a baby, Natasha. It's called nurturing."

"Well, I call it spoiling," she said with a smirk.

Biting her tongue, she said as nice as could be, "Well please excuse me, Natasha, I haven't seen her in a few months. I think you can let it pass just this once. I won't ever let it happen again."

"Well, it was your own choice not to see the kids. And just to set the record straight, I do appreciate you watching the kids as much as you had been. You could have said no if it was *that* big of an inconvenience." Eva couldn't help but be shocked at her attempt of an apology. However, before she could acknowledge it, she noticed her sister-in-law eyeing her up and down, and knew this nice moment was about to pass as quickly as it came.

"So, you sick or something?"

"Excuse me?" Lydia was squirming, so she let her down but not before she gave her a kiss.

"Well, any person can see you've lost weight, Eva. Inquiring minds want to know, or at least this mind does. How did you do it?"

Eva knew that if anyone noticed any change, she would be asked that question. But coming from Natasha, it had a negative resonance to it. Her sister-in-law always made her feel inferior, and this was one thing that wouldn't get Eva down. With her head held high, she said firmly, "I'm definitely not sick. It's all by diet and exercise, Natasha."

"No kidding," her sister-in-law said, disbelieving.

"Yup, no kidding," Eva said with an eat-me smile. The timer on the stove went off, saving her literally by the bell. "If you would be so nice, Natasha, would you set the table? The china and silverware are sitting on the hutch in the living room."

"Yeah. Sure." Natasha walked away slowly, looking back

to Eva as if she might miss Eva's nose growing from telling a lie. Once she left the kitchen, Eva chuckled to herself. If that was the reaction she got from Natasha, she couldn't wait until she met up with her mother! This might prove to be her best Christmas ever.

After dinner and the presents were all opened, the kids played with their new toys by the tree while the adults sat around the dining room table, drinking their hot toddies, all accept Eva. She stuck to water. If she was going to waste calories, it was going to be on a few cookies, not alcohol! Eric had been in a strange mood all day. Waking up that morning, he made himself breakfast while Eva ran to the gym before it closed up for the holiday. She was feeling great, breaking her two mile run mark. And when she got back, her joy diminished when Eric barked at her for leaving the garage door open for any yahoo to come along and steal their stuff as he quickly passed to leave to get alcohol for the get together. By the time he returned home, he had forgotten all about being mad and helped her dress the turkey when he saw that she could use the help, all the while making small talk. Before leaving the kitchen he pulled her into an embrace, kissed her and told her how much she meant to him.

When they were all sitting around making small talk, Eric said, "Well, I have some exciting news..."

Instead of all eyes on Eric, they all flew to Eva. With a smile that reached his eyes, Eric's uncle said, "Say it isn't so!"

Confused, Eva asked, "What isn't?"

"Are you pregnant, my girl?"

Eva's eyes bugged out of her head while Eric saved her from further embarrassment. "No Uncle Ben. That's not it!" At that, all eyes were back on Eric, relieving Eva. "Beginning next week, I'm starting a new job."

"A new job?!" a startled Bart asked.

"What are you thinking, boy? Don't you know that is a risky thing to do, the job market like it is? You have it made at Solid!" his uncle said, visibly alarmed. After all, his uncle got him the job at Solid Steel in the first place.

"Don't worry, uncle! I've done a lot of thinking about it, and it's going to be a great opportunity."

"What's the name of this company?"

"Malmac, Inc. They are a European company. I'll be traveling state to state working on machines like the one I'm running right now."

"But what about your benefits, Eric? What about the great insurance you have there? And the seniority?" his uncle asked.

"They are meeting my benefits and then some. It's going to be hard work, but I'll get compensated for it. The only downfall of the job is that I'll be on the road a lot and the training is overseas for a few months."

"Where overseas?" Natasha piped in, suddenly interested.

"Italy, in a city near Milan. I don't remember the name."

"Wow! Milan!" she said, enthusiastically. "That's like the fashion capital of the world! Now we have no excuse not to get to Europe, Barton! With Eric there, we'll have someone to stay with that will cut the cost down like a lot!"

Bart rolled his eyes, saying sarcastically, "Sure, 'Tash, sure!"

"I'm serious, Bart! You owe me one hell of a vacation! If it's all right with your brother, that is," Natasha blinked her false eyelashes at Eric, and then added, "And we aren't taking the kids!"

"We'll talk about it later, hon-ny," Bart bit out through clenched teeth.

"Well, I don't know how much extra room I'll have to accommodate you. The only thing I know is that they are setting me up with an apartment within walking distance to not only the plant but the train station and all the amenities the town offers."

"Well this old boy has seen his share of oceans and continents. I'll see you when you get back, son. Be sure to call me from time to time. If I don't answer, I may be dead. Be sure to send someone to check on me."

"Oh Uncle Ben, like we don't check up on you regularly! Do we really neglect you so much?" Eva joked.

Patting her hand across the table, he said, "Eva, my girl, you have *never* neglected me!"

Eric tapped his glass with a knife that was sitting on the table. "I have one more gift to hand out." Getting up from his chair, he opened the doors beneath the hutch and pulled out a rectangular gift wrapped box and handed it to Eva.

"But Eric, we promised we wouldn't..."

Putting his finger to her lips, he shushed her and said, "It's not from me."

"Then who is it from?"

"Jessup Totiono, my new boss."

"Why?" Eva looked confused.

"Just open it up. He said it was for us both, but you were supposed to open it."

"Well, okay." Carefully, she undid the wrapping, wanting to savor the moment. Inside the box was an envelope. Glancing up to see everyone watching her, she peeled it open. Peeking inside, her eyes got big. "Plane tickets!!! He gave me open ended tickets!"

Smiling from ear to ear, Eric said, "Perfect!"

She got up quickly and embraced him. "Looks like I'll be visiting you!"

Later that night after making love slowly and tenderly, he held her in his arms and kissed her head. "I'm going to miss this."

Adjusting herself so she could look into his eyes, she said, "I'm going to miss *you!*"

"When do you think you'll come to visit me?" he asked while stroking her hair.

"When would you like me to come?"

"Well, you know, our anniversary is coming up..."

"I could talk to Barbie. It would be almost like last minute, but I'm sure she'd be okay with me taking a week off. I have it coming." Although, she thought to herself, she was trying to save it just in case she would have to use it for morning sickness or doctors appointments, but this was a once-in-a-lifetime opportunity.

"A week, really? That would be awesome! I just hope we will be able to see each other and do a few things while you are there. I don't know how much extra time I'll have."

"It will work out. I'll talk to Barbie on Thursday."

"I'm a lucky guy."

"Oh? And why is that?" Eva asked jokingly.

"Like I have to answer that! I'm proud of you, baby. You are toning up nicely. I don't know if I want those Italian studs ogling my wife!"

"I only have eyes for you!" After a few minutes snuggling into him, she asked with a chuckle, "Do you think Bart and Natasha will visit?"

"God, I hope not!"

"Sorry, that's not a good thought to fall asleep on. How about this?" and then she whispered something sweet into his ear which made him smile and drew her closer. "Uh, uh uh, Eric! We have to get up in a few hours for the sunrise service."

His kiss lingered, but he broke away and said, "Fine."

"Goodnight, she whispered.

"Goodnight," he repeated and once they were back to their own sides of the bed he said, "And Eva?"

"Yeah?"

"I love you."

Turning her head to meet his, she smiled. "I love you, too."

*   *   *

Christmas and New Years with Eva's family proved to be interesting as always. Luckily her always cheery, never-had-a-problem sister, Joelle, made it home for their family celebration. Her little girl, Tyla, was a two-year-old ball of energy. She was just enthralled with little Moon, and couldn't stop touching and wanting to hold her. Somewhere along the way Heidi became a 'germaphobe'. Anyone who wanted to touch Moon had to wash his or her hands five times before even coming near the new born. Everyone fell in love with that little girl, and Eva noticed her once reclusive sister open up a little more with the family as a result.

Bunny noticed Eva's thirty-two pound weight loss right away. But unlike last time, she wasn't as boisterous about her observation. After Eric acknowledged her mom's presence, he found refuge in her dad's company, leaving Eva alone with her mom. "Eva darling, you look simply wonderful," she said while gathering Eva to her. "You are positively glowing. What have you been doing?"

Smiling, Eva said, "Exercising and eating right."

Patting her daughter's cheek lovingly, she said with care, "Well, keep up the good work. I know I haven't told you since we last spoke, but I am sorry for the remark about thinking you were pregnant. Sometimes my mouth is too fast for my brain."

"We all have that problem, mother. Besides, it's forgotten. If anything, I should be thanking you. I knew my weight was getting out of hand, but your comment made me realize it and take some action. I'm so glad I did. I really do feel much better." No way would she ever tell her of the real reason for her trying to lose weight. Her mom would try to fix it, and it was the last thing she needed or desired.

"That's wonderful, darling," her mother said sincerely.

"*Oh my gosh!!! Evalynn, is that you?*" a shriek of the familiar voice of Eva's baby sister behind her.

"Hey Joey!" Eva said as they stood in an embrace that went on forever.

"You look great! You *have* been working hard!" Since Joelle was the sports enthusiast of the family and had a degree in nutrition, Eva called her about what she had to do to get started. She and Joelle set up meal plans every few days that Eva stuck to religiously, and after their second phone call her sister advised her to get a personal trainer. That's when she hired Bryce, her personal trainer/bonus nutritionist/Godsend.

Noticing a little bulk beneath her sister's sweater, Eva stood back and assessed her. "Please don't take this the wrong way, but either you took to drinking too much beer or you are going to have another baby."

Smiling shyly, Joey said while rubbing her tummy, "We are due in March."

Tears sprang to Eva's eyes. Yes, she was genuinely excited for her sister, but again the jealousy came along side it. She wished she could be honest with her family about her struggles, but it was just too hard to talk about, and nobody there would really understand what she was going through or how she really felt. Now all the women in her life got to experience what she might never get to, and she knew that if things didn't go according to her plan, she just may have to tell them. Until then, she'd have to cover well, which she did so brilliantly this time around when she pulled Joey into another embrace to cheerfully congratulate her.

"Isn't Moon just precious? I forget how little they are!" Joey said excitedly as they made their way over to the baby.

"Yes, they are precious at that age, but I love seeing every stage they go through. I'm just sorry that I haven't gotten to see Tyla grow. Pictures are not the same, but they are better than nothing," Eva quickly added, noting the sadness in her sister's eyes by her comment. She knew how hard it was for her sister to live so far away from both her and Gavin's family.

After supper and the gift opening, Eric and Eva sprung the news about his new job. For the first time ever, Bunny seemed genuinely impressed by Eric. Eva wondered for a minute if she stumbled onto some alternative universe, because her mother recognized her own appalling behavior towards Eva *and* apologized for it, not to mention respected Eric on the same day? She almost couldn't believe it. Yet, with God all things are possible, and this was nothing short of divine! It sure rounded the holiday season on a good note.

* * *

Her time was getting short with Eric. In two days he would be gone, but she wasn't trying to think about it. Instead she kept busy with work, spending as much time with him as possible and making memories that would have to last a few weeks until she got to visit him in Italy. They were both excited for this experience. Everything was working according to plan. Before he left, he agreed that when he got back from Italy they would make a serious go of starting a family. She just knew that this was God's will for their life. Everything was going so smoothly.

Eric flew out early on New Years Eve Day. Embracing her before the security gate, he said, "I'll see you in nine short days!"

"I can't wait! Be safe!"

"I'll call you when I get there, no matter the time, okay?"

"And leave a message even if I don't pick up. I know how you hate leaving them."

Rolling his eyes jokingly, he said, "Okay, fine." Time was ticking away fast as he glanced at his watch. "I really should get to my gate, babe. I love you!"

"I love you too!"

"And keep up the good work. You look great!" he said as he held her close.

"You can count on it. Go before I make you stay!"

With one last kiss, he walked through the gate.

* * *

Snow fell continuously for two days, concerning Eva more and more as each flake accumulated. So far, twelve inches lay on the ground with another eight to ten to come over night. Eva was due to leave for Italy the next evening, and she was praying for a miracle that she would be able to leave on time, if at all. But she wasn't getting her hopes up. Barbie had shut the salon down, due to cancellations left and right. The night before the storm started, Eva went to the grocery and movie store to prepare for the worst. Eric missed it all by a little over a week. Up until he left, the little bit of snow that had come around the holidays was quickly depleting. Luckily, he made sure that one of his buddies with a snow plow would be there for Eva just in case they needed snow removal before he left, which she was forever grateful.

She was really worried that her workout schedule would get all messed up due to her being snowed in, so she called her trainer to ask him what to do since she wasn't able to make it to the gym. He told her to shovel in the meantime for some cardio as well as a few indoor activities to increase her heart rate, but he stressed that she just keep moving and beware of snacking too much. When the snow let up a little, she took the dogs for a much needed walk. They were getting quite accustomed to getting their exercise, and with Eric gone they had been moping around so she took them to a park a few blocks away; and since it was safe to do because they were the only ones out, she unleashed them so they could roll around in the snow.

When she returned, Eva heard the phone ring as she got inside the garage. Kicking off her shoes quickly, she picked up the nearest phone. "Hello?"

"Oh my goodness, Eva! Thank God you are there!"

"Char? What's going on?"

"How possible would it be to get over here, like now?"

The plows had been out just enough to get a single lane of traffic going, but no way could she get out of her garage. She was too snowed in. "I don't know. Why, what's wrong? "

"Well, my water just broke," she calmly said into the phone, but then Eva heard her cry out in pain. "I'm sorry, Eva. I just had a contraction. If you can't get here, may Charley and I drop the kids off at your house? I am totally not prepared. This baby is coming way too soon!" Charlotte had asked Eva months ago to watch the kids when she delivered, and thinking that she had plenty of time to get to Europe and back before this blessed event came into play, she didn't even think about the 'what if's'.

Eva could hear the fear in her friend's voice, so she tried to calm her down by saying, "Everything will be okay, Char.

Settle down. Since Eric isn't here to shovel me out, not to mention that I don't have an alternative for the dogs, why don't you drop the kids off here on your way to the hospital?"

"Oh, Eva! You are a Godsend! Oh, why of all times did this have to happen *now*???"

"Just think: it will make one heck of a great story!"

That made her chuckle. "That it will! Okay, we will be there as soon as we can!"

A half hour later the Featherstone clan darkened her doorstep. Charley had baby Brake in his arms, and he was trailed by Indy and the twins all bundled to survive sub degree temperatures. Glancing over to the minivan in the snow-covered street, Eva watched Char noticeably concentrating on her breathing while waving to Eva with a forced smile. "Good luck, Charley! Call me as soon as you know something. I'll be praying for you!"

Transferring the baby into Eva's arms, he kissed each one of his kids and told them to be good and then gave her a quick peck on her cheek in appreciation. "Thanks again, Eva! I'll let you know!"

The boys and Eva waved to their parents as they drove off. "All right, let's say we get inside and make some hot cocoa!"

After helping the boys off with their coats, boots, hats and mittens, Eva sat them down in the living room, turned on the television and went to the kitchen to make the cocoa. "Eva, the TV has snow on it too!" complained Indy.

"Okay, hang on! I'll be there just a minute!" Luckily Eva had her stash of old Disney movies as well as the new Shrek movie she picked up at the video store.

She threw in a bag of popcorn for a snack as well and minutes later the five of them were cuddled on the sofa with the dogs begging at their feet, while watching their first movie. "Please, no feeding the dogs, all right?"

Four sets of little hands hid their food from Reddog and Bruiser, who continued to drool at their feet.

"This is so cool! Mommy and Daddy never let us eat in the living room!" Wheeler exclaimed.

"Well, I don't have any fancy furniture or carpeting to ruin," Eva responded with a chuckle.

After hearing the name, Chase asked, "Can I call mommy?"

"No, stupid! She's having a baby!" Indy chimed in before Eva could answer.

Patting Chase's head, Eva said lovingly, "We are all going to have to wait to talk with her and your daddy. But I know they will call as soon as the baby is here. So in the mean time, why don't we finish the movie?"

The twins got restless after fifteen minutes so she agreed to let them play quietly with their train set that they brought. Baby Brake fell asleep in her arms, while Indy watched the rest of <u>Shrek the Third</u>. By eight thirty the twins were tired so Eva got them ready for bed. Since there wouldn't be school the next day for Indy, she let him stay up to watch another movie while the other three went to bed. Luckily for Eva, they went without a fuss.

Settled in next to Indy on the sofa, Eva was starting to doze off, but the phone next to her woke her up. She grabbed it and answered quickly, thinking it was either Charlotte or Charley.

"Hey baby!" Eric's voice cheered on the other end.

"Eric! Hi!" It had been a few days since she last heard from him. She knew a storm was coming, but hadn't mentioned it knowing how wrong the forecasters had been in the past. But now that she had him on the phone, she knew she had to tell him what was going on.

"Gosh, I miss you terribly!"

Stifling a sob with the back of her hand, she choked, "I miss you too!"

"Oh, 'hon, I didn't mean to make you cry!"

"I'm okay, really I am. I'm just so happy to hear from you!"

"I got all your messages, but this training is kicking my butt. I'm up at six every morning and out the door by seven. I don't get back to my apartment until at least six at night and after I eat something I'm out like a light. They are training us to get us out on the field sooner, so the good news is it's looking like it's going to be closer to three months instead of four!"

"Oh, babe, that's wonderful!"

"I thought you'd want to hear that."

"That totally made my day!"

"So I heard there is a storm moving through the Midwest. Are you getting hit at all?" he asked, anxiously.

"Unfortunately, yes. So far twelve inches, but they are talking about another eight to ten over the next day or so."

"Have you checked on your flight?"

"Yeah, and so far my flight is still running on time. But they have cancelled every flight for today according to the news. I'll keep you posted. I'm packed and ready to go!"

"And I'm ready for you to come. This place is unreal. You'll love it."

"I can't wait!"

"Has Opie come over to plow yet?"

"Not yet, but he must be crazy busy. As it is, there is only one path plowed on our street so far."

"But you are ok, though, right? Are you able to get out and shovel at all?"

"I've tried a little bit but it's really heavy. I shoveled a little path from our garage to the mailbox, but of course they aren't delivering anyhow so I don't know why I even bothered! I've been taking the boys for a walk to the park. They love it!"

"I bet! Will your sister be able to make it from the cities to watch the dogs still?" he asked, concerned. Probably more for the dogs' safety than for her sister's, Eva thought with a chuckle. Oh, how he loved those pups.

"She hasn't called, so I imagine she's still planning on it. If not, I'll ask Lucielle from next door to keep an eye on them. You know how much she adores them."

"Just make sure you tell her not to feed them chicken bones again. It almost killed Red last time."

"I think she learned her lesson the hard way, Eric. It took the poor woman months to even look at us in the eyes."

"I suppose you're right."

Indy stirred next to Eva and asked, "Is that Eric?"

"Yes, do you want to say hi?"

"Yeah!" he said with excitement.

Into the phone, Eva said, "Someone wants to talk to you. Hold on!"

Handing the phone to Indy, he quickly said, "Hey, Eric! Are you really in Italy?"

"Who's this?" Eric inquired, confused.

"It's Indy!" the boy said, giggling.

"Well, hey bud! Yeah, I'm really in Italy. Do you know where that is?"

"Kind of. I know it's far away and you need a plane or boat to get there."

Chuckling, Eric said, "You are right about that. So, what are you doing at our house?"

"My mommy's having her baby!"

Hesitating, Eric said, "Wow, Indy! That's great!"

"Yup! And Eva said we have to wait patiently until my mommy or daddy call to tell us when she had it."

"Yeah, that's the hard part, isn't it, bud?"

"It sure is!" Out the corner of his eye, Indy noticed that his favorite part of the movie was coming up. "Oh, Eric! I gotta go!" he said quickly before pushing the phone back to Eva.

Chuckling, Eva said, "His movie takes priority over talking with you!"

"Wow, I totally forgot that Char was even pregnant! That pregnancy sure went fast!"

"Well, as you remember, she didn't find out until she was like four months along and she is six weeks early," Eva said, whispering the last part.

"Well, I sure hope everything goes well."

"Yeah, I was hoping that you were them calling. But I have to say that this was a pleasant surprise!"

"I'm glad to have made your day! But who is going to watch them tomorrow if by chance your flight is on time?"

"Oh man, I totally didn't think of that. When they call, we'll get a plan in motion."

"I'm sure everything will turn out all right. Let me know if something changes! I hate to run, but I have to go! I love you!"

*   *   *

Two days later and it was still snowing. Not only was her flight cancelled, her food supply was dwindling, her snow banks were staggering and Charlotte and Charley were yet to pick up their kids. Outside the hospital parking lot, the roads weren't plowed so they were trapped there with their new baby girl, Summit Jane. When Charlotte called the next day crying, she thought something tragic happened. But when she finally got out that they had a little girl, it all made sense.

Leave it up to those two to have chosen such a unique name. Apparently they were going to name the baby Summit either way, because they figured it sounded unisex and it was in tune with the common theme of their kids' names; all had to do with racing. The baby was only five pounds and was jaundiced so she had to stay, they figured, for at least a week before they could take her home. So Eva figured that the snow issue didn't cause a major stir for them.

Eva didn't have time to get upset over missing her trip, due to Charlotte's kids, lining someone up to come dig her out of the snow up to the windows and taking care of her pent up dogs. Eric was undeniably upset that she missed her flight, not to mention not being with each other for their eleventh anniversary. He understood it was out of her control, but he was really looking forward to seeing her. Now, due to thousands of others who were inconvenienced, her flight was completely cancelled. The airlines told her that her ticket would be credited and could be used within the next year, so she told Eric she would have to use it another time. But in reality she knew that it was a lost opportunity because this was her last bit of vacation until July. The whole scenario didn't set well with him, because he was missing home and needed her there so much. Eva was frustrated too, but there wasn't anything she could do. She didn't appreciate the attitude he was giving her either. Yes, she had a job that she didn't have to punch a time clock for, but he was forgetting that it was her livelihood to be available for her clients. And the less she was there the more they tended to move around to other stylists. To avoid just that problem when she booked this trip to Italy, she took the slowest week off to miss the fewest people as she could. The salon was planning on a busy end of January, February and early March because of Easter being early this year, so this would have been a perfect time to take leave. She didn't tell Eric, but realistically she didn't see a way she could make it over before he got back. "Maybe a miracle would happen," she thought. And boy could she use a couple of those!

Chapter 10

Eric was lonely. Sure Jessup, Jess to those who knew him well, kept him busy at work but at night he missed his wife's warm body. Even though Eva and he hadn't been talking a lot before he left, it was still nice to have someone near just in case he wanted some conversation, and more importantly, some physical contact. And his pups, boy did he crave their smiling eyes, wagging tails and hot, stinky breath. He'd even go for their annoying high-pitched bark at this moment. He tried so hard not to get angry over Eva not being able to join him, but failed almost every night by cursing her, and God.

Although learning about his job was exciting, nothing else was. The allure of Italy wore off about the second week. It had been three weeks since he stepped off the plane into this foreign land and he was aching for an English conversation. He didn't know a lick of Italian, even though some of the words were close to Spanish; a language he had once learned in high school. Yet he was still clueless. Luckily everyone he worked with spoke passable English, enough for Eric to grasp not only what was going on, but for much appreciated conversation. So far he had learned six out of the thirty machines inside and out. Jess wanted him trained and ready to go out in the field by the end of March. The projection was good, and Eric was feeling confident. His boss was a very uplifting man and what Eric would guess to be in about his late fifties. He was shorter than Eric by a few inches, had thinning black/grey hair, dark complexion, friendly eyes and was thick in stature. More times than he could count, Jess told him that he was the fastest learner he had ever had and was excited about his placement in the company. There were three other men who were training with him; one from China, one from Africa and the other from Canada. The only one who was struggling was the man from Africa because English was a problem for him, and no one spoke his native language. When swapping stories on how they ended up there, they all had similar stories; they were all working on one of Malmac's machines and were asked to apply due to their knowledge of the apparatus they ran. All three were married. It was really hard to understand Akwahi Lahunar, the man from Africa, so Eric didn't go out of his way to engage in conversation with him. But Xing Chang kept Eric laughing by his off the wall jokes and trying to imitate American accents. He was a very intelligent man, but over-thanked a lot and was a perfectionist which made the training process for him take a little longer than most. Daryl Hammond from Canada was an egomaniac, thinking he was God's gift to Malmac, Inc. However, because he was the type who thought that they knew it all and never asked for help, more times than not he ended up screwing the machines up so royally it took a team of experts to iron it back out. He was also a sexist pig. The guy was supposedly married but within minutes of meeting he was bragging about his many infidelities, which told Eric he was either an idiot for admitting it let alone doing it at all or was a complete liar. Like him or not, he was the only one who spoke English as their first language, and Eric would look past a lot of annoying traits to get a little morsel of his home language.

Two weeks after they all got there, on a Friday after their last day of training for the week, Jess invited all the men over to his house for an Italian barbecue. Eric wasn't ever much for mingling with higher-ups, but knowing how long the weekend could be, as well as how laid back this management team was, he accepted. His boss sent out a town car for the men, Eric being the last to be picked up. It was a twenty minute scenic drive. Trees he'd never seen before leaned onto the road, and the rock clad mountains in the background took his breath away. Jess had a cooler of assorted beer for them to drink along the way, by far the best Eric had ever tasted. Eric was envisioning a much more luxurious house than what awaited them. His boss's home wasn't any fancier than what he had seen already in Italy. The thing that set it apart was the cobble stone privacy fence with grape vines growing up the sides around the perimeter of their yard (one could only imagine how many grapes grew when in season) where about twenty people were already gathered; most of whom Eric had already met. Jessup's brick house overlooked a nice sized lake, and Eric couldn't help but wonder what kind of fish were in there. The house from the outside looked really small and compact, but inside it had such depth and a great use of space. He loved the ingenuity: solar power, heated floors, wood burning stove, and a hidden compost pile next to the house. Eric noticed a small wooden boat turned upside down by the dock, and his boss noticed him eyeing it.

"You fish?" Jess asked.

"Yeah, I used to. A lot in fact."

"One day, I take you fishing here."

"Yeah?" Eric's eyes brightened.

"That would be nice, no?"

"Yes, it would. What kind of fish? Trout?"

"Yes, a lot of trout. But we no eat them."

"Catch and release then?"

"Yes, yes. Come now, I show you real Italian food!" Jess said, slapping him on his back.

That was another thing Eric couldn't complain about: the food. It was beyond words. Nothing against Eva's cooking, she made a mean dish of manicotti, but nothing came close to the authentic food of Italy. Jess had a few different styles of meat on the grill, one including lamb which Eric had never tried. Everything was laced with herbs from Jessup's wife's garden and the vegetables were so succulent they didn't need anything on them to spice them up. Loading up his plate and grabbing a beer, he took a seat on the top of the knoll overlooking the lake. He didn't intend to segregate himself from the crowd, but nobody seemed interested in taking in the cool, clear night next to the lake like he did; they'd rather sit inside Jess's four season glass porch. Evening's like these made him think of home. It had been a long time since Eric got the chance to use his boat or even to cast his rod into the many lakes near them; work and 'life' had taken over. When would he get the chance to do that again, he asked himself with a frown. It didn't help that Eva had never shared his love for the great outdoors. Yes, she went fishing with him a few times, but he knew she was there for him, not the love of the sport which in the end spoiled it for him. His brother and uncle had no interest and all his friends he used to do those things with had gotten on with their lives, and fishing to them became part of their past as well, but it was something he really enjoyed and suddenly had a longing to do it again.

"Mind if I sit by you?" a female voice sounded behind him.

Turning around, Eric saw that it was Jess's daughter, Claudia. He had met her a few times during his training, since she was the marketer of the outfit. Eric could tell that she was a no-nonsense business woman; a woman who took her job very seriously. At the shop she resembled a school marm, slicking back her dark hair in a severe bun or ponytail, wearing clothes that covered her body fashionably, yet studiously, and adorned with big black framed glasses that overshadowed her petite face. The fact that she towered over her dad and half the men that worked there was slightly intimidating as well. But now, 'holy cow' his brain was screaming. Her hair looked like black silk that cascaded half way down her back in wavy layers, and her big brown eyes stood out against her long black eyelashes without any barrier of clunky glasses. The white fitted sweater that she had overlapping her snug jeans, not that he was noticing or anything, made him temporarily lose his speech. Until this moment, he saw her as everyone else he worked with. Now, all he could think was that he should open his mouth and tell her that the spot was taken because the thoughts that were cruising through his head at the moment would get him into trouble if they escaped through his mouth. Instead of saying anything, he simply nodded.

With a plate of food in one hand and a beer in the other, she sat down quite effortlessly. Kicking her long slender legs out in front of her, she laid her plate on her lap and started to eat while looking out at the water. "So, how do you like the job so far, Eric?"

Finding his voice, he said simply, "I love it." When she smiled over to him, he realized that she had the whitest teeth he'd ever seen on anyone.

"I'm glad to hear it. My dad just raves about you," and then she paused before saying, "I have something to confess..."

Eric glanced her way cautiously, not knowing where this conversation was going. She continued, "My dad wanted me to drill you with questions, to make sure you are happy with us. But by your one response, I know all I need to know, so no more questions about work."

He was honored by their concern over his happiness there, but her beauty was still making him devoid of any intelligent conversation at the moment, so all he could say was, "Okay."

Claudia chuckled, and he noticed the gleam in her eyes when she did. "You don't talk much, do you?" she asked.

"I guess it depends on the subject," he said, finding his voice.

"Well, I suppose if I wanted a discussion with you I better ask you better questions; ones that don't require a yes or no answer."

That got him to smile. "I suppose so." And at that they both chuckled, loosening him up a bit. "How is it that your English is flawless, and your accent minimal?" he asked after taking a bite and swallowing it.

"I studied in New York my sophomore through senior year at a private high school, and then stayed on at NYU for my bachelor and master degrees in communications and marketing. Everyone gave me crap for my accent so I tried hard to lose it."

"Well, I'd say you succeeded."

"Thanks."

"How about you? Do you know any other languages?"

"Just a little bit of Spanish, but I don't remember much now. That was like sixteen years ago. Man! That is a long time!"

"Yeah, somehow those years go by without knowing how fast they are moving until one day you wake up and are like, 'wow, I'm twenty-eight, single and still live at home with my parents while all my friends are married with at least one kid.'"

"Welcome to my life, except I'm almost 31, married with two dogs instead of kids, not to mention half way around the world and not knowing exactly how I got here."

"Well, I can tell you this, you are here because of fate. My dad has been looking for you for a long time. This company is his baby. He started it ten years ago, but actually got it launched five years ago with him, my uncle and Lars and was known in only three countries. Now we are almost twenty-five employees strong and hopefully by the end of this year we will be getting into our twentieth country."

"That's gotta feel like a great accomplishment."

"We are all proud to be a part of it. You should be too."

Eric smiled, feeling honored. "How did your dad and Lars meet?" he asked since it had been nagging his thoughts for a while now.

"Believe it or not, on holiday when I was a kid."

"On holiday?"

Claudia laughed. "I forget you that you Americans don't do that. For two weeks every August practically all of Europe shuts down for vacation."

"Wow! That's crazy. But how do businesses make it? If there's tourism, how can they close?"

"They work together and stagger it so someone is always open."

"So your dad and Lars clicked and kept in touch or what?" he asked.

"That's pretty much it. We would visit him and his family in Norway and then they would stay with us."

Before Eric could ask another question about it, Darryl plopped himself down beside Claudia with his heaping plate of food and two beers in his hand and said, "Hey, pretty lady, would you mind if I sit here?"

"Of course not."

Eric noticed Claudia's uneasiness to Darryl's approach and watched her ease closer to Eric as an effect. "So, either of you guys up to going out tonight?"

"We are 'out', Darryl," Eric put in sarcastically.

"Oh, you know what I mean, man. This is Italy! We have to live it up while we're here. You must know of some hot spots around town," he said, speaking to Claudia.

"Well, I used to, but it's been a long time since I've done the club or bar scene."

"What? A hot little number like you? I thought you were single," he asked in confusion.

Claudia ignored his blatant comment and addressed her single status. "Not every girl who is single is hanging out at clubs. I happen to take my career seriously. It's a six day a week job for me, sometimes seven, and drinking the night away certainly isn't going to help my performance any."

"How do you expect to find a man hiding away behind closed doors? You are too fine to be wasting away," he said, eyeing her up and down with no remorse.

Subconsciously flipping her long black hair so it covered her chest, she said with confidence, "And what makes you think I desire to find a man? Is it that crazy I'm satisfied being an independent woman and that I don't need a man to make me whole?"

Wow! Eric thought. He was really beginning to like this woman! "She told you, man!" Eric chided with a smirk as he continued to scarf down his food.

Obviously flustered, Darryl got to his feet and started to walk away, but glanced over his shoulders and said, "The offer still stands, Wahler. I'm heading to Bella's after this."

"I'll keep that in mind."

Once he was out of sight, Claudia and Eric looked at each other and started to laugh. "Is he always like that?" she asked.

"Yup, pretty much."

"And he's married?"

"So he says. Although if I were him I wouldn't admit it; makes him look like an idiot. But then again, maybe that's his angle. The women he meets seem to thrive on his marital status and being treated like a piece of meat."

Shuddering, she said, "That's just wrong. I pity his wife."

"Yeah. You were wise not to encourage him. I admire the way you stood your ground."

Her eyes shone over to him, but in a bashful way, and her voice quieted when she said, "I believe in monogamy. I've been cheated on too many times to go through that pain ever again, hence why work has become my life. You don't meet anyone but drunks and losers out at clubs." Eric sat there stunned. No way could he imagine any fool cheating on the intelligent, beautiful girl beside him. She continued, since he wasn't saying anything. "I even tried dating men from church, but even they were just as shallow. Marriage was the last thing on their mind, and the only reason I'm interested in dating is to find a potential husband. It's just really discouraging when you get to be my age and knowing that the pickings are getting slimmer by the day."

Eric was getting uncomfortable with the turn of their exchange. It had been a long time since any woman besides his wife opened up to him like Claudia was. It didn't seem right, yet something about her intrigued him. He had nothing to say. Encouraging her didn't seem right for some reason, yet sitting there like a bump on a log made the momentary lapse of silence deafening.

Claudia said quickly, "I'm sorry. I don't know why I confessed all that to you. Like you care about my dating status. Tell me about your wife. Do you miss her?"

Her question jolted him. More so in the surprise that at the moment Eva was the last person he was thinking about, which made this whole scenario seem all the more wrong. Eric had to come up with something fast. "Yes, I do. She was supposed to come over for a week but she got snowed in back home," was all he offered.

"I'm sorry to hear that. Will she be coming over soon?"

"Unfortunately, no. She only had a small window of opportunity, and it's gone now. Luckily, I'll be out of here sooner than expected, so it won't be that bad."

"Men are resilient that way. I think women are more dependent on the man being around. I'm sure she misses you very much, Eric."

"I'm sure she does, but she's always been a very busy person. I rarely saw her the way it was." Why he offered her that information so willingly, he didn't know. But what he saw in Claudia's eyes right then told him he made a mistake in telling her that. He definitely needed to watch himself around her because he had a feeling that if he ever needed a shoulder to cry on, or a hug, she would offer it to him quite willingly, even though her words spoke differently.

Looking down at her hands, she asked, "How long have you been married?"

The way she asked him felt as if his answer would depress her either way. Or maybe that was what he wanted to believe? His thoughts were insane. "It was eleven years two days ago."

Her head popped up with surprise. "Eleven years? You guys were young, huh?"

"We were nineteen."

"Wow! That was young," she commented, pondering it for a second before asking, "Why the rush if you don't mind me asking?"

The sun was going down rapidly, and the reflection off the lake was breathtaking. So he focused on that while saying, "Guess we didn't think we were rushing into anything at the time. We just wanted to be together."

"That's really sweet. And are things the way you imagined it when you planned for your future?" She asked sincerely.

"Are they ever?"

"Yeah, good point." She mulled it around in her head a few seconds before asking, "But is that disappointing to you? Again, just tell me to shut up if I'm being too nosey. It's just that I've never met anyone who has married so young before and has made it this long. I mean…sheesh! I'm just putting my foot in my mouth, aren't I? I didn't mean it to sound like that..."

Chuckling, Eric said, "No, it's all right. I guess in a way I'm disappointed; more in myself than anyone. I'm glad for this opportunity because for the first time in my life I feel like I'm not failing Eva. She's a wonderful wife. I couldn't have asked for better. But I feel like she could've done better."

Claudia's hand gently touched his arm. "I'm sure she doesn't feel that way."

Her touch sent electric waves throughout him, and because he didn't want to be rude he let her continue to touch him but he looked away, trying to separate himself from what it made him feel. "Well, we are our own worst critic."

"Isn't that the truth."

The moment her fingers released his arm, he got a chill which made him look at her. Her face was flushed and she looked as if she were going to stand. So he quickly stood up and offered her his hand. "Thank you," she offered with a smile.

"You're welcome".

"Let me take those for you," she said, taking his plate and empty beer can. "Listen, I don't go out much but if you ever want to or just need to talk..."

"Yeah, thanks. I'll keep you in mind." Boy would he ever, Eric thought, which led him to believe he was in big trouble!

Chapter 11

"Am I seeing that right?" Eva asked as she stood on the scale at the doctor's office.

Janine, Dr. Kratz's nurse, smiled and said, "Yes, Eva. It says 151. You are officially down forty-nine pounds. Congratulations!"

Beaming from head to toe, Eva exclaimed, "Wow!"

"Let's just go into this room and I'll take your vitals."

Everything appeared normal to Eva's delight. Before the weight loss her blood pressure was verging on the high side, and given the drama in her life in the past week it was a miracle it wasn't into the danger zone.

Soon after Eric had left, Natasha was back to dropping the kids off on the weekends again. She was always quick to pick them up before Bart got back into town, but Eva knew that it wouldn't be long before he caught wind of what was going on. Eva never asked questions to her goings on. The less she knew the better off she was. And she had no intention of letting Bart or Eric know what Natasha was doing. For one, it was much easier taking the kids quietly without the threat of WW3 and since Eric wasn't around there wasn't a threat of him finding out. The truth was that she missed Eric and the kids helped fill that void.

It was the end of February, and Eric had called to tell her that he only had at most another four weeks left to go. She was excited. It was all planned out. She would get this doctor visit over with, ask her questions, set what appointments up that needed to be set up to get the baby process moving along and by that time Eric would be back so they could get started. Eva was so ready. She had done her part when it came to the improvement of her health, and if all the tests came back how she was predicting they would, she would be ready to go.

Then Sunday happened. After Natasha dropped the kids off the day before, they took the dogs for a walk to the park and they played for a few hours since it was a balmy fifty degree day. Then they ventured over to Charlotte's so the kids could play together, and that Eva could have a catch up time with her friend. It had been weeks since they had a heart to heart, and a lot had happened.

"You are fading away to nothing, girl!" Char said as she and the baby hugged Eva.

"Hardly, but I'm getting there!"

They took a seat in her living room. While watching Charlotte nursing her baby, she fought the envy away by saying, "She's so beautiful. I'm still trying to process that you have a little girl. It just doesn't seem right!"

Charlotte adored little Summit with such love as she lightly stroked her tiny peach fuzzed head. "We love her so much. And here I thought we were complete after baby Brake. I can't imagine life without her."

"Well, I bet you are kept busy. I just want to thank you again for watching the kids last Saturday. It helped me out a lot!"

"It's no bother. After five, what's three more?"

"You are amazing, Char."

Her friend looked at Eva with astonishment and then shook her head. "You are the amazing one, Eva. I'm forced to be with my kids, but you so willingly and lovingly take in kids that aren't even yours. Now that, my friend, is bordering on sainthood!" she joked.

"I'm their aunt. Someone needs to look out for them. I don't know what's going on, but something tells me there is going to be a coming of heads real soon. Please pray I'm not caught in the crossfire. I have enough on my plate."

"You know I will, 'hon. So what else is going on in your crazy scheduled world?"

"Oh, you know, the same ol' same ol'. When I'm not working, I'm at the gym, taking care of the dogs, running to help out wherever I'm needed and making sure I'm there for these kids. I did ask Kristin to keep an eye on them as well, just in case I'm missing signs of distress. She's so astute when it comes to children's behavior."

126

"Yeah, we were blessed to get her. My kids just love her!"

"So do Bart's kids," Eva said thoughtfully, and then added regretfully, "As much as I love having them around though, I am feeling a little burned out lately."

"You have way too many irons in the fire, girl. You do know that you don't have to volunteer to do everything, right?"

"Well, I feel guilty saying no, when I know I'm able and can find the time; especially when Eric isn't here."

"Yeah, but Eva, you have been this busy ever since I've known you."

"Have I?"

Laughing at her as if she were crazy, Charlotte said, "Um, yeah! Hello!"

"Man, I guess I don't even think about it. I just do it."

"Well, do less. I'm telling ya, you are going to definitely burn out fast going at the pace you are setting, especially taking care of those little ones. Speaking of little ones, Summit seems to have nodded off. Wish I were able to fall asleep that quickly!" Even though sleeping, Charlotte still tried burping the infant. And surprisingly a big belch erupted from that tiny body without waking. "Would you like to hold her?"

"I'd love to!" Eva exclaimed.

The baby settled right into the crook of her arm, right under her own breast. She smiled at the thought that someday this is what it would be like having her own child; such a precious life. The joyous process of conceiving, carrying, delivering and raising such a life filtered through her head until Charlotte's voice interrupted her thoughts. "Mitch Carter has been hanging around here a lot."

"Oh?" Eva concentrated on the baby rather than committing herself to Char's statement.

"Yeah. He mentioned that he sees you at the gym."

"Yeah, I see him around."

"He mentioned that you are looking great."

"Wow, really?" Eva's head popped up in surprise, and a blush rose quickly behind it.

Charlotte appraised her friend warily, and said, "Yeah, he

also says he talks to you; a lot."

The way she put it made it sound like Eva was doing something she shouldn't have and it made her defensive when responding, "Yeah? So?" Sure she committed a few hundred sins every time she looked Mitch's way and even more when she talked to him (not necessarily in what she said, but what she was thinking she'd like to say). He was a wonderful man. Many times she caught herself thinking, 'if only' and 'what if', which spoke volumes, and scared her into repentance every time. The time she gave into and acted on those thoughts, she knew she was in trouble. She knew now more than ever how important it was to stay on the right course with God's Word, and what she was going through was a major test of her will and obedience to Him. So far, Mitch Carter remained a temptation she disguised as a coincidental friendship that she held at arm's length.

"So I suppose he told you that he's separated from his wife."

"Yeah, he mentioned that."

"So then you must know that he gets the girls on the weekends and has moved to Red Wing permanently."

Still staring at the baby to avoid Charlotte's gaze, Eva said,"Yup."

After a long pause, Charlotte said, "Be careful, Eva. Loneliness is a great avenue for Satan to attack, no matter how on top of your game you are..."

Eva finally looked at her friend as if she were clairvoyant. "You don't have to remind me how Satan works. Mitch is only a friend. Nothing indecent is going on. Plus, I haven't had *time* to be lonely, so no worries there, sister!" she tried to add as a joke.

Smiling, but seriously Charlotte said, "I'm not saying there is something indecent going on, but there is potential there, my friend. He speaks highly of you, and I don't know why but it's made me sit up and pay attention. I don't have to mention that you both are in really vulnerable places right now. With Eric gone, and Mitch newly separated, well, you know. The two can combine forces and take you both by storm. We know he has a strong faith, as do you, but it's not good to put yourself in a tempting situation. And believe me, I know just how tempting he is! I know you love Eric, but even when our mate is near it's so easy to fall prey to lust. And it's all the more alluring when a prospect is near and tangible while our mate is far away."

"Char, with all due respect, everything is just fine. No worries, all right? If you feel the need to pray about it, please do. I won't lie and tell you I don't think impure thoughts when I'm around him, but that's as far as it goes. And I'm not foolish to think that he doesn't have lustful thoughts about women either, and that probably includes me; but neither one of us has ever crossed that line, and I'd like to think we never will. As for Eric and me, we're doing fine."

"Well, good. I feel better now that it's all out in the open."

"Good," Eva said with a smile. She knew her friend meant well and didn't mean to offend. If it were anyone else she might've gotten her feathers ruffled, but not with Charlotte.

To give Charlotte a break, she offered to take Indy and the twins home and meet up with them at church in the morning. Seth and Noah were really excited to have their friends sleep over. It would be the first time, and it would be a test of patience and ability for Eva. After a few screaming matches, which put Red and Bruiser's high-pitched barks to shame, and a tearful phone call home from Wheeler, it all went well. Eva never felt as content as she did that night. To her, that is what life was all about; getting to share your time and love with others.

After church that Sunday, the kids were crabby from the lack of sleep from the night before so she put them all down for a nap once they got home; even Seth. Within fifteen minutes, they were out like a light. She took that time to get into her Bible study assignment that she wanted to wrap up since her following week wouldn't allow a lot of time for when she heard a car pull up into her driveway. It was only noon, which was too early for Natasha to be picking the kids up. Normally it neared the six o'clock hour when she darkened her doorstep. Looking out the window, she was shocked to see Bart. Dressed in rumpled up clothing and looking like he just got off a week long drinking bender, he made his way up the sidewalk. "Uh oh," she thought, "this isn't good!" Eva met him at the door.

"Bart, this is a surprise."

His normally brilliant eyes were bloodshot, but they met hers when he said, "Can we talk?"

He caught her off guard, but she said, "Of course. The kids are asleep. I just put them down. Why don't we go into the kitchen?"

He followed behind her silently and pulled up a chair next to her at the table. "So, what's up, Bart?"

Even though she could tell something was really weighing on his mind, he mustered up a smile and awkwardly looked at her as if it was for the first time. "Wow, Eva. You look great."

"Um...Thanks..."

"No, I mean it."

Chuckling uncomfortably, she said, "I believe you. But I have to wonder as we sit here why you don't look like your usual together self."

That's when she noticed the tears in his eyes; Eva knew it wasn't good news. "Bart, what is it?"

"Natasha left me."

"She *what*?"

That's when she witnessed something she had never seen before: Bart honest to goodness crying. "That's why I'm home so early. I took the first plane out this morning. She left me a voice mail. Do you want to hear it?"

"Um, I don't know. Do you want me to hear it?"

"Yes, because then maybe you can help me understand it."

"Why? Is it cryptic?" she asked seriously, not knowing what end was up at the moment.

"No, it's just typical Natasha. But I want someone else to hear it just to make sure I'm not imagining all of this."

"Well, okay then."

Putting his phone on speaker phone mode, he got to his voice mail and the next thing she heard was a bored sigh and then Natasha's crisp voice saying, "Barton, it's me. I just wanted to let you know that the kids are at Eva's. I'm not coming home, as in ever again. I'm sick of playing wife to a husband who is never here and mother to kids who I'm just sick of. I want a divorce. I signed with an agent in the cities and he's gotten me some jobs in Chicago. He's going to make me a star, and I certainly can't make that happen *and* be a mother and a wife. The papers will be in the mail shortly. I don't want anything from you other than an uncontested divorce, and I'm relinquishing all rights to the kids. They won't miss me much any way. Goodbye."

Eva sat there stunned. "Wow!" she said with big eyes.

"So it's not a bad dream?"

"The woman couldn't have been more blatant! Oh my goodness, Bart, I just can't believe she'd do this!" Eva's eyes watered, trying to imagine what would be going on in Natasha's head to do such a thing. And poor Bart; he looked so defeated.

"What am I going to do, Eva? How am I going to tell the kids? What am I going to tell the kids? Am I really supposed to tell them that their mother left and is never coming back? Do you think she is really serious? I mean, I knew she was unhappy. But I never would have imagined that she would abandon the kids. Oh my God, what am I going to do?" he cried into his hands with his elbows digging into his thighs.

Eva's mind was whirling.

Pray with him, my child. Encourage him. Tell him that I am here in your midst.

He won't let you pray for him. If you ask, he'll say no and then turn around and laugh at you! Then he'll tell Eric and he'll be mad at you for throwing your religion on his family! Do you really want to stir that pot? Besides, why would he let you pray to a god who would let this happen to him?

There is no fear in my perfect love. Trust in me. Just ask him.

He's not going to let you.

Trust me, my precious daughter. Open your mouth and I will fill it.

Eva cleared her throat, and was visibly nervous when she said, "Bart, I'm so sorry. This is all a little overwhelming. I wish I had the answers for you. The only thing I can offer is my help. I can help you talk to the kids. If you don't mind, I'd like to talk with our youth pastor, who has a lot of expertise in this area. She counsels a lot of children of divorced parents. I don't want to over step any bounds, but just know that you aren't alone. Eric and I will be here for you and your kids." She reached over and touched his limp hand that was resting on his leg.

Her touch brought his teary eyes to meet hers. "Thank you. I don't know what I'm doing..."

"Bart, would you be interested in talking with Kristin, the youth director, yourself? She really is fantastic, and the most nonjudgmental person you'd ever meet. She might have the words you need for the kids..."

"I, suppose. I mean, what choice do I have?"

Eva could only look at Bart in pity. She knew this split was coming, but like Bart had said, never in a million years would she imagine it would be quite this extreme. After a few moments, Eva said with a boldness that only the Spirit of God could give, "Bart, I'd like to pray with you."

"Wh...what?" he looked uneasy.

"I said I'd like to pray with you. You don't have to say anything, but I do feel the urge to pray right now. Will you bear with me for a few moments?"

"O- okay..." he said hesitantly.

She scooted her chair closer to her brother-in-law and reached out her hands. With a smile of encouragement, he clasped his hands into hers. Bowing her head to start, he followed suit. "Father God, we humbly come before you with heavy hearts. Lord, we don't know why Natasha has done what she has done; only You know her heart. But as we stand in the wake of the devastation here, I know that you are here. I trust in Your promises, and You have promised to never give us more than we can handle. I know You are in control, even in the midst of chaos. Father, I pray that you give Bart the peace and comfort that only You can give. The answers might never come as to why this has happened, but we know from

Your word that all works together for the good of those who love you. And Father, please give us the right words when telling the children and give us the right time to tell them. Protect them from the evil of this world. Let them feel the love of Your people. Father, I love You, honor You and trust You with all my being. You instructed us to give thanks in everything, and even though it's hard, Father I thank You for this. I pray that good will come out of it. Thy will be done. In Jesus name, amen."

Tears were streaming down both their faces, and in seconds they were out of the chair, clinging to each other.

"Thank you."

Relieved over his reaction, Eva could only say, "You will get through this, Bart."

Sitting down again, Bart said, "I don't even know where to begin. I didn't give her enough credit. She did so much. I never paid attention. Eva, I have no idea how to raise those kids by myself!" he cried hysterically.

Grabbing a leftover beer of Eric's from the refrigerator, she handed it to Bart. "Well, the first thing you have to do is calm down. And the second thing you have to do is tell me when you are going to need me to watch the kids. You know that I'll help you with them, so don't worry there."

Taking in a deep breath, he said, "Okay. I leave for Denver on Wednesday, so I'll need someone to watch them until I get back Sunday evening, but I'll try to revise my schedule."

Eva mentally went over her week's schedule and shuddered inwardly. It was going to be an even busier week. First things first were those kids. "Don't worry if you can't. Just tell me what works for you, okay?"

"Are you sure? That's a lot to ask, Eva."

'Wow', Eva thought sarcastically, 'Bart with a conscience? Wonders never cease!' "They are my nephews and niece, Bart. Enough said."

Shaking his head with wonder, he smiled. "Thank you."

Smiling back, she said with ease, "While you nurse that beer, I'm going to call Kristin." She didn't give him a chance to

133

argue, and a part of her thought that he wouldn't anyhow.

Kristin Eastlund had been the youth leader at the church for a year now. She came with a bachelor degree in psychology as well as a two year degree in youth ministry, so the church just ate her up when she applied. At the time she was twenty-nine and engaged, but right before she stepped into her leadership role she broke off her engagement. Because she was part of her Friday night bible study, Eva got to know her really well, including the personals of her life. Her break up with Mathew was hard, but she knew it would never work. After a lot of prayer and discussion with him, they tearfully decided that they were better off going in separate directions and staying friends. He was a minister in Wisconsin and dating a member of the church, as where Kristin hadn't resumed dating yet, which gave her time to devote to her kids; all sixty-seven of them aging from preschool to seniors in high school. They all just adored her. She knew Kristin loved Bart's kids as much as she did and would do anything to help. And she was right. If Bart was up to it, Kristin encouraged both Eva and him to come right over.

When the kids woke up from their nap, they were so excited to see their dad. Well, at least Noah and Lydia were. Seth held back a little and watched the other two cling to him for dear life until Bart reeled him in too. The kids didn't know why their dad was crying or hugging them so tightly, but they ate it up. In fact, they didn't even ask why he was crying. There were a lot of 'I love you and missed you's' shared. Eva teared up at the sight. Never before had she seen so much love exude from her brother-in-law. At that moment, Eva knew that God had something in store here; something great.

After calling Charlotte and asking a huge favor, again, she dropped the kids off and told her that they would be back in a few hours. Up until they dropped off the kids, Charlotte hadn't a clue as to what was going on. Now that she saw Bart, she appeared even more intrigued. While in an embrace, Eva whispered, "I'll tell you about it later. Thanks again! We'll be back soon!"

They then drove over to the youth director's apartment. Kristin thought it would be less intimidating if they met in a homey atmosphere. She was renting a side of a small one bedroom duplex a few blocks from the church. Bart was getting anxious as they neared. "I don't know about this, Eva."

"Relax. She's not going to bite. Just give her a shot. You never know, she might give you some good ideas."

Kristin opened her door before they even got to the steps. Her long brown hair that usually was left hanging straight below her shoulder blades was now in a high ponytail, which made her appear a lot younger than she was. She didn't have a stitch of make up on, but her cheeks were flushed as if she just finished a good workout and her lips were moistened by some clear lip gloss; cherry from where Eva was standing. Her cornflower blue eyes were friendly, and her casual attire, inviting. Reaching out her slender hand, she said, "Hi, I'm Kristin Eastlund."

Normally Bart was outgoing, but he was really out of his element here. So with hesitation, he met her hand with a weak shake and said, "Bart Wahler."

Smiling, she said, "It's great to finally meet you! Why don't you two come in? Would either of you care for something to drink? I've got some beer, a wide variety of pop and flavored waters."

"You drink beer?" Bart asked, stupefied.

Laughing, her eyes lit up when she replied, "Not a lot, but of course! I'm from Milwaukee."

"And you are the youth leader, of a church?" Bart's expression was priceless. He appeared as if he were about to look around and see if aliens were going to join them in the room.

"Yeah. I mean, it's not as if I get drunk on the stuff, but I sure enjoy one on a hot summer day, and of course when the Packers play the Vikings!"

Bart visually loosened up by the time he entered the living room. Must've been the mention of football and beer, Eva thought jokingly. Both Eva and he declined a drink and settled on the couch where Kristin directed them. After getting a cup of coffee from the kitchen, she took a seat in front of her overstuffed chair instead of sitting in it.

Eva and her brother in law looked at each other over her choice of seating and chuckled. Eva joked, "Would you like us to join you on the floor?"

Blowing over her hot cup, she smiled. "Only if you want. I just feel more comfortable sitting on the floor when I'm discussing difficult things."

Bart shifted on his side of the couch and he found his voice. "How old are you, exactly, if I may ask?"

"Thirty. Why?"

He appeared shocked by either her age or her boldness, but he responded quickly, "You just seem young is all. No offense. I'm not saying that you don't do a good job at what you do, not that I would know, but this is very difficult for me, to the point where I have a hard time believing that a thirty-year-old , and I presume you are single?" she nodded in silent affirmation before continuing, "that you would know how to help me."

Eva sat back and just listened. The more she watched the two of them talk, the more she was impressed with Kristin. She'd known that kids and adults alike at church adored her, and knew she had counseled kids in the past. But it was interesting to see how calm and collected she was at receiving Bart's brash comment, as if she heard it a thousand times. No offense was taken, which was a blessing because Eva knew how Bart would react to any signs of weakness. He would have high tailed it out of there so fast their heads would have spun!

"Well, I may not be able to help you, but I know how to help your kids. They are beautiful children. Seth is such an intelligent little boy who makes friends so fast. And little Noah is so sensitive and shy, but is so quick to trust. And that Lydia of yours would melt the hardest of hearts. She's growing up so fast. Every little kid out there just wants to be loved, first and foremost. That goes without saying. But their sense of security comes in a close second."

"Y-you...you seem to know a lot about my kids," Bart said with guilt.

"I've gotten to know them. They are great. And I know they are resilient. Kids are a lot smarter than we give them credit for. How you deal with this will totally shape how they react. Now, I don't need to know all the details. Eva filled me in a little bit over the phone, as you know. And what we are dealing with here is going to be tough, I'm not going to lie to you. Seth and Noah are going to be the ones who take it the hardest. When are you planning on telling them?"

"I..." Bart was never one to stutter or look away, but Eva felt his uneasiness as he suddenly perched at the edge of the couch with his hands folded tightly between his knees and his head hanging low. In three words, he looked defeated. With a small voice, he finished by saying, "I have no clue."

Compassion was written all over Kristin's face. "Bart." When he didn't look up, she said his name again and waited. It took a few seconds, but when he looked at her his eyes were watery and Eva knew it was wreaking havoc with his ego. Kristin's soft features portrayed sincerity and luckily didn't come off as calloused or pitiful. "You don't have to figure this out on your own..." And after a few seconds of silence, she asked, "What is the probability of your wife coming back?"

"I don't know. She's never done this before, even come close. This is way out of left field..."

"I see..."

After a few seconds, he shook his head in defeat. "I realize I have to tell them, but I guess I need to know how to tell them delicately. I mean, I know what it's like to be abandoned." Eva knew of Bart and Eric's past, but she never heard it from Bart's perspective before. Ever since she walked in Kristin's house, she was just a fly on the wall, but his words made her want to turn invisible. She paid attention to every word, but Eva tried to act as nonchalant as she could while Bart continued, "I was six when my father ran out on us, and all I remember was that I hated him. And over time I hated that I hated him. He liked to hit a lot, especially my mom and me, so when he left it was sort of a relief. Yet a part of me missed having someone to call 'dad'. I always said I wouldn't be like him, but ya know what? Even though I never hit or left like he did, I'm just as bad. Natasha had been telling me how unhappy she was for months but I wouldn't listen. I lived for my job and my family came second. I can see that now, but at the time I thought providing for their needs was what my job as their father and husband entailed. Man, have I made a mess of this! It's my fault that my kids don't have a mother now. I'd love to blame her. But I know it's a lot to do with me."

"But, Bart, she is the one who left, not you. If there were problems there are better ways to do it than leaving your kids," Eva said, not able to hold back anymore.

"Yeah, I know, but in her defense, her mom ran out on her when she was young so I guess it's somehow ingrained. But I guess what got me totally blindsided on this was she swore up and down that she would never do that to her kids. After all, we both came from homes like that and we knew how much pain came from it."

Kristin spoke up by gently saying, "Well, one good thing is you have personal experience with this. Try to think back to when you were going through it, and remember what helped you the most. Now luckily your kids are a little younger. I'm not saying that they won't have a tough time with it, but they are still at an impressionable age. You are still the puppet master and they are puppets if you will. Now, I have no idea of your faith, but I do know about your kids. They love Jesus and they know how to pray. Regardless of how you think and feel, encourage them to pray for whatever is on their hearts; especially for their mother, to keep her safe etc...They will know how, I've heard them do it."

Bart looked up from his folded hands down to Kristin who was still lounged out on the floor. "Wow, I don't even know my own kids...yet you, a perfect stranger to me, know them. Sad picture, huh?" he asked, destroyed.

This is what hitting rock bottom looks like, Eva thought, and it's not pretty. Luckily Kristin had the right words. "Of course you know your kids. This is just another part of your kids' lives, that quite frankly, a lot of fathers are just as guilty of not knowing. Now is not the time for a pity party. Those kids are going to need you to be strong because it's going to be straining and stressful and ugly at times, but in the end they will remember your love and strength. All the other crud will be forgotten. And if there is anything more I can do for you, anything at all, please don't hesitate to call me." She got up, went over to her dinner table which was butted up against the corner wall and retrieved two business cards, handing them to him. "Day or night. And here is a number of a male colleague of mine if you would be more comfortable talking to him. He's also available any time."

Standing to receive them, he shook her hand. "Thank you."

And then Kristin addressed Eva while in an embrace. "And you, my dear, call me so we can do lunch someday within the next couple weeks. Maybe Char could join us."

"For sure. I'll talk to her about it. Thanks for everything. I'll for sure see you on Friday!"

The only thing Bart said on their way over to Charlotte's was, "She gave me a little food for thought. And you were right, she was nice..."

Eva just nodded her head in agreement and prayed that they would all weather the storm which was in the making.

Chapter 12

Friday. Another week gone by. Ever since Jessup's dinner party, something in Eric opened up and he decided that he wouldn't waste another minute alone. He started to frequent a few of the pubs near his apartment where sometimes Daryl or Xing would join him, and when they didn't he found that the locals were really friendly and spoke enough English to have a nice conversation; they really enjoyed learning about where Eric came from and the company he worked for. Before long, his new Italian friends started introducing them to a new club every weekend, starting Friday night; even Claudia tagged along when she could. But given this Friday was unseasonably warm for the end of February, he decided to forego the pub and accept his boss's invite to go fishing instead.

"It is not the best to fish, but we will see," Jessup said.

"That sounds great!"

"I leave now, but my Claudia come same time as you, no?"

"If she will drive me, that will work for me, sir."

After shaking hands, his boss walked away and Daryl came up behind him. "Another job well done as usual, brown noser?"

Daryl became the least favorite to hang out with, yet he seemed to be the most available. As much time as they spent together people would've thought they were becoming best buddies, which was hardly the case. The guy was obnoxious and Eric couldn't wait to be free of him. He spent more time chasing women, and that included Claudia whenever she went along, than in conversation with him. Claudia just laughed it off, treating it like a joke, but Eric knew that one of these times she was going to have enough and tell him where to take those proposals of his.

Whenever she'd go out with them, Eric found himself fending off the leeches if she had trouble not making herself clear. The rest of the guys, outside of Daryl, were there to have a couple drinks and relax; not to play bodyguard, so that's where he came in. Daryl hadn't been the only one knocking on her door unfortunately; there were plenty of them popping up. Come to find out, Italian men were even bolder and more obnoxious than Daryl was, if one could believe. Though Eric enjoyed Claudia's company, he was really getting tired of competing for her attention. Just once when she went with, it would've been nice to have an uninterrupted conversation with her. Instead, they were constantly being bothered by lame pick up lines. The last time they were out, one of her admirers who outweighed Eric by at least fifty pounds tried to be Mr. Tough Guy. Claudia's instinct was to just ignore him, but when he kept on she turned to him, hanging on to Eric closely and said, "I'm sorry, but as you can see I'm already taken." Luckily the other guys from work weren't around to see the exchange, other wise the rumor mill would've been in motion.

That was the first and only time she had touched him sensually, but with that one innocent gesture, Eric felt a jolt of electricity go through him and it concerned him. Out of coincidence or out of consciousness, they hadn't been out together since.

Since week one, everyone pegged Eric as the class favorite and Daryl teased him relentlessly about it enough to where he was liable to snap at the slightest annoyance. He never liked to be set apart from the crowd, even if it were for his positive attributes. And ever since Claudia had been hanging around them more after hours, he noticed that the teasing increased. So, when Daryl asked if he did another job well done, he said a tight lipped, "Yup." Like he was going to admit what he and his boss were discussing. If Daryl caught wind of Eric's invite from the boss it would just egg him on even more.

Eric started to walk back to his machine to shut everything down and noticed that Darryl followed. "Want to meet me at Bella's after work? I hear Jarvis's band is playing tonight."

"Oh, sorry dude, I'm not in the mood."

"Oh come on! You are always in the mood."

"Not tonight," Eric said with authority.

"But Xing is punking out on me too!"

Laughing as he started to clean around his machine, he said, "That's your problem, man, not mine..."

"Well, I'll ask Claudia then. She seems to have turned over a new leaf all of a sudden. For someone who claims she doesn't like the club scene, she's quick to say yes every time we invite her out!"

Wanting so bad to remind Daryl of his last failed attempt at asking her out, something stopped him. Eric knew the Canadian was one inappropriate remark away from being canned for sexual harassment, and he was so annoyed at this point he would've liked to see it all go down. Eric worked his way around the machine and said, "I guess it's worth a try. Good luck!" And with a final crank, his machine was properly shut down.

"Right. Well, I better get back to my station."

"Yeah, you do that," Eric said indifferently.

"Catch ya later, man."

"Yup."

Eric shook his head all the way back to the break room with a grin on his face over the fact that Daryl acted like a whiny little girl and was completely clueless to how the world around him actually thought of him. After grabbing a coke from the machine, he sat down and propped his legs on the table.

True to form, legs that seem to stretch for miles came walking in on the highest heels Eric had ever seen. "Hey, Eric! Daddy said I was to drive you home."

Sliding his feet back onto the floor, he said, "Yeah, you don't mind, do you?"

"Of course not. Do you need to go home and get a change of clothes or anything?" she asked, all the while moving around picking up litter left by random people.

"Actually, that would be great. I don't think your dad is expecting us for another hour or so."

"Great. I'll meet you at my car in five minutes. I have to close up my office, and I'll be right out," she stated, turned and walked out of the break room.

"Oh, Claudia, wait!" Eric said quickly, which made her turn

around abruptly and cling to the metal doorframe, which gave him too much of a view of her shapely figure. It took everything he had to pry his eyes away from that and hold them on her face. Walking over until he was within ear shot, he whispered, "I have to warn you that Daryl is on the prowl. He's going to ask you out again."

Chuckling, she answered, "That information would have been useful about three minutes ago when he cornered me next to his machine. Poor guy actually thinks that I would go on a date with a married man. I do hold some standards when it comes to men."

Smiling in a teasing manner, he said, "But I'm married and you go out with me..."

"Yes, but that's different. You aren't trying to get into my pants." After staring at him an awkward moment too long, she said, "Well, I'll see you in a few," and walked off.

Eric respected Claudia; as a woman, as the boss's daughter, as a colleague and as a friend. Besides Eva, she was his closest girl friend and he didn't have girls as friends. It really did confuse the lines when he thought of her at times. She radiated a sexual air; one that if he were single he knew they would've already been together and even though her words told him that she enjoyed his company as a friend only, something in her eyes every once in a while told him otherwise; just like they had right before she turned and walked away. This concerned him very much yet he didn't say or do anything about it. If anything, he tried to ignore it.

Eric had no idea what was going on in Eva's life. Of course that was nothing unusual. The last time he talked with her, she was unseasonably busy at work and had confessed that she helped Natasha with the kids a little bit on a weekend a few weeks ago, but he was too exhausted to get mad about it. He hadn't talked to his brother since he left and only called his uncle once, but it was a quick call since his uncle was in the middle of watching the Super Bowl. That was the last time he felt homesick. Eva and Eric always had somewhere to go on Super Bowl Sunday. He knew she would be over at

Charlotte's, having another one of their infamous parties, and the sudden pang of jealousy thinking about that acquaintance of Charlotte and Charley's. For the life of Eric, he couldn't remember the guy's name but he sure remembered how he looked at Eva and how much he didn't like it. He never had a trust issue with Eva. Her word was always as good as gold, so he put off his irrational feelings and focused on his job and his own day-to-day struggles. The only thing he missed was someone to warm his bed at night, and it was getting down right lonely. Claudia filled some of that void just merely with her presence. The only thing getting his mind off her physically was the countdown to go home and the reality that came with that.

Once at Eric's building, Claudia declined the invitation to come up to his apartment. So he hopped out of her car and told her he'd be back soon. The first thing he did was listen to his messages, five in all, while he searched for something clean to change into. Four of the messages were from Daryl, begging him to join him for a drink again. The other one was from Eva, asking him to call her. Looking at the clock, he knew it was almost midnight and she had an early morning so he wrote himself a note to call her as soon as he could the next day. It was the common theme with them; phone tag. When he started to change his clothes, he got a whiff of himself and it was no job for simply deodorant to fix. So he went in with the notion of taking the quickest showers, after questioning himself whether or not he should call down to Claudia and let her know what was taking him so long. But in the end he thought by the time he got done wasting the time telling her, he'd be out of the shower and dressed already.

Funny thing about showers and Eric: as soon as the warm water started to flow, he lost all sense of time. He got to day-dreaming about how awesome the water felt on his worn out body, then wondering what Eva was doing and did she even miss him?; and then of Claudia and the conflicted feelings he had towards her. All in all, he was in there about fifteen minutes. Quickly realizing his error, he whipped back the shower curtain and searched for a towel. Forgetting that they were all dirty, waiting to be laundered, he swore and went to the hamper in the main room to dig a soiled one out. Just about the time he found one, his front door opened.

"Eric? Everything all right in here?" Claudia asked as she stepped inside. Within an instant, she found him naked, except for the sorriest excuse for a towel that quickly covered his essentials. "Oh my...." She quickly turned around and finished, "I'm...I'm so sorry! I'll be out in the car."

Blushing and heart beating out of his chest, Eric said to cover up all embarrassment, "I'll be out in a second."

Without turning back, she hurried out the door.

Well, that was borderline humiliating he thought as he got dressed in the speed of light.

By the time Eric got to the car two minutes later, Claudia had her hands on the wheel in the ten and two position facing forward. Even after starting the car and taking off, she didn't say a word or look his way. He noticed that her dark skin held a pink glow.

"I hope you aren't half as embarrassed as I am right now," Eric said to break the ice.

"Oh! No! You...I mean...." covering her face with the hand closest to him, she said hysterically, "I, mean, yes! That was so embarrassing! And it was totally my fault! I shouldn't have walked in like that without knocking."

"And I should have let you know that I was going to take a quick shower, which wasn't so quick. I'm sorry."

For the first time she looked at him with her big brown eyes. "No, I am. But don't worry. I didn't see much."

"Gee thanks, I was always told that I had a..."

She clamped her hand over his mouth and they both giggled like school kids. "You know what I mean."

"Yeah. Forget that anything happened. It's not a big deal."

"Really? Promise?"

Smiling, he said, "I promise."

By the time they reached Jessup's house, the embarrassment of the 'walk-in' was almost depleted and they were back to normal. The smell of sizzling meat filled the air as well as an Italian ballad coming from the outdoor speakers. Instead of going in the front door, Claudia led him around the side of the house, through the steel gate separating the grape hedges and the house to the back yard.

Jessup had on a pair of casual pants and a windbreaker, apparently all ready to go fishing right then and there. He was turning what looked to be a slab of lamb on the grill. Noticing them right away, he went to his daughter and kissed both cheeks lovingly without touching her with his mitt or spatula. "Hello, love. Momma wants you in kitchen. You best go."

"Yes, poppy. Smells good!" she said with a smile, kissed her father once more and turned to wave quickly at Eric.

"So, you try lamb before?" Jessup asked.

"Yes, sir. The first time I was here."

"Ah, yes, of course. Well, you want drink?"

"Yes, thank you."

"Beer? Wine? Water? We have much to choose from."

"Surprise me..."

A moment later Jess brought out his stash of fine wine from Portugal, Italy's best whiskey, and specialty beer from Switzerland. "You choose," he said, pointing to his options.

"I'll try that beer."

He sat at the table, leaning back in his chair as he took a swig at the malt liquor. "Not bad," he said. Even warm, it slid down nicely. He admired Jessup's spread of land and house. It wasn't outlandish, and it had a homey feel to it. And he loved the fact that a person wouldn't have a clue that his boss was as well off as he was. Eric felt special being embraced by such a man. He was a person to look up to.

Maria, Jessup's wife, came out carrying bread in a basket in one hand and olive oil in the other. "Oh, hello," she greeted Eric with friendly eyes.

"Hello, ma'am."

Setting down the food in front of him, she went over by her husband who was preparing to take the meat off the grill. She whispered in his ear with a smile and then kissed his cheek before heading back into the house. After thirty-five years of marriage, it was encouraging to witness such affection for Eric. It reminded him of the better times with Eva, which set in a pang of sadness.

Snapping him out of it, Jessup said, "Another beer?"

"Oh, no thanks."

Nodding while setting the dinner down on the table, he yelled, "Okay, we eat!"

Within seconds, Maria and Claudia were settled at the table; Maria across from him and Claudia to his right. She had changed into a pair of jeans and a NYU sweatshirt and had her hair down. Eric had to tell himself not to look at her. She was even more beautiful when she wasn't all dressed up.

"So, poppy, what are you going to fish for?"

"We try for trout."

After a nicely prepared dinner, Jessup and Eric walked down the short bank to untie his fishing boat from their small dock. It was a little cooler out than Eric had planned for so Jessup loaned him a jacket and he was putting it on as they descended the hill. Once they were both situated in the tiny boat with their gear, which consisted of fishing rods and oars, Jessup asked, motioning to his fly rod, "You know how to use this?"

"Yes, we use them mainly for stream fishing in Minnesota."

"I hear much of the 10,000 lakes. It is true how many lakes they say?"

"I'm sure at one time it was true, but I know some have dried up. But there is plenty of water to choose from. You should come sometime. I'll show you some great fishing!"

"Yes, that be nice," Jess said sincerely.

After finding a spot, they anchored and then began to set up their flies. "So. You miss your wife, no?"

It wasn't the inquiry out of the blue that shocked him, but the question itself. In fact, it had been a while since he really thought about missing Eva and instant guilt set in. But he came up quickly with, "Oh, yes sir."

"Well, only few short weeks, no?"

"Yes, but it hasn't been too bad. The time has gone fast..."
He would need that much time to get these wonderful people
out of his heart and mind; if not longer.

Jessup cast his rod out in front of him in rhythmic
movements, and Eric watched the fly at the end of the rod skid
across the water like poetry. Eric was almost hypnotized,
sending him back to his youth where he would watch his friend
Opie make the same actions with optimal results. They never
were in lack of fish at his house in those days needless to say.
Fishing always seemed to relax Eric, and it had been entirely
too long since he treated himself to such pleasures.

"My Claudia no like to fish. And Maria, well she come with
me if I ask her, but this is my quiet place. You know?"

Smiling, Eric said knowingly, "Yes, I sure do."

"But, it's nice to share with someone who loves too, no?"

"I agree," Eric responded with a nod.

Eric finally got his fly tied onto the end of the line and
started to cast but got it tangled at the first flick of the rod. It
had been almost eight years since he fished that way when he
got to thinking about it. No wonder he was rusty at it. He was
untangling the line when out of the corner of his eye he saw a
fish jump clear out of the water near Jess's fly.

His employer's eyes lit up. "Wow! Big!"

"Well, we know they are in there anyhow."

Instead of fishing the same side of the boat as Jess's, Eric
thought he'd try the other side. After twenty minutes of
figuring out the rhythm of the fly rod, Jessup missed at least
four fish.

The silence was comfortable, and he was meditating on the
experience when Jessup asked off-handedly, "So, you make
family soon then?"

Eric jerked his head to Jess and for a moment he didn't say
anything. It was nice, for a while, not hearing about babies or
the desire to make babies. The pressure was off for once.
He'd never talked to anyone about his inability to provide
children for his wife of eleven years. But for some reason, he
felt comfortable telling Jessup, knowing the information

wouldn't get past the boat. Eric saw how devoted he was to his wife and daughter. Jessup loved them, heck not just them, but everyone he met. He'd never known a man like his boss before. No, that wasn't true, he thought. Eva was a lot like him, but at times he resented it. He just wished sometimes that she remembered he needed to be paid attention to as well; everyone else got so much more from her than he did.

Choosing his words carefully, Eric said, "I don't think it's in the plans."

"Oh, that is too bad. Children. They are blessing."

"Yeah, well, I guess the Big Guy upstairs," Eric said, pointing up, "overlooked us in the baby department." He realized what he just revealed and hoped that it would get lost in translation. It didn't.

"Oh, I'm sorry, son....Your wife no like to adopt?"

That got him in the gut. It wasn't Eva's fault for not having a child, it was him completely. Even though her body rebelled against her, it was him who denied her. He wasn't about to let Jess think that it was her fault. "Oh, she would. I wouldn't."

"No?" Jess asked as if he couldn't believe his ears. After a few minutes, he drew in a big breath, released it and said matter-of-factly, "My Maria can have no baby either. We try many years, but nothing. So we adopt."

The hair at the back of Eric's neck stood on end. It couldn't be. "Claudia? She's not yours?"

"Yes, she is ours. She no come from our bodies, but she be ours since she was three. We had Matteo too, but he die when he is ten from flu. My Claudia and Matteo, they are mine," Jess said, holding his fist against his heart. His words were spoken with such affection that it made him feel guilty for feeling the way he did about adoption. Not enough to sway him though.

Shaking his head, all he could say was, "Wow."

Just then, the fly that was lying in the water beside Eric took off. "Fish on!"

Chapter 13

The Sunday morning service was packed and Eva felt the praise of God's people, lifting her weary heart. It had been a long week, and she was looking forward to church like a man who craved a drink after running ten miles in a dry desert. She went every Sunday to get her spirit refilled to make it another week, but this last week she was depleted by Monday morning. There was no time for her daily reading of her worn-out Bible and her prayer life was brief excerpts of 'Help me's' and 'I can't do this'. There was nothing praiseworthy about her prayers, but instead all of them were cries of desperation. After almost four months of creating and living a healthy new lifestyle and losing fifty-nine pounds, she had regressed in a big bad scary way. After Bart left with the kids the Sunday Natasha left, she went to phone Eric to no avail. She was uncontrollably angry for so many reasons; so angry that it scared her. How could Natasha do this? How could she leave those precious kids? That woman had everything going for her: a beautiful home, a husband who supported her and her kids so she could stay home with them, every material possession known to man and three healthy beautiful children. Eva couldn't understand it. And where was Eric when she needed him? Until this point she had done all right on her own, but right now she needed his strength and wisdom. He would know what to do. And if she knew her husband right, he'd be on the next plane home once she told him the tale.

She worked out, but her diet fell way off the wagon. Instead of eating the chocolate and bread like it was going out of style, something she would've done before, she practically starved herself. A piece of fruit here and a veggie there was all she consumed and her body after a few days got worn out. Even her trainer commented on her performance, or lack thereof. Eva was dog tired and had no extra energy to give excuses. Instead of confiding what was going on in her life, she told him that she was sick and went home and got ready for work.

Work was too busy to call in, so she pulled herself up by the bootstraps and went. Thank God for a little comic relief from Stephanie, her receptionist. Charlotte, Kristin from church, Barbi and Stephanie were the only people who knew about Natasha's disappearing act, and she asked for it not to be public knowledge. Since Bart had to get back to work, Eva told him to drop the kids off Tuesday night so he didn't have to run like gangbusters to get to the airport on time the next morning. They worked it out that when she was at work, they were with Uncle Ben. Luckily they didn't mind going to the gym with her, but by Thursday the schedule got too much for her so she thought she'd take a day off which didn't help her cerebral state. She was used to going to the gym for a stress reliever and mental therapy as well as physical, but too much was weighing on her mind to get done what she needed to do there. The rest of the week had gone by fairly smoothly with the kids, but she knew that there would be a time when the questions would start. And she was worried if she would have the right answers.

Of course she had committed to do a violin solo at this morning's service months ago, and she hated to back down due to all the added stuff on her plate. So after dropping Seth and Noah off at Sunday School and Lydia in the nursery, she took her place in the choir loft next to the pulpit. As always, she and her violin were at one with each other. It wasn't until after high school and after the stress of being graded on her talent that she enjoyed the instrument. She had to close her eyes when tears flooded them as she played her version of 'Great is Thy faithfulness'. In her head, the words resonated through her soul, especially the chorus:

'Great is Thy faithfulness,
Great is Thy faithfulness
Morning by morning new mercies I see
All I have needed Thy hand hath provided
Great is thy faithfulness, Lord unto me!'

Before she knew it, her eyes opened to people singing and more than half had their hands raised to the sky to an awesome God who *had* provided new mercies every morning; who *had* provided everything they needed. She didn't know why she chose to do that song that day. After all, it was one of many she had to pick from. But now she knew. It was a great reminder of the big God they served.

She was packing away her violin after the service when Charlotte came up to her and gave her a hug. "That was beautiful, Eva. I just love that song!"

"Thank you." It took Eva years to accept compliments about her musical talent, but she learned that a simple word of thanks wasn't conceited like she always feared it would sound. She smiled at her friend.

"Where have you been, girl?" Charlotte asked, still keeping a warm hand on Eva's shoulder.

"All over! Bart has been in California since Tuesday and when he's not working, he's trying to find Natasha. And in the mean time, I've been watching the kids. Sorry I didn't let you know about not being able to make it to Bible study."

"Yeah, we were all curious at what happened to you, but you were in our prayers. Has he found out anything?"

"Just that she's definitely made up her mind."

"So he found her," Charlotte stated and not questioned.

"Nope. He was served papers right before he left for Cali. And with her not asking for anything, it sounds pretty cut and dried."

"Oh, man! Poor Bart. What does Eric say about all of this?"

Eva got a funny look on her face, almost one of disgust before saying, "I've been trying to get a hold of him for a week now and he never seems to be there. It's not something I can leave on his answering machine either. It's so hard because of the time difference and the different schedules we keep."

"Sheesh! How busy can the man be to not pick up a phone?"

Quickly defending her husband, Eva said, "He's probably busy socializing. It sounds like he met a few people; an annoying guy from Canada and a guy from China. And I'm glad because he was sounding pretty homesick before."

"But doesn't it bother you not knowing what he's doing when you don't hear from him?"

Chuckling, Eva said, "When do I have the time to worry about that? I work, take care of the dogs, make sure the kids are not only okay emotionally but try to entertain them as well and then try to find time for a workout. Thank God for Uncle Ben! He's really stepped in to help me and the kids just adore him."

"So I take it Bart talked to the kids about Natasha?"

"Yeah."

"How'd that go?"

"Seth is really quiet about it. He's maybe a little distant with me, but not alarmingly so. No unusual acting up though. And the only time Noah cries for Natasha is when he's tired. And I think they are really enjoying their one-on-one time with Ben. He's been so patient and loving towards them and has been a great role model. They aren't used to seeing Bart too often, which I guess is good when it comes to this transition. I thought for sure they would be extra clingy to him when he left, but they didn't seem to be phased by it. Luckily, Lydia doesn't know what's going on, thank God. Out of all of them, Noah is the most confused. Just yesterday he asked if he could call me mommy now. As much as I would love to claim him, I told him that I'm still his auntie. Then he asked me who was going to be his mommy and that almost killed me. I just explained to him that he still had a mommy, she just wasn't with him right now and that he needs to pray when he is sad."

"Oh man, Eva. That's just heartbreaking!"

"It is, but I'm certain God has His purpose for letting things happen. For one thing, I'm seeing a subtle change in Bart. He's definitely been humbled by this experience and is asking difficult questions, as if he's reevaluating his life. He told me he's been talking to Kristin on the phone a lot and asking her a lot of questions about the kids and about her faith. He's even talked to me for a while after phoning to speak with the kids. There's so much grief I hear in his voice; it's heartbreaking."

"Hi, Mrs. Featherstone! Hi, Eva!" Mitch's daughter, Shayla

interrupted them with her joyful greeting.

Eva embraced the dark-haired beauty. "Hey, beautiful! How was Lydia today?"

"She always had to be held," she said with a frown.

"Let me guess, she favored your sister?"

She nodded her head with watery eyes.

Brushing the child's cheek tenderly with her fingers, Eva said with a smile, "Babies are temperamental." When Shayla gave a confused look, Eva explained, "They go through phases. She'll probably scream when your sister holds her an hour from now. Don't take it personally." That caused Shayla to crack a smile. Eva hugged the girl to her side.

"Hello ladies," sounded a familiar baritone voice. With Eva's arm still around Shayla, Mitch put his hands upon his daughter's shoulder and rested on Eva's arm in the process. The touch made Eva instantly aware of his masculinity. "Hey," she said, smiling back to him but just as much in a hurry to move quickly from his reach.

"Hey, Mitch." Charlotte said, giving Eva an inconspicuous raised eyebrow. Eva ignored her. "Well, I hate to go, but I have to round up Charley and the rest of my entourage!" Hugging Eva quickly, she said, "I'll call you soon! My hair is in an emergency state again!"

When she left, Mitch said, "Mine too."

"What?" she laughed, thinking he was making a joke.

"Look at how long it is!" he insisted, pulling at the hair that spiked out in front.

"You were just in, silly. It looks just fine."

Ignoring her comment, he turned his daughter to face him. "Princess, why don't you rally up the other kids? We'll wait for you right here."

"Okay." She said enthusiastically.

Eva laughed after her. "She puts the word bubbly to shame."

"Both she and her sister give me a run for my money, that's for sure!"

"Whatever keeps you young, right?"

What started off as a smile faltered a bit after studying Eva.

His expression turned more reserved, and then he added a slow, "Right. Listen, Eva, I have to tell you something before the kids get back here."

Oh no, she thought. She wasn't sure she was ready to hear what he had to say. Their relationship was strictly platonic, which was what she kept telling herself anyway. Lately though, she was wondering if they were on the same page. Ever since his separation he had an aura of vulnerability, and it brought out more sex appeal in him than she'd care to admit. She wasn't deaf, dumb, or blind. These thoughts scared her to death. She should hightail it out of there, but her legs felt like lead. Choking out, "What is it?"

"My divorce is final next Tuesday."

"Oh, Mitch, I'm so sorry," Eva said sympathetically, touching his arm. "I really thought she'd come around." Eva had been praying earnestly for his situation. Apparently a few months back his wife came home from one of her girls' weekends and asked for a separation. He wasn't all that stunned when she callously told him that she no longer loved him. He told Eva that he wasn't sure what he felt for her anymore either. Their trial separation made him realize how unhappy he was in their relationship. However, he did vocalize to Eva how much he missed the companionship and that he was hoping over time he and his wife would work out their differences and get back together; if at least for the sake of his girls. But comments made by his long time friends and even his girls about how happy and relaxed he now seemed, he recognized that maybe his wife was right, they should continue on to a divorce. At times he was confused, he admitted, since now after a year of silence and fights, he and his soon to be ex got almost along like when they were first together. For a short time he was hopeful that the separation was a good thing and things would work out. But the more time went on, he was getting complacent of being on his own and the thought of going back into that environment started to give him stress. Sure things were all right now, but what if he moved back and they went back into the same old routines? He once questioned

Eva. She didn't say anything, merely just listened. She could hear the dilemma and didn't have the nerve to give her opinion. After all, at one point she'd been so frustrated in her relationship with Eric that she was about to leave him, but when it came down to it she knew it wasn't God's will for her to do so. At times, Eva felt the need to encourage him to work it out with his wife because of what the Bible said about it, but she didn't feel it was her place to offer her opinion on the matter either way. So she would continue to listen when he told her another reason he felt it was right to end things was because he felt like a more attentive dad knowing that he only had a few weekends a month with his girls who were growing faster than weeds. It worried him how they were slowly slipping away from him with distractions of their friends and, God help him, boys.

Ever since Charlotte inquired about Eva and Mitch's meetings up at the gym, Eva made a conscious effort not to run into him. Charlotte's point got driven home that it did appear bad to anyone who happened to be watching and the last thing she needed floating around their small town was vile gossip. In her mind, they were just friends. But in reality she had lived long enough to see how friendships like the one she and Mitch shared could possibly turn to something more in a heartbeat and the devastation that it would leave in its wake. There was nothing wrong with their friendship as of now, and she intended to keep it that way. The only thing that could create a problem in the scenario was that the more weight Eva lost, the more confidence she got. And at times she found herself daydreaming that a good-looking, successful man such as Mitch would certainly give her a second glance. And if things were different, she could see them together. But so far she was grateful that she never forgot that she was a married woman. Not ever. Not once.

Disappointment was written all over Mitch's face when he said, "Yeah, I thought she would change her mind too, but I guess God had other plans."

"Do the girls know yet?"

Shaking his head while his hand went through his still neatly cropped hair, he said, "Not yet. We are telling them tonight when I bring them back. I'm not anticipating any drama. They've had time to get used to the idea. Now we have to talk about the living arrangements. We decided that instead of fighting over them, the ball will be in their court how they want to split up their time. I'm preparing myself just in case they decide to move in with me."

"Wow! Well, I'm sure everything will work out all right. Your kids are great and have adjusted well. I'm just so sorry you all have to go through this, Mitch! It's so discouraging hearing of couples breaking up all around me. It makes me wonder if Eric and I will make it."

"Now don't go thinking like that. Marriage is tough, but it takes two. I guess I just wasn't willing to do all the work myself is all. I just wanted to thank you for listening to me. You have no idea how you've helped."

"I'm glad I could be there for you!" she added with a smile.

"And it sounds like you've had quite the load. Is that why I haven't seen you at the gym?"

"Auntie!" Seth screeched as he came running towards them. "Look what Mrs. O'Donnell gave us!"

Saved by the bell, she thought.

In his hand dangled a decorative bag of assorted candy. "Well, isn't that nice. Are you going to share with your brother?"

"Yes. That's what we have to do. It's good to share 'cause that's what Jesus would do."

Hugging the five-year-old to her, she kissed the top of his head. "You are such a good boy, Seth."

The child beamed, which made Eva's heart break, because this was just one time out of many that Natasha would miss out on. These kids were just too precious for words.

Within seconds, the rest of the gang were there, Lydia hanging onto Mitch's oldest, Peyton, and Noah holding onto Shayla's hand.

"How would you guys like to go to Liberty's with us?" Mitch asked, aiming his words more to the kids than Eva.

Cheap shot, Eva thought. Seth and Noah were quickly asking, "Oh, can we, auntie?"

"Oh, I don't know you guys..." Eva said, not wanting to deny the kids but knowing it wasn't the best idea.

"Pullllleeeaaassseee, Auntie?" Seth begged.

"Yeah, pleaase Auntie?" Noah echoed.

"Not this time, kiddos. Your daddy will be home soon and we have to let Reddog and Bruiser out before they destroy the mud room like they did on Wednesday."

Seth over dramatized a pout, which became contagious to the other kids. Mitch ruffled up Seth and Noah's hair and said, "That's all right, guys! Maybe another time!"

Noah tugged on my arm. "Auntie, can Peyton and Shayla come over for macaroni and cheese and chocolate shakes then?"

Every kids' eyes and smiles brightened at the suggestion. Seth asked, "Yeah! Can they, Auntie Eva?"

Looking from kid to kid, then to Mitch who gave a hopeful shrug, Eva's defenses went down. "Oh...I suppose so."

"Don't feel pressured, Eva. I can take the girls out like I had originally planned."

"No, it will be fine. Why don't you guys just follow us?"

"Can I ride with Mitch, auntie?" Seth asked.

"Yeah, me too!" added Noah.

This was too much, Eva thought. She had to nip it in the bud. "Not this time, buddies."

With quick voices of displeasures, Mitch squatted down to their eye level and said, "It would take too much time to switch your car seats around. So how about we help your auntie get her stuff together and be on our way to enjoy that macaroni and cheese and chocolate shakes?"

"Okay!" they all screamed excitedly.

After packing up her violin and Bible, Mitch grabbed his daughters' hands and winked at Eva saying, "We'll see you at your house then."

"All right. See you!" she added, ushering the boys to the car all the while holding Lydia as well as her bible and violin.

By the time they reached her house, the kids were wound up

tight. Knowing that Red and Bruiser would be just as hyper, she opted to come back for her stuff in the car. As soon as she opened the garage door, they heard the dogs barking making the kids laugh. "Hold on to your hats, kids! The dogs need to go potty quickly!"

So they all hid behind Eva as she opened the door to the frenzy of barking and wagging tails. "Hey sweeties! Go potty now!" And at her command they ran out just when Mitch was pulling up the driveway with the girls. Instead of emptying their bladders, they went to sniff the company. The girls giggled when the dogs sniffing got a little personal. "Reddog! Bruiser! Down boys! Come here! Right now!" They were just too excited to listen to her so she went closer to them and repeated the commands. That time they came and she told them to sit which they did the first time. "That was just the Wahler welcome wagon."

"They are so cute!" Peyton squeeled.

"They are like twins!" Shayla cooed. "Can we get a dog, Daddy?" she asked Mitch who was coming up behind them.

"We'll see," he said, not committing to anything.

"Why don't you all go inside and make yourselves at home and I'll make sure the dogs do their business. Seth and Noah can show the girls around."

"Yeah, come on!" Seth said excitedly.

By the time she got back inside, Shayla and Seth were playing with the dogs while Peyton was holding Lydia and helping Noah stack blocks in the corner and Mitch was making himself at home by starting the macaroni and cheese. "I hope you don't mind, but I raided your cupboards. They are looking a little bare, by the way."

Laying down her stuff from the car onto the table, she said, "Well, after a few days with the munchkins running around here, it's easily depleted. I'll stock up right before they come again."

"Smart. Well, I'm making three boxes, which will wipe you out completely. I hope that was okay."

The way he moved around her kitchen seemed so natural it almost took her aback. She quickly took over by throwing the empty boxes away and going through the freezer in hopes she had something to go with the entree. "What are you looking for?" he asked behind her.

"I was hoping I had an extra package of hotdogs..." she was saying when behind a frozen pot roast she spotted some. "Ah, hah! Here they are. Not quite Liberty's fine dining, but it should do."

"It will be just fine," he said as he took the package from her and added, "If you point me to another pot, I'll get these boiled up before you know it."

Trying to reach for them back, she said, "You are our guests, Mitch. You shouldn't lift your hand while you are here."

Holding the frozen hot dogs above his head, he said with a knowing smile, "That's just not my style."

"What if I'm not comfortable with the prospect of you cooking for me?"

Stepping closer to her, which suddenly felt like an intimate gesture, "But I'm not just cooking for you. I'm cooking for the kids as well, two of which are mine. The only way I'm letting you cook for us is if I pay you back for the food..."

Thinking about it, Eva knew she would feel more uncomfortable if she asked him to pay for it, so she relented at letting him cook for them.

"Why don't you go in with the kids and I'll yell when it's ready to go?"

"Are you sure?"

With a shoo of his hands, he said, "Go!"

Eva smiled as she left the room. Mitch just gave her a romanticized vision of what being married with children would be like. But in her reality, it would be her in the kitchen and Eric on the floor with the kids, or would it? All Eva knew was, she loved this reality right now. Even though the kids who were before her now weren't hers, and the handsome man in the kitchen wasn't her husband, she fantasized for a moment that they were a family and it left a huge smile on her face and her heart. For the first time, it didn't give her pause. This whole scene felt so comfortable. And when Mitch yelled from the kitchen that it was chow time ten minutes later, she just took it all in and ran with it. Her little table hadn't been this crowded since Christmas, but this was a way different feel. The reality was that there were two families here, each going through their own struggles, yet when together there was so much laughter and happiness. And when Eva asked for everyone to grab hands for the prayer and Mitch's youngest asked to lead it, Mitch and Eva nodded approval.

Eva could tell that she had never prayed out loud in front of anyone before because she sounded so timid. "God," she drew out. "Thank you for this food. Thank you for Daddy, and Peyton and Seth and Noah and Lydia and especially for Eva who let us come over today. Oh, and thank you for Jesus. He's so nice. Amen."

Eva glanced over to Mitch who was gleaming from smile to tears in his eyes at his daughter. Shayla shyly smiled back to him, which told him not to make a big deal out of it. "Okay, let's say we dish up and eat!" he said.

The dogs laid under either side of Lydia's highchair, hoping to catch any food that she was liable to fling their way. Usually you could hear their tails beating the floor in anticipation, but today the sound was drowned out by the chatter of everyone's voices. It was one of the most fun times she had with the kids and by far her most relaxed afternoon she'd had in over a month. She would be sorry to see it end.

Just as Mitch was packing his girls in his car to leave, Bart pulled in the driveway which excited his kids. "Dad!" They cried out, running towards him with open arms. The only one who didn't run was Lydia who was still in Eva's arms.

Swiftly picking them up, they locked their arms around his neck tightly. "Hey! You're choking me!" he said playfully, but it was enough for them to let up.

"Hey Bart. Do you remember Mitch Carter? You met him at the Featherstone's a few months back."

"Oh, yeah, hey," Bart said with a nod.

"Hey," Mitch parroted. "Well, thanks again Eva. We had a great time. Bye kiddos!"

"Bye Mitch!" both boys yelled while waving.

It didn't take a psychic to see the question on Barton's mind after Mitch's car pulled away, so she quickly explained, "His girls wanted to spend some time with the kids, so we invited them over for lunch."

"Uh, huh," he said, not quite buying it.

Not wanting to discuss it, she turned her attention to the kids, "Are you ready to go?"

"Nooooo!" Noah scrambled down from his dad's arms and came running over to Eva.

"Come on inside and let's grab your bags." As the kids dragged their feet to the bedroom, Bart came behind her, startling her when he asked, "So do you wanna tell me why that guy was really here, Eva?"

Eva spun on him quickly. "I told you the truth. I know it looks bad, Bart, but it's totally innocent."

Bart just studied her like he was trying to find a crack somewhere on her and then he asked, "When was the last time you talked to Eric?"

"When was the last time *you* talked to him?" Eva countered back to him.

He hesitated before saying, "Well, he doesn't know about 'Tash yet if that's what you are asking. Have you told him?"

"No. We haven't talked since right before she left. Why, do you want me to?"

Raking his hand through his hair, he said, "No. I'll get a hold of him soon."

"Well, good luck," she said sarcastically, "I've been trying to get a hold of him to no avail. If you talk to him before I do, will you let him know I'd like to talk to him?"

"Sure, Eva. No problem. But hey, listen, I want to thank you for watching the kids for me. They cried for hours after we left last week. I almost think I'm better off leaving them here and visiting them than uprooting and upsetting them further."

Touching his arm, Eva said, "Don't say that. They love you and you need them just as much as they need you."

"Yeah, that's what Kristin says too. Thanks for introducing

me to her. She's been a major help."

"She is wonderful, isn't she? She's been talking to the boys a lot, making sure they are doing all right."

"Yeah, she told me that too. She says they are doing well under the circumstances. I'm the one who needs his head shrunk. I don't know what I'm doing half of the time anymore. It was like I was going through the motions before, but now with her gone I'm feeling the weight of the responsibility and I don't know if I can take it. Yet I know I can't live without them either..."

"Who says you have to have this figured out all right now? You have Uncle Ben and me to help you. This isn't just your battle, so don't think you have to fight it alone, okay?"

He took her into an embrace and said into her hair, "Thank you, Eva. I've never told you this before but something about you brings about such peace in me."

She pulled away from him and with tears in her eyes, she said, "I'd love to take the credit, but it's not me who gives you that peace, Bart. It's God."

Chapter 14

Eric and his boss, Jess, stayed out on the boat until midnight after finding out that the night bite was the way to go. Once the sun went down, the moon acted as a brilliant lantern on the lake making it easier for them to see. Fishing after dusk was a new experience for his boss. Before, he had only gone in the early morning or just after dinner, and was impressed that the fish bit that late.

On their way back to the dock, Jess suggested that he stay overnight instead of driving him back to town. It was really late and his boss didn't think he'd be very safe on the road due to his exhaustion level. Eric accepted the invitation without hesitation.

"You take my Matteo's room," flicking on the light in the room right off the kitchen. At first Eric's response was hesitant thinking he was about to walk into a shrine to the deceased beloved son, but was instantly relieved when he saw it was converted into a den/spare room. Simple art in swags of blue decorated the beige walls, and not an artifact was left of the previous occupier to Eric's notice. His wife must've anticipated his stay because the full-sized futon bed was freshly made and turned down for use.

"Bathroom is down the hall. Towels and new toothbrush is on table. Use what you need. We see you tomorrow. Caio."

"Thank you, Jess. Caio."

After the long day at work, then his all night fishing adventure, he should have been beat but he was wide awake. So after he heard his boss close his bedroom door down the hall, he walked into the kitchen and grabbed a glass of water. Leaning back against the counter and taking in his modest but beautiful surroundings, he smiled thinking about how three months ago he would have never thought in a million years he would ever have come all this way and experienced the things he had.

That is how Claudia found him. "Oh! You guys are back! You must've done well. I've never known Poppy to stay out that late, but because of the high moon I didn't worry."

"Yeah, your dad did well, but we didn't get any pictures."

She chuckled. "And no stories about the one that got away?"

"Not this time. It was great to see your dad in motion."

"And you?"

"My technique needs some work. It's been a while."

"I'm glad you had a good time. My dad used to take my little brother fishing a lot, but he hasn't showed much interest since he died. That boat has seen the water only a handful of times since...."

"Yeah, I'm sorry to hear about your brother. How long ago was that?"

After grabbing a cola, Claudia pointed to the leather couch in the living room and they both found an end and faced each other. "He died eight years ago. Mattie had been sick from the moment we got him. We didn't know anything about his history except that he was found wandering the streets, almost naked, malnourished...." Claudia just shook her head as if trying not to remember.

"Oh my gosh, Claude. How old was he?"

"They think he was about two. He didn't know but a few words and he was really tiny, yet he was able to walk so the authorities had very little to go on."

"*Two*? That poor kid! What is wrong with people!" Eric felt revolted. He might not have had the most ideal childhood, but at least he had someone to watch out for him. He couldn't imagine letting a two year old out of his sight, which made him think of his nephews who were once that age and a niece who was rapidly approaching it.

Claudia chimed in quickly, sensing Eric's defensiveness. "I can't imagine our life without that boy. Everyone warned my parents not to adopt him because of his unknown past. But the moment we met him, we all knew that he was supposed to be a part of this family."

"So you were a part of the decision?"

"Of course. Mama and Poppy always included me in their decisions. They even let me name him."

"He didn't have a name?"

"He was only there a day before they called us. You see, back then my parents took in wayward children, but this was the first time they took in someone so young. After three months of caring for him and loving him from almost the start, my parents inquired about adopting him. No one had come forward for him, so within a matter of a few months he was ours."

Shaking his head in astonishment, he said, "Wow, I've never heard anything like that. I've only heard the horror stories about adopted children; you know, rebelling when they find out they were lied to and stuff."

"My parents never lied to Mattie and me. From the time we could understand, they were telling us what they knew about our birth parents, and to thank God that He brought us all together to be a family. I've never felt insecure or had the need to search for my biological parents. And I never had any real need to rebel. Okay, maybe a little when I was in the states, but that was when I was a teen and testing the waters kind of stuff."

"I know all about that. But, wow! Thanks for sharing that with me." Just then a yawn escaped him.

"Oh, Eric! You must be exhausted. I can let you get to bed."

Standing up and stretching his arms above his head, his tee shirt came out of his jeans and he missed how Claudia stared at his nicely toned abs in admiration. "Yeah, I think I'm going to sleep like a rock tonight."

Standing as well, she said with a smile, "Well, goodnight then." And before he knew it, she went to him, placed her hands gently on his strong shoulders and slowly kissed one cheek, then the other. Her mouth was only inches away from his and her eyes darted between his and his mouth.

Being around her made him forget where and who he was anymore. One moment she was like his sister, and now all he could think about was kissing her. All these weeks of pent-up sexual frustration was at the surface ready to burst out, and here was one gorgeous, intelligent, caring woman in his arms. With a little hesitancy, he gently pulled her to him so their bodies met; both their eyes closed and their mouths brushed. Sparks flew and hearts pounded. Instead of kissing her again, he pulled her tighter into an embrace and whispered harshly, "What are we doing, Claudia? This is so stupid!"

He felt her tremble, but she didn't let go. "I know, Eric. I know you belong to someone else and I know that you love her. I see your devotion to her, and that's what I love about you. It's so unfair! I've never met a guy like you in my life, and I kept telling myself to stay away but there is just something about you that I just can't resist."

"You paint me like I'm perfect. I'm not, Claudia." He pulled away from her just slightly so he could look into her lovelorn eyes. "It scares me how bad I want you right now. And I'm beginning to think this isn't just a physical connection either. I've been tempted by others before, but never this strongly. This is so wrong," he said, yet pulling her into another embrace. "But I can't seem to let go."

"Do you want me to?"

"I should say yes."

"But?" she asked, looking up to him in anticipation.

His mouth came crashing down on hers in a fevered passion, and she was very receptive. After a minute into their intimate embrace the chime of the clock made them jump apart, and then realizing what it was they both held their chests and chuckled. Taking her hand in his, he lifted it to his mouth while smiling seductively.

"We should probably say good night."

Shakily, she agreed. "So, we should probably just forget this ever happened..." she said and looked down to their adjoining hands.

"I won't forget it, Claudia," he said, which made her eyes meet his. "But how do we continue from here? We made some powerful confessions right now and in all honesty, I really don't know how to digest it. I don't want to hurt you, and I especially don't want to hurt Eva."

"I understand. Just know that even if I just have this memory, it will satisfy me for a lifetime. I have no regrets," she added with a smile.

Reeling her into another embrace, "You are going to make it hard to deny you, Claudia! Go to bed. I'll see you in the morning."

After kissing him again, she ran down the hallway to her room leaving Eric more conflicted than ever. What was he thinking? Eva probably was at home missing him at every turn and just now, after he had violated his vows, did he think of her.

"Oh crap! I forgot to call her!" he muttered to himself as he sat down hard on the bed he was given for the night. Then, the weight of what just happened opened up a dialogue with himself. "Oh God, what did I do? She's a breath of fresh air. I've never known anyone like her. Would it really be so bad if I slept with her? She's aware of the playing field, right? No way would Eva even find out. I know I could trust Claudia that much. What's the harm if she never found out? This is so messed up! I know I need to get her out of my head. But how?"

Just then he heard his door open, and there she was. Claudia shut the door behind her and she leaned against it all the while staring into his eyes. "I heard you, Eric."

Quickly standing up, he blushed. "I didn't know I was talking out loud."

Claudia took slow steps towards him, and that is when he noticed her attire. All she was wearing was a NY Yankee's jersey that covered her bare essentials. "Even if you weren't, I knew what you were thinking. I was pacing in my own room debating whether or not to come, and the next thing I knew my legs were leading me to your door and then I heard my name... Eric...."

Suddenly, they were both trembling, not quite sure if it was out of fear or excitement, but it was Eric who reached out the rest of the way for her. "What?"

"It really sucks you are married!" She cried into his shoulder.

Kissing the top of her head, he murmured, "I know."

"Can we be stupid one more time? Then I'll promise to leave you alone forever."

"I don't know if that is realistic, hon. You deserve a man who can devote all of himself to you."

"Know what the sad thing is, Eric? The little bit I've had of you is more than all of the men I've had in the past combined. If this was the only night I'd have with you, I'd cherish it until I die. And if I walk out of here without being with you, I fear I'm going to regret it for the rest of my life."

Kissing her forehead, he whispered, "You deserve so much more than I can offer you."

"But the question is, are you offering me anything at all?"

"I'd love to say yes, Claudia! But there's no way I could promise tomorrow."

"I know and understand, Eric," she said, looking straight into his eyes. "Please make love to me."

"But your parents are…"

Placing her forefinger on his lips, she whispered, "Sleeping like rocks. An earthquake could come and they wouldn't be fazed by it." She then pushed him back onto the bed and stepped back.

Eric's heart was beating so hard his ears hurt. Everything that was in him that wasn't attached to it was crying for Claudia's touch. But he knew once he saw her last stitch of clothing hit the floor, there was no turning back. If he was going to stop things from progressing he needed to do it now.

And then the Yankee's jersey hit Eric's feet.

*   *   *

"Well, it's about time, bro!"

"Yeah, sorry about that, Bart. I just got home from spending the weekend with my boss and his family. What's up?" Eric asked as he toweled off from his long shower.

"Oh gee, I don't know. My life is in shambles while you are half way across the world doing god knows what with god knows who! Thanks for checking in," Bart said sarcastically.

"Whoa, whoa, whoa, bro! Slow down. What happened?"
Eric's pulse instantly increased, imagining the worst. Did he
lose his job? Were one of the kids sick? Or worse, dead?

"So Eva didn't tell you. I thought for sure she would beat
me to it, but I'm glad she didn't."

"Spit it out, will you? What didn't Eva tell me?" Eric was
starting to get agitated from being left out in the dark.

"Don't yell at me, dude! I can't take it right now, all right?"
Bart uncharacteristically calmed himself down and practically
whispered what he had to tell Eric. "'Tasha left us."

"Are you joking?"

"Nope."

"And when you say 'us', you mean the kids too?"

"Yup."

"Oh my god, I need a cigarette," Eric said, and then dug
through pockets until he found his pack of Marlboros.

"I finally quit. I was smoking so much I was making myself
sick, so I guess one good thing came out of this."

"Well, if you ask me, she did you all a favor."

"Excuse me???"

"It's no secret that everyone hated her," Eric said and then
exhaled a plume of smoke from his lungs.

"Oh gee thanks, bro. Is that supposed to be your idea of a
pep talk?"

"Just stating the facts. I feel bad for the kids even though
she was hardly what you'd call a mother."

"I swear to god I'm going to pound you so hard for
disrespecting my wife-"

"Soon to be ex-wife, I hope," Eric interrupted.

"You are such an insensitive prick!"

"Man, I'm sorry, but I'm not going to lie and say I didn't see
it coming. It was going to be one out of the two of you, and
honestly? I'm just glad it wasn't you who bailed. Like I've
told you before, I don't think I could ever forgive you if you
did." After he said his piece, he wanted to withdraw his whole
side of the conversation. From the time he got home he had
been on cloud nine with nothing on his mind but Claudia and

their amazing time together. Knowing how dysfunctional his brother's home life was, this wasn't exactly a shocker. So he knew his words were sounding really calloused, and it was just a matter of time before his brother would blow his stack; amazingly enough though, Bart didn't overreact to his last comment. In fact, he didn't speak at all for at least a minute.

Eric could practically see his brother shaking his head in astonishment when Bart laughed and said, "You know, it's amazing to me how many times I've heard you get all over Eva for being 'holier than thou' and self-righteous, but right now dude I've never wanted to throttle someone so bad for thinking that they have all the answers and judging something that they have no idea about! And just for the record, that wife of yours is an amazing woman! I've never seen a more caring and giving person. She's been the one who has saved my sorry ass these past few weeks. I'm grateful that the kids have her as a mother figure; she's the best one I could ask for! So instead of casting stones my way, why don't you do everything in your power to get home so you aren't sitting in the same position as I am."

"What are you talking about?"

"I'm talking about that guy, Carter, sniffing around your wife and my kids."

"Whhhhhhat?" Eric growled.

"Yup, the boys talk about him constantly as if they see him all the time. I know Eva's intentions are good, but I hear that his divorce just went through and from what I can see, he seems to be pining for your wife."

Steam was rolling out of Eric's ears. "I'll see to it."

"Just get home, bro. Family first, right?"

"Right," he said through clenched teeth.

"When was the last time you talked with Eva?"

"I don't remember; obviously too long ago."

"Give her a call, man. She misses you."

"I will."

Nothing like crashing the amazing mood he was in. How dare Eva hang out with Mitch Carter, knowing how he felt

171

about him? Bart just confirmed every worry he had about the man, and the fact that Eva didn't have enough sense to walk far, far away from him made his blood boil. The guilt that he felt over what happened between him and Claudia somehow seemed justified now. And boy, would he get his say as soon as he got hold of her!

Chapter 15

"Oh, hi, Mitch! What are you doing here?" Since it had been a beautiful spring day, she thought she'd skip the gym and take the dogs for a run. They were all a bit cooped up being in the house and needed some fresh air. What first started out as a mile walk around the neighborhood when she first started her fitness program almost six months prior was now a four mile jog. It got her blood moving and her dogs tuckered out; it was a win, win situation. She figured since she didn't have Bart's kids and she got off a little early, she'd get home, try Eric once more (to no avail), jog and get back before it turned dark.

Mitch was jogging towards her and stopped as he approached. "Hi, beautiful! I'm renting a house a mile that way," he said, pointing in the way he had come.

"I thought you were just going to hotel it..."

"That's what I thought too, but a guy from the office was trying to sell his house to buy another and I happened to be walking by when I heard him comment that it would take a great stress load off if he could find someone to rent it until it sells and the rest they say is history."

"Oh, wow!" The dogs sniffed his shoes and Bruiser was gravitating towards his crotch when Eva pulled back on his leash. "Bruiser! Down! Now!"

Mitch laughed and petted both their heads. "Don't worry about it, they are okay."

There was an uncomfortable silence which motivated Eva to say, "Well, great to see you again! Enjoy your run!" as she jerked the dogs away from Mitch.

"You too!"

Eva sent him a quick smile, then headed on her way but turned quickly when she heard her name. "You have plans for supper?" he asked.

173

"I have a garden salad with my name on it at home!" she joked, running backwards.

"Would you like company?"

"Well...I..." She knew she should say no and get it over with. She didn't have the kids as a buffer this time and it would look really wrong if anyone saw him coming or going from her house.

"I could really use the company," Mitch added, which pulled at her heartstrings. What kind of friend would she be to let him bask in his loneliness? She asked herself.

"I'll bring a chicken," he added.

She had to stop the dogs because they were pulling her too fast and she was afraid of landing on her rear in front of him. "A chicken?" she asked, laughing.

"I picked up a rotisserie at the deli along with some coleslaw and potatoes. It's a little too much for just me. How about it?"

"Come on over around 6. I'll have our salads waiting."

Winking, he said, "Sounds good!"

*　　*　　*

It was 4 o'clock in the afternoon when she returned from her run. She refilled the dog's food and water, which they lapped up quickly from their exercise. All she wanted to do was take a nap or have a nice soak in the tub, preferably at the same time, but because she committed to this dinner her relaxation went out the window. But she did need a shower desperately.

It was in between shampooing and conditioning her hair when she heard the phone ring. Not wanting to break her rhythm, she just prayed that whoever it was would leave a message so she could get back to them.

There was a message. It was Eric, and he sounded irritated. It had been two weeks since she last spoke to him and just about three months since she last saw him. She missed him and couldn't wait for him to get back, yet she knew she was getting complacent since he had been away and there would be a time of major adjustment when he returned. Judging by the tone in his voice, she really debated calling him back. The last thing she wanted was a confrontation over the phone, but she knew that if she waited for him to call her back, it would double his irritation.

He picked up on the first ring. "Hey, honey!"

"Where were you all day long? I called the salon and Barbie said you left at three and when I couldn't reach you at home I was thinking the worst!"

His words were accusing which prompted her to snap back rather sarcastically, "I do what I always do on Monday, getting off early or not; it's my errand day. I just got back from taking the dogs for a jog. And not for nothing, I did try calling you right after I got home not to mention a million times over the last two weeks. It's just as frustrating for me to try getting a hold of you, you know!"

"Yeah, I know. This arrangement is really getting old!"

"I'll second that! Did Barton call you?"

"Yes, he did; last night."

"So, he told you about Natasha then?"

Letting out a string of breath, he said, "Yeah. Wow! Everything all right on your end? He's not overstepping his bounds with the kids, is he?"

"No! Absolutely not! In fact, between him, Uncle Ben and me, we've devised quite the schedule that works for all of us."

"And how are the kids? Are they going to be all right?" Eric asked tightly.

"Honey, they will be fine. We are all trying to keep the lines of communication open, making them feel comfortable to talk with us. Kristin is working with them every chance she can get and she says they are adjusting remarkably well."

"Who the hell is Kristin?"

"Kristin Eastlund, the youth minister at our church. I've talked about her a million times. Don't you remember?"

"No, I guess I don't. But then again, you talk about so many people from there I can't keep track of them all," Eric said

175

snidely, but then paused and retorted, "I'm sorry, Eva. I just seem so far removed from home, from you, and this whole situation that I feel like I'm on the sidelines and it really sucks."

"It's all right. It's totally understandable," she responded sincerely, relaxing a little by his apology.

Chuckling lightly to himself, he says, "I'm just surprised that Bart is letting anyone from your church interfere with his family."

"Actually, he has been calling Kristin a lot about the kids. He seems to appreciate her help."

"Oh no! Please don't tell me that my brother is becoming a holy roller!"

Eva bristled. "And what would be so bad about that? I think that if Bart can find any sort of peace or contentment in his life right now, it's a good thing. Do I see him praising Jesus from the rooftops or speaking in tongues at this point? Hardly. But I don't begrudge him finding answers to life's difficult situations. I personally think God is knocking hard on the door of his heart right now, and if Kristin or I can help him in any way to find a way to open that door, we will."

"Maybe you and your friend should mind your own damn business! You need to stop focusing so much on my brother becoming a Jesus freak and pay more attention to the goings on at your own door."

"And what's that supposed to mean?"

"I didn't appreciate hearing that you've been hanging out with that Carter guy."

Eva's heart began to beat out of her chest. Placing her hand over it to try slowing it down, she gulped and asked, "What are you talking about?"

"Oh! So are you denying it?"

"No, not exactly. We've seen each other at the gym and at church, and he came over for lunch with his girls one time, but I would hardly call that hanging out." As soon as she said the words, she knew how it must've sounded and it wasn't good.

"What would you call it then?"

"I...I know how it must seem, but it's totally innocent, Eric. I swear it is!"

"I don't want you hanging out with him. And let me clarify that since you seem to have lost your common sense, all right? I don't want you to go out of your way to talk to him, be with him and I sure as hell don't want to hear that he's been in my house again, with or without his kids!"

Tears were streaming down Eva's face and she was shaking. "Eric, why are you being like this? Don't you trust me? I've been nothing but faithful to you. I can't promise that I won't see him or his girls again."

"I hear that he's newly divorced. Does he think we're separated? That you are a free agent because I'm gone? I trust you, but I'm sorry, Eva, I just don't trust that guy or any guy that hangs around married women without their husbands around. I know in your twisted little religious bubble you think guys and girls can be just friends, but it just doesn't work that way. Guys, especially lonely guys, look at girls who are their 'friends' as potential bed buddies," Eric said gratingly.

"But that's not how Mitch is. He knows I love you and that you are away on business. I talk about you all the time."

"I'm telling you, Eva. Stay away from him!" he said, ignoring her statement.

Instead of fighting, she just said a defeated, "Fine."

"Good," he said, satisfied that he made his point clear.

"So when are you coming home?" She asked with longing.

"I hope soon. Jess will let me know by the end of the week."

"And then what?"

"He'll let me know then. It sounds like I'll have the entire continental USA for now until they can train another tech. It's going to be a 24/7/365 day a year job."

"That's what you signed up for. But you like it, right?" she asked hopefully.

"I love it; best thing to come my way!" For the first time that night, he sounded upbeat.

"That's awesome, hon!" And since he was back to a good mood, she thought she'd tell him her exciting news. "Guess what?"

"What?"

"I wasn't going to tell you until you got home but I just can't wait! I just got off the pill! My doctor says we can start right away. If you are home by next week it will work out perfectly!"

"Whoa! Don't you think you should've talked to me first? I mean sheesh, Eva! I'd like to know how taxing this job will be before we venture into parenthood!"

"But I thought this was the plan. When you got back, we'd try again. That's why I've been busting my butt for all these months. I'm down sixty-five pounds, Eric. Dr. Anderson says I'm in great health to conceive, and best of all she couldn't see any cysts! I'm still on my fitness and healthy eating plan, and intend to stay this way until way after God blesses us with a child!" For the first time in the conversation, she was honest to goodness angry. His words were a big blow. Once again, they were not only on separate pages but completely different books.

"We'll tackle all that when I get home. But for now I have to get to bed! It's almost midnight."

"I want a baby, Eric," she stated boldly. Eva needed to be heard and the statement cut right to the chase.

"I know. I have to go now. I'll talk to you soon, all right?" he said, sounding exhausted.

"Okay. Good night. I love you!"

"You too," he replied quickly, and then the sound of the line going dead punctuated their turbulent conversation.

Tears clouded her vision as she gently laid the phone down. Eva knew she should've called Mitch and cancel their dinner plans right then and there. Given her state of mind, she could almost envision how things could transpire between her and her dinner guest if he were to come over, and it should terrify her, but disappointment, resentment and anger fueled her decision; and the sad truth of the matter was she knew exactly whose hands she was playing into. And at this point she didn't care. She was sick of the fight.

178

Chapter 16

Once he hung up the phone with Eva, Eric paced his small apartment, lightly banging the phone against his head in frustration. He really had no right to say anything to Eva about Mitch Carter, knowing very well that she would never entertain the idea doing anything inappropriate with him. It was he himself who crossed the line in that department, big time, and he knew he was in trouble with a capital T. If it were just one kiss, or even one caress, he could forgive himself and go back to Eva with a clear conscience. But knowing that they took it to a place where souls connected, five separate times to be exact, he knew how hard it was going to be to face Eva and contemplated a separation from both women until he got his head on straight. Eva telling him about wanting to get right to the baby-making process when he got home panicked him the most. Now more than ever he was certain that it wasn't the right time. He didn't even feel fit to be in a mature relationship let alone being responsible for an innocent human being.

Eric was grateful that Claudia wasn't a stage five clinger. She was as confident and cool as ever and never let on in front of her parents once that something was going on between them. After their first time making love, Eric thought for sure the guilt would come on him, but it never did. Everything just clicked with her, from their attraction to each other, to her unique relationship with her parents to her laid back attitude about practically everything. It was as if they had been together forever. Not once did he compare her to his wife. He knew they were two completely different women, and he loved them both. It just took that one time with Claudia to know that it wouldn't be the last time they'd be together. There was no way he could give her up, and when she showed up at his apartment just a few hours after last seeing each other, he took her into a tight embrace and told her as much. He knew it wasn't fair to her because unless he made the decision to leave Eva he'd have to let Claudia go eventually. It should have helped that Claudia knew the rules and would play by Eric's set, but her willingness to comply made him love her even more. He was trapped by his own volition.

Midday after the phone call with Eva, Eric requested a meeting with Jessup to tell him of his family's recent drama. Part of him was desperate to hear that he was ready to go out on his own so he could escape from this affair before it got completely out of control, yet the other part of him ached to stay so he could eek out more time with Claudia. But his boss gave him the okay to head on out at the end of the week. He felt that Eric grasped all the machines ins and outs and would be ready to get to work. After shaking Jess's hand, he gravitated towards Claudia's office, which was on the way to the training center. He was disappointed to find that she wasn't there, but knew he'd catch up with her eventually.

Darryl was loitering at Eric's machine when he walked into the center. "Hey, Wahler."

"What's going on, Darryl?" Eric asked without interest as he grabbed his clip board with his check list.

"I'm knocking off early. Walter went home sick so I have nothing to do. Want to meet up later for a drink? I'm getting really sick of seeing the inside of my apartment."

"Oh man, I'd love to, but I have so much sleep to catch up on!" he said with a fake stretch and yawn to stress a point.

Darryl just stared at him and Eric could see that he didn't believe a word he said. Instead of calling him on it, he asked, "Hey, you are pretty chummy with Claudia. She dating anyone yet?"

That made him tense and he hoped it didn't show when he rebuffed Daryl by saying, "Dude, you're married. Seriously, get over yourself."

"So what? It doesn't stop you!"

Eric puffed out his chest and looked him right in the eye. "As I've told you before, we are just friends. She's not interested in sharing a man. She deserves better than that." He spoke every word with conviction, but there must've been a flicker of something in his eye because Darryl jumped on it.

Eric shuddered at the devilish laughter coming from the man inches away from him. "Well, well, well, looks like I arrived too late. She's already taken, isn't she?"

Pushing at Darryl's shoulder so he could get past him, he said through clenched teeth, "I have to get back to work."

"I judged you wrong, Wahler! Looks like you *do* know how to get it done." he practically yelled, following behind Eric.

Eric whirled around on him and pressed his pointer finger into Darryl's chest. "Be careful what you start accusing people of, asshole! Stay out of my business!"

"A hot reaction only shows guilt, Wahler," Darryl yelled after Eric as he exited the room.

Grabbing his cigarettes, Eric headed outside and took a seat on a ledge next to the parking lot. The last thing he needed was rumors flying about something that was so true. And if he knew Darryl like he thought he did, the rumor mill had already started and it would be a matter of time before Jessup had another meeting with him. He didn't know if he could lie to his boss, whom he loved like a father, if confronted.

Fortunately, his fears were put to rest as the remainder of the day went without a hitch and by six o'clock he was showered and relaxed on the couch in his apartment. He knew he should've called Eva to make amends after last nights conversation, but he was too exhausted, and in all honesty, didn't want to talk to her. But the woman he did want to, seemed to have disappeared that day, which both concerned and relieved Eric. He missed her beautiful smile, her laughter and her presence, not to mention those gorgeous long legs. But he would have to survive more long days like he had today in the future without seeing or hearing from her.

At eight o'clock, there was a knock on the door and he knew instantly who it was. As much as he knew he needed time alone to clear his head, his desire for her was so intense that he couldn't and wouldn't turn her away. As soon as the door cracked open, without looking he reached beyond it and pulled her to him, pressing an urgent kiss to her mouth.

After a few seconds he finally opened his eyes and laughed, "I'm sure glad you weren't someone else!"

Kicking the door closed behind her, she went into his embrace again but just loosely draped her arms around his neck and smiled up to him. "I missed you today."

"I missed you too. Where were you?"

"I had a last minute meeting in Milan with some potential buyers in Germany and Austria. If it goes all according to plan, we will need three more techs on the job."

"Wow! I bet your dad is really happy about that."

"It's exceeding all their expectations."

Kissing her again, he said, "So, to what do I owe this visit?"

Tears sprung to her eyes. "Daddy told me that you'll be leaving on Friday."

"Please don't cry, honey. We knew this was coming."

"I know. I just didn't think it would be this soon."

He let go of her to get some air. Running his hands through his long hair, he said, "I told you that I couldn't promise tomorrow!"

"So is today tomorrow?"

"I honestly don't know, Claude. You mean so much to me..."

"Yeah, yeah, yeah, I know the rest. 'But it's not you, it's me. Can we still be friends?'"

"Can we?"

"Four days ago when this situation was all in theory I'd have said yes. Now, I don't know how that would be possible."

Pulling her onto the couch with him, he tucked her into his side while kissing the top of her head. "Tomorrow isn't until Friday," he whispered.

Looking up to him with watery eyes, she asked hopefully, "Really?"

Kissing her, he replied with a smile. "Really."

* * *

How they made it through that week without getting caught was a miracle. To Eric's relief, if there was a rumor going around about them it didn't reach them or Jess. But rumor or not, the fact was that he was leaving a woman he had grown to love just as much as the wife he left three months ago and he still didn't know what he was going to do about that.

Jessup had a party for his 'graduation' at his place the night before he left with the three bosses and his fellow trainees. It went well into the night. He didn't want it to end. His boss hired a driver to get him home that night, and before he left Claudia took him aside and told him that she'd sneak over that night. It would be their last night together and they both needed one last unadulterated taste.

She worked it out to look like she left early for work for her parent's sake, but really, she snuck out after her parents went to bed and spent hours making love with him, and then insisted that she take Eric to the airport. At first he tried urging her to go back home, not to raise any suspicions. But she wasn't taking no for an answer.

It was a quiet ride to the airport that morning. All Eric could think about was what would happen next. Would they remain in contact? Would they remain long distance lovers? Would he ever see her again? Would Eva know with one look that there was another woman? And if she did, would she kick him out? Would Claudia have him then, or was he a challenge that was won and as soon as he left the magic between them would vanish? Every answer to these questions plagued him beyond measure.

Claudia walked him into the airport hand in hand and before he went into the secure area, he pulled her into his embrace, knowing the chance of anyone knowing them would be slim to none.

"Call me when you arrive?"

"I will," he said affectionately.

Looking down, she asked softly, "Will she be there to pick you up?"

Lifting her chin so she was forced to look into his eyes, he said, "No. She doesn't know I'm coming."

"Do you still love her?"

"Yes, I do," he said regretfully. "Look, I know this whole thing is hard and confusing and to be totally honest I don't know what will happen when I get home. I wish I could promise you something, but I can't. Just know that I'll *never* forget my time here with you."

"Me either!" She hugged him closer. "It's probably best you are leaving. One more moment with you and I don't think I'd ever let you go!"

"Speaking of going, I better..."

"Just one more moment..." She whispered into his ear and took in the scent of him.

He lightly kissed her once more before separating from her. "Take care of yourself, all right?" he asked, brushing his index finger over the tip of her nose.

"You too."

With a final wave, he was past security and out of sight.

Chapter 17

Eva was still fuming about her phone call with Eric when Mitch arrived at their scheduled time and she tried masking it by brightly welcoming him. She insisted that he take a seat in the living room while she did the meal preparations.

But it was when she was in the kitchen that she turned into a mad woman, slamming the cupboards and swearing when she couldn't find the right salad bowl. "Whoa, whoa, whoa, girl! Slow down!" He said, coming up behind her and putting his hands on her shoulders to calm her.

She took in a deep breath and closed her eyes before responding. "I'm sorry, Mitch. I'm not in the best mood right now. I'm afraid I'm not going to be the best company tonight."

"Nonsense. How about this? You sit down and I'll get everything set up. Something tells me that this has nothing to do with whatever you are trying to do here. Right now I think that you need to keep away from sharp objects. Let me take over," he said, teasing her.

"Fine. Whatever...," she said in a defeated tone, not even cracking a smile at his joke.

Eva sat down hard onto the kitchen chair, which prompted both Bruiser and Red to prod their noses at her arm, making her pet them. This was one of those times where she didn't need them to be high maintenance.

"They don't need much encouragement, do they?" Mitch asked as he began setting the plates and silverware on the table.

"Rarely. I was hoping that they would be dead tired after the run I just took them on!"

"From the look on their faces, I suspect that it's almost their dinner time too. Are we okay to dine in here or do you want to take this out to the living room?"

"I don't feel like battling the chow hounds. Let's stay here."

"Great! What would you like to drink? It looks like our choices are going to be water or milk. Which would you prefer?"

"Milk, but I can get it myself, thank you."

Blocking her way to the cabinet where the glasses were, he said, "I realize you can do things for yourself, Eva. But let me get this for you. Please." There was something in the way he was pleading with her that made her let him. He wasn't being patronizing, he was sincere and it brought tears to her eyes and she looked away before he saw. It had been a long time since anyone had made a gesture so small, yet so incredibly sweet.

Once seated, Mitch asked, "Would you like me to say the prayer?"

Smiling, Eva nodded, and her heart warmed by yet another kind gesture; something she could never see her husband ever doing. Comparing the two of them was futile, since there was such a vast difference. And the more time she spent with Mitch, the more she added to her long list of things she loved about him. The highest of which was the fact that he was a believer like herself. She could talk to him about anything pertaining to the Lord; nothing she could do freely with Eric without being mocked.

The second she hung up with Eric, she knew where this night might lead if Mitch came over. Eva knew they were good friends, but did she really want more? It sure tickled her thoughts every now and again, but she had been with Eric for so long it was scary to think about doing something physical with someone other than him. As handsome as Mitch was, she really couldn't see herself doing anything like that. But she was really enjoying the attention he was lavishing on her at the moment, so much in fact that she didn't hear a word of his spoken prayer.

It was silent for a minute while they took their first bites, then Mitch asked jokingly, "So, are you going to tell me what has you in a bad mood, or am I just supposed to sit here and assume?"

Eva put down her fork, took a sip of her milk and then slowly looked over to him. "Eric called before you got here and we had some words."

"Ahhhh, I figured as much."

"You did?"

"Eva, it wasn't so long ago I was married. I remember how fights affected us. However, you should be getting along the best when you are away from each other. That was when Laurie and I actually had better dialogue."

"Well, we aren't passing the test. This is the longest we've been apart since we were sixteen and I miss him, and yet I don't; especially when he gets so angry at me. He just found out about Natasha and the kids, and apparently it was all my fault that he was just finding about it now even though I've been trying to reach him since it all happened and he was either never home or just avoiding my phone calls which makes me question his devotion and love for me since its been almost two weeks since we last talked and almost three months since we last touched and I just want his support but all I get is yelled at and I'm just so tired of dealing with it all..." Eva said breathlessly, and then broke into a sob.

Mitch slid over in his chair and hugged her to his chest. "Shhhhh, it's all right, baby. It's all right. It's good to get it out."

"I'm sssorrrry, Mitch. You shouldn't have to listen to me ramble," she spoke into his chest.

"What are friends for?"

Eva inched away from him, yet not too far away that he was still touching her. Wiping at her eyes, she asked seriously, "Is that what we are, Mitch? Friends?"

They stared at each other for a long moment and Eva could see her question registering in his eyes. He loosened his arm around her a bit, cleared his throat and he said, "Of course. What else would we be?"

Shaking her head, she replied, "I don't know, all right? I sometimes get confused when I'm around you."

Pulling back he asked, "Confused how?"

"Maybe that's not the right word. Let's see if I can get this out right without offending you..."

"Darlin, you could never offend me."

"You are too nice."

"Is that an offensive statement?"

187

Eva laughed. "No. It's just that I'm not used to such flattery all the time."

"Well, it's in my nature."

"I like your nature; very much. And I like our friendship; to me it's all right, but others around me don't think it's right which makes me wonder if we are doing something wrong."

"But we haven't done anything wrong. You are a great friend to me and I enjoy your company. Those people you are listening to have no idea what they are talking about."

"But tonight for instance when you asked me to dinner, a scripture came to mind and I'm not able to get it out of my head."

"Oh yeah, what's that?"

"'Avoid all appearances of evil.'"

"So you think people would see this as evil."

"I know they would."

"Even though this is just a dinner between a brother and sister in Christ."

"A divorced brother and married sister in Christ."

"So what you are saying is you think I should leave," he said almost defensively.

"See??? You *are* offended! I knew I shouldn't have said anything!"

Mitch caught himself and changed his attitude quickly. "Oh Eva, I'm not offended. I just see it differently. For our situation, I don't feel convicted and I don't worry about what other people think. If it appears evil to them, that's their issue. I know I'm not doing anything wrong, and neither are you."

"Yes, but, to be honest...."

When she stopped, he encouraged her by saying, "Yes?"

With tears in her eyes, she said, "My thoughts are impure a lot when we are together. A lot of 'what if's' come to mind."

"You aren't the only one who struggles with that."

"I hate to ask, but does it happen to you when you are with me?"

"Of course, Eva. I'm a guy and you're gorgeous and so unbelievably sweet!"

Snorting, she said, "You're the gorgeous one with so much going for you. You could get any woman you choose and here you are wasting your time and energy on a married woman who is unavailable. It confuses me. I guess the burning question is, why *are* you here?"

"You give me way too much credit. I'm not really interested in meeting another woman to make my life complete right now. I guess I'm enjoying being single, and you give me a safe alternative when it comes to getting companionship with the opposite sex."

"When you say 'safe', you mean..."

"I mean there isn't a chance of falling in love."

"Oh. But what about intimacy? Don't you need that?"

"I get that with you, without the physical element, that is."

Eva leaned back hard in her chair. "Wow. That is something new. I have to chew on that for a second."

"What?"

"About intimacy; here I thought that it meant being strictly physical."

"Nope."

"So you have no interest in getting physical with me? Is that what you're saying?"

"Oh, every fiber in my being would love to, but that would be crossing a line which would confuse our relationship, which is pretty perfect the way it is by the way."

Eva blushed, but became bold when she asked, "What would you say if I asked you to make love to me right now with no strings attached?"

"I'd say thanks for the great offer, but I couldn't do that without strings with you. Too messy. But I will say this to you my darling Eva: if Eric ever disappears from your life I will be on that offer so fast you won't know what hit you!" he said, his mouth inches from hers.

The room's temperature rose twenty degrees after that statement. Eva's heart was beating out of her chest, and the drums in her ears were about to explode from the pressure. Breathlessly, she said, "We should finish our dinner."

Mitch brushed his lips against her cheek and scooted back over to his plate. "Good idea."

Chapter 18

The sun was going down when Eric landed in Minneapolis-St. Paul airport. He hadn't thought about how he would make the track from the airport to Red Wing which was a forty-five minute drive until he was sitting at the Chicago airport. He had a three hour layover, which gave him time to call his brother from a payphone.

"Hey, what's going on?" His brother answered as if he knew who he was talking to already.

"Where you at?"

"Home. Where are you?"

"Aren't you traveling this week?" Eric asked, ignoring his brother's question.

"I'm not traveling anymore."

"What? Since when???"

"Since I quit on Tuesday."

"How could you up and quit? Do you have another job lined up? What are you going to do for money, man?"

"I've made a lot of contacts, bro. I'm not worried about money. I'm worried about my kids. They really need me right now. And don't worry, I've already had three interviews and they all look good. The best part is any one I choose I'll be working close to home and will be here every night for the kids."

"Wow, Bart. That's really cool."

"Where are you, dude? I can hear a lot of people in the back ground."

Eric looked around, not aware of his surroundings. "I'm in Chicago. I'll be in Minneapolis by 7. Could you pick me up?"

"Why me? Can't Eva pick you up?"

"She doesn't know I'm coming, and I don't want her to know."

"Oh, you going to surprise her? She'll love it! And you are going to be so surprised when you see her, man! She looks amazing!"

"Yes, I suppose I want to surprise her, but if it's not too much bother, I'd like to bunk at your place tonight. I have to get my head together before I see her."

"Uh oh, dude, I don't know if I want to get in the middle of this..."

"There's nothing to get in the middle of, man. I just need some time to myself before she sees me. So will you do that for me please?"

"Yeah, I'll be there. I'll ask Uncle Ben if he'll watch the kids over night so you'll have some peace."

"Thanks, Bart. See you soon!"

One phone call down, one to go. He needed to talk to Claudia. She was all he dreamed about every time he dozed off on the plane. After waking up from every one of his naps, he was certain he made the worst mistake by leaving. By the end of the flight, his head was a mess.

She answered on the first ring. "Oh my god, I didn't think you'd ever call!"

"Hey baby! I said I would, didn't I?"

"Yeah, but it was the longest eight hours of my life. I miss you!"

"I miss you too. This is going to be hard, I can tell already."

"What are we going to do, Eric?"

"I'm trying to figure that out. All I can promise is that I'll try to call you whenever I can. All I could think about was you forgetting about me and moving on to someone else..."

He could hear the tears in her voice when she said, "No one could replace you. *No one.* I wanted to tell you this at the airport, but I couldn't get out the words. But I love you, Eric. What you do with that is up to you, but know that I would snap you up in a second if I knew you were a free man."

He couldn't answer for a minute, but when he did he had to press his head against the phone booth to cool his forehead. "You are an amazing woman, Claudia, and if I were free there would be no issue as to where I'd be right now."

"Oh God, I love you!"

Eric wanted to say it back but knew it would be a cruel thing to do. "I only have one minute before my card is used up,

191

baby. I'll call you as soon as I'm able, all right? Please get a good night's rest. I'll be dreaming of you!"

"I will."

"I have to go now. Sweet dreams, Claude!"

Eric heard her say something, but he had the phone in its cradle before he could respond. It was one of many regrets which he was sure to come. He had to confide in someone before he exploded; someone with wise counsel.

* * *

As soon as Eric saw Bart at the baggage area, he embraced him hard. He hadn't realized how long it had been until he saw his brother at that moment. Bart had aged ten years over night. He looked haggard. Eric couldn't ever remember seeing his brother's hair that long, both on the top of his head and face. And it was the first time he noticed that his temples and even some of his facial hair were sprinkled with white. He decided against giving him grief over it and just relished seeing a familiar face. "So good to see you, brother!" Eric said with tears in his eyes.

"You too, kid, you too."

"I brought home some awesome liquor from Switzerland. Can't wait until you try it! Best stuff I've ever had!"

"Well, let's get home so we can break it open then!"

Eric began telling him about the company he was now working for and about the bosses and staff so enthusiastically that Bart had to slow him down. "Wow, dude, sounds like you made a wise choice there."

"I love it! It's right up my alley, and the pay is great!"

"Sounds like it, bro. I'm happy for you."

Eric was taken aback. "You are?" His brother was the most selfish person, besides Natasha, that he'd ever known. For his brother to be happy for Eric was nothing short of astounding.

"Of course. Why wouldn't I be?"

"Um, cause you never were before."

"Yes, I was."

"No, you weren't. It was always about you, your job, your kids, your wife and your things. Any time I ever wanted to tell you something about me I got cut off. Never once did I hear from you how happy or proud of me you were. Ever."

"Yeah, I am pretty self-involved. Sorry about that. I'm working on it. Getting help as we speak."

Eric was taken aback by his brother's humbling words. Getting help? From who, he wondered. "Wow, bro. I'm impressed. May I note that whatever you're doing, its working?"

"Thanks."

Eric just looked at him funny, as if he couldn't believe his ears. "Wow! Thanks too?" Looking around frantically, he joked, "Am I being punked here?"

"Oh shut it! Don't give me a hard time. It's difficult being selfless."

Shaking his head and chuckling, Eric said, "You are a class act. So what's going on with Natasha if I may ask?"

"The short of it is we'll be officially divorced in ten days."

"Ten days? How is that possible? She just left a few weeks ago."

"Yup, and her lawyer boyfriend is seeing to it that I go away quickly and quietly."

"So she *was* seeing someone else."

"Yeah, well, what can I say to condemn her? So was I."

"You were?" Eric was astounded.

"I had a girlfriend in Arizona, but I broke it off right before 'Tash left. She was putting too much pressure on me. It was hard and confusing living a double life. I realized I just wanted simplicity in my life. Even though what Natasha and I had wasn't perfect, I decided that's what I wanted. And then she left..."

"Wow bro. Did she know?"

"I never told her, and she never accused me. But then again, we never did really talk unless it was to yell at each other."

"I sometimes wondered with how much you were away, but to hear that you actually went out on her blows my mind."

"Yeah, so from one cheater to another; who is she and how

serious is it?"

"Wh-what do you mean?"

Snorting, he mimicked, "'I have to get my head together before I see Eva.' Bro, I know what that's all about, but I didn't have anyone to help me sort out the feelings."

Eric was deflated. He couldn't deny it. He was a terrible liar. "She's a girl I worked with. And it got pretty serious."

"But you ended it, right?"

"Not exactly. But she knows I can't leave Eva."

"So where are you then?"

"Confused and miserable and feeling extremely guilty."

"You gonna tell Eva?"

"No way! I don't want to lose her!"

"Well, if she finds out another way, she'll leave you too. But then again, your wife is an amazing woman. Now that I know a little more about the way she is, I'm pretty certain she'd forgive you."

"But it's not as if I just kissed this woman once. I slept with her numerous times, and I wanted so badly to tell her that I loved her. She's just as amazing as Eva, bro; but different."

"I'm sure she is, man. But right now you have to ask yourself, is she worth the hurt it will cause her and everyone around you? Unlike Natasha, everyone loves Eva."

"I know I opened Pandora's Box on this one. And I know someone is going to get hurt eventually. I've known it all along. I'm so messed up right now it's not even funny. Sleep deprivation isn't helping either."

"Well, we're almost to my place. Get a drink in you and get a good night's rest. I'm sure when you see Eva again it will all come clear as to what you should do."

Eric just looked over to his brother and stared, trying to figure out what happened to his brother that made such a change in him.

"What???" Bart asked when he noticed his brother staring.

"Nothing. It's just that you sounded....so parental."

Bart punched him in the shoulder and grinned. "There, now we're back to being brothers."

"I like the change."

Paying attention to the road once again, Bart smiled. "I don't know, bro, ever since Natasha left something out there told me that there would be good that came out of this. It was a lot of Eva's influence, but I have to say that her church has really put themselves out there for the kids and me. If it's not Eva or Uncle Ben helping out, it's Charlotte or that youth director Kristin. I never knew people could be that...nice and supportive to a complete stranger; especially for an A-hole like myself. But all their chatter about that stuff about Jesus, I'm starting to think they might be making some sense. There's something that makes me wonder: what's the reasoning behind people who read the words in that book that motivate them to do as it says? I mean, is the story that real? I used to think that your wife was a weak-minded person, clutching onto an invisible man in the sky for who knows why. But to have witnessed what she does in a given day between work, church, working out and taking care of my kids all by herself and not to have broken down once when just looking at her makes me want to run away fast if anyone expected it of me? I am starting to believe that this Jesus is what she truly believes gives her strength to move on. It's just hard to believe that I might've been wrong in my thinking. I mean, it's hard to imagine that there is more to this life than women, work and beer!"

"Wow, that was deep, Bart. I'm excited for you in this new exploration of the what if's of life and everything, but could we hold church hour for when I'm not almost asleep already?" he asked with a yawn.

Shaking his head, Bart said, "Yeah man, whatever."

"Thanks," Eric said, closing his eyes.

"You really fallin asleep?"

"Uh huh."

"Fine," Bart replied, cranking up his hard rock, putting Eric completely asleep.

Chapter 19

It was Easter weekend and you could tell by the numbers at the salon. Barbie had taken a two week vacation, leaving Eva in charge since she was the acting manager. There had been no time to sit and read magazines or even chit chat with the other girls, since her boss gave her a to-do list a mile long on top of getting all of her customers in. She could've worked until ten that night, but her body was happy when three o'clock rolled around.

It was a blessing that Bart had the kids that week because she didn't know how she would've swung everything. But she sure did miss them. It had only been a few weeks, but they had gotten into a routine that worked for everyone; everyone but Bart. Even though Eva could see that he was becoming somewhat softer, especially towards the kids, she noticed at times how lost he looked and his impatience flared at times which only told her of how really stressed he was. But she appreciated the time he took now for his kids, hugging them more and paying more attention to them when they talked than he ever had in the past. She was proud of him.

Kristin, the youth director, talked to her after the Good Friday service, telling her how well she thought the kids were doing under the circumstances. Eva knew that Bart had been calling her for kid advice, but her ears perked up when Kristin started asking questions about her brother-in-law-and-soon-to-be-ex-sister-in-law's relationship. Like did they fight a lot in front of the kids? Did they ever show displays of affection? Was Bart good to Natasha? Part of her thought that maybe Kristin was just trying to evaluate how the kids would form unhealthy ideas about relationships, but when she asked Eva what Bart had seen in Natasha in the first place and if Natasha was as pretty as the kids said, Eva sensed that Kristin might be falling for Bart. She would never bring it up to her friend though; after all, she knew Kristin was a lot wiser than that. The only way her friend would consider dating a man was if he was a Bible-believing Christian who walked closely with the Lord. And they both knew Bart wasn't even close to fitting that profile.

* * *

Eva was finishing counting the drawer when Stephanie came to the front. The other girls had left already, and as usual her receptionist stayed with her to close up. Her young friend had been a busy girl, being a boys' basketball cheerleader, which just finished a few weeks prior. It had been a long while since they had gotten caught up on events.

After locking the door, Stephanie reclined back on a few chairs which lined up against the front window, kicking her feet up. "You in a hurry to get home?"

"Not really. I was thinking about going over to Bart's to see the kids on my way home though. Why do you ask?"

"I have to go shopping, but I'm not really jazzed about going alone. Jennifer and Rachelle, you know, the twins, and I planned on going together but they had to go to their grandparents for the weekend and my mom is working. Pretty much everyone I tried is busy. Just wondering if you are up to it," she said unenthusiastically.

Snapping the cash register shut, Eva looked over to her and asked, "What are you looking for? Anything in particular?"

"Yeah. A prom dress."

"A prom dress? You're going now? What happened to 'the prom can take their flowers and dresses and shove it where the sun doesn't shine?'"

"Yeah, I know. But then Justin got his head out of his rear end and asked me finally. A few months late, but better late than never I suppose."

"That's a good attitude. So does that mean he wants to get back together with you or is this just a 'date'?"

"Who knows. To be honest with you, I'm still sorta pissed

off about how things went down, ya know? He sidestepped asking me to prom like someone dodging a cow pie. At first I thought it was because I wouldn't sleep with him, like at all, and that especially included prom. After he broke up with me, I heard he went out with Shae Winterbourne which didn't put those fears to rest because she is the sluttiest girl in our class. Just knowing where his lips might have been makes me want to vomit. You know, the more I talk about it, the more I just want to stick to my original sentiment and tell him to kiss off."

Eva laughed. "But you'd regret it and you know it."

"Yeah, I'm sure I would. So, you willing to battle the stores with me or not?"

"Sure, why not. Let me get this in the safe and we can go."

Stephanie popped up from her relaxed composure, and said, "Oh! I almost forgot!"

"What?"

"Mitch dropped these off for you."

Stephanie held out a small square envelope to Eva. "Mitch? When was he here?"

"About ten o'clock this morning. I'm surprised you didn't get a hot flash; everyone else in here did!"

Smiling, she opened the envelope. "Two tickets to 'Amazing Grace' at the Sheldon Theater." Eva was confused as to what that was about. She had heard that the play that was being put on by a local church was incredible. It was written and directed by a couple who attended there.

"Wow, that's nice. Who are they for?"

"I have no idea. If you don't mind, I'm going to call him quick."

A few rings later and Mitch answered happily. "Hey beautiful! How was your day?"

"Great! Say, what's up with these tickets you left me?"

"I'm glad you got them. I was going to drop them off at your house, but I thought that you wouldn't miss them this way. I'm taking the girls tonight and had two extra tickets. I figured you could either join us by yourself or find someone to bring with you."

"Oh, that's great! Thank you. Maybe I'll invite Steph. We

are just about to go out shopping for her prom dress."

"OOO prom! That seems like a hundred years ago," he said, nostalgia in his voice. "That should be fun!"

"I'm going for morale support."

"And I'm sure you will be. Well, I hope to see you tonight."

"I'll be there unless something more attractive comes my way!"

"Cute," he quipped and then asked jokingly, "So I'll see ya?"

Laughing, she said, "Yeah, you'll see me!" and hung up the phone. She really did look forward to it.

*　*　*

"You have to try it on, Eva! Come on!" Stephanie encouraged playfully while she herself stood in a black and white strapless, very fitted, above the knee dress.

Eva held out from her a tiny black sequence frock and it was a size 6. There was no way she could fit into a size 6! It was adorable, but she hadn't been able to squeeze into anything fitted in years. "I hardly think so," she said, putting it back on the rack.

Instead of listening to her, Stephanie grabbed the size 6 and 8 in the same style and put it in the dressing room next to hers. "You have earned this moment, Eva. When was the last time you tried on a prom dress?"

"Oh man, thirteen years ago? And about thirty pounds?"

"Stop being sarcastic and humor me, will you?"

"Oh...oh fine!" Eva shut the door accidentally hard, making her wince. She started to shuck off her clothes while saying, "Tell me again why I agreed to go shopping with you?"

"For moral support I heard you say a few times, but you have to admit it's a lot of fun!"

Eva stood in front of the mirror in just her underwear and stared. And then she stood a little taller to iron out those few spots on her flesh where she could still see flab. Instead of putting on the dress and modeling, she looked at herself straight on and then turned to see her profile; sucking her gut in and out. 'There is no way I'm going to fit into a size 6!' she thought to herself.

"Hey Eva, don't you even think about trying on the size 8 first. I'll bet you a hundred dollars that you fit into the 6."

Eva snapped out of it and started to take the size 6 off the hanger. "You don't have a hundred to spare."

"Okay. If you fit into it, you pay for my dress. If I lose, I call drag-my-feet-Justin and tell him he's out of luck."

Eva just laughed. "You are going to be sorry you made this bet, but you're on." There was a zipper closure in the back, so she had to step into it. Well, so far so good, she thought, but wasn't expecting it to zip up at all. Once she got the dress up and over her toned legs and hips, her arms slid in to the spaghetti straps and she reached around to find the zipper. She got it as far as her lower back and then she was stuck. Frustrated that she was right, Eva said, "Nope, doesn't fit."

"I don't believe you!"

"Well, believe it. I can't even get this stupid zipper up any further."

"Let me see."

"No," she said through the thin door.

"Open up, Ms. Wahler."

Rolling her eyes, she said, "Fine."

Stephanie's eyes got big when she saw her. "The heck it doesn't fit! Turn around!"

"It doesn't-"

"It does too! Turn around so I can zip it up!"

Eva reluctantly turned around and within two seconds Stephanie zipped it up the rest of the way. It wasn't loose, but it sure fit like it was made just for her. Eva gasped, bringing her hand up to her mouth while turning so she could check herself out in the mirror. "No way!"

"Told ya so! You look amazing!"

Eva turned slowly in a 360 turn not believing her misty eyes. "I haven't been a size 6 since high school, Stephanie! Oh my gosh!" She cried triumphantly.

"Wait til Eric sees you! He's going to gobble you up whole!"

Hearing her husband's name warmed her, even though she was still a little hurt and mad at him. She made a mental note to call him when she got home. "I can only hope!" she said with a full-fledged smile.

For the next half hour, Eva tried on every size 6 dress in the place with no intention of buying, just to make sure it wasn't a fluke; and it wasn't. Stephanie decided on a salmon colored cocktail dress, the only one of its kind left. Eva tried to make good on their bet, but Stephanie wouldn't let her buy it. She was just glad that Eva found out how small she'd really gotten.

Eva couldn't have had higher spirits than when she walked in the house that afternoon. She was so out of it that she didn't notice the dogs not barking or the TV on in the living room. Instead, she picked up the phone to call Eric, and was hoping he'd answer.

"Who are you callin'?" The person in question said from behind her.

Eva dropped the phone in shock. "*Eric!* Oh my Gosh! You're home!!!" She ran over to him and hugged him hard and then kissed him feverishly. "I've missed you so much!"

"I've...missed...you...too..." he said in between kisses.

She stepped back but still in an embrace, she asked, "Why didn't you call? How did you get here?"

"I wanted to surprise you, which I see I did. And Bart picked me up."

"When? This morning?"

He paused before saying, "No, last night."

"Last night? And you didn't call? I could've picked you up!" she said in a motherly tone, instantly regretting it.

He pulled away from her and grabbed a can of newly stocked beer from the refrigerator. "Look, I just wanted to surprise you. Can we not fight tonight? I'm really tired and just want a relaxing couple days to get back to normal. Is that too much to ask?"

Eva's eyes stung with tears and it took everything within her not to lash out. "I'm not lookin to fight either. I'm glad you're home."

"It's good to be home," he said quickly then took a long swig of beer.

He looked so ruggedly handsome she couldn't stay away any longer. She took the beer from his hand, put it down on the counter behind him and snuggled in close. "You look so good! I've missed you so much. I dreamt about your touch every night. It's what got me through...." She inhaled his fresh showered scent and then said, "I want you. Right. Now!"

Eva started to kiss him again, but she noticed that his hands remained idle on her waist while she was all over him like an untrained animal. "What's wrong?"

Eric stood there closing his eyes for a minute while she waited for an answer. When they opened, they were full of regret. "I'm just too tired, Eva. As much as I'd love to ravish you right now, I don't think I can. I'm sorry."

Eva let go of him like he was on fire and turned away. She wanted to cry...to scream...to run far, far away...

"All right," she said in a small voice. "Get some rest. I'm going to take the dogs out for a run."

He didn't even try to stop her. And for the next hour and a half she ran until her tears and her energy were depleted.

Chapter 20

As soon as Eva left with the dogs, Eric fell back onto the couch and it took everything in him not to chase after her. He knew he crushed her and it killed him. He was amazed at how thin she had gotten, and he could have kicked himself the most for not telling her how proud he was of her. For a second he thought they had gone back a decade. She was just as beautiful now as she was back then. It almost took his breath away.

He knew without a doubt that if he wanted to be physical with Eva ever again, he had to end it completely with Claudia. There was no way that he could move forward with Eva with the dark cloud of Claudia looming over his head and remain sane. He just hoped that Eva would be gone for a little while longer because he needed to clear the air as soon as possible. He picked up the phone and dialed Claudia's number and was getting a little nervous when she didn't pick up right away. It would've been almost two in the morning her time, but knew she was a night owl.

Groggily, she answered, "Hello?"

"Hey, it's me," he whispered, not thinking it strange to do so when no one was listening in.

"Oh! Heyyyy. How's...everything?" she asked cautiously.

Eric covered his eyes with his middle finger and thumb, pressing lightly as to the start of a slight headache coming on. "To be honest, not good. I'm just going to come out and say it because if I don't get it out we'll start talking and I'll lose my nerve and I'll never say what I have to say."

She cut him off by saying, "Eric, just say it."

Breathing out, he said with tears in his voice, "It's tomorrow."

There was a pause and then she said in a soft voice, "Okay."

Eric's head popped up. "Okay? That's all you have to say?"

"What else am I supposed to say, Eric? You told me that you can't promise me tomorrow, and I knew that. Am I supposed to cry and fight for you? You know me better than that. It was destined that someone get hurt. She's a lucky woman to have you. I still think I'm pretty lucky to have had a taste, but I'll respect your decision. Look, I was going to call you on Monday but since I have you on the phone, I'll give you the run down. But from now on, to make it easier, I'm going to have Veronica be your correspondent. I hope you don't mind."

"No, I totally understand. I'm so sorry, babe. Our timing sucks. You are an amazing woman, you know that?"

She snorted, "Apparently not amazing enough..."

"That's not true, Claude..."

"Enough Eric. I need to go before I do start crying. But daddy said your phone and computer should be there by Tuesday, and he said that he doesn't have any work as of yet but you'll be on call once you receive them. Do you have any messages for him?" She sounded so professional all of a sudden, and he realized that this phone call just ended a really great friendship. But he knew it needed to be done.

"No, nothing. But say hi to him for me, will ya?"

"Yeah, I will. And Eric?"

"Yeah?"

She paused before saying, "Take care of yourself."

"Yeah, you too, Claude. Again, I'm so sorry."

"Don't be. Thanks for the memories. Bye."

She hung up before he could say another word.

It was finished.

* * *

Eric knew he needed to mend the fence and the best way he knew how was to make supper for Eva, which consisted of ordering from their favorite Chinese takeout place. He wanted it to all be ready by the time Eva was back from her run, so once he was back from town, he set the table with plates and forks and the little white containers sitting between them and waited impatiently.

To his calculations, an hour and a half went by and he was starting to get nervous that she had taken the dogs and left him for good. It had just started to turn dark when he heard the pantry door open and the sound of the dog's paws across the floor. Instead of running to greet him, they took a quick drink of water from their bucket and collapsed on their dog beds.

Eva's hair was drenched, her face was red and her breathing was labored when she walked into the kitchen. She just stopped in her tracks and stared at Eric sitting at the kitchen table with his hands folded, and all he could do was think about not screwing up anything the rest of the night.

"You hungry?" he asked hesitantly, hoping she wouldn't turn away from him.

"Yeah, I am." No smile, but no glare either. That had to be a good sign, Eric thought.

That's when he stood up and pulled out her chair for her, something he'd never done before but thought he'd give a try.

Instead of walking over to him, she said cordially, "Thank you, Eric. I'll be right back," and then left the room.

A part of him felt paralyzed and deflated over her rejection, but the other part wanted to go after her and demand that she talk to him. It had been a long time since she got like this and he knew it would be a while until he was out of the dog house.

Ten minutes later she was freshly showered and in a sweat suit that he'd never seen before. It took everything in him not to start eating without her because after all he was starving. And he wanted to kick himself when he forgot to get up and pull out her chair again, but he wasn't used to the gesture and she was too fast for him.

"I ordered sesame chicken, pork fried rice and beef lo mein. I hope that's all right."

"I'm fine with whatever," she said indifferently, and then got up and poured herself a glass of water.

By the time she got back to her place, he had the containers opened and waited for her to scoop her portions onto her plate.

She folded her hands and bowed her head and the gesture wasn't lost on him. Nothing had changed since he'd been gone, he thought, and he thought of his brother's comments about Eva; about how his brother was beginning to understand her when it came to her faith. He never would, but promised himself that he wouldn't harass her about it anymore; he owed her that much at least.

When he saw out of the corner of his eye that she was finished offering up her prayers, he asked, "You have a nice run?"

"Uh-huh."

"How many miles did you do?"

"Six."

"Did you run them all?"

"Yup."

He could tell this was going to be like pulling teeth. Only when she was hurt or mad did she pull out her one word answers. Instead of ignoring her or yelling at her to snap out of it like he did in the past, he thought he'd try something new.

"Eva, I'm sorry about earlier. There's no excuse. I'm just so sorry." She just nodded her head without looking at him. "Please look at me, hon." Her eyes were stony, a look that he'd never seen before and it kind of scared him. "I'm so sorry. I'm such a jerk. You don't deserve to be treated that way. Please forgive me!"

With that he was on his feet, took her by the arms and lifted her from her chair until she was in his embrace. This time it was her arms that hung limp by her side as he hugged her. "Please say that you forgive me, Eva. Let's start this night over!" He started kissing her and when she wasn't responding he pulled away and said, "*Fine!*" in a huff.

"You hurt me, Eric," she said in a small voice. Instead of sitting back down like he did, she leaned back against the counter and hugged her middle, looking sad.

"I know, babe. And I'm really sorry," he responded in anguish.

"I feel like I'm walking on egg shells around you all the time. I can't say or do anything right. I don't wake up every day and say to myself 'let's make Eric's life a living hell today'. This separation was hard on me too." That's when she finally looked at him. "Do you think I enjoyed you being gone? It was lonely. I missed you so much and every time I talked with you on the phone, it was like I was interrupting you. I felt like you forgot about me. Weeks went by without a word and it wasn't for lack of trying to get a hold of you. Don't you know how much that killed me? Every night I fell asleep wondering if tomorrow would be the day I heard from you, and when I did, it was nothing but jealous fits of no merit. I imagined a million and one scenarios of your homecoming but what I got was something I wouldn't have dreamt of in a million years. I felt like a piece of garbage. You didn't seem to be excited to see me, even though you said you wanted to surprise me, which you did, but I don't know; something was off. What hurt the most though was the fact that I've been working my tail off trying to get fit and you didn't even notice! And today for the first time in a long time I felt truly beautiful, but in the matter of five minutes you had the ability to reduce me to an ugly duckling."

"Eva, I'm so so-"

"I know. And I forgive you, but I had to say my piece. And I'm tired of fighting. I just want to get along."

"I do too. Will you come and sit down?"

She walked slowly over to her chair and sat at the edge of it. "I noticed right away, Eva. You look beautiful. You look just like you did when we first met."

It was the first time she cracked a smile. "Not quite, but I'm on my way. Just twenty pounds to go."

He reached over and grabbed her hand and started to rub the top of it with his thumb. "You look great right now. I'm proud of you."

"Thank you," she said and then averted her eyes to her plate of fast cooling food. "We should really eat now. I'm starving."

"Yeah....me too."

But suddenly he wasn't talking about his food.

Chapter 21

Eva was so grateful that it went a lot smoother after dinner the night before, and then they made passionate, familiar love until they were exhausted. She was just so relieved that he was well, was home and the tension between them gone for a moment. His apology seemed genuine and she could tell that he was trying hard not to rock the boat. But as they sat there watching the television afterward, getting right back into their old routine, she couldn't help but be a little sad about the fact he had to try so hard. Should it be that difficult? Sometimes she just didn't know what she was doing wrong to make him so edgy and had hoped that time away from each other would've helped. And maybe it would in the end; after all, it had only been a few hours since he'd been back.

At nine o'clock the phone rang and Eva reached for it on her side of the bed. "Hello?"

"Eva! Oh good, you're okay. I was a little worried when you didn't show."

Oh no, Eva thought wildly, the play! "Oh my goodness! Mitch! I'm so sorry. Things got a little crazy around here tonight. Eric surprised me this afternoon. He's home!"

There was a pause, then a happy, "Oh wow! That's great!" Eric sat up straighter in the bed when he heard Mitch's name mentioned, which made Eva glance over to him; he was wearing a scowl that looked like a wolf about to go crazy.

"Yeah! I hope the play was as good as everyone said it was."

"Oh, it was. You missed out! But I totally understand why you weren't here." Eva then heard some talking in the background. "The girls say hi."

"Tell them hi back. I'm so sorry, Mitch."

"No problem, I understand. Have a nice night. Hope to see you tomorrow."

"All right. See you," she tried to say as nonchalantly as

possible knowing Eric hung onto her every word.

When she hung up the phone, all she could feel was the hot stare of her husband. With a clenched jaw, Eric asked, "What the hell was that?"

"You obviously know it was Mitch."

"Don't treat me like I'm stupid, Eva. Just tell me why he was calling my wife."

"There you go again, talking in the third person and acting like a jealous fool. I'll tell you, but are you willing to listen for once?"

"If the roles were reversed, darling wife," which he spit out, "I'm sure you would be reacting the same way."

"I doubt it, my darling husband," she said sarcastically, "Because unlike you, I trust you. You could tell me that you went skinny dipping with the Dallas Cowboy cheerleaders and I wouldn't care because I know you would never touch them, no matter how hot they were because you are an honorable man."

Something flickered in his eyes and he looked away. "I'm not *that* honorable..."

"You know what I mean, Eric. I trust you and I wish you would trust me after all these years. Mitch Carter and I are just friends. And that phone call was because he gave me two tickets to see a play tonight, which I totally forgot with all this excitement and he was just calling to see if I was all right. You know, what a friend would do."

Shaking his head, he said in defeat, 'I just don't like it, but what am I going to do? I obviously can't stop you from seeing him."

"No, you can't. I'd really like for you to get to know him. He's a really down-to-earth guy. I think you'd like him if you'd give him a chance."

"Not going to happen, so you can just forget it," he spat.

"What are you so afraid of, Eric? That I may be right for a change?"

Eric got up from the bed, grabbed his pillow and said, "I'm done with the conversation. I'm going out to the living room. Don't wait up for me."

Eva wanted to cry for the second time that night, but she waited until he left the room and shut the door. After a few minutes of shed tears, she got on her knees and cried out to the Lord with her face in the comforter that muffled her words, "Father God, I know I have sinned against both You and Eric. I know that this relationship with Mitch is affecting my marriage, but I can't see deserting him now. He doesn't have a lot of people in his life, and he trusts and needs me as a friend."

So does your husband, my dear child. Mitch has others. Don't use that as an excuse.

"Okay, maybe I just like the way he makes me feel. I can't do anything right in Eric's eyes. Help me to love him as You have loved me. Give me the grace to make it through this."

I will never leave you or forsake you, daughter. Lean on me, and I will give you the peace that passes all understanding.

"I desire Your peace so badly. I'm so sorry for not coming to You with all the things that are going on in my life sooner. Be with Bart and the kids; let them lean on You instead of the world and its trappings in what it considers true happiness. They are such a blessing to me. But I want a child of our own so bad, Lord. And Eric doesn't even want to talk about it."

I know the desires of your heart.

"But doesn't Your Word also say that you will give it to me as well? How Lord? When? I've done my part, and I'm living a healthier lifestyle...I'm so tired of waiting."

My ways are not your ways. Everything works out for good of those who love Me according to My purpose.

"This I know to be true, and I praise Your Holy Name for that! Father, sustain me while I wait on You. Thank You for the miracle I know You have in the works. In the meantime, help me to be the best wife I can be. Help me to be an effective witness to him, Lord. I pray that You may move in him that he come to one of tomorrow's services. I'm not going to force him, but I also know how important Easter Sunday is for those who don't believe. It's not a story that ever gets old for me. Thank you for sending me a Savior, Redeemer and Friend who took on all my sin so I may be redeemed in Your eyes. I'm so sorry for even flirting with the idea of being with another man other than my husband. I'm humbled by what

You did for me on that cross! Thank You for your resurrecting power. Without Your Spirit leading me, I honestly think I would've left Eric by now. Thank You for showing me the Truth in what You desire for my life and constantly reminding me to deny myself, pick up my own cross and follow You."

You know the secret to my Peace and Joy, my precious child. Love as I have loved. Forgive as I have forgiven. My Grace is sufficient for you.

"It is, Father. Just please work a miracle in my marriage. I'm so tired of fighting."

Rest in Me.

And with that she slipped into bed, shut off the light and fell into a restful sleep.

* * *

Eric woke up when she was dressing that morning and she found him smiling at her after she got her head out of the neck of her blouse. "What?"

"God, you're beautiful," he said, propping his hands behind his head.

Her face brightened by the compliment. "Thank you," and she went over and kissed him and he quickly grabbed and pulled her across his chest.

"I'm sorry I get crazy thinking about another man getting close to you."

"No man comes close to what I have with you, Eric. Trust me."

Kissing the tip of her nose, he said, "I do. And I'm sorry."

"You're forgiven," she gave him a quick kiss and stood up to finish getting dressed. "It's Easter, you know."

"Yeah, I know. Bart is picking me up with the brats for the 11:30 service."

Eva stopped and looked at him. "Really?" That would have been the first time she'd have seen Bart enter a church. Eva

211

didn't question it, but instead offered up a silent word of praise.

"Yeah, I know. Weird huh? I wasn't going to go, but Bart said that he wanted to bring the kids and asked if I wanted to join them. How could I pass up witnessing a lightening bolt through the ceiling on an Easter Sunday?" he asked sarcastically.

Eva ignored his joke and said instead enthusiastically, "I think that's great!"

"Yeah, I'm sure you do," he said with a smile, and for once there was no disdain dripping from his words.

"I play all three services. I'll find you guys after I'm done, all right?"

"Sounds great. We'll save you a seat. Good luck."

He was full of surprises this morning. Never once had he wished her good luck in anything pertaining to her church activities. Her prayers from last night were fast-acting she thought. "Why thank you," letting a kiss linger on his mouth before saying, "I gotta get out of here. I'll see you later!"

He smacked her on her behind as she turned around. "I love you! Now go!"

"I love you too!"

* * *

The moment that Eva saw her husband's family enter the sanctuary a burst of excitement coursed through her veins. The kids started waving excitedly at her and little Lydia screamed with animation when Eva waved back at them. She wondered how long it would be until the baby would be ushered to the nursery, but for the time being she was being good. Bart was holding onto her and Eric had Noah's hand. They smiled at each other and he winked, making her stomach flip for the first time in a long time.

The choral director signaled for her to start the intro with her violin so she snapped back into focus. On the last of the three songs the piano and choir would join her. There was a lot of chatting from the parishioners before she started to play, but once she began silence filled the room. Years ago she got nervous knowing that so many eyes were on her, but now she just got lost in the music.

Luckily the choir sang almost right away once the service began so she could find her seat next to Eric and his family. Little Lydia scurried over every lap until she was on Eva's and the baby gave her a big sloppy kiss. Eva whispered, "How are you, love bug?"

"Ma! Dadamamamama!" Lydia screeched, making almost every head turn their way. And she didn't stop there. She wanted a conversation with Eva right then and there, and after motioning to Eric that she was going to bring her to the nursery, they were off.

Kristin, who normally took care of the education wing during this service, was the nursery leader along with three senior high girls assisting her. "They roped you in to work today, huh?" Eva asked as she handed over a very talkative Lydia.

"Yeah, Shelly Obermeyer called in sick. So I volunteered to take over. How's Lydia today?" she asked the happy child in her arms.

"Really chatty, that's why we are here. And I see that you've got your hands full already," as she looked around at all the toddlers ambling around. There must've been twenty of them. At least they didn't have any newborns to look after as well.

"Yeah, but the girls are great with them."

"Yeah, I enjoy the duty every once in a while, but with this many I'd get overwhelmed!"

"Oh, I think you'd manage. I heard you play earlier by the way. Beautiful as always. I envy your gift."

"Thank you! But hey, I better get back before the sermon starts. Give auntie a kiss, Lyddie," she said, puckering her lips at the child. Lydia leaned forward and gave her a noisy smack. "See you after the service," she said to Kristin.

"Okay," she replied joyfully, over exaggerating the wave for Lydia's sake.

The church had just hired a pastor out of seminary a few months prior and the head pastor gave him the last service on Easter since he had to get out of town and it gave the young man practice preaching to a large crowd. Eva couldn't help but be nervous for him. Chad "Chappy" Chapman was twenty-seven years old and was a former wrestler in college with a medium, stocky build. He still looked like he could pass for eighteen with his spiky brown hair, bright blue eyes and a light-the-world smile. The teenage girls went ga-ga over him, and it didn't help that he was single. There were a few bold senior girls in the youth group who flirted with him which put him on high alert. Everyone, young and old, loved his energy and apparent love for the Lord, but a few had questions where the opposite sex was concerned and how he would handle their advances. So far, he handled it with grace.

His message was personal, talking about the fact that for the first twenty years of his life he was one of those kids that sat in the pew every Christmas and Easter and heard the story of a baby who was sent to earth by God, lived a perfect life, died and rose again. It was a great story, he said, but he left church feeling the same year after year, not knowing how this 'good news' affected his life. He went out of obligation to his parents, who as well went to all the Christmas and Easter services their whole life out of obligation to their parents and etc...

When he was a senior in high school he received a scholarship for wrestling at the University of Minnesota. Wrestling was his life; he ate, breathed and dreamed it. When he went to college, it was his goal to work on his wrestling, aspiring to eventually get into the Olympics, which his coaches had high hopes for him. And with his education, he wanted to get a degree in education with a minor in history. He loved learning about different countries' histories and he loved tutoring kids, which brought him to the conclusion he'd make a good teacher. His freshman year in college, he was paired up with a random roommate, which happened to be someone who was there on a basketball scholarship. His name was Shem Lamont. Meeting that man changed Pastor Chappy's life.

Shem was involved with Campus Crusade for Christ, and every Wednesday night he'd ask Chappy if he'd like to go with him to one of their meetings, and every Wednesday night Chappy always had 'other things to do'. After a short while he knew his roommate had something genuine going on with his faith; when he wasn't studying or playing ball, he was out with his Crusade buddies, was reading his Bible or praying. At first it took him back walking in on this 6'5" huge black man on his knees, but Chappy had to respect that; admire it even. They had a lot of talks about God and what He was doing in Shem's life. One day they were discussing life goals, and his roommate's response puzzled him. He said, "Chappy, I know what I'd love to do, but my life is not my own."

"How is it not your own? Whose else is it?" he joked, not understanding.

"You see, when I was fourteen I gave my heart and life to Jesus. I live for Him, and He directs my way."

"I don't get it. How exactly does He do that? Can you actually hear His voice?"

"No, not audibly. The best way I know how to describe it is this: To me, the Bible is my GPS for life. Everything I need for direction and success is in there. If I mess up, I get into His word and It helps me reconfigure my position. He's also equipped each one of us with specific gifts and talents to be used for His glory. For instance, two of the best gifts He's given me are the skills to play basketball and the love and understanding of the Bible. I had a dilemma which direction to focus on once I got to the college level because I had the pull to go to seminary, but I also had offers to play ball too. So I prayed that He would shut doors that are meant to be shut and open others wide for me to see Him on the other side for me to go through. Well, a few months after that prayer and still not knowing what direction to go in, I got a full ride scholarship here. There were a lot of offers thrown my way, but this was the only offer of an all-expense paid education. My choice was pretty much signed, sealed and delivered right then and there."

Pastor Chappy told the congregation that he and Shem had

been roommates for two years and had become really close. Shem even got him to go to the campus church a few times toward the end of that second year, and it was a lot different than the traditional church he'd gone to his whole life. It was a little uncomfortable for him, not knowing the lyrics to the songs which were on the wall instead of a hymnal, not to mention not knowing exactly what they were talking about due to his lack of scriptural knowledge. But it was refreshing and tangible for him. There were life messages that helped him on a day-to-day basis.

When he got back from winter break, Shem had been talking to Chappy about seriously leaving the U to go to the Moody Bible Institute in Chicago the next school year. After nagging his every thought for two months, Shem applied last minute for the following semester just to see if it might be God's will to do so. It seemed like such a long shot, but when he got in, it seemed to confirm that it was where he was supposed to be. He'd be giving up the rest of his full ride scholarship to follow a higher calling. Chappy knew how nice the scholarship was because he was benefiting from it as well with his wrestling, so he knew what his friend would be giving up. Shem didn't seem concerned about the loss. So, the last week of their sophomore year he announced that he wouldn't be attending the U the following year, making Chappy a little panicked because he was counting on Shem as a roommate in their very first apartment. The last words Shem spoke to him were, "Do not worry. God is in control. If He can get me into Moody last minute, He will certainly find you a new roommate before the end of summer is over. And just remember Chappy, if you want a clear direction for your future, read your Bible!"

Shem was in a head on collision on his way home that day, dying on impact. Every word his friend uttered of God all those years ago still echoed in his head until this day. But it was at his friend's funeral where God had become real to Chappy, feeling as if He had sent Shem as his own personal angel here on earth. Here Shem could have gone to Moody right out of high school, but God had bigger plans for his short life. And apparently it wasn't just Chappy who thought so either because when they gave an invitation to come forward to receive Jesus Christ, seventy-eight others stepped toward the altar without hesitation. Chappy realized that he may think he ran his own show, but after looking at what God did through Shem to get Chappy's attention, he knew differently.

A seed was planted that day, and he surrounded himself with people who were wise in the Word and attended a Bible-based church, going to every Bible study available. It was there that things started to make sense to him: the importance of that little baby in the manger, the Savior of the world. Without Him, there would be no hope: no hope in moving on from this tragedy, and no hope in seeing Shem again. In death we think about life; life that without the death of Jesus, or His resurrection none of us would have it, or the true life which God desires for each one of His creation. And as a history buff, Chappy never knew how much was at his fingertips until he opened the cover of the Bible Shem had given him for Christmas the year he passed on! Remembering from their early discussion, he prayed to God the same as Shem did about opening and shutting doors to his future plans. He fell in love with the Bible, and he didn't know if it was because it was his friend's dream or if it was becoming his own, but he had the urge to apply to Moody that September and he got in for the next fall. The rest, he said, was history.

His message received a lot of hallelujah's and amen's.

Eric sat looking bored out of his mind during the moving sermon, but it was Bart who looked like he received the message loud and clear. But when they gave an invitation to those who haven't received Christ as their Lord and Savior to come forward, he remained seated. There were eight people who came forward, which received a lot of praise Jesus' and more hallelujah's. Both Eric and Bart seemed curious as to what this entailed, since neither of them had ever witnessed an altar call.

"I wanna go up there, daddy!" Noah exclaimed.

"Shhhh, you don't know what it's for," Bart said feeling

slightly embarrassed for his loud son.

"Yes, I do. I want Jesus to come into *my* heart!"

"You can't, Noah. You are too young..." was all Bart said, and it took everything in Eva not to butt in.

"But..." Then his teary eyes looked over to Eva, "Auntie? Can't I go up there?"

"I'm sorry, sweetheart. You have to listen to your father."

Instead of letting it go, Noah scooted past Seth, Eric and Eva and peered into the aisle, watching those who were now at the altar. When the pastor asked them to kneel and bow their heads, Noah followed suit right where he was and Eva couldn't have been more proud of that little boy.

"Eva! Stop him!" Eric hissed.

Eva just gave Eric a quick look and then put a finger to her lips. She saw out of the corner of her eye Bart's leaning forward with his elbows on his knees with his head in his hands. The pastor began, "Repeat after me: Father, I know that I'm a sinner and I'm in need of Your son as my Savior. Please forgive my sins. I invite the Holy Spirit to live in me to help me know Your ways so that I may not sin against you. In Jesus name, amen."

Noah's little voice was heard and people who were around him had their hands out as to send their support his way. It was a beautiful sight and in her silent prayer, she prayed that Bart and Eric would leave the poor kid alone. If they couldn't encourage him, at least don't put him down for his decision. Eva knew it was her responsibility to help cultivate his new-found faith in Jesus.

Chapter 22

Eric was so glad to get home. It was a pretty decent service until the 'incident' with Noah. It felt really cultish to him and he just wanted to get out of there. Not to mention that all he could think about was Claudia and how bad he had to have hurt her. All this talk about sinning, he couldn't help but feel exposed somehow. He knew what he did was wrong, but in his mind he made it right by cutting it off. That made everything all right, right? That's partly why he went so willingly today; to make it up to Eva in a way. Not that she'd ever find out about him and Claudia, but it made him feel better to know he was putting Eva first. All he wanted to do was to make her happy and would do almost anything to make it happen; everything but what he knew she really wanted. Besides a baby, he knew she wanted him to get 'saved'.

He knew the baby subject was going to pop up soon, and he was preparing himself. Now that Claudia was out of the picture he really shouldn't have anything to lose by trying again, but a part of him couldn't think about bringing an innocent human being into the world knowing the uncertainty of life. And this whole getting saved business was for those eccentric people who needed the spotlight on them. Eric believed in God and Jesus, but he didn't need to get all fanatical about it. Getting up in front of a bunch of strangers to profess it seemed a little showy to him. He didn't need the attention.

He panicked when he saw Noah fall for it hook, line and sinker. As for his brother, he had no idea where his mind was. Outside of his first comments to Noah, he just let it go by not addressing it again. But Noah was all smiles, hanging onto Eva afterward. She kept telling him how happy she was for him and that all the angels in heaven were celebrating because of his decision. Filling the kid's head with that kind of fantasy was harmless usually, but to influence an innocent child to cultish behavior seemed almost abusive, but he wasn't going to get into it now. In fact, he probably wouldn't ever bring it up because it's an argument that would have no end. Been there, done that. It wasn't worth the fight.

Eva had invited Bart, the kids, Uncle Ben, Kristin the youth director and her sister Heidi over for lunch. He was relieved that they wouldn't have to see the rest of her family for a while. Heidi wasn't so bad. He hadn't seen her since she had the baby, who was five months old already. But from the sound of it from Eva, she had changed quite a bit. And he wasn't too excited to find out that his wife invited the youth director over. He had had too much church for one day and wasn't looking forward to another revival hour in his living room.

By the time they got home, Uncle Ben was in the kitchen carving up the turkey Eva had put in the oven before church. He had also made the potatoes and green bean casserole. The troops rolled in one by one, with Kristin hanging onto Noah's hand.

"Hi, Uncle Ben! Thank you for helping out!" Eva said, kissing him on the cheek.

"Yeah, thanks Uncle Ben!" Eric said, shaking the old man's hand.

"Well, hells bells! The lost has been found. How are you, son?" he asked with a proud smile.

"I'm great. It's good to be home!"

"Well, thank goodness the time passed by quickly. With these kiddos running around, time flies by at warp speed!"

"I bet. They are like little tornados."

"Hey, Uncle Ben!" Seth said, hugging the old man's waist.

Ruffling Bart's oldest son's hair, he smiled and said, "Hey, trouble. Wanna help me set this on the table?"

"Sure!" Uncle Ben handed Seth a platter the size of him full of turkey and everyone was ready to step in and help him if he were to get into trouble.

Kristin, Bart and Eric guided the other two kids into the living room and all took a seat but Eric who flipped on the TV to see the pre-game showdown between the Vikings and the Cowboys. Addressing his adult guests, he asked, "Can I get you anything to drink? Water, soda, beer?"

"I'll take a beer, bro."

Kristin added, "OOO, that does sound good! But I think I'll stick with water for now."

Eric's questioning look speared laughter from his brother. "I know, right? She's from Milwaukee," Bart said, which should've explained every thing but didn't. Instead it remained an inside joke between his brother and Kristin.

"All right. I'll be back."

Was this some sort of alternative universe he walked into? Since when does a youth leader of a church drink alcohol? Wasn't that some sort of cardinal sin?

About the time he brought the beverages back to them, the dogs were going ballistic at the front door, signaling the last of their guests had arrived. After pushing the pups out of the way, he opened the door to a strange woman holding an angel of a baby in her arms.

"Hey Eric! Welcome home!"

"Heidi?" The hair she had left on top of her head, which was about an inch long all over, was bleached white and was spiked every which way. She was actually dressed normally for once in baggy kackis with a tangerine blouse that hung like a light weight afghan. To him, she was actually quite stunning.

Pushing her way inside, she joked, "Yeah, it being Easter and all, I thought I'd dress up a bit."

"You look great! And who is this little pumpkin?" Eric asked, smiling at the baby which made her giggle.

"This is Moon. Say hi to your uncle, precious!" With that, she handed the light-weight child to him and she snuggled right into his neck. "Awwww, she likes you!"

"She's a cutie. Quite a bit bigger since we saw her at Christmas time! Well, come inside, you are just in time for dinner. Can I get you anything to drink?"

"How about a glass of water? I'm parched after that long ride!"

"Sure!"

Both Bart and Kristin stood up at their entry. "Bart, Kristin, this is Eva's sister Heidi."

Bart nodded. "Yeah, we met at my brother's wedding."

Heidi just smiled and then looked over to Kristin as Eric exited the room to get her a drink.

"Hi, I'm Kristin. I go to church with your sister and she took pity on me and invited me over since I wasn't able to get home."

"Nice to meet you. She took pity on me too. My other sister who normally has me over is in Florida with my mom and dad so here I am!"

"Heidi!" Eva screamed coming from the kitchen and already had Moon in her arms when she came to give her sister a hug. "You made it! Wow, sis, you look great!"

"And look at you, baby! You are fading away to nothing!"

"Not quite, but I'm almost where I want to be."

"Well, you look wonderful!"

"Thanks! Let's all sit down. It's time to eat."

Eva gave a short blessing for the food, and the eating commenced. It was a snug fit around her table, but Eric could see how happy Eva was. She really was in her element when she entertained, which wasn't that often.

He was impressed at how much Heidi had changed. She was still her aloof self, but motherhood seemed to agree with her. When Moon fussed, she scooped her up and was attentive as any mother would be.

And once Uncle Ben found out the youth director's dad was a former career marine chaplain, they discussed military life which surprised Eric since his uncle never discussed that part of his life. It was a closed subject, but now his uncle seemed to recollect the beautiful places he saw, the dives he had for housing on base, the friends he made and the few that he still talked to, more information than Eric learned in the last twenty-one years living with the man. Kristin was a genius at what she did for a living, Eric thought. He was so impressed by the little bit he heard of their conversation, but it was hard to hear everything because he was also trying to carry on a conversation with the kids. They just couldn't wait to see what the Easter bunny had gotten them. Eva told Bart that she had it all taken care of so he wouldn't have to worry about anything. So after the meal, the kids dug into their new treasures, the ladies cleaned up the kitchen, and his uncle went to take a nap on the couch while he and Bart went outside for a smoke.

"I thought you quit," Eric said as he handed over one of his cigarettes.

"I did."

When Bart inhaled his first puff of smoke, Eric laughed. "Yeah, looks like it."

"I just needed one, okay?"

"Okay, okay..." he said, holding up his hands.

Bart observed Eric closely. "How are you doing, bro? You look beat."

"I am. Not used to so much commotion. It's been a while."

"Heidi looks a lot different than what I remember," Bart commented.

"That's because she is. She's grown up a lot I think."

They sat there in silence for a few minutes and when Eric glanced over to see what his brother was doing, he found Bart staring intently at him.

"What?"

"So?" Bart asked, expecting Eric to know what he was talking about.

"So, what?" Eric repeated, confused.

"I can't believe you are going to make me spell it out. Eva's not dumb. She's going to figure it out," Bart said forcefully just above a whisper. "This tired routine is only going to work for a few more days and then she's going to get suspicious."

"Oh," Eric said, finally understanding what his brother's problem was; where he stood with Claudia. "There's nothing to figure out. It's over. I ended it."

Bart put his hand on his shoulder. "It's for the best, bro. It's hard as hell, but you won't regret this decision."

"I know. It's just, oh I don't know. Now that 'Tasha is gone, you ever think about going back to the girl out west?"

Bart blew out a plume of smoke and said, "Yeah, at first I did. But now that I've been away I realize that she isn't what I really wanted. I loved being with her because she was so carefree and fun. She knew I was married with kids. And at first she was fine with that, knowing that I'd be kept at a distance and she wasn't even close to ready for any type of commitment. At the end when she started putting on the pressure, she said it was her or my family. I knew if I chose her, I would never see my kids. She wasn't into them; kinda a theme I have with women, huh?"

"Well, at least you caught yourself before getting in that crap storm of another mess. There is no way I could see my girl being like that. She's a career woman, sure, but I can't see her not embracing someone else's kids."

"Well, luckily you don't have to worry about any of that. You just have Eva to worry about."

"Yeah, so lucky." Eric was done with one cigarette and was quickly onto another. "These taste so damn good I could smoke the whole pack! I've been going through cigarettes fast since I've been home."

"Well, slow down, bud. Don't wanna have to see you in an iron lung before you're forty!"

"Yeah, yeah..." It was a beautiful spring day. The sun was still shining high in the sky and Eric was anything but enthusiastic to get back inside. So he grabbed a few folding chairs which were hanging up from the winter and placed them in the sun, which was half way down the driveway. "Take a seat."

Once seated, Eric said, "Kristin seems all right."

"Yeah, she's cool. Looking at her and talking with her you'd never know she was a Jesus freak, ya know?"

"Yup. It's kinda refreshing. Hope she rubs off on my wife," Eric commented sarcastically.

"What's up with you? What has she done that's gotten you so miffed?"

"I can't believe you'd ask me that! Did you not see your son today? She sat there encouraging him instead of doing something to stop it. And afterward she just sat there, smiling like the cat who got the canary."

"Well, maybe I was wrong to tell him that he couldn't. It's not a horrible thing."

"But it seems wrong to do that to a kid. It's like he's being indoctrinated. He doesn't even know what he was doing."

"Actually, I talked with Kristin about it on the way over here and she said that he most definitely knew what he was doing. She did the same thing at his age and look at her now. She doesn't remind me of someone who is in a cult. Like Eva, she genuinely cares about people and she says it's all about 'soul saving'. I totally don't get it yet, but it's not as scary of an idea as I once thought. She invited me to their Wednesday night adult program and I told her I'd think about it."

Eric looked over to his brother, not believing his ears. "Are you joking?"

"No. I'm seriously thinking about it. I mean if my son is going to get caught up into it, I should know more before I ruin my kid's life even more by ripping him away from people who love him."

Eric stood up quickly, lit another cigarette, feeling instantly agitated. "All of you have gone nuts! I go away for a few months and everyone has gone religious on me. I can't escape it!"

Bart's leg started bouncing up and down, signaling that he was getting irritated as well. "I'm hardly a religious nut, you ass! But I'm not as close-minded as you when it comes to it. What's the harm in it?"

"Nothing...just nothing...just don't bring it around me if you have a 'saving' moment in the process. If you get around too many of them at once it's like they draw you in and you start to lose yourself, just remember that."

"You know more than anyone that no one can change me. I'm stubborn. The only person who changes me is me!" And with that, he left Eric to stew.

Chapter 23

Getting back into a routine with Eric around took some getting used to, especially since he had no set schedule. His laptop and phone arrived Tuesday morning and it was so foreign to Eva. Everyone she knew had them, but both she and Eric really had no use for any type of computer or a cell phone. And after the internet installers came the next day, they were all caught up to the twenty- first century. Eva was just glad she didn't have to mess with any of it because it intimidated her.

By the following day she was ready for him to get to work. On something; anything! He was going stir crazy which was affecting her life more than it ever had before. She had a routine she had gotten into while he was gone and he was messing with it. But instead of complaining about it, she rearranged her schedule so that she worked out every morning instead of some evenings because Eric longed for her to be at home with him at night. It was nice to have him want her, since it was quite the contrast from his initial homecoming. In fact, it was as if he couldn't have enough of her.

Saturday night they were invited to Charlotte's for dinner. He griped a little, but quit when he saw that it meant a lot to her for them to go. But at the last minute, Charlotte called really upset.

"What's wrong?"

"I'm so sorry to have to do this, Eva, but I have to take Summit to the emergency room. We think it's the croup but we have to find out for sure. Tell Eric we're so sorry!"

"Hey! Don't worry about it! Just get that baby well. I'll be praying for her; let me know what happens!"

"I will!"

Eva had just gotten home from work when she got the phone call, so she hadn't even begun to get ready which was a plus. Eric was tinkering on the computer, getting more excited as he played with it. "I don't know what we did before without this thing! You can look up anything on here!" he said as she came into the living room where the computer sat on his lap.

"That's good, hon...That was Charlotte. They have to take the baby to the ER so they had to cancel."

"Awwww, that's too bad," he said, unaffected by the news, but changed his tone when she delivered one of her disappointed looks. "What do you want to do now?"

"I could make us some salads."

"Oh come on! I'm so sick of rabbit food. Let's go out and get some actual human food! I'll take you to The Bierstube. It's all you can eat fish night there. That's still healthy for you."

Instead of pointing out that it would be fried in grease and would be far from healthy, she bit her tongue and then said, "Fine. I'm going to take a shower. I'll be ready in a half hour."

"Fine...fine..." he said, already back engrossed in surfing the internet.

*   *   *

She decided to wear one of her new dresses which made her feel youthful and sexy. She may be a married woman but it wasn't a sin to look good for her husband she thought. And the look on his face when she came out of the bedroom told her that he was paying attention.

He set aside the computer and went to her, grabbed her around her shrunken waist and kissed her passionately. "Was that easy to put on?" he asked.

"Yeah, why?" she responded, giggling.

"Just wondering if it will be just as easy to take off!"

"Eric!" she screeched, trying to fight his advances off. "Aren't you getting hungry?"

"Yup, but my stomach can wait. There are other parts of me that can't."

A half hour later they were scooping their clothes off the floor and reapplying them, this time with a little more challenge from being sweaty.

With a smile, Eva said, "I'm ovulating, you know."

Eric sat down on the edge of the bed hard. "Oh, come on, Eva, not now..."

"Why not now?" she asked, turning to him once her dress was in place. "When's a good time to talk about this? What would be so wrong if we conceived tonight?"

"Eva, our life is just getting on track. I know you want a baby, but I'm going to be gone a lot now...it's going to be like raising it alone..."

"What is this???" she asked, getting hysterical. "You told me that you'd support me! If you didn't want a baby, why encourage me into thinking that it was a possibility when in fact it wasn't?"

"Actually Eva, if you were listening to me I didn't encourage you; not really. Look, if it happens tonight we'll deal with it..."

"*If* it happens? *If* it happens? Let me tell you something, *if* we created life tonight, I can deal with it; with or without you here. I don't know if you were paying attention to what has been going on in my life for the last three months, but I managed quite well on my own thank you very much."

"Listen, hon, I didn't mean to get you upset. I'm just trying to tell you that I don't think I'm ready to be a dad yet. Why can't we just adjust to my new job and see how it will work?"

"How what will work exactly? Our marriage?"

"No! Our schedules and such. If we are going to have a kid I want to be around to see it grow!"

Tears started to slide down Eva's cheeks as she sat down on the bed, defeated. "I'm so tired of waiting, Eric. I feel like we only have a small window of opportunity here. I want your baby so bad!" she said in a small, tired voice.

He slid beside her and held her next to his chest. Kissing the top of her head, he said, "I know, hon, I know." He didn't say any more, to which Eva was grateful. This night was exhausting. "Let's get something to eat," he suggested.

"I'm not hungry," she said like a sulking child.

"Well, I am. Come with me and watch *me* eat."

"Let's go if we are going to go then," she said quickly, exiting the room without looking back. She refused to prolong the fight.

*   *   *

On Monday he had gotten his first assignment in Seattle and would be gone all day but would be back that night. He had been excited to get into it and gave Eva a big kiss before he left for the airport. It had been a busy Monday for her up until the last hour before she left, which gave her time to catch up on the latest tabloid gossip. And after fifteen minutes of scanning the pages, Stephanie came in and drama was written all over her face. "Wanna tell me about it?"

"Justin's a loser."

"Oh no! What now?"

"He 'forgot,'" using her fingers as quotations, "that he asked another girl to prom. 'And he's really sorry'."

"No way! What a dirt bag!" Eva felt for Stephanie. It was hard being a teenager, but then again it was hard being an adult too. If she had to choose, Eva wouldn't turn the clock back for anything. The growing pains were agonizing.

"Yeah. I should've gone with my first instincts and told him to go suck an egg."

"So are you still going to go?"

"You bet your ass I am! In fact, news traveled so fast that by lunch I had another date lined up," Stephanie said proudly.

"Good for you, Steph! Who is he?"

"His name is Norm Kilts; he's a junior, and a smart junior at that. He's also a great athlete and super hot. I could've done worse," she joked.

"Wow! How'd that all go down?"

She laughed. "We have trig together and he came up to me before class started, told me what a fool Justin was and said if I needed a date he'd love to go with me. It's funny, I noticed him before, but he was kinda untouchable, ya know? As far as I know, he's never really dated either and is one of those really focused guys who doesn't have time for girls. I'm sure I'll find out a lot more about him when we go."

"Are you going with a group or just by yourselves?"

"That's the funny part; he knows some of my friends, so we are going with them."

"Well, I'm glad that dress won't go to waste!"

"Yeah, me either. It should be fun, after I get over being mad at Justin, that is. It's just good to know all guys aren't a bunch of jerk wads!"

"Yeah, I got lucky the first time around; although, Eric has his jerky moments too. I think they are all designed with that gene; it just depends on whether or not they have parents or older sisters to whip them into shape. It doesn't sound like Justin had enough knock downs."

Stephanie smiled. "Gotta love your insight!"

"Glad I could help," Eva said in an upbeat voice. "I think I'm going to go now. Barbie should be here in a minute. I'm craving a workout. My trainer is waiting for me at the gym."

"Have fun!"

"Always do!" she said with a wave and was out the door.

* * *

Eric had taken day trips the rest of the week and was usually home by nine. It was like he was back in Italy except she got to sleep next to him every night which was a plus. Her schedule was back on track, which made her happy. However, the following week he was in San Francisco when he called her to tell her that he'd have to stay the night because one of the machine parts wouldn't be there until morning so it was more affordable to stay out there. They both knew events like these would occur so it was just something to get used to.

It was the day he was coming home that she got the bad

news; she got her period. For the past week she tried not to concoct false pregnancy symptoms like she did in the past whenever she was late. Her breasts got tender a few days after her period was due, and after six days without getting it still she tried not to get giddy but she failed miserably. Disappointment flooded through her the next day though when she started to bleed; it practically ripped her heart out. Was this her answer? Was she just being too stubborn not to hear God in all of this? After all, how many times did she hear that her body would probably never produce, or the fact that she didn't even have Eric's support? At that moment she honestly doubted that a baby would ever exist for them. She called in sick because she was so distraught and when Eric walked in that night he found her scrunched into a ball on their bed.

"Eva, what's the matter, baby?"

Her nose was plugged up and she sounded nasally when she choked out, "I got my period today."

He didn't say anything for the longest time, just looked away. But then he said tenderly, "I'm sorry Eva. I really am, but maybe this just isn't the right time for us."

With that she started wailing so hard that it was getting hard for her to breathe. "Just....leave....me....alone!"

"I hate it when you hurt. I wish I could take it away..."

"Leave me alone!"

She didn't even think about how her words affected him as he got up and walked away. Her heart was broken and his words all but crushed it more. He didn't care, she thought. It was impossible to think about how to move on from this point in faith. She was broken.

Chapter 24

Eric loved his job. For the last few months he was traveling every day of the week somewhere along the west coast ranging from Seattle to Dallas, mostly Seattle. However, he was called into his old work one time for maintenance which was a hoot for him since he was on the other side of the business now. The guy they had running his old machine was an old friend who had taken over his former position and he was really frustrated with it. Like they did to Eric, they crammed two weeks of training into two days, and he had been floundering ever since. But the problem was, unlike Eric, this guy was not mechanically inclined. By the time Eric got to the machine, he had to basically de-program everything and start over from scratch and give his friend a 'how to run a cold-saw for dummies' rundown. After a few months on the job, he found that nine times out of ten, it was the same story wherever he was called to. There usually wasn't a major problem with the machine, just operator error. If he could change one thing about how these companies ran their operation, it would be adequate training time. He wrote in his notes and even wrote a letter to the office requesting the go ahead to inform companies that there will be at least two weeks of training on any machine purchased by Malmac, Inc. It would not only benefit the men running the machines but him as well. He figured he wouldn't be called as often to fix stupid errors, and it might save the company money in the long run with traveling expenses as well as hiring a new tech. He hadn't heard from the office, but he took that as a positive sign that they hadn't said no at least.

He was pretty much his own boss, and the only time he had to check into the main office, via the internet, was when he logged his actual working hours and the parts used. What he did in between jobs was his business. It was one of many great perks.

By the end of his first month, Eric found himself doing a lot of overnight trips due to the office trying to stack up his rounds while he was at his destination. It was a great escape from the continuing drama at home. His brother took on a new job closer to home, but he still had to travel within Minnesota and the schedule overwhelmed him quickly. Eva volunteered to take the kids any time he needed her to, which seemed to be every time Eric was home. It was great to see the rug rats, but all he wanted after being gone was to come home to a quiet and orderly house. That wasn't so with the kids around. A few weeks ago Eva had Charlotte's three older boys over as well, which made him want to run for the hills. Eva was really great with them, taking them to the park with the dogs and having painting and clay projects for the older boys and a coloring book for Lydia. He got nervous when he saw her setting up for it in the kitchen, but was impressed when the kids listened to Eva's rules and then followed up by obeying them. Eric was just an onlooker, occasionally stopping in to sing praises on their master pieces. But this was Eva's show and he didn't mind her having it. Being around those kids seemed to be the only time she really was happy lately. And he was all about trying to appease her these days.

It took her about a week to get back to herself after she got that first period once off the pill and she was quickly back into the baby-making mode again. When he complained that he was feeling like a sperm donor, she started to cry and told him how much he didn't care about her or her desires. He just wanted to run away. Being honest with her just hurt her, so avoiding her and the subject made the most sense to him. Would their life ever get to a point where he wouldn't have to hear about making babies every other day? He was beginning to think she'd never give up the mission, and he didn't know how much more he could take.

And it didn't help that he couldn't get Claudia out of his head. He hadn't seen or spoken to her in three months and it was killing him not knowing how she was fairing. He knew he made the right decision, but knowing that he altered someone's life negatively made him feel so guilty. All he wanted to know was if she was all right. Had she moved on? He thought about asking Veronica how she was doing, his contact at the main office and mutual friend of Claudia's, but thought it might raise some eyebrows and he didn't need any more tongues wagging than necessary. After all, what's done was done. Claudia's silence was evidence of that.

It was after the Fourth of July when he got a call from Veronica telling him that he had a new intro class to give, only this time it was in Buffalo, NY. It was exciting for him to get away from the West Coast for a change and he'd always dreamed of visiting New York. He'd done more traveling in the last few months than he had in his whole life and wasn't taking a single moment for granted.

The exciting news was he was green flagged to spend five days instead of the ordinary two to do the introductions, which would give him a reference point of comparison to give to his bosses. Hopefully, there would be an improvement in the men's understanding of the equipment that would show in their work and how often he'd have to go back to make corrections.

It also meant he would be almost a week away from home. At first Eva was a little disappointed but he promised that they would do something together on Friday when he got home. It seemed to appease her, which would make his time away a lot less stressful. For the last month, she'd been a whirl wind of emotions. One day she'd be really happy and then the next four she'd be in a funk. It was like constant PMS and he wanted to pull his hair out. She didn't even want to sleep with him anymore, which told him one of two things. She was either pregnant so she no longer was in need of his sperm or her body hadn't changed all that much inside, which meant that the cysts were forming again, making it impossible for his swimmers to take. They'd been through this two other times, and if his instincts were right, her cysts were back and 'Aunt Flow' had been visiting and wasn't going away any time soon. He figured that if she were pregnant she would've had it sky-written. He didn't know how much longer she'd be optimistic about this. Given her mostly depressed state, he was guessing she wasn't far away from giving up hope, but this time it broke his heart to see her finally realize what he did all those years ago. When she finally confided in him through tears that her doctors wanted to put her back on the pill because her body was out of whack again, she begged Eric to think about adoption, which killed him because his answer would always be no. All he could do was pull her close and say nothing. It was the most uncomfortable silence ever, but it must've spoken a thousand words because she hadn't brought it up again.

*   *   *

It was a beautiful morning when he landed in New York, where he then picked up his rental car and followed his GPS to the shop. He was scheduled for noon and was there with fifteen minutes to spare. It was a peaceful, clean environment and the men were serious learners. But by the time he got to his hotel that night and checked in, he was exhausted. He was walking to the elevator with his duffel bag slung over his shoulder when he thought he saw a girl sitting in the lobby who looked strangely like Claudia. He shook his head, telling himself that he had to stop thinking about her. But just then she looked up and their eyes connected. It was her!

Slowly he walked to her as she stood up abruptly; clutching her multicolored oversized handbag against her chest for dear life, and the look on her face told him that she wasn't there by accident. She was dressed professionally in a red silk blouse, black skirt, hose and high heeled shoes. To him, she was just as beautiful as the day he left her all those months ago.

She was forcing a smile, giving him the impression that she was uncomfortable being there which put him on alert. "Claudia? What're you doing here?"

"I booked this training for you and I knew you'd be here. I had to see you. Can we go somewhere to talk?" She blurted out in a run, batting at the tears that were suddenly falling from her eyes.

He took her in his arms where she remained stiff. "Oh God, what's the matter?"

Pushing back from him, she said, "Eric, please...don't..."

"What? Why?"

She just shook her head and asked again, "Can we please go somewhere private?"

Eric was confused as to what this was all about, but he wasn't going to waste another moment wondering. Pulling her towards the elevator, they only had to wait a few seconds before it opened. It was a silent ride up to the third floor. Eric could only look at her as she kept her eyes to the ground and her bag tightly anchored across her chest. When they got into his room, he threw his bag down on the ground and turned to her. "What's this all about, Claude? Why are you in New York?"

"I work here now."

"There's an office here now? Since when?"

"There isn't an office here. I left the business."

"You what? Why?" Eric sat down on the bed as she remained standing.

"I had a friend who found a job for me in marketing. I had to leave there, Eric. I had no choice." She turned away, and Eric knew she was crying not by the sound she was making but from her shaking shoulders.

He went to her, but sensing him coming, she put her hand out to stop him. "Please...don't..."

"But Claudia..." Eric felt helpless. He was still standing near her when she turned around with now red eyes and a tormented face. "What is..." And that's when she dropped her oversized purse. Beneath it laid the problem. She was obviously pregnant. "Oh, my God..." he said, dropping down hard on to the king sized bed. Looking from her swollen abdomen to her disgruntled face, he got the full picture. But he could barely take it all in. After a few minutes of silence, he opened with, "Please forgive me this question, but is it....is it mine?"

All she could do was nod, holding her mouth and muffled, "I'm so sorry!"

He went to her and hugged her, not letting her push him away. "It's not your fault, baby! It's not your fault." He kissed the top of her head.

"Yes, it is," she mumbled into his chest. But she moved back just enough to look at him in the eyes. "I lied to you. I was never on the pill. That first night things went so fast and I didn't want to stop...and then I figured it was too late to come clean. I thought for sure that it was the safe time of the month. It's never failed me in the past..."

"Oh my God, Claudia..." he said, letting go of her and went to go look out the window. He should've been furious with her, but all he could think of was no matter how it happened, she was pregnant. She didn't get that way by herself. "Oh man," he said as he leaned his head against the cool window and closed his eyes. "So, what did your dad have to say about this? Is he going to can my ass?"

"He doesn't know. I left before he or mama found out. It would shame them so much. I couldn't do that to them! That's why I had to leave and take this job."

"How are you going to keep it a secret?"

"The baby is due the beginning of December, which will give me a few weeks to recover before I go home for Christmas...."

"And what then? Hide the baby in your suitcase? They are going to find out sooner or later, Claude."

"They won't ever know. I'm giving it up for adoption..." she said in a small voice.

"Adoption?!" Eric went over to her and grabbed her shoulders. "No way, Claudia! No kid of mine is going to be adopted out like a puppy."

"What do you suggest we do, Eric?" she snapped at him for the first time since they had known each other.

"I don't know, all right?"

"Well, I do. I'm not ready to be a parent. And I sure as hell am not ready to be an unwed mother."

"We could get married!" Eric hastily interjected. He saw how serious she was about this whole adoption idea and he was

237

desperate to find an answer.

"You already are married, Eric," Claudia stated sarcastically.

"Well, I'm going to have to divorce her. I will not have my child being a bastard!"

Claudia was angry. "For one thing, you made up your mind four months ago when you made that phone call to me; you chose her. And to be honest, you did us both a favor, because even if you did leave her for me it wouldn't have worked out. I would never have your whole heart, because some of it would still belong to her. I'm not now, nor will I ever settle for second best. I was just disillusioned for a few weeks there. As far as our relationship is concerned, it has been dead and buried." He was grateful that she didn't sound bitter; just tired. But there was definitely a finality to it which he took sadly to heart for the second time. It hurt less hearing it over the phone. "And secondly, our child won't be a bastard. He or she will have a loving mother and father. I know there is someone out there who will love it the same way Poppy and Mama loved me," she said with watery eyes. "My mind is made up, Eric. I figured you had a right to know about the baby and my decision, but I wanted to give you an option..."

"An option? An option for what?"

"This baby is either going to go to loving strangers of my choosing or to you..."

"Me?!"

"Yes. You."

Shaking his head and raking his hand through his hair, he said adamantly, "No. There is no way!"

"Why not? I thought you said that you and your wife wanted kids?"

"We do, but...but there is no way. There is no way she'd consider it after knowing the truth."

"Why does she have to know the truth?"

His head snapped up quickly. "You mean lie to her at whose child this is?"

"Not lie exactly; just omit."

"Lying." He stated harshly. "I don't know if I could do it..."

"But you'll think about it? Keep the baby, I mean?" she

asked hopefully.

"I don't know, Claudia. This situation is just so....crazy!"

Eric was now sitting on the bed with his fingers pulling at his hair. Claudia took a seat next to him and said tenderly, "Listen, I know I put you into a really tough place and I'm really sorry. When I found out, one of the first things I did was go to mass because I had thought more than once of aborting it and was in agony at what to do. But when I was on my knees praying and crying out to God the thought of you came to mind. I had already said goodbye to you in my heart, but He reminded me that this child was part of you too. After you left, Poppy and I had talked about you and your wife and he brought up the fact that you weren't able to have children. And I believe a seed was planted that day even though at the time I wasn't interested in hearing anything about you and your wife; especially about your fertility problems. But it was when I was staring at the Virgin Mary that I got such a clear picture of what I was to do. Like Mary, I'm just the vessel used to bless someone with this miracle. It's a little twisted, I know, but you and your wife came to my mind. It was the first time I had some sort of peace about the situation. I walked away that day feeling like this could be sort of like an atonement for what I did. I've always wanted kids, but for some reason I have no desire for this one. It may sound cold to you, but I can't explain why that is... Eric, I hold no ill will towards you. I knew what we were getting into, but it was a mistake that will take a while to forgive myself for. I hate the fact that I was almost a home wrecker, and I guess that's why I'm all right if this secret stays between us forever no matter what happens. No sense in people getting hurt that don't have to. I felt that I had to see you and tell you in person, and I just hope that you'll at least think about it."

"Yeah, I'll think about it. But I seriously don't think it will work. *If*, and I mean *if*, I decide to keep it, you are right, there is no way I can tell Eva that it's mine. Not only would it kill her to know that I was able to impregnate someone else and not her, but it would prove that I was unfaithful. She would leave me and I'd have to raise it on my own; and she's the one who is great with kids! I'd be like my brother, Bart, who carts his kids off to the safest relative or friend to have days on end breaks!"

"I think you'd be a great dad. That's why I'm hoping you'll consider this, Eric. As for your wife, it's really up to you how you handle all of this. But I just want you to know that I don't want anything to do with the baby. Once I hand it over to you, it's closed. That's another reason I had to leave the company. It will be easier to stay away, and the chances of us running into each other will be nil."

Eric's eyes started to tear up from how clinical she was being. He knew she had to be that way due to the subject matter, but at the moment he didn't see how she couldn't be affected by being alone with him again. There were still feelings there for her in him and he was trying hard not to let on. This baby was definitely a complication, and it was hard to sink in that it was his. "I understand. I really need to think about this, okay?"

"Okay...But can I ask you to do me one favor please?"

"What's that?"

"I have my first ultrasound on Thursday. I scheduled it knowing you'd be here and in hopes that you'd come with me..."

"Oh, I don't know. I'll be training almost all day..."

"It's at four o'clock. I made sure to allow you enough time to get through your class. Would you please come?" she asked unashamedly.

"Sure, I guess it wouldn't be a bad thing to do...."

She gave him a hug, which brought to mind too many memories. But he knew he had to get rid of them quickly and remind himself that what they had was dead. "Thank you, Eric. I'll pick you up here at 3:45. The clinic is only a few blocks away from here."

"Okay..."

Claudia picked up her purse, looked back and smiled sadly. "Whatever you decide, Eric, it will be right...Just pray about it..."and she was out the door.

Chapter 25

Eva had finally confided in Charlotte over the battle she faced, shortly after her first attempt at making a baby; even though it took Charlotte to force it out of her. Her friend poked and prodded Eva after bible study when she noticed the usually chatty Eva just going through the motions throughout their discussion, and Charlotte was determined to find out why she was being so quiet. At first Charlotte asked the obvious questions: "Is it Eric? The kids? Heidi? Your mom? Work?" But when Eva shook her head to each inquiry, Charlotte stood her ground and said she wasn't leaving until Eva told her what was going on; she was concerned.

Tears ran down her cheeks, and Charlotte hugged her, rocking her back and forth as she would any of her children when they hurt. "Tell me what it is, sweetheart!"

After what seemed like forever, Eva confessed, "I can't have children!"

Eva could only hear her friend's intake of breath as she held her close and then she said with emotion, "Oh Eva! I'm so sorry, baby! I'm so sorry!"

They both cried more tears and when they separated, Charlotte asked, "How long have you known?"

"For years. That's why I started losing weight. The doctor said that it might help with getting pregnant..." Eva went on explaining her condition along with the fact that if all else failed even adoption was out because of Eric's refusal. "And I thought for sure it would happen this time naturally. I worked so hard! I understand that everything happens for a reason, but this is the desire of my heart; it's what I've been dreaming about ever since Eric and I got married. Instead, I'm watching every one else around me live my dream...and it's so hard!"

Charlotte hesitated, but then spoke with sadness in her voice. "I don't have a clue at what you've been facing. As you well know, I have quite the opposite problem," she added with a chuckle, but it was lost on Eva. "I'm sorry, Eva, had I known..."

"That's why I haven't said anything. I don't need pity; I just need a miracle!"

"Then we shall pray for one!"

"Don't you think I've been doing that? It's all I've been doing since I found out all those years ago!"

"But there is power in numbers, my dear sister! Let us agree in Jesus name, shall we?" Charlotte only had to smile at Eva and they were soon following by bowing their heads. "Father, we know the challenge our bodies sometimes gives us, but we pray that you open up Eva's womb in Jesus' name, and if it be closed, Father I pray that you work on Eric's heart. Soften it so they may adopt a child that you have prepared for just them. Help Eva to move forward in faith and we thank You for the miracle we know that You have in the making here. Give Eva the peace and grace to get through this. May this be the start of healing to her body, soul and spirit. In Jesus name, amen."

"Thank you, Char! I don't know why I've kept this to myself this whole time; it's been such a burden!" Eva said as she hugged her friend.

"Satan loved every minute of your torment too. Let it be a lesson to both of us to not be afraid to burden each other. It feels great to be there for someone, other than the kids and Charley for a change. I sometimes feel useless as a friend. Thank you for trusting me with this!"

"Thank you for listening!"

Eva left that conversation a million tons lighter. She had a new sense of hope and did move forward in faith. No matter the outcome, she knew that God wouldn't give her the desire without following up on it somehow. However, when she started her period that second month and it didn't stop for almost two weeks, she knew her answer. She had been preparing herself for such a reality, but knowing that this was it, it was hard and she needed a shoulder to cry on.

Taking her friend's advice, she showed up unannounced to utter chaos. Both baby Summitt and Brake were screaming their heads off in each of Charlotte's arms and the twins were playing cops and robbers very loudly; the scene only made Eva laugh, breaking her pathetic mood.

"Need extra hands?"

Handing Brake over to her, she said, "I have to somehow put them down for a nap, and Summitt here needs to be fed. Would you mind trying to calm the twins down on their bean bags?"

Brake was still fussing in Eva's arms but wasn't as hot as when Charlotte first opened the door. "Sure," she said, kissing Brake's forehead. It made the baby smile. "Come on, little guy. Let's go chase your brothers!"

It took Eva an astonishing fifteen minutes to gather the twins and settle them down on their bean bags for a nap. Eva had to promise them another over nighter really soon for them to at least pretend to close their eyes. After looking on them for five minutes, she knew they were out like a light. And by that time, Brake was resting his head on her shoulder so she brought him to his crib and laid him down. He fussed, but she just sang him the 'David and Goliath' song, which was his favorite, and he was asleep in no time as well.

Eva found Charlotte in Charley's Race Room, lounging on the couch with the baby huddled under her shirt. "They are all asleep."

Charlotte simply smiled, but she was exhausted. "You have the magic touch. Can I hire you? Those boys are going to be the death of me! I'm just glad I get a little break when Indy is at his friends..."

"It seems overwhelming, but they are sweet. If I didn't love my job so much I'd say yes to your offer in a heart beat! Any time you guys need a break, send them over!"

"Careful what you offer, girlfriend!"

"I'm serious. I figure I can live vicariously through you..." Eva tried holding back the tears, but a dam of them broke forth.

"Oh no! What is it?" Charlotte asked, very concerned.

"I just got back from the doctor...."

"And?"

"And I have to go back on the pill. Losing the weight wasn't the answer. They do, however, give me a 30% chance of conceiving if I do fertility, but the kind they want us on would be out of our own pocket and we just can't afford it. Plus, we decided long ago that I couldn't risk it; too much threat of cancer."

"Oh Eva, I'm so sorry."

"Yeah, I can't question God at this point. I just wish I knew what He was doing. My patience is running out."

"Well, I guess we'll just have to keep up hope that God does His work on Eric's heart."

Eva snorted sarcastically, "The day I hear Eric agree to adoption will be the day I never question God's timing ever again!"

"But in the meantime, wanna watch the kids on Friday night?" Charlotte asked with a witty smile and a wink.

* * *

Surprisingly, Eva was in a good mood considering everything that had transpired at the doctor's office, outside her one desperate plea to Eric about adoption which got her a flat nowhere. Silence was new for him, which only gave Eva some sort of hope that he was at least thinking about it, and she didn't want to rock the boat so she didn't bring it up again. He had called almost every night since he'd been in New York, and he seemed really tired. He didn't have much to say; just that he was really busy. So busy that he wouldn't be back until Saturday now. Something came up where he had to stay an extra day. She was relieved because she offered to watch Charlotte's gang and didn't know how Eric would feel having five kids in the house after a long week.

It was an overwhelming thought at first having all five kids at once, but when Charlotte pulled up to her house and started to unload the van, she got excited. Charlotte and Charley hadn't gone out on a date since the baby was born which was six months ago already. So, she offered to have them overnight. The stipulation was that she had to pick them up by eight the next morning because she had to get to work.

Charlotte had dropped them off around four with instructions a mile long, mostly for the two babies. After reassuring her that she would call if she had any problems, Eva rounded up the troops to the living room. Reddog and Bruiser were so excited to see the kids and she was grateful the dogs were good with them. One less worry.

She had hot dogs and mac-n-cheese ready to go, knowing they were all fans of the food. Indy was such a help with the babies, but found him to be a hindrance with the twins. Knowing it would be a challenge to keep them occupied due to the lack of electronical equipment, she had art projects ready as well as fun games to play.

Around the seven o'clock area, her front doorbell rang, making the dogs go nuts. Indy answered it before Eva could say, "No!"

"Seth! Noah!" Indy screamed excitedly.

"What are you doing here?" Seth asked in astonishment.

Before long, Bart and his gang filled the front entryway. Noah came running towards Eva, hugging her legs. "Hi auntie!"

"Hey buddy!" She had Summitt in her arms and baby Brake was wobbling behind her. Bart had Lydia in his arms and all the boys were conversing at once. Speaking loud enough so Bart could hear, she asked, "What's going on?"

"I needed a break. But I see that you aren't in any position to watch any more..."

She saw how tired he looked and she took pity on him. "Need a drink?"

"Sure..."

He kept Lydia in his arms even though she tried grabbing for Eva as they walked by. Looking back before going into the safe haven of the kitchen, she said, "Indy. Seth. You two are in charge. We will be in the kitchen. No rough housing, all right?"

"All right, Eva," Indy said respectively.

"Okay, auntie," Seth said quickly and then went to playing cars with the boys.

Bart had already helped himself to a beer as Eva found a seat around the table. Lydia was squirming to get out of Bart's arms and into Eva. Summitt was content, and Eva was scared to move her, but said anyway, "Want to trade?"

"Sure, why not. It's been a while since I've held a baby of that size." It was true. Summitt was only fifteen pounds, a very petite baby with very little meat on her bones, but she was as sturdy as a six month baby should be. However, after a few minutes, he set her in the bouncy chair that was sitting on the table.

"Hi baby girl," Eva said, snuggling Lydia in her arms and kissing her cheek.

"Hi!" she said clear as day.

"Well, aren't you a smart little girl!" Eva said, laughing, mystified how quickly they go from being babies to toddlers. She heard Bart opening the beer, which reminded her of his presence. "Been a hard week?"

"You have no idea! Well, I guess you would. I'm just not good at this parenting business..."

"You get an 'A' for effort, Bart. You don't have to be perfect you know."

"I'm not even close. I came so close to slapping Seth tonight, I was so angry with him. The fear I saw in his eyes reminded me of me and my own father. I can't be that man! I'm afraid that I'm screwing those kids up more than if I gave them up to someone who was actually good at this..."

"You aren't your father, Bart. You stuck around when the tough got going and even if you did hit Seth it won't kill him to be punished. I'm a firm believer in spankings when it's merited."

"I never had to discipline them much in the past. That was Natasha's area. I hated it when she hit them and I vowed I wouldn't. But tonight...tonight I came way too close."

"Well, I'm glad you came over."

"Yeah, me too. If I'd known that you were watching the Featherstone kids..."

Batting a hand in the air, she said, "In the words of Charlotte, 'what's a few more?'" and they both chuckled. "But seriously, if you need to get away for a few hours, I can hold down the fort."

"You are an amazing woman, Eva. But no, I wouldn't do that to you!"

"Well, you are more than welcome to stick around if you want. We were about to make ice cream sundaes."

"You are going to need an extra pair of hands for that."

"If you are willing, I'm ready!"

Bart's answer to that was yelling toward the living room with a smile, "Who's ready for some ice cream?" which received screams and yells from every kid in the house.

Chapter 26

Pray about it, Claudia said. For his wife it was something she did hourly, but for Eric it was a foreign concept. What's praying going to do? But because he was about to lose his mind after Claudia walked out the door, he gave it a whirl. The earth was shifting so fast for him that he took a seat on the toilet, just in case he had to use it to deposit his last meal. And that is where he started his prayer. "Oh God, what have I done? What am I going to do? I can't let my kid go to some stranger! But I don't think I can face Eva with it either!"

She doesn't need to know the specifics.

Eric chewed on that for a long time, trying to concoct a believable enough tale that Eva would somehow buy. Maybe he'd run it by Claudia to see what she thought. But then again, she didn't seem interested in how he'd fair in all of this. She had made it clear that she didn't want to have anything more to do with him outside of this baby. What they had together was a mistake. It hurt to hear the truth. He knew it, but had a hard time admitting it to himself.

This decision was the most important decision of his life. To him it paled in comparison to getting married, taking his new job and his choice to have an affair. This was an innocent child who could potentially be put in a bad situation if the truth were to be revealed. He knew Eva was a forgiving person, but there was no way in Eric's mind that she'd be *that* forgiving.

For the next few days, Eric was glad to have work as a distraction. He worked long days, but the environment was abnormally peaceful for a factory. Usually there were undercurrents of tension between the general laborers and the management teams. Eric didn't know if it was different there because it was a non-union shop or if they all just got along that well. Two nights after Claudia's announcement, he happily accepted an invitation to one of the supervisor's house for supper. Normally when he was asked to dinner they'd take him out to a nice restaurant, but after convincing Eric that his wife was the best cook in town, he couldn't refuse the offer. There was nothing like home cooking to Eric. David Reiche had a young family, with two little girls ages two and four. Eric could see how much he loved to be at home with them. It was as if the office work never walked through the front door with him. David was the same at work as he was around his wife and children, which impressed Eric. He and his wife, Shelly, were really interested in learning about Eric, but he wasn't one to dish no matter how nice someone was. He needed to know someone a while before he really opened up to them, so he kept his responses pretty vague without being rude. Last night at the hotel he felt like he was losing his mind thinking about Claudia and the important decision he had to make, so Eric was grateful for the Reiche's dinner offer; being alone did him no favors. It was a great distraction.

* * *

Eric hadn't heard from Claudia since she left the hotel Monday night, but knew she'd be where she said she'd be. He was in the lobby of the hotel at 3:40 on Thursday and she entered right at 3:45 like she promised. She was in casual attire, wearing mid length jean shorts and a light blue and white checkered pregnancy blouse. Her long dark hair was pulled back into a high ponytail and it swung back and forth as she walked. Again, her oversized handbag was planted in front of her, masking the evidence of their affair.

"Ready?" she asked, sounding as if she wasn't ready herself.

"Ready as I'll ever be."

"I figure we could walk? I need the exercise."

"I could use some too."

On their way, Claudia asked how the training was going, keeping it light between them. "It's actually been a great work environment. They are grasping the material okay, maybe a little slow on the take, but I tell ya it makes all the difference in the world if you have good management. This place works like a well-greased machine."

"Yeah, Poppy was telling me that he had a great conversation with the owner; Edward I believe his name was."

"Yeah, he's a hands on owner. Plus his head supervisor is a stellar guy. Has a great business sense, is fair and is really patient. I don't see that a lot, especially in big companies like this outfit." As the clinic neared, Eric's stomach started to flip over. When Claudia continued talking about Malmac, Eric had to stop her. "I'm sorry, Claudia. Can we give the topic of work a rest, at least for a little bit? I have to get my bearings..."

"Oh...sure..."

Eric saw that he stunned her by his abrupt words which made him feel awful. "This is so overwhelming, for both of us. How are you taking this all so in stride?"

"I've had three months to digest this, Eric. I really appreciate you coming with me. I thought talking about work would be a safe subject for us..."

"I know. It's just; this is major! I can't think about anything else right now..." They walked up to the clinic doors, which Eric held open for her. "Well, here we go!"

After Claudia signed in, they were only waiting a minute before being called back. The nurse came in and asked if she had a full bladder, which she did. After Claudia got situated on the hospital bed, the nurse turned off the lights, pulled the curtain and asked Claudia to expose her belly. "Nothing like getting right down to it," Eric joked quietly, which got a chuckle out of Claudia.

"Now how far along are you?" the nurse asked as she got everything situated.

"Sixteen weeks."

"Well, okay. Let's get started. This gel will be warm." Eric looked down at her swollen belly and was amazed that it could stretch that much. He couldn't imagine another five months of growth on her small frame. There were horizontal red marks from her navel traveling south. "Are you moisturizing? Your skin looks irritated," asked the nurse.

"No, I haven't. It's just been this past week that it has been itching."

"It's from your skin stretching. Try using cocoa butter; it's really soothing."

"Oh, all right."

"Ahhh, here we go!" the nurse said excitedly. "See there? That's the head, and there's the hand..." Eric was so surprised that it was so lifelike. It was being photographed in 3-D so it took a few seconds per frame. It was after she took the picture of the foot that she stopped and gave a, "Well, would you look at that!"

"What?" both Eric and Claudia asked, squinting at the screen trying to see what the nurse was pointing out.

"See that there? That shadow?"

Eric had to move closer to the screens, but he saw it, but he didn't know what he was looking at. The nurse continued cautiously, "I might be mistaken, but I think there might be another baby! Let me try another angle."

Claudia looked at Eric with terror in her eyes, and he grasped her hand with both of his. He didn't have to say anything to let her know that no matter what she wasn't alone in this. The nurse now had the wand right above her navel where she got a shot on the other side of the baby. And that's where they all saw it. The babies were back to back, which cast a shadow in the original picture. As excited as the nurse was, Claudia snapped, "But how can that be? When I had my last appointment they only heard one heartbeat!"

"That happens once in a while. Sometimes their hearts beat in sync."

"Oh. My. God," was all Claudia could say.

"Twins?" Eric asked just to make sure he wasn't seeing or misunderstanding things.

The nurse took their reaction to mean that this wasn't the best news ever, so she took her cue and left the room, telling them that she'd be back with the pictures.

"Could this get any worse?" Claudia scolded herself.

251

"Not by much," Eric responded, leaning back into his chair.
"I suppose you are going to run for the hills now..."

"I didn't say that," he said, sitting up.

"Your look says everything, Eric."

"My look, as you put it, is still digesting everything, Claude.
My God....twins! We are going to have twins!" he said with a
half of a smile, mystified.

"Um, correction, Mr.Wahler. *You* are going to have twins."

Standing up and pacing, he vented, "I can't believe even
after seeing our children on that screen that you'd still be up
for all that you suggested. There has to be a way to keep you a
part of their lives!"

"Eric, there isn't. I'm telling you, this is for the best. I
know you'd do a great job in raising them!"

"I don't know, Claude....Twins! This is a lot to think about..."

"And I hate to rush you, but I'd really like an answer soon. If
you aren't for it, I have to get going on finding prospective
parents for these babies. Twins are a hot commodity these
days!" she joked.

"That's not funny, Claude."

"I'm not entirely joking, Eric. I want to know your decision
soon. The only way I'm going to make it through this
pregnancy is knowing that these babies are going to a good
home and I don't want to waste any time if you aren't
interested."

The nurse came in right then and handed them the pictures.
"One set enough for you?"

Eric just looked at Claudia, who just nodded in response to
the nurse. "All right then, you are free to go."

Claudia walked Eric back to his hotel in silence but didn't go
inside. Instead she hugged him briefly, handed him the
pictures and said, "Call me soon, okay?"

"Okay," he said, half smiling.

"If you have any questions, or anything about this, just call
me. Anytime."

"I just may do that."

"Bye, Eric."

"Bye..." Claudia turned to leave and he stopped her by grabbing her hand and whirled her around. Putting his hand under her hand bag, he felt her stomach for the first time. It remained there while he aimed his words at her belly, "I'll be thinking of you, little ones. If I decide to be your daddy, it will make me the happiest man in the world. But if you get someone else as your daddy, just know that I'll always love you...and I'll never forget you..." He then kissed his other hand and placed it next to the one lying on her belly, and then turned and walked away with tears in his eyes.

Chapter 27

It had been a month since Eva's last doctor's appointment where she had gotten the news that her condition hadn't improved. God had closed the door on her having her own child, but she still held out hope that Eric might change his mind on adoption. She wouldn't think about the possibility of Him never coming around on that. Instead of focusing so much on the day that Eric would change his mind, she kept busy doing almost everything she'd always done.

Ever since Eric had come home from Italy, she had tried cutting down on her extra activities by prioritizing them. Bart's kids, working out, church and her Friday night Bible study were the four things she wouldn't give up outside of work. It pained her to do so, but once the school year ended in June she told the choir director that she had to step down from being in the choir and as the violinist, but promised that she'd be willing to do a special number once in a while. It just so happened that a few weeks after she resigned that position, a new family joined the church that happened to have a daughter who was an experienced flutist in the high school band. She did a beautiful job and Eva was grateful that someone else stepped up to offer up their talents.

She was a little sad that Mitch gradually disappeared from her life, but knew that it was probably for the best. The last time she saw him was at church the last weekend in June. He caught up with her after the service, inquiring why she wasn't in the choir anymore.

"I just don't have time."

"Oh, well; you are missed," he said with a sincere smile, but something in his eyes were different.

"Mitch, is something wrong?"

"No, why?" he asked, but as soon as he looked away she knew he was lying.

"Tell me," she coaxed.

Shrugging his shoulders, he said, "I don't know. I've just been lonely lately. We never see each other any more. Not that I depended on you for my sole entertainment, but it sure was nice to have someone like you to talk with; to be my sounding board. I don't feel like I'm welcome to call or stop by anymore..."

Eva knew what he meant. There were times during the day when she'd think of him or his girls, but she slapped her hand when they touched the phone to call him. "Yeah, it's probably good that you didn't. Eric has a problem with us being friends. It's nothing against you personally; it's just any man who would befriend me. He's been going through a jealous phase and I'm not sure where it's coming from."

"I'm sorry, Eva. I don't want to get you into trouble with your man. That was never my intention."

"Don't worry about it. I'm sorry if you feel I've been avoiding you. It's just that I don't want to do anything to rock the boat right now. Flaunting our friendship would probably tip it right over."

"I understand. I'd probably be the same way. I just want you to be happy."

She simply smiled...and lied. "I am."

"Good," Mitch added quickly.

There was an awkward silence, which Eva hated so she said, "Well, I should probably get home. Maybe I'll see you at the gym or on the road!"

"That would be nice...And Eva?"

"Yeah?"

"Take care of yourself. I'm always a phone call away if you ever need to talk."

"Thanks, Mitch. I'll remember that!" Eva wanted to say the same to him, but she thought telling one lie was enough. If she wanted her marriage to survive, there could be no more communication between them. This, she knew now, was God's will.

But at the moment she didn't worry about it too much

because her number one priority was to work on her marriage. With Eric gone so much it was almost like it was when he was in Italy. People joked that they were still together after all these years because of how much time they spent apart, but the truth was that this was one of the most challenging times in their marriage. It was hard to communicate by phone. Half the time they were playing phone tag, but unlike Italy they were both making better attempts at reaching each other. For the first few months she was okay with him being gone so much, but now she was getting lonely again. Instead of complaining about it, she buried it deep and focused totally on him when he was home; even if he was grumpy. She tried putting herself in his shoes and knew it couldn't be easy living out of a suitcase, living in airports and hotels alone, and being away from the people you loved. So she ended up biting her tongue a lot and prayed.

* * *

Eric had been gone Monday through Friday for three weeks in a row since his trip to New York and she missed him. She was pleasantly surprised to see him rough housing with the dogs on the living room floor when she came in with the groceries the first Friday afternoon in August because she wasn't expecting him until later that night. Smiling, she said, "You're home! I didn't think I'd see you until tonight!"

He stood up, went to her and gave her a quick kiss. "I got an earlier flight."

The groceries in her hands were getting heavier by the second. "Here, let me help you with those," Eric said.

While they were unloading them, Eva noticed how thin Eric had gotten. Traveling must be taking its toll on him, which made her take the cans out of his hand and say, "I can handle the rest of this. Why don't you sit down and relax? You must be tired."

Stealing the cans back, he snapped, "I'm not a damn invalid, Eva."

Putting her hands up, she said, "I never said that you were. You just look tired; I was just trying to help."

After placing the cans into their proper place, Eric shut the cupboard doors and just stared at them for the longest time before he turned to her and gave her a hug. "I know; I'm sorry. You are too good to me."

Something was wrong; she could feel it. "Eric?"

Eric only held her tighter.

"Hon? Um, I can't...breathe..."

"I'm sorry," he whispered, letting go of her. "I guess...we need to talk."

Eva's heart started to beat really fast. The troubled look on Eric's face told her that whatever he had to say, she wasn't going to like. But calmly, she said, "All right. Let me put the eggs and milk away..."

Eric walked out of the room without another word and Eva found him sitting on the couch with his elbows on his knees, staring at the floor. When he heard her come near, his head snapped up and she saw that his eyes were red. It worried her. Sitting next to him, she put her hand in between his. "Please, just tell me!" Her eyes glistened with tears. Her mind was racing....Did he lose his job? Is that why he's home so early? Was he sick? Did something happen to Uncle Ben? Or the kids? Dear God, not the kids!

He didn't look at her when he said, "A few weeks ago I ran into my boss's daughter in New York. Actually, she found me to tell me something..."

Eva was listening, trying to follow every word, relieved that it wasn't about any of her initial worries, but still not knowing where this was going. "What was it?"

That's when he looked at her and hesitated. "Now I know that you'll say yes in a minute but before you do I have to tell you everything..."

"What is it?" Eva asked hysterically. The suspense was killing her.

"She's pregnant, with twins...and she wants us to adopt them."

"*What?*" Eva asked with part excitement but part unbelief as well. There was no way it would come this easy.

"Now listen, nobody knows besides me. She was working for her dad in Italy but when she found out she was pregnant she moved here until she had them. She found out it was twins when I was in New York with her. When her dad and I were fishing one day I had told him that we weren't able to have kids and that information must've gotten to her. She told me that she was going to abort it, but one day in prayer she thought of us. I told her I'd think about it and that I'd have to talk to you..."

Wow, if that wasn't divine, Eva thought, but instead she asked, "Oh, Eric, are you serious? How serious is she? Like, you don't think she'll change her mind, do you?"

"No. She's dead set on it."

"What about the father? Isn't he in the picture?"

"Not anymore. She said that wouldn't be a problem. In fact, there might be a way around all the legalities."

"What do you mean?"

Taking a deep breath in, he asked, "Before I say anything more, are you interested in doing this?"

"Are you kidding, Eric? It's all I've been praying for, for years!" Eva was literally shaking with excitement. She could barely contain it. All she wanted to do at that moment was hug Eric silly and shout from the roof tops how awesome God was!

"Okay, but you might not like this part..."

"What part is that?" Eva asked, not fazed a bit by his tone of voice.

"She wants me to be on the birth certificate as the father."

"What? Is that legal? Doesn't there have to be proof?"

"According to Claudia, and yes she's done the research, all the hospital needs is for me to be there to sign it. And with that, Claudia will sign over all rights to me and all we'd have to do is go through the paperwork to have you as their legal mother."

"Whoa, whoa, whoa, slow down. What are you not telling me here?" Eva wasn't in so much a fog that she didn't see red flags all over the place.

"I'm telling you everything. Claudia has checked with legal counsel about this. As long as I'm on the birth certificate, the babies are legally mine. The minute she gives birth to them, her lawyer has already drawn up papers for her to sign over full custody to me as well as giving up her rights to them. Within six months, they will be ours forever."

"It just sounds too easy...and too good to be true," Eva said skeptically.

"It does, but believe me; it's legal. That's why it took me so long to talk about it with you. I wanted to know that we wouldn't end up in prison over it."

"So you've been carrying this around, for what, a month now?" Eva didn't know if she wanted to kiss him for trying to protect her while he did the research or throttle him for not telling her what was going on sooner.

"Only a few weeks," he said quickly. "I just didn't know what I wanted to be honest. But when she showed me the ultrasound pictures, it became real to me that these babies could be ours."

"Do you still have the pictures?" Eva asked cautiously.

"Yes," he said, and then gulped.

"I want to see them."

Eric went into the bedroom and came back with a large manila envelope. There were four pictures, showing two perfect babies. It brought tears to Eva's eyes. "Please tell me that this isn't some sort of a joke, Eric."

"It's no joke."

"Is this what you want? I mean, really want? Because just a few months ago you didn't even want to talk about the possibility-"

He cut her off by saying, "It's what I want. Opportunities like this don't happen very often. She is the daughter of a great friend and boss. She trusts us to keep this secret. No one is to know who she is to them."

Those were simple terms, Eva thought. She was finally going to be a mom! "Oh, Eric! We are going to have twins! God is so good!" Eva cried into his chest.

"Yes....Yes, He is," he whispered into her hair.

Chapter 28

"You told her what?" Claudia asked, not amused.

"I told her that my name will be on the birth certificate."

"And she has no idea that you're really the dad?"

"None," he said with confidence as he reclined back on his hotel chair. Eric had called Claudia because he had no one else to talk to about this. It was a huge weight on his shoulder and for now he had her to be a sounding board. He was about to tell Eva the truth, that he was the father of the babies, but the lies rolled off his tongue so fast and easy that he couldn't stop himself once he got started. Eva bought every one of them. The only truth to what he said that day was that everything they were doing was legal. He knew he had a few months to come clean, and he might, but for now everything at home was peaceful and happy. Eva was beyond being overjoyed and back to her normal self. Knowing he was the cause of this was enough to take the edge off the guilt for a while. But when he was alone in the hotel he thought of every possible bad scenario that could arise from this, which almost made him pick up the phone that night and tell Eva the truth. There was power when he wasn't face to face with her. But instead, he called Claudia whom he hadn't talked to since that Friday night in New York when he called to say that he wanted the babies. It took him another few weeks to figure out what to say to Eva, even though it didn't go quite as he imagined.

"I'm happy that you are taking them, Eric." She was in New York and he was in San Francisco but it felt like they were right next to each other.

"So am I. It's overwhelming. I don't know how to do this without putting you on the spot, but I told Eva that I'd ask you..."

"What is it?"

"She wants to meet you."

"Not possible," Claudia said abruptly.

"That's what I told her; that you wanted to keep this as private as possible. She just wants to thank you in person..."

Eric faded off, knowing how this must sound to the woman who was carrying his babies. It was a lot to ask, and it put them both in an awkward situation. Claudia said, "I'll tell you what, how about I call her and talk to her? Do you think that would appease her? I just can't face her, Eric. She would see through this whole farce in five seconds by just looking at my guilty face. At least over the phone I can fake it 'til I make it."

"Would you do that? I know it would make her day. This really has been a dream come true for her...But I also know this has got to be so hard for you." Eric felt both sides of this situation and was so conflicted.

"It is, but knowing that they are going to be with you is making it easier to accept. All I can do now is enjoy the process. I felt them move for the first time during a meeting the other day. It was so beautiful I started to cry. Since my colleagues all know my dirty secret now, they understood my emotional state."

"God, Claudia, I'm so sorry I put you in this situation."

"We're totally over the apologies, Eric. What's done is done. Let's move forward, shall we?"

"I hate your positive attitude," he joked.

"I'm hoping that I rub off on you soon." He could hear her smile in her words.

"Thank you for listening to me. I don't really have anyone else to go to with this."

"I don't mind. It's nice having someone in your corner when you are feeling all alone in crises. I'm confident that all this will work out though. I hope you are getting there too."

"In ways I am, by how easily Eva agreed to it. But there is a fear that the truth will come out. I'm not confident in knowing Eva's reaction."

"Who is going to tell her? Not me, I hope you know."

"Yeah, I trust you. It's just a fear I have. So many times tonight I wanted to pick up the phone and tell her, but something stopped me. That's why I called you. I need to hear that I'm doing the right thing by keeping this from her."

"Honestly, Eric, I'm just as confused as you are. It's killing me not to tell my parents about this. But I know in the end it's for the best all around that they don't know. I know they would encourage me to keep the babies and would help me raise them. But every fiber in my being screamed "NO" every time I even thought of it. As far as I'm concerned, these babies aren't mine. I'm just carrying them for you and your wife," she said clinically.

Eric paused and pondered what she just said and it angered him. "I don't understand how you can be so nonchalant about all of this, Claudia. I know what we did together was wrong, but children were conceived here. *Our* children. I resent the fact that you treat our time together as if it never happened and this situation as normal. It's *not* normal. Its hell knowing that you live with our mistake every day, and I'm going to reap the reward in the end. And where will you be? How is this really going to affect you in the end? See, this is what I think about all day long. Just because I chose Eva in the end, doesn't mean that I don't care for you."

"Eric, yes I live with our mistake every day, but I try not to remember what we had. It hurts too much," she admitted softly, but then dramatically changed when she said, "Dammit, I resent the fact that you won't let what we had go. It has to be forgotten for us to move on from this. I have to be detached because what matters most is these children, not us, and not how they were conceived."

Eric never cried so much in his life. Her words hit home. Clearing his throat, he said, "Okay. Enough said."

"Good. Look, I don't mind being here for you, but this has to stay completely about the babies. If at any time the conversation ventures to us again, I'll hang up on you."

"I totally understand," Eric said with a lump in his throat. He dreaded the answer to this question, but he asked anyhow, "And after they are born? Will I hear from you again?"

"No. I think it's for the best if I just disappear, don't you?"

"Whatever you decide, I'll respect."

"Thank you, Eric," she said with gratitude and then asked, "So, when is a good time to call Eva?"

It was the first time he heard Claudia call Eva anything other than his wife, which took him back for a second. Swallowing another lump in his throat, he said, "She's involved in a lot, so it's hit or miss with her. It's probably best to try Sunday afternoon."

"Would it be easier to just give her my number?"

"Would you mind?"

"Would I ask if I did?"

"That would be great, Claude! Thank you!"

"You're welcome. I'm tired, I'm going to bed now."

"Good night."

"Good night, Eric."

After he hung up the phone with Claudia, he closed his eyes and thought of their conversation. He understood why she was saying and doing the things she was, but it still hurt after all they had shared with each other. It would take him a lot longer to forget about her than it was for her to forget about him. He realized now that what they had was a product of loneliness mixed with a whole lot of lust and hormones. But now he would love her for bringing children to him and Eva where they probably wouldn't have had them. Claudia was a catch, no doubt about that, he thought. But like she pointed out, if he'd chosen her over Eva, there was no way that she'd get all of his heart. As he prayed that night, he asked God to forgive him for keeping the truth from Eva, and he made a deal with Him that if his secret was never found out, he'd promise to go to church every Sunday...once the twins were born. No need to be hasty, he thought.

Chapter 29

Before Eva said anything to anyone about the adoption, she had to talk to this Claudia. It still seemed like it was too good to be true. How could someone just give away their babies so easily? she wondered; especially someone coming from a wealthy family who would have all the resources to raise a child. Eric gave her the few basics that he knew of the girl. She just turned 29, was adopted herself when she was a toddler and had a degree from the University of New York in marketing. As far as Eric knew she wasn't dating anyone, and couldn't tell Eva anything about the father. There were so many questions Eva had for Claudia, and she hoped that she would not have to wait a long time until she had her answers. As it was, two weeks had gone by without a word as to when they would meet and it was making her nervous. She didn't want to rock the boat with Eric, fearing that he'd put a kibosh on this whole thing if she got too demanding.

Luckily the salon had seen the school rush they were anticipating, but by the end of every work day Eva was exhausted. It was mid September and the excitement of homecoming was in the air. It was all lost on Eva because all she could think about were the twins. *Twins*! It took everything in her not to call up Charlotte and let her in on it, but she had to know for sure before getting her hopes totally up.

Eric left for Montana that Wednesday morning and said he'd be back that night. Their relationship had improved so much over the last month or so, getting back to how they were when they were first married. Her heart throbbed once again. The stars were lining up, and she felt truly blessed. She still couldn't believe that he changed his mind about adoption; and so suddenly. Even though they weren't his lineage, he talked as if the twins were already theirs which warmed her heart.

Eva couldn't take it anymore. When Eric got home that night, she asked him if he talked to Claudia and if he did, what did she say about meeting up with them?

"Yeah, I asked, but she said that it would be easier on her if you just called her. Here's her number," he said, taking a scrap of paper out of his wallet.

"Can I call her anytime?"

"I assume so. It's her cell phone, so I imagine she'll have it on her."

Eva looked at the clock. It was 8 p.m. which meant it was 9 New York time. "Do you think it's too late to call tonight?"

"No, she's a night owl."

"How would you know?"

Eric suddenly busied himself in the kitchen, putting dishes away. "She told me so when we talked. I guess it's hard for her to sleep...being uncomfortable and all that..."

Eva was appeased by his answer and was too excited to wait any longer. "I hope she is doing all right. I'm going to try calling her."

"Go for it," he said, kissing her before leaving the room.

Eva took a seat on the couch and dialed the number on the scrap piece of paper. It only rang twice when she heard a sweet feminine voice say, "Hello?"

"Hi, is this Claudia?"

"Yes, it is. Who is this?"

"Um, this is Eva Wahler, Eric's wife?"

There was a pause then, "Oh yes, I've been expecting your call."

Eva's eyes instantly filled with tears. "Wow, this is really happening! I don't know what to say, or ask, but I guess I just want to say thank you! I've been praying for this for so long, I was about to give up hope!"

"Well, I'm just glad that you guys are agreeing to this. It's nice knowing that they will be going to good parents. Eric talked about you all the time. He told me how good you were with kids."

"Eric is great with them too; you should see him with our nieces and nephews!"

"Yes...yes I can imagine."

There was a small pause, in which Eva prayed quickly to

find the words. "Claudia, are you sure you want to do this? I mean, Eric said that you are adamant about it, but I'm just scared that you'll change your mind. I've been through a lot when it comes to this roller coaster ride of trying to conceive that I don't think I could take it if you did. I've heard of horror stories of adoptive couple's planning on getting a baby and the birth parents getting cold feet. I guess I just need to know that this is really going to happen."

"Rest assured; I've never been more positive about anything in my whole life."

"Really?" Eva asked hopefully.

"Really."

"What about the father?"

"He's okay with it," she answered in a monotone voice.

"Are you sure he won't come back for them?"

"That's why Eric's name is going on the birth certificate. That way, no one has claim over them but Eric and me until I sign off on them."

"And this will really work?"

"Of course. My attorney has all the paperwork drawn up. You and Eric will be able to take them within forty-eight hours if all goes well."

"Wow!"

"Yeah, pretty cool how that system works."

Eva really liked Claudia. She seemed really calm and collected and seemed to know what she was doing, which appeased her. "So I can start telling people?"

"Tell away," Claudia said happily.

Eva was beaming one minute and then suddenly she felt Claudia's burden. How must it feel to carry babies and to know that you'll be giving them up for someone else to raise? So with compassion she asked, "How are you feeling?"

"Besides getting fat and really emotional I'm great. The babies are great. Any more questions?" Eva could tell that Claudia was anxious to get off the phone.

"Yes! Too many! But do you think I can think of any right now?" Eva laughed and cried at the same time. This was really going to be a reality.

"Well, before I go I have one for you. Do you want to know the sexes of the babies?"

"Ooooo, good question! You know, I always said that I'd want it to be a surprise, but knowing that it's twins I have two to get ready for. So I think I'd love to know!"

"Right now?"

"You actually know right now?" Eva asked excitedly.

"Yes."

"Oh my! Let me get Eric on the line."

"Okay, I'll wait."

Eva found Eric lying down on their bed with his eyes closed. "Eric? Are you sleeping?"

"No," his eyes remaining shut.

"Do you want to know the sexes of our babies?" she asked with a bright smile.

Eric popped up so quickly she was afraid he would hurt himself. "She knows?"

"Yes! Get on the other line! Quick!"

By the time she got back on her phone, Eric and Claudia were talking. She heard Claudia say, "...to know."

"Hi, I'm back!" Eva said happily.

"All right. You both sure you want to know? Or do you want to guess first?"

"Just tell us," Eric said.

Eva thought it would be fun to guess, but at this point she didn't really care. Claudia said, "It's a boy and a girl."

"What more could we ask for?" Eva said through tears.

"That's great, Claudia," Eric added with emotion.

"Thank you both for doing this. Like I told Eric, Eva, these are your babies. I know you will both love them as if they were your own. Even though I know this, the reality is that it's going to be difficult for me. So with all due respect, I can't see you guys when you come to the hospital for them. I'll call when I go into labor. Since Eric's name is going to be on the birth certificate, he needs to be here within hours of the delivery. Thank you again, Eva, for letting Eric do that. It will cut down on your expense and red tape."

"It makes sense to me," Eva said, but really feeling conflicted over all the secrecy.

"And another thing," Claudia added.

"What?" Eva asked.

"After all this is over? You don't know who I am, you've never talked to me, I don't know you; which is another reason I can't meet you. It's nothing against you. Under other circumstances I would have loved to get to know you, but I have to do this in order to heal. Even though I know Eric, he knows that after this there will be no communication between any of us."

"I understand, Claudia. We respect your choice."

"Thank you. And if you have any more questions or anything before then, call me. I'll get back to you in one way or another."

After ending the conversation, Eva just sat there. This was going to happen! Eric came out and sat next to her on the couch, pulling her close. "Feel better?" he asked.

"Much. She is so nice!"

"Yeah...she is..."

"And you are sure you want to do this? No turning back?"

He paused before saying, "I'm not going to change my mind."

"Good. Because I'm already in love with those babies!"

Eric was silent, but continued to hold her. Eva loved being close like that and hoped this was the new start of their lives.

* * *

Eva decided to tell her Bible study group that Friday night. Usually at the beginning of the study, people would ask for prayer as well as give testimonies. All Eva came before with was prayer requests a mile long for her family, but after she listened and took notes of people's prayer requests this time, it was finally her turn to share. All ten of the women who showed up religiously were there and all were her dear sisters in Christ, ranging from 25-60, only one of which knew her struggle with infertility. She started, "Well, I have a praise report..." That seemed to get everyone's attention. "But first of all I have to confess something, something that Char already knows." Charlotte's eyes filled with tears and with an affirming nod, coaxed Eva to continue. "I've been trying to have a baby for almost eight years now with no success. To make a long story short, I have a lot of female problems and I thought I had them solved after losing all this weight, but God had other ideas. Ever since Eric and I got married, I've desired to be a mom so bad, but when it wasn't happening let's just say I've been broken over it more times than not, and up until a month ago, Eric was against adoption..."

"No way! He changed his mind?" Char asked excitedly.

Eva nodded, and then added with happy tears, "And it gets better. His boss's daughter is pregnant out of wedlock with twins, and she wants to give us her babies."

The room was filled with, "Oh Eva, that's wonderful! Congratulations! Praise God!"

Kristin asked, "When are they due?"

"December first. We will have them by Christmas!"

Charlotte came over and hugged her. "What a timely gift! God is so good. He doubly blessed you guys! And Eric is really cool with all of this?"

"Strangely, yes. That's the true miracle here."

"Well, if God can part seas and move mountains, He can change the heart of a man!" Charlotte proclaimed.

"Amen," the ladies chanted.

Instead of getting into the study that night, Eva's testimony was talked about and dissected the whole hour. It gave them all hope knowing that they served a big God who listened to prayer. It wasn't always in our timing or how we thought it would go, but He is always making a way, working in ways we can't see to make everything come together for His glory.

By the end of the night they had already scheduled a baby shower for the middle of October at the church. For once, Eva was on the receiving end of it. Because there was no evidence of a baby anywhere near her it felt a little weird agreeing to it, but the girls were insistent on it.

She didn't tell Barbie at work until the following week. Her boss was happy for her until Eva told her that she'd be taking a three month maternity leave. Eva was one of the top earners at the shop, which put Barbie in a bind. Eva didn't know how she'd be able to afford being off that long, but she knew there was no way six weeks would be long enough; especially with twins. Eric was making better money now that they were able to stick a lot of it away for her leave. She would miss her work if she didn't get back to it, so she assured her boss that she would be back.

The only people she was afraid of telling were her family. She knew her dad, Heidi and Joelle would be all right with the concept, but it was her mom and Andrea whom she feared. There never seemed to be a great time to tell them all at once, since there weren't any holidays coming up. If she waited until Thanksgiving, she might have the babies to tell of themselves, and Eva thought that maybe that was the way to go. In the end, she confided in Heidi and Joelle and made them swear to secrecy until she found a way and time to tell the others. They were both excited, but mad that she never let on any problem in the fertility department. Eva agreed that it was selfish of her, but focused on the exciting news of the twins.

Eva invited Bart and the kids over for a Saturday night barbeque in celebration of their announcement. Eric kept silent almost all night, which only made Eva worry that he was rethinking their decision or that he was embarrassed to tell his brother he wasn't able to have kids with Eva and had to resort to adopting. For the first time, it took the edge off her excitement, replacing it with shame. But when Eva announced that they were adopting twins, Bart seemed genuinely happy for them, giving them each a hug. The kids were a little confused as to what it all meant, so Eva sat down with them on the floor while holding Lydia and said, "There is a girl who your uncle knows who is going to have twins. She isn't able to care for them, so she is going to let us raise them for her. She is the birth mommy, but I'm going to be the mommy who sees them every day and takes care of them."

"Kind of like how you are our mommy?" Noah asked.

"No, you dummy! She's our auntie. We don't have a mommy any more! The one we had was stupid, and I'm glad she's gone!" Seth said with more anger than she'd ever heard out of him.

Out of the corner of her eye, Eva saw Bart walk out of the room, which told her that she was on her own on this one. "You don't mean that, Seth."

"Yes, I do!"

"Well, one day your dad might meet a woman and get married again. Then she would be your mommy."

"I don't want another mommy! I don't need a mommy!" he said in defiance.

He was within arm's reach so she grabbed him and hugged him to her side. She had to let him know that she cared and understood him. "I love you, Seth. I know you are hurting right now, but getting angry won't help you. Remember what I told you what to do when you get mad?"

"Yeah, you said I needed to talk to God about it."

"And do you?"

"No," Seth said, pouting his lips.

"Why not?"

"Because it doesn't help. I tried."

"Would it help if I prayed with you?"

Seth just shook his head, and she wasn't going to press it. So she said, "All right, love." and kissed his head. "I have a question for you."

"What?" he asked with big eyes.

"Would you be willing to help me out when the babies come home? You are so good with Lydia that I'm going to need you."

Smiling again, he said, "Sure!"

Noah piped in and asked, "What about me? Can I help too?"

"You sure can, sweetheart," she said, smoothing down the cowlick in the front of his head. "Are all of you all right with

271

this? I mean, you three have been the most important people in my life. I don't know how I could do this without you!"

Noah and Seth hugged her and Lydia from both sides. "I think it will work out just fine," Seth said matter-of-factly.

"I think so too. Just think, guys, they will be your very first cousins!"

"Wow!" Noah said, liking the sound of it.

"Neato!" Seth said with a full-fledged smile.

Lydia screamed from the excitement.

Eva's sentiments exactly.

Chapter 30

It was a beautiful night to grill, and Eric was known for his awesome burgers. And it was a great distraction from the news Eva just announced. He had been so nervous to say anything to Bart, not wanting to get ribbed for choosing to adopt. Not that he had much of a choice, for the simple fact that they were his own kids. It killed him not to confide in his brother, but he knew it was for the best that the truth remain buried... under all the lies.

Bart joined him on the deck and watched him flip the burgers and hot dogs, but Eric noticed that he seemed more agitated than normal. "What's up?" Eric asked.

"Seth. That kid has been grating on my nerves. Lately he's been such a defiant little brat."

"Payback is a bitch, man," Eric said with a chuckle.

"Yeah, just you wait bro!"

"We have an advantage though. We've been watching how you've been doing it for years and taking notes on what we will and won't be doing when it comes to raising *our* kids."

"You know? You are real funny. I'd watch what you say since it seems to me like my kids have been raised mostly by *you*," he added, trying to raise Eric's blood pressure.

"Wow, that was almost a slam," Eric answered in unabashed sarcasm.

Shutting the lid on the grill, he took a seat next to Bart. Staring straight ahead, his brother said, "He hates Natasha."

Eric was surprised to hear the sadness in Bart's voice. "I thought you'd like that fact. She did royally screw all of you over."

"I know, dude. But she's their mother no matter what that paper she signed says. She wasn't ready to be a mom, I get that now. I'm not mad at her. I'm just sad that it took abandoning three kids to find out how really unhappy she was."

"Dude, I think y'all need counseling."

"Yeah, probably so. Luckily Lydia isn't affected at all; she's too young. And Noah takes everything in stride. He cries for her sometimes, but he seems to be appeased by praying about it. I'm glad he's found peace in all of this; I'm kinda jealous of him actually. But Seth is just so angry. I guess I'm the easiest target. He knows I hate it when he brings her up, so he keeps on until I'm about to burst. I'm so scared what I'll do to him one of these days."

"Just send him our way. Eva seems to know what to do."

"Yeah, she'll be a great mom."

"Yeah," Eric said with a proud smile. "She's wanted this for so long."

"So it was a no-go for you guys to come about it naturally?" Bart hesitated in asking.

"She has a lot of medical problems."

"After a while I figured that something was up, but I didn't ask 'cause I didn't think it was my place to."

"Yeah, no one knew. We were both kinda embarrassed."

"Hey, it happens. But adoption huh? You sure?"

Eric took a deep breath in, trying to think of the right response not to tip anything off. "Yeah, I'm pretty sure. It was the last thing I was looking for, but the birth mother being so close to someone I admire; I couldn't say no. She was so insistent on us taking them."

And the lies continued…

"So, what, you worked with her in Italy?" his brother asked, fishing for more information.

"Yeah, her dad is my boss; great family, but strict Catholics."

"Ahhhh, doesn't believe in abortion then?"

"Nope,and she doesn't believe in being a single mom either."

"Where's the father?"

"Not in the picture."

"He gonna create a problem? I've heard of stories…"

Eric cut him off by saying, "No problem in that area." Nobody but Eva and Claudia knew about Eric being on the birth certificate, and every time he was asked by anyone about the father being a potential problem he perfected down-playing the question as if it had no relevance.

"Well, good luck, bro. You will make great parents! My only word of advice is to keep your traveling down to a minimum. Before you know it your oldest is 6 going on 18 and you've missed their life."

"I'll keep that in mind, bro."

*   *   *

"Eric! I'm so scared! It's too early to have them!" Claudia cried into the phone. Luckily he was just a state away in New Jersey if he had to get to her. It was just a fluke that he happened to be there when she called.

"Calm down....Tell me what's going on." Eric had been reading a book on pregnancy so he was familiar with some of the terminology.

"I'm having major contractions, and they are eight minutes apart."

"Did your water break?"

"No, but I'm really scared it will!" She was thirty-two weeks along and the last time they spoke she was doing fine, and the babies were developing well. Time had been ticking fast for them, and Eva had almost everything ready for their arrivals. The church had thrown Eva a grandiose baby shower the weekend before. It was so overwhelming for Eva when over a hundred women showed up bearing gifts from diapers, outfits, and toys to swings and car seats. Everything was in pink and baby blue or red and blue. Eric had never seen such an awesome display of generosity in his life. It was getting more real by the second that he'd have his children in his arms soon.

From what Charlotte was saying about twins, it was common for them to come early, but he knew that eight weeks was way too soon. So, he calmly said, "Claudia, I want you to hang up and call 911. More than likely it's just false labor, but you need to get to the hospital. I can be there in four hours if you need me."

"Okay...Okay, I'm hanging up now."

"Keep me posted no matter what, okay?"

"Yes...okay." Eric could tell that she was trying to be brave, but heard the fear in her voice. He wanted to call Eva because she would be able to calm him down; this was getting too nerve-racking. But until he knew what was going on for sure, he wouldn't burden her with it.

Two hours went by and he was beside himself with worry. "Oh God, I wish she'd call!" And then as if she heard his request, the phone rang which he picked up before it could sound again.

"Hello?"

"Eric, I'm fine. It was false labor. I'm on an IV, and I'm going to have to stay the night. But they want me on bed rest for the rest of the time. What am I going to do?"

"You don't have anyone to help you?"

"No. No one..." Claudia started to cry.

"Let me help."

"How?"

"I have six weeks of vacation yet to use..."

"You are going to need that for when the babies come. I can not have you do that..."

"Well, I can't have the mother of my children fending for herself when she is supposed to be on bed rest!"

"Eric! Stop it!" Claudia snapped, her voice suddenly turning cold. "You can't come here. I'll figure it out. Don't worry about it."

"Ha! Don't worry, she says! If you don't want me to worry, stop calling me with all of this!" he yelled, highly agitated at her hardened words, and over the fact his hands were tied.

"Fine! I won't! I'll call you when it's time."

"Fine!"

She paused before yelling back, "Fine!" and ending the call.

*   *   *

Eric didn't hear from her again until she called three weeks later when her water broke.

Chapter 31

Eva knew that it could be any day when Claudia would go into labor, but when Eric called her from Dallas she had just walked in the door with the dogs after their run. Every day she was working on tying up loose ends before this day came. They had turned their spare room into the nursery, deciding to paint it yellow with a Raggedy Ann and Andy border. It was inspired by the dolls, given to her by Kristin who said they were her favorite dolls when she was a kid. And she thought it fit, considering they were having a boy and girl.

Everyone wanted to know what they were planning on naming the babies, but she and Eric wanted to keep it a surprise. Besides they weren't one hundred percent sure. They thought they'd wait to see them before deciding.

They hadn't bought anything, other than the paint and border for the room, since every baby item imaginable had been given to them. It took three cars to transport all of the gifts home from the shower the church threw her, and within days after mentioning the news of the adoption presents from her clients, coworkers and co-workers' clients poured in like a third world country in need. She felt so blessed. It was really sinking in that her time to become a mom was about to come and every day she got on her knees and praised God for answering her prayers. Never again would she ever question God and His timing. Everything was working like clock work; from her just about giving up hope, to Eric having such a change of heart that she barely even recognized him anymore, to such an overwhelming positive response to what they were doing. Even Andrea and her mom were excited. Okay, maybe not at first, but after telling them that she was unable to have them naturally, they accepted it warmly.

It was Monday when they got the call, which meant she had to call her prescheduled clients. Eva had been talking to her

278

clients for the last few months, telling them of her three month leave and if Claudia might happen to go into early labor, her clients would be diverted to one of the six other girls working there.

Eric had requested a two-week vacation, informing the company that they were in the process of adopting. They told him to let them know the dates he needed.

Eric's boss called the house a few days later and Eva picked up. "So I hear that you finally get a baby," he said in a jolly happy tone. She could practically picture his ear to ear grin and was suddenly nervous for the fact that she had a secret that he'd never know. It was such a pity too. Between Eric's rave over the man and this one sentence spoken to her, she knew how genuine and nice he was.

"Yes, sir." She didn't want to say too much, but she didn't want to seem unfriendly and stiff either. So she added, "We are excited."

"That is glorious! I left message with Eric's phone. I can tell you now too."

"What is that, sir?"

"You tell him to take two weeks. After that, we keep his schedule light for little bit more, yes?"

"Oh, Sir! That would be wonderful!!! Thank you so much!"

Jess chuckled and said, "You welcome. One day I hope to meet this child."

"Children. They are twins," she added with pride. She figured it wouldn't hurt anything to tell him that much.

"Oh, wonderful! They will bless you."

"Yes, I believe they will," she choked, knowing that her babies wouldn't know this sweet, wonderful man as their grandpa. Adoption had so many facets; especially secretive adoptions. It was a blessing to the adoptive parents, but such heartache for those who wouldn't see the child, and in this case, children, grow.

They were both happy with Jessup's message, and relieved in the fact that they would have some time to get acclimated with the twins before he got to traveling hard again. She was so happy that Eric was so involved with the process. When this first began, a part of her thought that she'd be on her own in everything, not knowing how on board he really wanted to be, but she soon found out how much of a willing participant he was, taking part in every area of planning which surprised and thrilled Eva. In fact, he'd been the main communicator with Claudia, which in ways made her feel left out. She asked him one time why Claudia never called her, and he said that she was adjusting to the reality that someone else would be her babies' mommy. Apparently talking to Eva would be too hard, which Eva could totally understand. Plus she knew that they had a friendship going before all this began. The way he talked about her, it was like she was the little sister he never had.

Eric caught a flight to New York that night out of Dallas, and the best Eva could do was get a stand by flight for the next day, hoping that she'd get one right away in the morning. She tried getting a red eye that night as well, but they were all booked. They had planned for events such as this, knowing that he'd more than likely be out of town when they got the call. So, she had a small duffle bag packed and ready to go with ten little outfits, diapers and wipes, and all other essentials for taking babies home and across country along with the two car seats. It would be a handful getting there, but once she met up with Eric, her load would be lightened. Since she had time to waste, she took out her to-do-baby-list and checked it twice. Everything seemed to be there, but as time ticked away and not being able to get any sleep, she felt like the only thing she was losing was her mind.

Eric had landed in New York nine o'clock her time and she called him every fifteen minutes for updates. After the fifth phone call, Eric told her that he'd call when the babies came. As far as the doctors could tell, the babies and mother were doing fine. She was fully dilated, and they were preparing her to push the last time she called. It had been an hour since she last heard from him and she couldn't take it anymore, so she called Charlotte. "What's going on?" Char asked frantically.

"She's in labor!"

"Oh my gosh, Eva! That's great! How far along?"

"Last I heard she was ready to push, but that was an hour ago and Eric said not to call; that he'd call me."

"Why aren't you on your way there?"

"I couldn't get a flight out until tomorrow; hopefully. I'm on stand by."

"Oh no! How are you holding up? Yeah I know; that was a stupid question."

"I'd feel a lot better if he'd call me no matter what right now. All I can think of is every bad scenario. I need to get some sleep, but I'm too dang excited!"

"Let's pray, shall we?" Just hearing that calmed Eva down, but she bowed her head as her friend said, "Father, we thank You for this miracle that You are bringing into Eva and Eric's life. We just pray that You be with Claudia and those babies. May she have a safe and fast delivery, and be with her as she hands them over to Eva and Eric. Give Eva the peace as she awaits the phone call that she's looked forward to all her married life. Keep them all safe in Your loving arms, in Jesus name, amen."

"Thank you, Char."

"You're welcome. Do you want company while you wait at the airport tomorrow?"

"I think I'll be fine. I'm hoping I'll get on the first plane in the morning."

"I'll be praying that you do. Congratulations, Eva. I'm so happy for you!"

"Thanks for being there for me."

"Goes both ways, girl!"

Eva picked up on the first ring when Eric called at midnight. She hadn't slept a wink and pretty much had her mind made up that after she talked to Eric, whenever that'd be, she'd head right for the airport. "Eric! I was getting so worried!"

"Sorry, babe. It was a fast, but hard delivery. Our babies are here!" he said in a jubilant but tired voice.

"How are they? Are they healthy?"

"Our girl is six pounds even and is doing well. But our boy is suffering from a little jaundice. Don't worry though; they are saying he'll be just fine in a few days. He's a healthy five pounds six ounces."

Eva's eyes filled with tears. "Oh, this is really happening, isn't it?"

"Yeah, and wait til you see them; it becomes more real..."

"I can't wait to get there!"

"Call me to let me know your flight times. Eva, I love you!"

"I love you too, Eric," she said, wanting to pinch herself to see if she was dreaming. "So, you were there when they were born after all?"

"Yeah, she didn't kick me out, which surprised me."

Eva was a little disappointed that she wasn't there too, but asked quickly to hide the letdown, "Do you have the names figured out yet?"

"No; I'll wait until you see them to decide."

"Sounds good to me," she said, finding it hard to contain her heightening joy. "And how is Claudia?"

"She had a tough go of it, physically and mentally. She only took one look at the babies and told us all to get out. I have a feeling that her lawyer is on his way as we speak."

"Is she still saying no to meet me?"

"Afraid so, babe. I tried, but she wouldn't hear of it; too tough."

"Is she sure she really wants to do this?" Eva asked reluctantly. It would kill her to hear that Claudia had changed her mind.

"I've asked her that a million times, and her answer is always the same. She's not their mom, *you* are."

"All right, well, I guess I'll see you tomorrow sometime. I can't sleep. I'm going to get a few more things done around here and then I'm going to the airport."

"Okay, babe. I'm going to get a few hours sleep at the hotel myself. G'nite!"

Once Eva hung up the phone, she collapsed on her bed with an ear-to-ear smile. In a matter of five minutes, she was a mom.

Chapter 32

Eric was working on pure adrenaline since he received Claudia's phone call that she was in labor. By the time he got to the hospital, she was writhing in pain due to the plain fact that she refused any pain medication. He had no idea if she'd let him in the delivery room as it was, but with her in the condition she was in he wouldn't have been the least surprised to be kicked out of the hospital let alone the room. But the fact of the matter was, she didn't even notice him....well at first, at least. One of the nurses asked if he was the father, and when he nodded she told him quickly that 'his wife' was a stubborn one. Eric was beyond making sense out of where Claudia's head was at lately and was concerned that this whole thing would blow up in his face. She put on a great front of being strong, but to him she was acting insane; this wasn't the woman he knew. This Claudia was unstable to say the least, and who knew what she was capable of if she ever saw Eva face-to-face. Whether or not Claudia was willing to meet Eva didn't even factor into this plot. There was no way on God's green earth that he'd put the two of them in the same room, especially after what happened during and after the delivery.

When Claudia finally noticed him in the room, she cried. "It hurts so much!"

"I'm so sorry, Claude. I wish there was something I could do," he said with guilt. She was lying on her side, holding her massive stomach which was protruding unnaturally. He wanted to hug her, but the look on her face at the moment told him to back off. But he asked anyway, "*Is* there anything I can do?"

"Yes! Get these kids out of me!" she yelled as another contraction hit. The monitor indicated that they were getting really close together. Eric knew there wasn't much time left.

"Didn't you take anything for pain?"

"No."

"Why not?"

283

"For one, I want to walk out of here as soon as I'm able...and two, I want to remember this pain so I'll never do something this stupid and irresponsible for as long as I live," she said through clenched teeth.

Eric ate up her words and it sliced his heart. Luckily they were all alone during this conversation, he thought. All he said back to her was, "Yeah, well, I wish I could take some of that pain for myself so that I may learn my lesson too."

Dully she looked at him and said, "I think the babies will be a constant reminder of that."

The doctor came in then and Eric took the chair by the head of Claudia's bed. Dr. Bruns was a woman in her early forties who had apparently delivered her share of twins from her many stories she told to lighten the mood in the oppressive room. It didn't take a licensed psychiatrist to figure out that he and Claudia may have made these children together, but that was all that they shared. Eric wasn't prepared when the doctor asked Claudia to roll over onto her back, flipped up the sheet that covered her legs and began checking her internally. He quickly looked the other way but was too late and saw way too much. "All right, it's game time. You are ready to go. The next contraction you can start pushing, okay?" Dr. Bruns said.

"Okay."

Eric left the room every time Eva called to give Claudia respect. After the fourth time, Claudia got perturbed. "What is her problem? Doesn't she understand that this could take all night, God help me?"

"She's just excited, Claude. I keep telling her that I'll call when it's all over..."

"Well, shut the damn thing off!" she yelled when a contraction hit.

He didn't, and when it rang again she gave him such an evil stare that it sent chills down his body. Once he got the message across loud and clear to Eva not to call again until she heard from him, he went back into the room where Claudia was starting to push. He gave her his hand to squeeze, which she used with evil pleasure. Her screams were so loud that he was surprised that Eva couldn't hear them in Minnesota. It was just as painful for him to sit by and watch as it was for Claudia to actually go through. Because of him she was going through this, and with every scream he could feel the hatred aimed towards him. It took forty-five minutes to deliver his little girl, who had a full head of black hair and had a pair of healthy lungs. She was a good-sized baby for being a month early and the doctor was surprised that everything appeared to be normal with her. Claudia started to cry, voicing that she couldn't do that again. But Dr.Bruns told her that the second one will come a lot easier. When he wasn't coming, Eric flinched when he saw the doctor's hand disappear into Claudia. "He's breach, so I'm going to turn him. This might be a little uncomfortable but I'll try making it quick."

"OhmyGodohmyGodohmyGod," was all Claudia could utter through tears.

"Okay, now the next contraction you can push," the doctor informed.

In the background Eric could hear his daughter cry, and the reality of the situation hit him like a ton of bricks. These were his babies. He would be responsible for them and he suddenly felt inadequate. But it was temporarily forgotten when his son emerged. It took him a little while to cry, which concerned Dr. Bruns. The baby looked a little smaller than his sister, but healthy nonetheless. After cleaning out the nose and mouth, she turned the baby over and slapped his back and butt a few times until he gave a cry, but it was short and sweet and apparently enough to appease the hospital staff.

Eric had imagined what it would be like to welcome his children into the world, and he was more than a little disappointed that the mother of them wouldn't even acknowledge them. He knew what Claudia had been saying all these months about not wanting anything to do with them once they were born, but he thought that once she saw them she would at least like to look at them. It had to be tough for her given all the circumstances, but not to even look at them hurt him more than he could ever express. When asked by the nurse if Claudia wanted to hold them before weighing them and putting them under a light, something that was standard for preemies, she shook her head and looked away. When delivering the afterbirth was mentioned, Eric said he was going to slip out and get some fresh air. That was something he didn't need to see, plus it would give him a chance to call Eva. In ways he wished she had been there to see the babies being born, but knew it was for the best that she didn't. As it was he was grateful that Claudia let him in to witness the event.

After his phone call to Eva, he ventured back into Claudia's room where she was alone, huddled into a ball on her side facing away from the open door. "Claudia? May I come in?" Eric asked after knocking on the door.

"Yeah..."

"Is there anything I can get you?"

She just shook her head. He walked to the other side of the bed so he could see her, expecting to see her crying. Instead, she was staring stone-faced out the window. There was nothing to see but a lit parking lot due to the hour of the night. He slid a chair next to her bed and sat on it. "You did a great job, Claude. I'm proud of you..."

She continued to stare past him, not saying a word.

"Are you sure you want to do this? One phone call home will stop Eva from coming here." A part of him kicked himself for saying the words, but he had to make sure for all of their sakes.

With that, she rolled over onto her back and slowly sat up, snapping out of it. "For the last time, Eric, I'm sure. You don't have to worry about me coming back for them."

"But I worry about *you*. Are you going to be all right?"

"I don't know. I guess time will tell...Just promise me two things..." she said with a desperate plea.

"Anything."

"Give them a good life, and no matter what, don't let my father know..."

Eric gulped down his emotion as he agreed to her terms. "Thank you, Claudia. If you ever change your mind about seeing them, or if there is anything you ever need..."

Holding up her hand, she said, "We can't ever speak again, Eric. And I mean that. If you try to call, I will hang up on you. Now, I don't blame you for what happened; please believe me when I say that. I just need to do it this way to help let go, otherwise I don't think I ever will."

"I understand....I'll miss you, Claudia," he said with tears, grabbing a hold of her hand.

Touching his cheek lovingly, she said, "You better leave now, Eric. My lawyer will be here soon. If you stick around out in the lobby or in the nursery, he will give you the necessary paperwork you'll need to proceed with getting them home as well as the adoption process."

Eric hesitated, but then stood up, leaned over and kissed her softly on the mouth. He lingered there probably a little too long, but neither of them pulled away. They both had tears rolling down their cheeks when they pulled apart. "Thank you, Claude," he whispered and then quietly waited down the hall for her lawyer.

*   *   *

After returning from the hospital at two in the morning with all the paperwork in hand, he collapsed, sleeping like a baby. He woke up at eight, took a much needed shower and headed straight to the hospital to see the twins. By the time he got there, it was almost ten in the morning. And when he approached the nursery, he saw that his little girl was out of the light already which pleased him. It was the first time after she was born that he got to hold her, and the moment she was in his arms he started to cry. He never thought he'd see any offspring of his own, and it overwhelmed him. It was harder because nobody was there to enjoy it with him. The nurse had informed him that Claudia had already checked out, and when he asked if she came to see the babies before she left the nurse just shook her head sadly. He knew it was stupid to ask, knowing it would only disappoint him more. But what it also did was reaffirm that the secret of these children paternities would be safe, which he hoped would help him move on as well.

After looking in on his son, who was doing remarkably well according to the nurse, he took off for the airport to pick up Eva. She never looked more beautiful to him. One would never be able to tell that she didn't sleep a wink the night before. As he hugged her, all he could think about was how he wished that the twins were hers, and he stopped himself quickly. They *were* hers; and his. Ever since Eva accepted this arrangement, she spoke of them as if they were her own flesh and blood, and for that he couldn't have loved her more.

Luckily their luggage, which consisted of the two car seats and the baby's duffel bag, was on the first turn of the carousal. So Eric gathered everything up quickly and they headed for the rental car, struggling to figure out how the seats worked. Eva laughed, "This was the one thing that I didn't prepare for. What happened to one click and you're done?"

"And I'm mechanically inclined! I can work on complex machines, yet putting in two car seats gives me trouble; go figure."

Once they conquered that feat, they were on their way to the hospital. Eva asked him all about the delivery, but Eric omitted a lot of it. All she needed to know was that it hurt a lot, and that Claudia walked away this morning with no regrets and the babies were coming along great. Even the little boy was due to be off the lights in a few days, which meant they could go home soon. Eric relayed the information Claudia's lawyer had given to him. It was really quite simple. The kids were his and Claudia relinquished her rights as a parent. Once they received the kids social security cards, they could proceed with the adoption. They would have a court fee and would have to make a court appearance to make it legal. Then it was all done and the kids would be forever theirs.

Eva started to cry as soon as she saw the little girl and even harder when she saw her boy. Eva picked up the little girl but not before Eric embraced Eva and kissed her. Once the baby was in her arms, she exclaimed, "Oh my, you are a little peanut!" and then kissed her sweet face. "Mommy loves you. I've been waiting for you for so long! Thank you, Jesus!"

Eric gulped down the sob lodged in his throat. How did he deprive her of this moment for so long? he scolded himself. She was meant to be a mom. He brushed his fingers over his son's head who was lying in the crib next to where they were standing. "So, what should we name them?" he asked.

Eva just stared at the baby in her arms. "I think she looks like a Rachel Joy, what do you think?"

"I thought you were stuck on Mckennah Rae."

Holding the baby out in front of her for a second, she confirmed, "Nope, I think she looks like a Rachel Joy."

"I think it's a perfect name for a beautiful little girl."

Eva leaned over to look closely at her son. "What about this guy?"

"I don't think he looks like an Aidan, Carter or Brendan, do you?" he asked. Those were their top three boy names.

"You are right. What name comes to mind when you look at him?"

"Matteo."

"Matteo?" she laughed.

"I heard it when I was in Italy and it kinda stuck with me." He never met the boy who stole Claudia and her parent's hearts, but his story about how he came in and out of their life made a lasting impression on him. He wanted to honor Claudia somehow in all of this even though she would never know and neither would Eva.

"I don't know about that one, Eric, maybe for a middle name, but I don't think I like it for a first name."

"Well, what have you come up with?" he asked nicely.

"I was thinking of Isaac. Isaac Matteo Wahler. What do you think?"

Eric thought about it. It was different enough, which they were looking for, but not too different that the boy would get teased. After all it would be something he would have for life. "Isaac is a strong name."

Eva smiled. "Yes, it is."

"Well hello, Isaac Matteo. Welcome to the world," he said to the sleeping baby and then kissed the little girl in Eva's arms, "And hello Miss Rachel Joy."

Eva handed Rachel over to Eric and then kissed him. "I love you so much. Thank you for making this a reality for us!"

Eric felt a stab of guilt but swallowed it away. He knew that if they were going to move forward, he had to forgive himself for the deception and let it go. So, he said what he needed to say to move on, "I love you too. This was the best decision I've ever made…"

Epilogue

The twins had slept the whole plane and car ride home, having to wake them every three hours to feed them. The first twenty four hours went smoothly since leaving the hospital. Eva was so taken with how attentive Eric was with the babies. A part of her feared that he wouldn't be able to bond with them right away knowing that they weren't his own, but the exact opposite happened. He was instantly protective of them both and was continuously kissing or holding them. Eva had awakened in the middle of the night at the hotel and saw Eric holding both babies; crying. It was such a beautiful sight that she didn't alert him to her state of sleep, or lack there of, but just stared at them with joy in her heart.

There was an entourage waiting for them at their house the day they returned home with the twins with banners streaming their living room in pink and blue saying 'It's a girl' and 'It's a boy'. Bart and the kids, Uncle Ben, Heidi and Moon, Charlotte and Summitt and Andrea were there, all anxious to meet their new addition. Bruiser and Red dog were trying to figure out what the commotion was all about, but once they saw their masters they ran up to greet them with loud barks and wagging tails. Eric set Rachel down on the floor in her car seat and both dogs came up and sniffed the baby but apparently she wasn't to their liking because they soon ran off. It was a concern of theirs how they would react to the babies, hearing horror stories of dogs attacking newborns when the parents were out of the room for a second. If this was any indication, they were in for a smooth ride.

Her sister Andrea fell in love with them, and then proceeded in giving a mommy 101 class. If Eva had to rate the most surprising reaction though, it would be from Uncle Ben who at first just stood back and took the whole scene. It was when the crowd thinned and it was just Bart, the kids and himself that he went over to Eric who had both of the twins. "Would you like to hold one of them, Uncle Ben?" Eva asked behind him.

"I don't know about that. I prefer for them to be a little sturdier."

"Oh come on, Ben, they don't scare you, do they?" Bart joked.

"Scare me? No…"

Eric handed him Isaac, who had just awakened once in his uncle's arms. "Oh, look at you…scary sight first thing in the morning, huh son?" Ben said in a high-pitched voice towards the baby. Isaac gave a big yawn in response but didn't lose eye contact with Ben once. "I'm not a man who thinks much of God…" he was saying while intent on the baby, "but I know a miracle when I see one. And I don't know two people who deserve these children more than you two…"

He was usually a man of few words, but when he spoke it usually meant a lot. This was one of those times to Eva. She hugged his side and said, "I love you, Uncle Ben. They will be so blessed to have you in their lives."

Ben had tears in his eyes when he said to her, "I'm the lucky one." By then it had quieted down and Eric's entire family was in the living room and had turned their ears on the man who played such an important, yet back staged role in their lives. Not once in the thirty odd years that they'd known him had they seen him shed a tear, let alone cry. After gulping down the lump in his throat, he looked between Bart and Eric when he said, "I haven't been the best guardian, I know. I've made some mistakes, had a few regrets, but I'm so glad that you included me in your life. Once you were eighteen I thought for sure you'd be gone from my life, and back then I couldn't wait for the day to get rid of you rug rats," he added by chuckling. "But then you brought this one home," he gestured towards Eva, "and I was so glad that you did. *If* there is a God, she is surely His angel. I never thought it was fair when year after year there were no children. I had a feeling that there was a problem, and I cursed the God that you believe in so much, Eva…and I'm so sorry," he confessed, breaking down.

It stunned them all, but Eva was fast-acting and took the baby from him, but encouraged with a hug, "Don't worry about it, Uncle Ben. I'm guilty of that too, but it all worked out in the end..."

"Yes, it did. I guess I just wanted to tell all of you how happy you make this old, crotchety man. I consider you boys like my own sons and all of these kids are like my grandkids. I just want you to know that there isn't anything I wouldn't do for any of you."

Eric had tears in his eyes when he went over and hugged his uncle with Rachel still in his arms. "Thank you for putting up with me, man. You are like the dad I never knew; even better."

"This is getting to be just a little too much for me," Bart said uncomfortably. "It's time to head on out, kiddos. Come on."

"Oh, come on dad! Can't we stay just a little longer?" Seth asked.

"Sorry, Seth. I have to work early tomorrow. We'll see them soon, don't worry. Share your hugs now..."

Eva didn't know what happened there, but if she had to guess, she just witnessed Bart peel back a layer he didn't know existed and he didn't know how to deal with it. Escaping always seemed to be his first reaction, but she'd kept that observation to herself.

Her church family fell in love with the babies. Offers came out of the woodwork to baby sit anytime they needed. Hand-me-downs arrived weekly as well as care packages. She hadn't realized how many friends she had until this happened.

Eric started attending the worship services with her once they got back with the twins for the first few months, and then it tapered off to just once a month, with the excuse of having too much to do. She was so hopeful back when he went every week, and even when he went just once a month. She was just happy that he went that often. He seemed to have stopped going completely when he saw how many extra pair of hands there were to help her with the babies, which made her think that the only reason he went in the first place was because of the kids. She was past nagging him about anything lately and their marriage had been the strongest it had ever been. This was exactly how she imagined it would be.

The twins were just over six weeks old when her parents and youngest sister met them for the first time over the New Year. Her dad was always a sucker for a new baby, and her mom usually was too. But it took her mom a while to want to hold either of them, and once she did she fell in love with them. It was also the first time Eva met Joelle's son, Zander, who was already eight months old. It was a wild bunch at Andrea's with Joelle's two kids and Moon who just turned one and went from crawling right to running. Andrea's kids remained well mannered as usual, but weren't a real help in managing the little kids like Eva hoped they would be. But they both thought the twins were fun to hold and poke at. Eric was overprotective as usual, making sure the kids weren't too rough with the twins. Eva's mom was the first to notice how attentive he was and was openly impressed for the second time since she had been married to him.

Rachel had been fussier than her brother around feeding times, but all in all for the first couple weeks they seemed to be on the same schedule. Or maybe she thought that because Eric was always around to help her. But when he went back to work, she found that raising twins wasn't easy. If she was holding one, the other would fuss and vice versa. Sleep was a luxury, and she really missed Eric when he did over nights. He called home more than ever just to see how the twins were doing and how she was faring. A few times she got upset because they had just gotten down for a nap and she was just dozing off when the phone rang. Those days all she desired was a half hour's rest. Working out became something of the past, but as much up and down and carrying them around as she did was enough exercise for her for the time being. One day she'd get back to it, she promised herself.

They were hard to leave once Eva went back to work three months after they were born. She decided to go back part time until they got a little older. Plus she didn't want to overwhelm Uncle Ben who offered to watch them. She'd always loved doing hair, but nothing compared to being a mom. It was hard and demanding and often went underappreciated but she wouldn't trade any of it. The good went with the bad; all a blessing from the God who sent them to her and Eric. Isaac gained weight quickly and surpassed Rachel within the first couple months. She might've been the first born, but he had been the first in everything else. He was the first to smile and laugh, first to roll over and he sprouted the first tooth. But within days his sister was mimicking him. As they grew, Isaac's black hair that he was born with faded quickly to blonde and had some curls at his nape where Rachel held onto her dark straight wisps. Isaac surprisingly had blue eyes where Rachel had brown. Everyone who saw them couldn't believe how different they looked, and would comment over how much Isaac looked just like Eva and Eric. In a way it was nice that people wouldn't know right off the bat that they weren't biologically theirs. But in every other way that was important they were.

The adoption hearing was scheduled to be on Eva's thirty-second birthday. She couldn't ask for a better present. Since the day she held Rachel and Isaac in her arms, they were hers no matter what a piece of paper said. But she couldn't wait until it was legal. Nobody knew the full story about the legalities of the adoption. As far as everyone knew, they were both going to be sworn in as their legal parents; not just Eva. Eric thought that it was best so that it didn't raise suspecting eyebrows, and Eva agreed. She almost confided in Charlotte one afternoon, but stopped herself, because she still didn't know if what they did was totally legal, and given Charley's profession Charlotte would be sure to find out. There wasn't a thing she'd risk at having those kids be legally theirs.

Charlotte was throwing Eva and Eric an adoption party/Eva's birthday party the Sunday after the adoption was official. The twins had turned six months old a week before and were scooting across the floor with no trouble. It saddened Eva that they were growing so fast, especially since she missed so much due to her being tired through it all. But it was par for the course of their first year of life.

She was a nervous wreck before the ceremony, thinking that something was going to go wrong. But the process took a total of three minutes and they were out of there with the signed documents that stated that they were both the legal parents of Isaac Matteo and Rachel Joy Wahler. They each held a baby as they hugged and kissed each other. "I love you," Eric said.

"I love you too. They are really ours!" she exclaimed.

"They sure are. Let's go celebrate..."

It was three weeks later when she noticed bruising on Isaac's arm. At first she thought that he might've bumped himself and dismissed it. But when she noticed a few more bruises on his stomach and legs as well as starting to spike a fever that over the counter medicine couldn't cut, she brought him to the emergency room. Eric took the first flight home from New Mexico and met her at the hospital. The doctors were concerned. His temperature was up to 103 degrees and they were doing everything they could to break it. It took almost forty-eight hours to do so, and after running a battery of tests, they didn't like what they saw so they sent him to the University of Minnesota. Although very rare in a child of six months, they were going to test Isaac for leukemia. Eva knew what it would entail from watching numerous science health TV programs on the disease. Depending on the seriousness, a bone marrow transplant would give him the best success rate and Chemotherapy would be an alternative, but it would be the harder route; especially on a child of his age. The best matches would be found in the biological parents or immediate family, and since neither she nor Eric shared the same blood type, Eva panicked knowing that their only hope would be to somehow reach Claudia for help.

Note from the author

Dear reader,

I hope you enjoyed this book. It was inspired by struggles I had with my own infertility. You could say that it was great therapy for me as I wrote it. Although very loosely based on my life, I want to stress that it is very much fiction and does not reflect the real relationships I have.

There were many years where I was crippled by the fact I may never have children, but unlike my character Eva, I was very vocal about it and received a lot of support from those around me; especially from my husband, my mom, church family and most importantly God's Word. It's a harsh reality, and my heart goes out to all those who are going through it. My advice to you if you are struggling; find a support system to help you cope, and I pray that God hears the cry of your heart.

As time moved on, I realized that God had other plans for me. Children still may be a part of our future, but as we wait on a clear direction I'm going to enjoy the journey I'm on now! For the last ten years I've been really enjoying writing, giving birth to many great characters through stories He's given me which translated into three different novels. This was the first one I felt confident in letting the masses read. It's still hard for me to imagine myself as something other than a hairstylist, but I believe the gift of telling a story was from Him alone.

As you know, Eric and Eva's story is far from over. I'm working on their continuing saga as well as introducing you to two new/old characters in my next book.

I'd love to hear your thoughts on 'Love Interrupted' or for more information on my next book, drop me a line at www.kimberlyanndockter.com .

In closing, my prayer is that you find the gifts God has given you and use them. You never know who it will bless or where it will take you.

Sincerely,
Kimberly Ann Dockter

About the author

Kim is currently a full time hairstylist in Andover, Minnesota and loves to read, write, and attend Bible studies in her free time. This is her first published novel with hopes of more to come in the future. She was born and raised in Red Wing, but now lives in a 107 year old farm house with her husband and three dogs in Princeton, Minnesota, and is very active in her small country church.